Praise for *The Fortunate Ones*

"A subtle, emotionally layered novel about the ways art and other objects of beauty can make tangible the invisible, undocumented moments in our lives, the portion of experience that exists without an audience but must be preserved if we are to remain whole." —*New York Times Book Review*

"Umansky's richly textured and peopled novel tells an emotionally and historically complicated story with so much skill and confidence it's hard to believe it's her first." —*Kirkus Reviews* (starred review)

"The Kindertransport, the recovery of Nazi-looted art, family ties, and adjustments to great loss. . . . In Umansky's first novel, they're brought together in an original and tremendously moving way. . . . [Umansky] sensitively addresses the complicated issue of survivor's guilt and leaves readers with a sense of hope." —*Booklist* (starred review)

"The restitution of art works stolen by the Nazis provides the background for this début novel. . . . Umansky shrewdly avoids letting the issue of stolen art crowd out other aspects of the story, to which she gives a feminist tilt." —*The New Yorker*

"A beautiful and complex story . . . [that] questions who art really belongs to, and demonstrates how even one work of art can inform and transform lives irreversibly. . . . This novel is elegant, engaging, and smart." —*Bustle*

"Must-read."

—Town & Country

"Umansky's multilayered novel asks the big questions—who are we and who are the people we love? What can we, and what should we, forgive? How does history write itself on our lives and our society?—with compassion, tenderness, and a deft touch.

—Hanya Yanagihara, author of A Little Life

"Ellen Umansky is an absurdly gifted writer, and her masterful debut is so smart, so compelling, so emotionally and intellectually and morally complex, it will make you see the world in a completely different way. I loved, loved, loved this book." —Joanna Rakoff, author of My Salinger Year

"In Ellen Umansky's remarkable first novel, two women from different worlds and generations search for the same stolen painting—a Chaim Soutine portrait that becomes a talisman for each. One of Umansky's many gifts to her lucky readers is the ability to illuminate the truly transcendent powers of art, but also its inherent shortcomings in the face of devastating loss. This is a stirring and ultimately uplifting debut."

—Helen Schulman, author of This Beautiful Life

"The Fortunate Ones is like the melody of a song that you can't forget. Its marvelous, utterly human characters will stay with you. In a story that spans decades and continents, Umansky takes readers on a journey that both challenges and affirms our notions of love, art, family, and sacrifice."

—David Gillham, New York Times
bestselling author of City of Women

"[A] beautiful debut novel. . . . The vivid characterizations make it hard to believe that this is Umansky's first effort."
—PureWow

"For both women, the painting comes to represent what might have been and the complex past. Umansky's vivid telling of the scenes in Vienna and life in wartime London are lovingly juxtaposed against the modern angst of Southern California."
—*Publishers Weekly*

"A touching novel that will appeal to readers who enjoy historical drama with a mystery that spans the years."
—*Historical Novel Society*

"A debut novel that is written with the prowess and force of a veteran storyteller."
—*San Diego Jewish Journal*

"On its surface, *The Fortunate Ones* is a gripping mystery about the fate of one painting and the two very different women who've spent their lives mourning its loss. Lucky for us, Ellen Umansky has gone further, weaving a potent exploration of grief, guilt, desire, and forgiveness. A lush, haunting debut."
—Anna Solomon, author of *Leaving Lucy Pear*

"With remarkable elegance and electric prose, Ellen Umansky has written a brilliant novel about a stolen painting, the Holocaust, Los Angeles, mothers and daughters, and the mysterious bonds of love. I stayed up all night reading this book and it left me weeping, in awe of her gifts and, more than anything, so lucky to be alive."
—Joanna Hershon, author of *A Dual Inheritance*

"*The Fortunate Ones* is a riveting, page-turning novel that investigates the true price of art and love and history. It is both magnificent in its sweep and intimate in its telling. And the end? It will take your breath away. Three cheers for Ellen Umansky's perfect debut."

—Jennifer Gilmore, author of *The Mothers*

"*The Fortunate Ones* is a rich and engaging debut. Ellen Umansky skillfully transports readers from war-torn Vienna and London to present-day Los Angeles, and the journey is intriguing, memorable, and worthwhile."

—Pam Jenoff, internationally bestselling author of *The Orphan's Tale*

"The characters in Ellen Umansky's beautiful novel are haunted not only by loss but by the way one loss bleeds into another and reshapes the world. They are masters of what Elizabeth Bishop called 'the art of losing,' but such is Umansky's own art that she manages, with enormous skill and empathy, to make her characters finders as well. If they seldom recover what they have lost, their quest for wholeness makes *The Fortunate Ones* a profound and moving exploration of sorrow and reconciliation."

—Jonathan Rosen, author of *Joy Comes in the Morning*

THE
FORTUNATE
ONES

THE

FORTUNATE

ONES

A NOVEL

Ellen Umansky

WILLIAM MORROW
An Imprint of HarperCollins*Publishers*

P.S.™ is a trademark of HarperCollins Publishers.

THE FORTUNATE ONES. Copyright © 2017 by Ellen Umansky. All rights reserved. Printed in the United States of America. No part of this book may be used or reproduced in any manner whatsoever without written permission except in the case of brief quotations embodied in critical articles and reviews. For information address HarperCollins Publishers, 195 Broadway, New York, NY 10007.

HarperCollins books may be purchased for educational, business, or sales promotional use. For information please e-mail the Special Markets Department at SPsales@harpercollins.com.

A hardcover edition of this book was published in 2017 by William Morrow, an imprint of HarperCollins Publishers.

FIRST WILLIAM MORROW PAPERBACK EDITION PUBLISHED 2017.

Designed by Bonni Leon-Berman

Library of Congress Cataloging-in-Publication Data has been applied for.

ISBN 978-0-06-238249-8

17 18 19 20 21   LSC   10 9 8 7 6 5 4 3 2

*In memory of my mother, Gloria Mark Spivak,
with deep, abiding love.*

And for Dave, Lena, and Talia, always.

COMFORT

VIENNA, 1936

OMA WANTED TO SEND A telegram to Papi in Paris, but Mutti said no. "He will be back in three days. He will know soon enough," Mutti said from the cot in the little room that would have been the nursery. She had moved in once the pains began. ("It's too early!" Rose had heard Mutti cry out.) The doctor had come and gone, the sheets had been changed, the blood scrubbed away. Without any evidence, it almost seemed to Rose as if it hadn't happened.

"She will be fine, won't she?" Rose asked Gerhard.

"Of course," he said. "She has been those other times."

"What other times?"

Gerhard shook his head. He had little patience for his younger sister. "She will be fine," he repeated.

They were seated at one end of the long dining table beneath the brass chandelier, eating apricot dumplings with cinnamon. Cook seemed to have forgotten that they had had strudel after lunch. Rose had already polished off her serving, but her brother had about half left. Between small careful bites, he turned to a composition notebook by his side, studied a list he'd written.

"What's that?" Rose asked. Normally she tried not to ask Gerhard too many questions. Her brother loved nothing more than to lord his knowledge over her. But right now she would do anything not to think of her mother lying pale down the hall.

Gerhard considered for a moment. "I am working out how to sell tickets to the Dianabad pool," he surprised Rose by answering. "Near the wave machine."

"But the Dianabad is public, and the season doesn't open for two more months," she felt compelled to say. "No one owns those spots."

He let out an exaggerated sigh, but it was no match for the glow of satisfaction lighting up his face. "You can sell anything, if you know how."

Rose heard steps and Bette's fair head appeared. "Gerhard, I could use your help." He got up and Rose did too, following them down the long hall, away from where Mutti was lying, and into their parents' bedroom.

The brocade curtains were drawn, the embroidered coverlet on the bed smoothed back, the pile of silk pillows just so. The room was chilly, and all the exactitude made Rose uneasy. "Why are we here?" she asked.

Bette sighed. "You don't have to be," she said, and to Gerhard: "She wants the painting of the boy."

"The painting?" Rose said, as surprised as if she had been told that her mother had arisen this morning and announced she was joining a nunnery.

Gerhard and Bette were already tugging at the gold frame. "She said she sleeps better with it nearby. And we are not to question her. Do you hear?"

Rose nodded. She couldn't imagine questioning her mother, today of all days.

Bette, thin-shouldered, only a few years older than Gerhard, strained as she tilted the heavy picture, scraping the plastered wall. "Gentle, gentle," she cautioned as Gerhard helped her heave it off.

Rose joined them as they carried it down the hall, and she considered it a victory that Bette didn't shoo her away.

Inside the little room, Mutti lay against white pillows on the cot. She wore a white nightgown, but the darkness of her hair, piled up on her head, stood out in contrast to all that white. Rose decided it gave her face definition. She was still reassuringly herself, beautiful. The room was cozy, the porcelain *kachelofen* chugging away, Mutti's brass lamp with the pink glass shade casting a warm glow. Bette must have moved it in, Rose realized.

A cane-backed chair sat close to the cot, and Bette and Gerhard angled the painting to rest on it. "Thank you," Mutti whispered. Her dark eyes fell on the picture, and Rose followed her mother's gaze. The boy in the painting was not pretty. He was too skinny in his red uniform, his face pasty and elongated. The paint was thick, thrown on; it looked as if the painter couldn't be bothered to slow down and pay attention. Rose didn't understand why her mother loved it so.

"Children, you are here." She said it wonderingly, not at all the sharp Mutti Rose knew, and it made Rose wish she had stayed at the dining table and not followed her brother in. Mutti motioned for her to come close, she laid a hand on Rose's head. Rose saw that the bedsheets were Mutti's favorite, edged with crochet. "My little *mausi*," she murmured, and Rose felt chastened.

"Beef broth, ma'am?" Bette said. "The doctor said you must eat."

"I could use a touch of something," Mutti said, and leaned back against the pillows.

Bette curtsied, and signaled to the children. "Come, let your mother rest."

Back in the drawing room, Gerhard picked up the volume about the Kaiser that he had been reading, sank into the wingback chair near the windows.

"Why does she like the painting so much?" Rose leaned against the chair behind her brother, playing with the fringed edges of the

Persian throw that covered the top of the cushion. Across the room, a glazed porcelain vase crowded with roses occupied a spot on the mantel. Why hadn't her mother asked for flowers instead?

"I don't know," Gerhard said, and he didn't look up from the book. "She does."

"Well, I think it's ugly."

"Of course you do. You're too young to understand it."

"I know *you* don't either," she said, coloring. And from the way Gerhard pushed his nose into the book, peered at the pages more closely, Rose could tell that she was not wrong, and it irked him.

"Who is the boy in the painting?" Rose ventured. "Does she know him?"

"No. She bought it in Paris on a trip with Papi, years ago," Gerhard said, not looking up. "You were just a baby. You don't remember."

Gerhard was right. She didn't remember. The painting of the boy had always been in their flat, along with so many other things. Rose loved the tapestry of the peacock with its lustrous blues that hung near the swords that had been her grandfather's, the velvet jewelry case with the silver clasp that had been Oma's, the small landscape of a waterfall that if you were attentive and looked behind the copse of trees (which Rose always did), you could detect the shadow of a bear.

But her mother doted on the painting of the boy, took considerable comfort from it. It disturbed Rose. "I wish it were gone," she said with coarse agitation.

1

LOS ANGELES,
DECEMBER 2005

LIZZIE MADE HERSELF LOOK. The pine casket was descending, the sun playing against its surface, metal railings guiding it into the ground. A knot of cemetery workers stood nearby, shovels in hand. She gazed past them toward a trio of slender cypress trees cutting sharp against the resolutely blue sky. It was not yet noon but already hot. Out of the corner of her eye, she registered smudges wheeling and darting. Hummingbirds? Possibly. They used to flit around the twisted vines of scarlet bougainvillea out by her father's pool. She could remember her father pointing to the tiny birds when she and Sarah first moved to L.A. "Hummingbirds don't hum," he had said. "Hear that? It's more of a *scratch-scratch*. No poetry there."

Now Lizzie squinted behind the oversized sunglasses that she'd purchased last summer on Canal Street, played with her father's watch. The Rolex was too big and loose for her wrist, but it was his. She looked again in the direction of the cypresses, but whatever birds had been there were gone. Or maybe they had never been there at all. She heard the rabbi chanting. She grasped her sister's hand.

This was a mistake. It could not be right. How could that be her father in there? How was that possible?

Lizzie had last spoken to him four days ago. She had left work that Thursday at a decent hour and was negotiating the crush of people on Sixth Avenue when he had called. He was telling her about a few trips he was planning. Next month to Iceland: he was talking about Reykjavík and eating fermented shark and how the first lady was Jewish, Israeli-born. The following spring he wanted to go to Seoul. Lizzie was only half listening, her mind focused on getting on the subway downtown so she wouldn't be late. (Another online date, another evening for which she was trying—unsuccessfully—to keep her expectations low.) Still she couldn't help but say, "So many trips. I thought you were concerned about money."

"No," he had said. "*You* think I should be concerned about money."

She half laughed, half snorted. "I do not," she had said, but that was the way it had always been between them. She was thirty-seven, and little had changed since she was seventeen.

An hour later, Lizzie thought her date was going fine, but after one round he stuck out his hand and said, "Good luck with everything!" (A banker and former ZBT brother? Just as well.) She went home, poured herself a glass of wine, settled on the IKEA couch that she kept telling herself she had to replace, and chanced on *WarGames* on TV. She reached for her phone and pecked out a text, all thumbs. "The only move is not to play," she typed. "Bullshit eighties propaganda. I'm jealous," Claudia soon responded, and Lizzie laughed, feeling better already.

The first two calls didn't wake her, but the third did, and Sarah's voice sounded high-pitched and strange: "There's been an accident, a car accident." Lizzie got on the first flight the next morning. She took a cab to JFK well before dawn and landed in L.A. just as the sun was coming up, the dishwatery gray of the sky turning a lurid orange. As she barreled over skeins of freeway to UCLA, she chanted to herself: *He'll be fine, he has to be fine.* But he never regained consciousness.

Now the rabbi motioned for the sisters to stand. Angela, on Sarah's other side, stood too, her arm around Sarah's shoulders. Lizzie clutched her sister's hand. She wished she were standing in the shade of those cypresses. She could hear the rush of cars on the nearby freeway, sounding like water. An unspeakable thought intruded: *What if the doctors had been wrong? What if for one moment when they unhooked the machines and covered him up, what if he had still been alive?*

The rabbi gestured for them to come forward, toward the fresh mound of soil beside the gaping hole. A shovel pierced the dirt, stood upright.

Lizzie remembered little of her mother's funeral, but she recalled that hill of dirt. She had been thirteen then. Lynn had been sick for about a year (and surely long before that, Lizzie realized after she died). During that year, while her mother got sicker and sicker, Lizzie and her sister continued to go to school and Hebrew school, taking ice-skating and clarinet lessons—pretending, fruitlessly, that everything would be fine. Their grandmother moved in. Joseph stepped up his visits, coming once a month. (She overheard her mother on the phone with her father: "No, no, Joseph, that's ridiculous. You need to be out there, working. I am *fine*.") He took them to the Ground Round and to Friendly's for Fribbles as he had when he and Lynn first split up and he'd moved into a rental in the city, before his friend convinced him to join his ophthalmological surgical practice out in Los Angeles, before there was the slightest inkling of Lynn's cancer.

During their mother's illness, Lizzie was the one heating up cans of Chef Boyardee for herself and Sarah, forging their permission slips, lugging up loads of laundry; she was the one who went to Sarah's soccer games. (Except for those times that she didn't, using the money her mother gave her for snacks to play Ms. Pac-Man at the arcade, slamming wrist against joystick and gobbling up those dots and cherries as if her life depended on it.) She always thought her additional domestic duties, emotional and practical, would be temporary.

She was twelve years old. Things would change. Never did she think they would change because her mother would die.

Sarah squeezed her hand, and the warm pressure of her palm, the tightness of her fingers, somehow enabled Lizzie to move forward. She took a step, stumbling slightly, but she righted herself when she took hold of the shovel's metal handle. It was heavier than she thought, but she pressed down and succeeded in flinging down a paltry patch of dirt. The hollow thump of the soil making contact with the lid of the coffin—a *pling*, really—was a harrowing, haunting sound.

Where was her father?

AFTERWARD, THEY DECAMPED TO AN art gallery at Bergamot Station. The long narrow space filled up quickly. The air grew warm. So many people, from so many different parts of her father's life: med-school classmates and cousins and ex-girlfriends and former patients and neighbors and the caterer who was also the mother of Sarah's friend from middle school (she and Joseph had probably dated, Lizzie realized with a start). Her father would have loved this. It almost felt like he was here. Max, Joseph's good friend, offered her a drink. She shook her head. "Coffee," she said. "Please," her voice sounding tinny in her ears.

Lizzie thought she spotted Claudia, but as she fought her way through the tangle of hips and elbows, the crowd closed in, tightening. It felt less like a memorial than an art opening. The space was so hot and packed; the loud voices seemed to warble, ricocheting against each other. She stood, uncertain.

"Oh, Lizzie. Oh, oh." Before Lizzie knew what was happening, a soft rotund woman rushed up and threw her arms around her. "I'm so so sorry about your father," she said. "He was wonderful."

"Thank you," Lizzie said, her cheek pressed into the woman's wiry earring. She smelled of baby powder. Who was she? And then it clicked: her father's former secretary Pat. She had worked for him for a year, maybe two, tops, ages ago. It was during the time when his practice was booming, when Joseph issued limos to bring patients in for their cataract surgeries. All the Beverly Hills ladies loved him. He was raking in the profits and was eager to spend—on trips to Hawaii and Morocco, two-seater Italian convertibles, artwork that he liked to show off during dinner parties. All Lizzie remembered about Pat was that she was a rabid Clippers fan and lived with her brother. In fact, Lizzie now recalled, the brother started coming into Joseph's office, hanging around until his sister got off work. *The patients don't like it*, Lizzie could remember Joseph complaining. *I don't like it*. Pat was still hugging Lizzie, an awkward intimacy. But Pat felt strongly about her father, and Lizzie held on.

"I hadn't seen him in months," Pat said, finally pulling back. "Maybe even a year. What kind of person am I? It had been so long. Why hadn't I made plans?"

"It's okay," Lizzie said. "I'm sure he felt the same way." She added this even though she couldn't remember the last time her father had mentioned Pat.

"But I should have known better. I *knew* better. And now he's gone. It's too late. I can't believe he's gone." Pat's voice trembled.

"I know," Lizzie said. She couldn't bring herself to say anything more. *Remove yourself*, she could hear her father say. Where was Sarah? Claudia? She wanted a rescue.

"He was still young. And now he's gone, just like that. I can't believe it. You poor girls." She gave Lizzie's hand a squeeze. "I'm going to miss him so much."

"Thank you," Lizzie managed, "I have to—" and with her sentence unfinished, she fled.

At the back of the gallery, she stood against the wall, praying that it was close to five P.M. They had called for the memorial to end then. There were fewer people back here, no one who seemed to recognize her, and that enabled her to breathe. It was hard to be around people. But she did not want to be alone. She gazed at a large photograph of a man's torso, elongated and stretched thin.

"There you are," Claudia said. "I've been looking all over for you."

"Found," Lizzie said as she threw herself into her friend's arms, desperate for solidity.

After a moment, Claudia pulled back, cocked her head to the side. "How are you doing?"

Lizzie touched the back of her head. Her hair felt frizzy, her body unclean, her eyes itchy from lack of sleep, all the coffee she'd been drinking. She kept waiting for Joseph to emerge from the crowd. "I'm okay," she said.

Claudia looked at her steadily and didn't say a thing. Finally she said: "Have you eaten? I have to say, the food is shockingly good. Your father would be proud."

"All Angela's doing." Lizzie's sister's girlfriend was the one who had reached out to the gallery owner, an old friend of Joseph's; Angela had set up the caterer, she hired the bartender and arranged for the chair rentals too. "I feel like I should be doing more," Lizzie confessed.

"Are you kidding me? Today, of all days?"

"I know," Lizzie said. Still, it made her uneasy.

"That's Angela. She's probably making you feel that way."

"I don't think so. She's been great."

"Uh-huh. I spoke with her earlier, and she seemed as prickly as ever."

"You're terrible," Lizzie said, laughing. It felt good to laugh.

"I'm right. You know, it stems from insecurity. She's just afraid your sister's going to leave her for a doctor or a lawyer."

"Angela *is* a doctor," Lizzie corrected her. "An anesthesiologist, remember?"

"Oh yeah. Well, then, a doctor with a dick," Claudia said, unperturbed. She chewed on a strawberry. "You didn't answer me: Have you eaten today?"

"A little," Lizzie lied.

"Come on," Claudia said. "Let's get you some food and libation."

Soon Lizzie was biting into a bagel that Claudia had loaded up, eating it for her friend's sake. She truly wasn't hungry. The bagel itself was dry, but the lox was fantastic, not too salty, buttery—where was it from? she found herself wondering. Then she realized her father would wonder. She turned to the lukewarm Chardonnay. Last night, despite the Ambien, she'd woken up in a sweat around four in the morning in her sister's guest room, her heart galloping, not remembering where she was or what was so criminally wrong. A maw of fear overtook her. Oh God, her father.

Claudia fished through her bag. She picked up her buzzing phone, rolling her eyes. "This had better be crucial. I told you I'm at a fucking funeral," she said. "Uh-huh, okay." She mouthed to Lizzie, *I'll be right back.*

Lizzie nodded but she felt a flip of panic. She couldn't handle another conversation like the one she had with Pat. Where was her sister? She eyed the narrow room. The crowd had thinned. She didn't see Sarah. She went to the bathroom, found the door locked.

As Lizzie waited against the wall, she looked at a nearby canvas: A large-scale painting, depicting a couple sitting on a boat-sized couch, watching TV. The man's feet were propped up on an ottoman, the woman sitting up straight, only inches apart, but a discernible distance. Sunlight spilled in from a window but their eyes remained on the glowing screen. They paid no mind to the largest object in the room: an elephant, standing to the right of them.

The elephant in the room. Lizzie let out a snort. It was funny, but it was more than that. The painting itself was beautiful: the elephant's leathery wrinkly hide, the polished elegance of his curved tusks. And it was this gorgeously rendered specificity, the fact that the painter was willing to bestow such attention, that made her think of Ben. He would like it too.

Did he know about her dad? She wanted him to know. And yet

she didn't feel like she could call him. It had been nearly three years since they had broken up. She still sometimes wondered if she had made a mistake.

The bathroom door opened, and an old woman Lizzie didn't recognize came out. She saw Lizzie looking at the painting. "What do you think?" she asked, her hands on her hips like a general.

"I like it," Lizzie said. "You?"

"Not really," the woman said. She was tiny, in a dark tailored suit with a brightly colored scarf at her neck. She spoke with a gravelly voice that made Lizzie think of peeling paint. It carried a hint of an accent—British?—that she could not place.

"You don't?" Lizzie asked. What was there not to like?

"She's not working hard enough. I'll bet you she's capable of more. At the end of the day, what are you left with?"

There was more to it than that. The joke was only the start. She could hear her father say, *Tim-ing, now that is everything.* But Lizzie only said: "I always thought being funny could get you fairly far."

The woman looked at her, her thin mouth expanding into a smile. "It's nice to finally meet you. I'm Rose Downes." She held out a hand. "I'm so sorry about your father."

Oh God, was she supposed to know her? Lizzie could be terrible with names. "Thank you. It was nice of you to come today." She hesitated. "I'm sorry; how did you know my father?"

Rose touched the silk at her neck and smiled inwardly. "You probably know me better as the woman whose family used to own *The Bellhop.*"

Lizzie couldn't have heard her right. "*The Bellhop?*"

"Yes."

"My Soutine?"

"Well," Rose said, and drew her lips in. "Some might argue it's *my* Soutine. It was my family's. But yes, that painting."

"And my father knew this?" Lizzie said thickly.

"Yes, of course he knew," Rose said with a touch of exasperation. "That's how we met."

"I'm sorry," Lizzie said. "I didn't realize—" She couldn't finish her thought.

Lizzie first saw the painting on the day she arrived in L.A. after her mother died. She hadn't been to her father's house in close to a year. He opened the front door and she was hit by the light, a blinding California light. The floor-to-ceiling windows in the living room were like a taut glass skin—a country of it, everywhere you turned. She walked to the windows, stuck her face up against the glass, and peered down into the mouth of the parched ravine, the yawning canyon far below. The depth to which she could tumble filled her with a bruising, voluminous peace. It was larger than her mother's cancer, bigger than moving across the country to live with a father she didn't really know.

She turned around and, with her fingers still pressed up against the glass, she saw him. Across from the fireplace hung a painting of a man. A young man, dressed in a uniform, a fancy red uniform with gold buttons. His face and limbs were elongated, his ears elephantine. His nose was crooked, as if someone had slammed a fist into it. His stance was awkward, his head too large for his body. He didn't seem to know what to do with his hands. But the colors! His face was a riot of swirls: when she went closer to the canvas, she discovered other hues in his uniform, dips of blue and white, streaks of gold and black and purple, as if whoever had painted it couldn't contain himself, as if he were unleashing all the pigment he had at his disposal. It was angry and ugly and dizzying and beautiful, all at once.

"You like that?" Joseph asked. "It's pretty nice, isn't it?"

She shrugged. "It's okay," she said, and sat down below it. All that red!

He cleared his throat. "For someone not interested, you're paying a lot of attention."

Lizzie gave another shrug, stayed silent. She made her father nervous, she was realizing, and she found, to her surprise, that she liked this feeling, the tart taste of power like a cold marble in her mouth.

"It's by a guy named Soutine. He was a French Expressionist. Which can refer to many things, but expensive is one," Joseph continued. "I first saw it years ago, in New York." He paused. "With your mother. She liked it too."

As Lizzie remembered, she saw Rose looking past her at the elephant in the room. "I thought your father told you, but perhaps I misunderstood," Rose said. "I truly liked him. My condolences to you and your sister." She nodded quickly.

"Your family owned the Soutine," Lizzie said, her mind too awhirl to settle on a question.

"We did."

"Where? Where are you from?"

"Vienna. My mother purchased it in Paris, in the twenties, and brought it back home."

"Oh," Lizzie said. The accent fell in place. "And then?"

"It was stolen. When the Germans came."

"Oh," she repeated. She did the math in her head. She understood. "I'm sorry."

Rose nodded. "I know it was taken from you too. I met your father, afterward. I read about the theft in the newspaper. There was a small item in the *L.A. Times*—"

Lizzie felt a familiar tightness in her stomach. She remembered reading that article months later, before she left for college. She was looking for stamps on her father's mess of a desk when she came across a short clipping from the paper, and the memories from that night came flooding back as surely as if she had been slapped. *Why was he saving it? Why was it here on his desk?* She crumbled it up, buried it deep in the wastebasket. But within the hour she stole back into his study, fished it out, ironed out the wrinkles as best she could, and placed it back where she had found it, feeling guilty once again.

"My husband read it," Rose was saying. "I couldn't believe it—*The Bellhop*, here, in Los Angeles! I hadn't seen it since I left Vienna as a child. I got in touch with your father. In the beginning, we met to talk about the painting and the theft. But—well, through the years, we just kept meeting. Not often, but we'd go to lunch or maybe an exhibit together. He always drove. I abhor driving. And he took me places I hadn't been."

"Really?" Lizzie asked, the tightness beneath her ribs easing up. She could imagine it, her father with Rose. "Where would you go?"

"Different places. The Bradbury Building, for one."

"Oh, I love that building." Her father took her there after she watched *Blade Runner* in her high school film class. She could remember the moment of stepping past the plain façade into the sun-soaked interior, all that gorgeous wrought iron. *It's even better in person, isn't it?* her father had said, and there was such delight in his voice; even if she hadn't liked it, she would have agreed.

"It's overrated," Rose said with a shrug. "Too much going on. You know the architect famously claimed he got a message from a Ouija board as to how to design it. It looks that way."

Lizzie let out a snort of a laugh. She couldn't help herself. She liked this woman.

"We went years ago," Rose continued, unfazed by Lizzie's laughter. "And to Grand Central Market afterward. This was before it was cleaned up, fancified. We tried four different kinds of *mole*, and all were delicious."

Lizzie could picture it precisely—her father leading past stalls filled high with dried chilies and avocados and mangoes, past the lunch counter with its neon sign advertising chop suey. The thought gave her a lift, made her, for a brief moment, happy. "I wish I could have been there."

Rose gave a hint of a smile. "Yes," she said, and they both fell into silence. Rose glanced toward the front of the room and Lizzie followed her gaze. The gallery had emptied out; Lizzie saw the

Ellen Umansky

bartender stacking glasses into an orange plastic crate. "I have to get going," Rose said. "My condolences again." She nodded seriously.

"No, you haven't met my sister yet—"

"Another time."

"Only if you mean it. I really would like to talk to you more."

"Of course."

But Lizzie couldn't shake the feeling that if Rose left, she would never see her again. She could just hear Sarah: *You met who? She claimed to have owned what?* And this fear lent a particular urgency. "You said you were born in Vienna," Lizzie said. "During the war—where were you?"

Rose touched the bright silk at her neck. Her eyes in her lined face were like polished dark stones. "I was in England," she said.

She said it so simply, seemed so matter-of-fact about it that Lizzie decided to add: "So you got out."

"My brother and I did," Rose said. "My parents did not."

"Oh," Lizzie said. It was terrible, what Rose was saying. She didn't have to say more. "I'm so sorry."

"It's happened," Rose said firmly, as if Lizzie were trying to convince her otherwise.

2

VIENNA, 1938–1939

THEY WERE NEARLY PREPARED. BETTE had filled the wooden bucket halfway with water and set it next to the tiled stove. A cast-iron ladle leaned against the bucket, and a collection of small tin balls nestled in a snowy dishcloth, as if preparing for the alchemy that lay ahead. Rose had purchased them earlier in the week with her own money, from the bounty of the two shillings that Oma had given her for her eleventh birthday last month, forgoing a chance to see *One in a Million* at the UFA movie house. When she slid her coins over the counter, the wizened shop clerk had cracked a lopsided grin at her. "And a happy new year to you, young lady." Rose pocketed the tin balls with a smile, feeling giddy and shy with belonging.

Now she fingered a pellet and rolled it around in her palm. It was light, to be sure, but it still felt substantial, hard. She liked the feel of the cool metal against her skin. "Are you sure it will melt?" she asked.

"Of course I'm sure. I've been doing it as long as I can remember," Bette said, and she punched the heel of her palm into the dough. "It's heat to metal; it's what happens."

Bette was from the country, nearly half a day's train ride outside of Vienna—a village where chickens ruled the dirt streets, water was drawn from a well, and a movie house was an inchoate fantasy. Rose thought of herself as having a good imagination, but when she tried to picture herself living in such a place, the movie in her mind simply stopped, unspooled itself off the reel.

Rose moved closer. "When can we start?" She felt itchy in the woolens that her mother made her wear, her feet sweating in her thick black boots.

"I need to finish my work first."

And my parents have to leave, Rose thought, but she knew it would annoy Bette if she said it. After Rose had bought the tin balls, she tucked them deep into her knapsack, never mentioning her purchase to her mother. *Lead pouring is an old wives' tale*, she could hear Mutti say. *That's what they learn in the country.* But how would Rose know it wasn't true unless she tried? Everyone else was having fun on New Year's Eve—Gerhard was staying at his friend Oskar's for the weekend, her parents were going to a party at Tante Greta's—why shouldn't she too?

Rose watched Bette's slender fingers ribbon the edges of the dough, the smell of the yeast tickling her nostrils. "Heinrich says too much bread isn't good for your constitution," she said.

"Is that so?"

Rose nodded. "He says in the future we'll probably swallow a pill instead of taking meals." She dipped her fingers in the water of the bucket and swished them around. She had just reported the entirety of one of her conversations with Heinrich. They had had two in total. She had met him last summer at the holiday camp she had attended at the foot of the Alps. He was a reedy redhead a year her senior who spent most of his time ferreting out shade to read Jules Verne. When she saw him crossing the grounds, holding his book like armor to his concave chest, such a fluttery feeling arose in her stomach—Rose had never felt something like that before.

"Only people who have an excess of food would complain about it," Bette said when: *brrring!* The bell sounded. Rose started. "Let's go see what the missus wants," Bette said, wiping her floury hands against her apron and heading toward the door. Rose followed. "Not *you.*" Bette let out one of those thin knowing laughs Rose hated. "She rang for me, not for you. I'll be back soon."

After Bette left, Rose tried to amuse herself by attempting to toss the tin balls into the bucket. But each time she failed. Finally she decided to go to her parents' bedroom, see what Bette had been summoned for.

She took the long hall—still harboring a new-paint odor—past the pantry and laundry and turned down the second hall that led to the drawing room and her father's study, guarded by the double swords her grandfather had purchased in Constantinople. In their old flat, the swords had hung in the drawing room, but her mother had argued that the new home demanded a new start. Nothing was where it used to be. The one exception, Rose thought as she cut through the sitting area to knock on their bedroom door: the portrait of *The Bellhop.* In the bedroom it remained, despite her father's objections. ("I should be the only man in here," he said.)

"Come in," Mutti called. For Rose, the shift was as great as stepping from the darkened movie house into bright afternoon sunlight. She registered the smell of lilies and the rustling sound of silk before she could take in the dazzle of her mother in her entirety.

Charlotte was giving her nose a final pat of powder. A smooth lock of hair dipped down below her left eyebrow, giving Rose the unsettling impression that Mutti was winking. She wore a navy silk gown that made her pale skin look paler, her dark hair darker. Her beauty made Rose feel light-headed and envious and wistful and proud, all at once.

"Where's Bette?"

Mutti tsked. "Manners, child. What kind of greeting is that?"

"I don't know," Rose said, and looked down at her toes. Her feet felt even sweatier, entombed in her boots.

"An honest one," Papi said. Wolfe was short but nimble, always in motion. He fiddled with his tie. "We should go."

Mutti shook her head—at Rose or Papi, Rose wasn't sure. "Bette is fixing the fastener on my cape. It should only take a moment."

Her father frowned. "We'll be late. We're expected at Greta's in less than an hour."

"And it will take us less than half an hour to get there. We're not in the nineteenth district anymore."

He looked away from her, gave his tie one last decisive tug. "Indeed we are not."

Her mother had pressed hard for the move to this apartment, Rose knew, to this neighborhood in particular. Now they were close to the embassy quarter, within walking distance of Ringstrasse and the Opera—her mother's dream. No one else had seen the point in moving. So what if some rooms in their old flat were forever hot and others forever cold? Who cared if their stretch of Liechtenstein-strasse was thick with leather and machinery shops? The man in the shop on the corner always gave Rose peppermint candy when she passed, and she loved playing in the walled garden of the hospital two blocks away. But her mother persevered—she always did.

"If we're late, maybe we'll miss Karl's speechifying," Wolfe said. "He makes it sound as if Schuschnigg is already at the gate, waiting to swing it open for Hitler."

"No politics," Charlotte said. "Not tonight."

Rose had studied the Great War in school. She knew that Papi had been a foot soldier in northern Italy, but he didn't like to talk about it. She heard him once telling Gerhard, "I fought a war so you don't have to."

Bette came in, holding Mutti's wool cape in outstretched hands. "Ma'am," she said, and offered it to Charlotte.

"Perfect," Mutti said. "Thank you." Bette gave a little curtsy and bob of her head and left. "I'm glad I noticed it before we left," her mother said.

"Yes, can you imagine? Someone might have said, 'Your cape fastener is loose. Horrors!'" Her father widened his eyes at Rose, who giggled.

Charlotte pursed her lips. "Someone should look presentable, don't you think?" She touched Rose's head. "You're a good girl."

"Thank you, Mutti," Rose said. "Good night."

"We'll see you next year," Papi said, and he too touched her head and they were gone.

SHE *WAS* A GOOD GIRL, Rose thought as she ran a hand over the polished brass handles of her mother's inlaid dresser. But not *that* good. She sat down on her mother's settee and yanked off her black boots and woolens, liberating her sweaty feet, the air delicious between her toes. Then she went over to her mother's closet, running her hand against her dresses—silk and worsted wool and light cotton.

She paused at a peacock-blue dress, linen with an Empire waist and beautiful white piping. Mutti had worn the dress at Bad Ischl last summer, when they ate pink ice cream in the café. Rose remembered how after the ice cream, they ran into Herr Schulman, her mother's piano teacher, near the river. When Charlotte's hat blew off, Herr Schulman leaped after it, retrieving it with speed, heaving, and handed it back to her with such a grin on his face, as if he'd won a grand prize. Now Rose tugged off her own dress and slipped into her mother's. It was enormous—the square neckline slipped off her shoulders—yet it felt wonderful, like sipping from a big glass of lemonade in the shade of summer.

Rose wound a long string of her mother's pearls around her neck, dusted her face with powder. She added her favorite scarf of her mother's, blue-and-purple silk with a pattern of birds perched on branches, others with wings open in flight. The material felt fine and elegant against her neck. Rose assessed herself in the mirror and spoke: "Why, thank you, Heinrich, I would love to dance." She gave a curtsy and held out her hands. She pictured Ginger Rogers and Fred Astaire. She spun in a circle. Once, twice.

When she stopped, she was in front of *The Bellhop*. The boy in the painting gazed at her. How many times had she looked at the picture? She knew Mutti had bought it on a whim in a Parisian gallery for far too much money—so said Papi. It had been painted by a man named Soutine, who was Jewish, her mother liked to say, as they were. (But *Ostenjuden*, her father would often add, not like us—an immigrant, from the east.) Rose had not changed her mind. She still thought the portrait ugly, but she couldn't stop looking at it.

The boy in the painting stood awkwardly in his red uniform, gold buttons glinting, a matching red triangular hat perched atop his head. His hands rested on his hips, legs straddled open so wide he looked as if he might topple over. His pale face was impassive, his dark eyebrows shot up high. There was a resentful look in his eyes, as if he didn't trust the painter, the endeavor altogether. The paint itself was so thickly piled on that Rose had the feeling it had been created in the middle of an argument—she heard shouting, she saw the flinging of color onto the canvas.

But now, none of this mattered. He did look awkward and unpleasant, but he was a boy only a few years older than herself, a boy who wanted more than anything to escape: his uniform, his life, his own skin. He didn't want to be unpleasant, Rose was convinced. She longed to help him.

"I'm sorry," she said. "I didn't mean to be rude." She curtsied and said, "Yes, I would love another dance."

Bette's high pitch cut through Rose's imagining. "Rose, where are you?"

"Coming," Rose called as she stepped out of the dress and left *The Bellhop* behind.

BETTE WOULDN'T LET HER HOLD the ladle. "You're my responsibility," she said, tossing her thin braid back. "Heaven forbid you burn yourself." But she did hand Rose a ball. "Now roll it around tightly, and shake well. My *oma* always said that this gives them your strength, your print."

Rose made a fist and shook. Then she placed the ball in the cast-iron ladle. Bette positioned the ladle on top of the stove's front burner. She held it with a steady hand over the flames. Every few seconds she angled the ladle from side to side, a graceful balletic move. Soon the lead ball was shuddering under the heat, no longer a ball but a silvery amoeba-like creature, slithering to spread to the edges of the spoon. Rose, peering close, thought of the fat caterpillars she and Gerhard spotted down by the marshy banks of the Danube. "Is it ready?"

"Almost," Bette murmured.

Rose felt the heat. The ball had lost its color altogether. It flashed iridescent, something otherworldly, like something out of Jules Verne.

"Okay," Bette said. "Now." And Rose didn't know how she did it, but Bette managed to keep the ladle steady and guided Rose's hands to her own too. "You slide it into the water," Bette said. "My *oma* says it's part of the fortune."

Although her stomach was careening, Rose obliged. She could feel an emerging, nearly drowsy sensation that took her a few beats to recognize as calm. Bette transferred the ladle to Rose, but kept her hands on Rose's, and it was this warmth too, this feeling of support and connection, that Rose cottoned to, would remember for years to come when Vienna seemed like a dream.

"Now!" Bette ordered, and Rose released the bubbling metallic mass. A bright, tinkling noise sounded as the hot metal hit the water. Though there was little splash, Rose tipped back. She wiped her sweaty forehead and peered over the pail. The metal had hardened immediately. She couldn't discern its shape. She was almost afraid to look. Over the past week, she had listened attentively as Bette described the possible shapes and their corresponding fortunes: Would they see a ship, which would indicate travel in the next year? (Rose very much hoped this would be the case.) A ball could mean that luck would roll your way. If the metal resembled an anchor, that meant that you must help someone in need; and a cross . . . "Well, let us hope we don't see a cross," Bette had said, making the sign of a cross.

But all Rose could make out was a bubbly surface: "That's money! That's definitely money," Bette said with true excitement, but Rose was looking down farther—more money would mean more movies, it would mean more travel too, wouldn't it? But then, oh, there was something else, a small little something, a thin piece of metal no wider than her thumb.

"Do you see that? What's that little piece, there?" Rose pointed.

But Bette had already turned, she had pulled out the spoon. "I saw it—that doesn't count—let's try again."

IN FEBRUARY, BETTE'S MOTHER FELL ill and she went home to take care of her younger brothers and sisters. In March, Chancellor Schuschnigg opened the gate for Hitler after all. Now instead of shillings and groschen, there were marks and pfennig. There were German soldiers in uniform on the street saluting one another. They spoke in funny accents, which Papi imitated with gusto at home, but fell silent when outside.

The Vienna spring of 1938 was unusually balmy. The lilac bloomed early, the chestnut trees preened with their gaudy pink blossoms, and the park benches sprouted new signs: NO JEWS PERMITTED TO SIT HERE.

In school, Rose and her Jewish classmates were moved to the back of the room, six of them occupying the last row, separated from the Christian students by two empty rows. They were a world apart now, the Jewish students. Rose hated sitting in the back. She hated class. And to make matters worse, Gerhard didn't have to go to school anymore. The new restrictions said that Jewish children the age of fifteen or older didn't have to attend. It was so unfair, Rose thought, why couldn't she stay home like her brother?

By June, Bette was no longer allowed to work for them. Wolfe's importing business—which Rose's grandfather had started when he was a young man living in Constantinople decades earlier—had been repatriated. Papi disappeared for hours at a time into his study, barricading himself behind the tall thin pages of the *Neue Freie Presse*. But more distressingly to Rose, nearly as significant as Bette's departure, was this: Rose wasn't allowed to go to the movie house anymore.

"I can't go to *any* movie?" she asked. For a moment, she could imagine a dividing line: *Snow White*, yes; anything with Deanna Durbin, no.

"It's part of the restrictions," Papi said. "Those are the rules."

They were sitting at the dark oak dining table after dinner, drinking coffee and eating tiny delicious choux pastries with cream filling that Tante Greta had brought over. Mutti kept the bell to the right of her, as if a new unnamed maid might miraculously appear if she rang.

They had been talking about visas. They were always talking about visas, Rose thought, tired. They weren't going anywhere. Tante Greta had come for a visit while Onkel George went to the American embassy. Everyone said there were no American visas available until 1950, but still, they went to put their names on the list.

"Can Ilse still go to the movies?" Rose asked.

"Of course. She's not Jewish," Gerhard said, waving a spoon at his younger sister. "Idiot."

Rose waited for her father to admonish her brother, but Wolfe only lifted his eyes skyward. Rose followed his gaze up to the plaster ceiling.

"She's a child," Charlotte said to her husband, plainly enough for everyone to hear. "You think they would bother a child?"

His dark eyes became slits. "Do you really want to find out?" he snapped.

Mutti shook her head, gaze averted. Rose shot a look to her brother, but Gerhard bent over his plate and ate uncharacteristically fast.

Papi looked at all of them, into that great bowl of silence. When he spoke again, his voice had dropped. "My apologies," he said. His strangled voice was far worse than his yelling. He pushed his chair back, hurried out of the room.

For a moment, there was only the sound of scraping: Gerhard's spoon against china, as he took great care to chase down every last morsel of whipped cream. Then Tante Greta spoke: "And, Charlotte, Rose should get rid of her movie-stub collection too; it's unhygienic to have all those old tickets lying around."

Rose stared at her plate, blistered by her fury. She hated every single member of her family, but her Tante Greta most of all; she truly did.

A WEEK LATER, ROSE, MUTTI, and Gerhard decamped from Vienna to spend the summer months with Charlotte's parents in the country in Parndoff, and for a while everything seemed normal, good even. Every morning Rose helped her grandfather tug his apartment window open and lower a string down to the street. Within a few minutes a boy would yell out, "Ready!" and Rose's grandfather, with her assistance, would haul the string back up, the day's newspaper attached.

Rose spent countless afternoons swimming in the Danube with Gerhard, who liked to ignore her but never said no when she tagged along. Rose would lie on the marshy banks, pushing her toes into the warm squishy mud, the sunlight against her bare arms a reminder that no, she hadn't fallen asleep. She wondered if Heinrich had gone back to the holiday camp. She listened to the drone of insects, she tried to ascertain the shapes of the gunmetal clouds scuttling above. She decided that the country was better than the city after all.

One afternoon she and Mutti went to the grocery store. As they were about to walk inside, Charlotte recognized a stout, redheaded woman fishing a triangle of cheese out of the wooden barrel out front. "Gertrude?" she said, "Gertrude Bieler?"

The woman looked up.

"It's Charlotte Zimmer. How nice to see you!"

With seeming ease, the fat woman spit at Mutti—a great hurl of saliva. Rose saw it darken a spot on her mother's lovely cotton blouse.

"What do you people want?" Frau Bieler hissed. "Why are you still here?"

Charlotte stood, a smile cemented on her face. She smiled and she didn't say a word.

"*Juden.*" Frau Bieler spit again, this time at her feet.

It was Rose who tugged at her mother's hand, Rose who sprang back to life first. "Mutti, Mutti," she said, the words tumbling out of her.

FALL, BACK IN VIENNA. THE days growing shorter, the sky paper white. Rose attended an all-Jewish school deep in the nineteenth district. It took more than an hour to get there by tram. There was discussion of keeping her at home. But for the time being, she continued to go. Everything, it seemed, now fell under the category of "for the time being."

Each day, a different embassy. This was how her parents spent their days, waiting at consulates for hours at a time—Canada, Argentina, Paraguay, Uruguay, Ireland, Cuba, China, it didn't matter where—lines snaking around corners, switchbacking up the sidewalk. A new dialect sprang up at home: Words like *affidavits, baptismal certificates, exit* and *entry visas* dominated the conversation. It was all the adults talked about: Try the Bolivian embassy in the late afternoon; avoid the man with the leathery face.

Wasn't there anything else they could discuss? Rose didn't want to hear their strained voices, the urgency with which they spoke. She missed Bette.

And Gerhard wasn't around to distract her. Her brother would disappear for hours at a time, sometimes saying he was going to meet Oskar, other times just slipping out without warning. They all knew he was going to see Ilse. "At least he doesn't look Jewish," Rose over-heard her mother say to her father. It was true; Gerhard was rangy and blond, and at sixteen he had a good couple of inches on their fa-ther, hitting six feet. Rose knew that Gerhard's looks brought her par-ents no small amount of comfort as they thought about him on the streets alone. She tried not to think about her own dark complexion.

In early November, a Jew murdered a Nazi in Paris. School was let out early, and Rose was told to hurry home, avoid the main thoroughfares and the trams. In the flat, they gathered around the wireless, glued to the broadcasts. Her parents wouldn't let her go out-side for days.

There were so many stories swirling: her mother's old piano teacher, Herr Schulman, had been arrested and was being held in Dachau. The Begeleisens had had their apartment repatriated—soldiers had come in the graying hours of dawn—and had been forced to move into a flat with three other families. Rose hadn't liked Peter Begeleisen; he had told her that witches like to yank teeth out of the mouths of little girls in the middle of the night, but still she felt bad for them. The Volkmans had managed to get out last week, their visas came through for Ireland. The husband had been able to land work as a machinist for a clothing factory outside of Belfast.

Their friends the Klaars had taken out a small classified adver-tisement in the *Jewish Chronicle*, seeking work in London, and Rose's parents decided to follow suit. They fought over the language in the ad. They fought a lot those days.

Wolfe wrote: "Would noble-minded people assist Viennese couple, capable of every kind of housework, knowledge of English, French, and Italian? Exemplary references upon request."

"No one cares what languages we speak," Charlotte said to Wolfe. He was sitting in the velvet wingback chair near the window, trying to balance the writing tablet on his knee in the watery light of the late afternoon. He now avoided his study.

"What do you suggest?"

Charlotte took the writing paper out of his hands. Wolfe played with the loose ivory threads from the Persian throw covering the velvet head cushion. His wide face looked slack, jowly.

She wrote: "Married couple, cook and footman, Jews, seek position in household."

"Everyone knows we're Jews," he said bitterly. "Why else would we be looking for work?"

"Then we shouldn't hide from it, should we?" Her mother said the words with such sharpness that Rose half expected blood to bloom.

ONE DAY IN JANUARY, ROSE came upon her mother in the kitchen. Charlotte wore Bette's old apron, which was too long on her. A jumble of pans and bowls and piles of snowy flour crowded the table. "What are you doing?" Rose asked.

"What does it look like? I'm baking." Charlotte pushed a strand of loose hair out of her glistening face with the back of her hand. "A poppy-seed cake."

"You bake?" Rose wouldn't have been more surprised if her mother had donned a pair of ice skates and broken out in song.

"Of course I bake," Charlotte said. "I do lots of things that you don't know about."

The next morning, Mutti dressed in her best suit, a houndstooth pencil skirt and flared jacket that Rose loved, with a creamy blouse with a scalloped neck. She looked like Greta Garbo. She muttered something about visiting Tante and rushed out the door, the poppy-seed cake held carefully in both hands. Rose watched her hurry down the street; the bare crooked fingers of the chestnut trees sliced the putty sky.

A week later, Rose found out where she had really been. The Kultusgemeinde, the city's Jewish community organization. Onkel George had a cousin who had a fiancée named Edith who worked for it. And because of this connection, Mutti said brightly, stooping to meet her daughter eye to eye, you're going to England!

They were in the drawing room, her father in his wingback chair, not saying a word.

"What?" Rose asked, blankly.

"You are going to England, where the queen lives with her two little princesses," Charlotte told her. "Remember Mutti showed you the pictures of the little girls in their beautiful dresses who live in castles?"

Rose stared. Her mother was speaking as if she were a baby, a girl of six years old, and not eleven. She wasn't making sense. England? How could she go to England?

But what she said was this: "You're coming?"

Her mother shook her head, soundlessly.

"I'm going alone?"

"No, no, not alone," Mutti said quickly. "Of course not! Gerhard is going too. Along with hundreds of other children. It will be a great adventure." She straightened the hem of Rose's middy blouse, flattening down the sailor collar.

"Where am I going to live?"

Mutti's eyes were glassy bright, her cheeks aflame. "You," she said, "are going to live with an English family. A *lovely* generous English family," she emphasized.

"Who are they?" Rose asked, her insides slickened with a hideous sickly sensation. She hadn't known this was possible, but now she realized that it was everything she feared.

"They are good people," Mutti finally said. "They are *very* good people. I know this, because they've agreed to take care of you."

"No," Rose said. "I won't go."

Her mother must have answered, Rose knew she did, but the roar of her fear descended and tore through her, like a train bulleting ahead. Mutti had done her best to comfort her, but try as she might, Rose could never recall what she had said.

3

NEW YORK AND
LOS ANGELES, 2006

HER DAYS WERE STULTIFYING AND long. The nights were longer. After she went home to New York, Lizzie took a week off from the new firm (she still thought of it that way, even though she had been there close to a year). Her senior partner didn't encourage her, but he didn't argue either. Those first days were a disaster. She picked fights—with the sweet Croatian owner of her dry cleaners when her cardigan wasn't ready, with a taxi driver for deciding to take Broadway downtown in the midafternoon. Small kindnesses could be her undoing. Her college boyfriend sent her a short e-mail saying how sorry he was, and there she was, weeping over her laptop. One evening after she came back from the bodega with beer, the nighttime doorman said, "Nice guy, your dad. I remember him helping you move in." And it was true, she remembered with a faint smile, Joseph had been there—directing the movers, saying to her, "You could have lived in a place with an elevator; why didn't you like that apartment on Ninety-Sixth Street?" The doorman said: "I'm sorry. My mom died five years ago and I still don't believe it."

She thanked him tearfully, hurried up the stairs. She didn't believe it either. Nothing made sense to her. Not lying on the couch watching reruns of *Freaks & Geeks*, not meeting a law school friend for lunch, not talking to Sarah or Claudia on the phone or pounding on the treadmill or downing cup after cup of coffee. The feel of the raw winter air against her face—that was the only thing that felt close to right.

One night, she was on her couch wearing a thin V-neck of her father's, leggings, and a pair of his wool socks, eating pad thai from Saigon Grill and watching *Double Indemnity*. She loved the movie, had seen it numerous times: she loved Barbara Stanwyck, who managed to be both steamy and coolly intelligent, and she loved poor hapless Fred MacMurray, who was no match for Stanwyck. Lizzie appreciated the ratatat dialogue and seeing Los Angeles as a city of noir, where nothing was as it seemed. But tonight, watching MacMurray race through the downtown L.A. streets, drive up to Stanwyck's house high in the Hollywood Hills, not the same hill where she'd grown up but not unlike it either, those spindly palm trees looking even more surreal and strange in black and white—she felt unnerved, seeing the city she knew so well, a city that wouldn't be the same for her ever again. Los Angeles was achingly far away.

Had her father ever seen the film? She switched the TV off. She called Sarah, but it went to voice mail, and she hung up before leaving a message.

Lizzie grabbed her coat, hat, and scarf from the hook, stuffed her keys, phone, and some bills into her pockets. Outside it was cold. The streetlamps threw out pools of anemic yellowish light. The moon was nowhere to be found. She began walking down Broadway, her gloveless hands clenched in her coat pockets, head down. She made her way past a pair of teenage girls wearing long thick sweaters, maneuvered around a stoic dog walker who held the leashes to four yelping, straining creatures. She passed newsstands and the little French bistro where her father and Sarah had taken her to celebrate the end of her first year of law school and the Starbucks that had been a Love's Pharmacy that had been—she had seen pictures—a butcher's shop.

And the pet supply shop that had been a video store where Claudia flirted with the teenage clerk, and she and Ben fought about which movies to rent.

She didn't know where she was going until she saw it. There was little inviting about the boxy Cuban diner, its fluorescent lights, but Lizzie went inside.

The waitress ushered her to a booth toward the back, but Lizzie shook her head. "Can I sit here?" She motioned toward a table by the door.

The waitress shrugged. "You'll feel the wind every time the door opens."

"That's fine," Lizzie said resolutely, and she slid in.

She had last sat at this table with her father. It had only been a few months ago, a quick weekend trip in October for the wedding of someone Lizzie barely knew, the son of a medical school classmate of Joseph's. The skeletal trees along Broadway she stared at now had been full and resplendent. He had ordered the bistec, a charred sirloin loaded with garlic and onions, and ate it with gusto, grousing about going to a wedding solo and asking her about dating. ("Are you using OkCupid? I love it; I've met lots of—" "Dad, please. Can we talk about something else?" "But OkCupid was started by Harvard students!") Now she ordered bistec, her second dinner of the night. When it arrived she ate and she ate. She scraped her plate clean, thinking of her father all the while. She never felt full.

As she was paying, feeling wobbly from all that food, she remembered her father telling her about a cousin of her grandfather's who had gotten off the boat from Poland, thinking he was in New York and only later realizing it was Havana. Joseph had called her after Castro had transferred power to his brother. "We should make plans to go to Cuba; it won't be long before Fidel is gone." She heard the tenor of his voice—it sounded so clear and distinct in her head—and something inside her cracked open. She attempted to zip up her jacket with trembling hands.

"You okay?" the cashier asked.

"I'm fine," Lizzie insisted as she pushed open the door. The brutal cold was a comfort as it hit her hot face, stung her lips, her skin.

The next morning she was up at sunrise, and for the first time in a week her mind felt sharp. She was at her office by seven thirty. An hour later, Marc, her senior partner, strode in.

"What are you doing here?" Marc said. "You look—" He paused. "You do not look good. Go home."

"Please," she said. "I need to be here. Please."

By the following week, she hit upon a viable angle for the Clarke appeal. Marc thought it was a solid approach, and even Clarke, who wanted to know every last detail in his weekly calls from prison in Otisville, chortled and said, "This might actually work." Lizzie should have been happy. But it felt beside the point.

Then Ben called, nearly three weeks after Joseph died. "I'm so sorry. I just heard," he said. It was so good to hear his voice, so specifically good, that Lizzie started talking—she told him about the blind curve on Mulholland and the SUV that Joseph never saw coming. ("It wasn't his fault," Lizzie said, "it wasn't anyone's fault.") She told him about the funeral and how she feared she didn't do her father justice with her eulogy, and then, she said, there was the woman who came to the burial in flip-flops. "Who goes to a cemetery in flip-flops?" she said.

He cleared his throat, didn't answer.

"You know, that was a rhetorical question," she said, feeling self-conscious, and tried to laugh.

"I'm just so sorry," he said. "I wish had known—"

"I should have called and told you."

"No, no, it's okay. I just—" He paused. "I liked him a lot. Your dad. He was a good guy."

"He liked you too," Lizzie said, and it was true. Joseph had been so disappointed when they broke up. She fought to keep her tears at bay.

She and Ben had met in law school, and moved in together after graduation; both landed jobs as associates at big, white-shoe law firms. It was as exhausting and all-encompassing as everyone had warned her it would be—there was nothing in her life but work—but she kept her head down; she was good at working. And she was pulling in so much money—she had gone from making zero to $175,000 a year. (She stared at that first paycheck, the march of digits incomprehensible.) Over her second year at the firm, though, something shifted. Her exhaustion metastasized into something darker, an anxiety that became her most voluble companion. Her senior partner now yelled at a new associate, and even this Lizzie took as a sign of failure. "Maybe you'd be happier at a smaller firm," Ben said. She made a face. What? Like she couldn't handle the work?

Their sex life sputtered out. They fought about the most superficial things. The way he would sometimes empty only the bottom half of the dishwasher made her want to scream. But they got engaged. She neared thirty-four. (As her grandmother loved to remind Lizzie, "When your mother was your age, she already had two children." Lizzie considered it a triumph that she didn't respond: "Yes, but she was also on the cusp of divorcing.") Then one sticky August night when Ben was out of town for a friend's bachelor party, she exited a bar through the back door and made out with a cocky summer associate in an alley off Baxter Street redolent of warm asphalt and garlic. She left his third-floor walk-up before dawn, feeling as if she had to vomit. Who had she become?

After Ben moved out, she walked around their apartment in a fog, feeling stunned and ashamed and small. How did she let this happen? She wasn't a dramatic person. She wasn't messy. Until she was.

Now Ben was talking about the time her dad insisted on taking him to the L.A. Auto Show, despite Ben's lack of interest in cars, and the spectacular dinner he took him to afterward in a tiny, eight-seat sushi bar that lacked a name on the thirty-seventh floor of a downtown office building. There Joseph held forth on the artistry of Vin Scully and his profound disappointment that Ben did not know him.

"*How can you not know who he is? How is that possible?*" Ben bellowed, imitating Joseph. "*He is not 'just a baseball announcer.' He is a master storyteller. He is a master of life.*"

The lights in her apartment were low. "Where was I during this dinner?" she asked. What she meant was: *Please keep talking.* Ben knew her father. No one would ever know him like Ben did.

"Oh, I don't know; gossiping with your sister, scowling at me."

A heaviness descended upon Lizzie. "I didn't scowl at you all the time, did I?" she asked softly.

"No, you didn't. I'm sorry I said that," he said, but he hesitated— Lizzie was certain—God, she had been awful to him.

"I'm really sorry," she said. "About everything."

"Listen, I did some scowling too. Stealthily, but I did."

"I fucked everything up, didn't I?"

"Oh, Lizzie."

She should stop. She didn't trust what she was feeling. But the more intensely she felt, the more convinced she became. She had messed up one of the only good things in her life. "I miss you," she finally said, alone on the couch that she and Ben used to share. "I probably shouldn't say that, but I do."

He didn't answer, and his lack of a response fed her conviction. "Come over," she whispered.

"Lizzie," he said, a plea airlifted with regret.

"I'm sorry," she said, speaking toward the ceiling. "I'm sorry for so much."

"It's okay. I'm sorry too."

"You have nothing to be sorry for."

"Not true." He let out an odd warble of a laugh.

"Let's both not be sorry," she heard herself say with sudden conviction.

"Okay," he whispered.

She closed her eyes. "Come over."

He didn't answer. She was too agitated to fill the silence.

"Okay, then," he finally said.

His hair was thicker than she had remembered and he was wearing that orange T-shirt that she loved, and the combination of new and old, rawness and comfort, felt so inevitable and right. When he fumbled with a condom, she said, "No, just let it be," because she could easily imagine it happening; she *wanted* it to happen. But he flashed her a hard, desperate look. "No," he said, and he tugged it on.

Afterward, they lay together, still. He was brushing her hair back from her face with a tenderness that made her ache when he said, "You know, I have to tell you something."

"What do you have to tell me?" she said teasingly, thinking, *He's a good man, a kind man.*

He shook his head. His gaze was fixed beyond her: on what? Did it bring him comfort to see that the window blind was still broken? Did he look at her clothes strewn on the wingback chair and think with satisfaction that she wasn't as neat as she liked to claim? Or was he thinking of the times he had pulled her into his lap on that chair? They had been happy then, hadn't they?

"I'm seeing someone. But you knew that, right?"

She closed her eyes. Even the air felt heavy, a trap.

"I should have said," Ben continued, "but, I—well, I didn't. But you had heard that, hadn't you? You knew."

"Yes," she said. "Of course. I know." And now she did.

ON ONE OF THE MANY nights that Lizzie couldn't sleep, as the delivery trucks rumbled down Broadway and the sky lightened to the streaky, cement-colored dawn, she watched bundled-up figures hurrying down the street, and she thought about Rose Downes.

Lizzie could remember asking her father all kinds of things about *The Bellhop* when she was a kid: *Was he famous? Was the man who painted him famous? Who picked out the frame?* (*You're a funny kid,* she could remember Joseph saying; *what kind of kid wonders about frames?*) But she couldn't remember asking him why he'd bought it.

Why hadn't she asked him? And she couldn't recall ever thinking about the other people who might have owned it before.

She decided to write Rose a note. She found a card she had bought at the Frick aeons ago, featuring an Italian Renaissance portrait of a young man against a sumptuous green background. It was easy enough to locate Rose's street address online. She wrote: "It's not our Bellhop but I've always liked him. I hope you do too. It was lovely to meet you. I'll be in L.A. in three weeks; coffee then?" She signed it with her name, her e-mail address, and all three numbers—cell, work, and home.

THREE WEEKS LATER, ON A Thursday, she took the last flight out of JFK to LAX, and she spent much of it working, reviewing a stack of cases she'd printed out from Westlaw and Lexis. She arrived after one A.M., flying in a cab over wide stretches of freeway to arrive at Sarah's house long after she and Angela had turned in for the night. Lizzie's body was jangly, buzzing with restlessness, in full-throttle protest. The next thing she knew, Sarah was standing over her, already dressed. "It's almost ten," she said. "We need to go."

Lizzie's left cheek felt as if someone had jabbed it with a stapler. She had fallen asleep on her laptop. "Okay," she said, rubbing her cheek, running her fingers through her knotty hair. "Just give me a few minutes and I'll be ready."

Sarah assessed her. "You look exhausted. You sure you're okay?"

"I'm fine!" Lizzie said loudly, which did nothing so much as prove Sarah's point.

MAX RAN HIS OWN SMALL law office from a Spanish stucco overlooking the thin ribbon of park on Ocean Avenue. For years, their father's friend had focused on criminal defense, but his current practice mostly consisted of longtime clients, many for whom he now settled business disputes, the occasional DUI, and even rarer, estate planning. Inside his office, Lizzie downed her second cup of coffee and picked at a cranberry muffin as Max went over the steps in painfully simple detail—filing the will with probate court, making an inventory of the estate's assets, paying off the estate's debts and taxes—yes, yes, she knew all this.

"Everything okay?" Max asked, as if sensing her impatience.

Lizzie felt chagrined. "Yes," she said, "of course."

"You know, your father chose me to be the executor because the laws in California differ significantly from those in New York, and more important: he knew it would be burdensome. He didn't want you—either of you—to have to deal with this."

"I'm so glad," Sarah said.

"Me too," Lizzie said, a lie. She didn't know why she cared about being executor. She didn't want to deal with Joseph's estate. It was likely a mess. And she wasn't expecting much. Joseph mocked cushions, 401(k)s, Roth IRAs, most fiscal plans that smacked of—well—planning. He had made a small fortune with his surgical eye practice, but the Joseph she knew was a spender through and through; he lived off the money's exhaust.

Still: when Max spoke about the second mortgage on the house (taken out, Lizzie realized as he went over the details, when she was in law school), she felt a flicker of unease. Then Max mentioned a real estate deal Joseph had made years earlier, a shopping mall in the Central Valley that had gone belly-up. The value had taken a nose dive when Joseph needed the cash the most, so he had to unload it with the mortgage underwater. It went into foreclosure. Max said there was little in terms of liquid assets.

How were his finances really that bad?

"There's still the house," Sarah was saying. "We can pay off what we need to with the profit from the sale."

"Yes," Max said as Lizzie looked at her sister anew. They would sell the house? Of course they would. Still, the thought of it gone made Lizzie feel hollowed out. She glanced out the window. A stone fountain dominated the courtyard, four muscular fish holding up a conch shell. Even the fishes' mouths looked parched.

She thought of all that money he had made through the years, so much earned and blown. Why hadn't he said anything? She could have helped. At least she should have pushed him harder to sock some away for himself (and yes, maybe a little for her and Sarah too). Lizzie had chosen to become a lawyer in part so that she could take care of herself. She did not suffer from want. Still, she sat in Max's office, feeling bereft, and thinking: *There wasn't anything?* She asked: "And the insurance money from the paintings?"

"That was quite a while ago," Max said, but his light-colored eyes settled on her face. There was sympathy in his gaze, an odd intimacy. She flushed, looked away.

Max went on to say that Joseph had requested that his possessions be split evenly between the two girls, with a few exceptions: He wanted Max to have the Ortiz collage; Lizzie the Julius Shulman photograph (he remembered how much she loved it, and this thought brought her back to herself, gave her a shot of pleasure); Sarah the Sugimoto seascape; and the West African funeral masks to Rose Downes.

"Rose?" Lizzie echoed.

"Who?" Sarah asked.

"The older woman I told you about, from the memorial?" Lizzie turned to Max and said, "I don't understand. They weren't close. Why give her the masks?"

Max shrugged. "Perhaps because of *The Bellhop*. It was stolen under his watch, after all."

"My watch, actually," Lizzie muttered. And after that, she didn't ask any questions.

IN FEBRUARY, THEY PUT THE house on the market. In less than a week, during a snowstorm that pummeled New York, they got an offer. The buyer was a Paramount exec around Lizzie's age—ob-gyn wife, two young kids—with the sort of swaggering verve that Joseph would have admired and made Lizzie annoyed. ("I want this house, I love this house," their broker reported him as saying. "I'll pay ask, all cash. The offer's good for forty-eight hours. After that, it goes down twenty-five thousand each day.")

A month later, she was flying out again. She and Sarah had to do a final cleaning to empty out the house. It made Lizzie feel queasy to contemplate, but she tried to remain pragmatic. Max had recommended an estate sales firm and she and Sarah lined it up. "Trust me, everything has value," Miller Perkins, the head of the firm, had said. "There's a buyer for it all."

At work, Lizzie learned that a similar case to Clarke's was being argued in front of the Third Circuit. Oral arguments were scheduled for the day after next. "You should go down to Philadelphia," Marc said. "Hop on the Acela and turn around the same day."

"I'm supposed to leave for L.A. tomorrow."

"Ah," he said, considering. Then he brightened. "Well, Kathleen can go instead." Kathleen was a hard-charging associate three years behind Lizzie. She was supposed to report to Lizzie on cases, but Lizzie often found her talking to Marc instead.

"Kathleen can go to L.A.?" Lizzie offered sweetly.

"She probably would, if we told her to," Marc said. "She'll be fine in Philly. She can be your ears."

"I don't need extra ears. Let me figure it out. There might be some wiggle room."

When Sarah picked up, Lizzie plunged forward: "I'm really sorry, but I can't come out tomorrow."

"What? Why?"

"Work." Lizzie let out a big exhale. "My boss is insisting that I go hear a case being argued in Philadelphia." Sarah didn't respond, and Lizzie added: "An important case. I don't really have a choice."

"Well then," Sarah said coolly. "Fine."

"I'm sorry," Lizzie said. "But I have an idea." She tried to lift her voice enthusiastically. "We're so rushed; what about postponing and getting a storage space? Then we'd have time to go through everything when we can." She had been thinking of the time she and Ben had gone to his parents' storage space on the Upper East Side. Lizzie and Ben had visited it to collect his tent for a July weekend in the Catskills (camping, Ben's idea). But camping seemed steadfastly beside the point once she stepped into Manhattan Mini Storage. So clean, so quiet, such a blessed rush of air-conditioning. Forget about North-South Lake or wherever they were headed, Lizzie had said, they should spend the night here, watching movies in the unit among the bank boxes of tax returns, ski equipment, Ben's clarinet from junior high, a Pack 'n Play that his sister's baby had used: all of it safe, untouched, waiting, for the future, for life to begin again.

"That's ridiculous," Sarah said. "Perkins is already on board. He's started getting the word out—"

"I'll pay for it," Lizzie said. "I don't mind."

"What? No. It's not about the money. I don't want the stuff in storage. I want to get it over with. I want it finished."

"Okay, then, okay," Lizzie said, regretting that she had ever brought up the idea. But when she actually forced herself to picture emptying out the house, getting rid of all her father's things—the thought made her break into a sweat. How could anything to do with their father be finished?

LIZZIE WENT TO PHILLY, WHERE, during court breaks, she would call Sarah back, steel herself to answer her questions. (*Yes, let's sell the side tables. No, hold on to his medical textbooks.* "You know, I could answer much faster if you could text me," Lizzie said. "It takes me forever to text," Sarah said, "all that up and down with my thumbs. Why can't I just call?") From Philly, Lizzie flew Denver to L.A. By the time she made it to Sarah's house in Los Feliz, Sarah and Angela were long asleep. Her sister had left the kitchen light on and a note on the counter. "Welcome," it said. "There's pasta if you're hungry."

Lizzie was. For the first time in a great while, she was ravenous. She opened the fridge. Inside were yogurts and bright juices and fresh berries nestled in bowls; two kinds of water (seltzer and flat) and two kinds of milk (almond and regular), and yes, pasta too, some olive, tomatoey thing. Lizzie, cowed by the bounty, ate standing— delicious, even cold. She should have put it in a bowl and heated it up, eaten like the grown-up she was. But she couldn't be bothered.

Wine, on the other hand, she could use. She opened cabinets, searching. Sarah and Angela had renovated this Craftsman house high in the hills when they moved in about a year and a half ago. For months, it was all Sarah could talk about: her sister, a social worker at a halfway house for girls, who used to rail against skyrocketing recidivism rates and people's idiotic notions of mental illness and psychopharmacology, now all she could talk about was baseboards and backsplashes.

Lizzie had taken to grousing to Claudia about Sarah's endless renovation talk, pointing out that this was a house Sarah never could have afforded on her own social-worker salary. "Being with a doctor must be pretty nice," she had said.

"You could have a nicer place," Claudia said.

"What's wrong with my place?" Lizzie said. She loved her apartment, even though it was tiny, with the kitchen the size of a TV, as Ben used to say, and only one true closet. But it was rent-stabilized and had been her home since law school. Why should she spend more? "You have no idea how crazy real estate is in New York."

"Uh-huh," Claudia said. And then: "Maybe Sarah's house will be annoyingly *Architectural Digest*."

Her friend looked at *Architectural Digest*? Did she know anyone anymore? "No, it's going to be beautiful," Lizzie said with uncontained wistfulness.

And it was. As she opened the white cabinets that only looked expensive ("IKEA!" Sarah had crowed), Lizzie admired and felt envious of it all: the dark-stained floorboards, the brushed-nickel pulls on the drawers that opened so smoothly, even the poured-concrete countertop, which Lizzie had secretly thought (hoped?) might be sterile, but turned out chic.

Behind the slim bottles of oil (olive and walnut and almond too) she finally spotted wine. She pulled out a Malbec. After she filled a glass, she kept opening cabinets in her sister's indisputably lovely kitchen, no longer sure what she was looking for. On a shelf above the sink, she saw squat bottles of medication and vitamins. There was the lithium that Sarah had been taking for nearly twenty years—"I'm a goddamn poster child for it," she'd say, sounding like their father— there was red yeast rice and folic acid and a prescription bottle for Clomid. Made out in her sister's name.

Lizzie stared at the label for the Clomid as if it would transform itself. She knew what it was. Claudia had been taking it for months ("popping it like candy," she had said) since she married Ian last spring. What would Sarah be doing with it?

She turned back to the Malbec and downed two more glasses in quick succession. Sarah didn't want a baby; Lizzie was the one who was supposed to have a baby. She climbed into the bed in her sister's guest room, unnerved and exhausted, trying not to dwell on it, wishing she did not feel like crying.

THE SUNLIGHT IN THE KITCHEN hurt her eyes when Lizzie padded in, wearing a worn T-shirt of Ben's and sweats she'd cut off at the knees. Sarah was washing strawberries; Angela, pouring coffee into a travel mug. Angela was already dressed in heels and high-waist trousers. She looked taller, more imperious, than usual. Lizzie was suddenly aware of her ratty T-shirt. She wished she had put on a bra.

"You got in okay?" Angela asked. There was a touch of bristle to her voice, as if she suspected Lizzie were about to complain.

"Just fine, thanks," Lizzie said with caution. She turned to her sister. "Hello, you," she said, brushing her cheek with a kiss, trying to be casual about her studied glance. Did her face look rounder? Was she hiding anything beneath her loose, striped T?

"I see you made yourself right at home," Sarah said, nodding at the not-quite-finished bottle of wine, perched alone on the gleaming counter. Someone had cleaned around it, Lizzie realized, and decided to leave it there.

Lizzie blushed. "I'm sorry. I meant to clean up."

"It's fine," Sarah said, and her clipped tone only confirmed her annoyance. "Perkins called me yesterday and told me to leave the cookbooks behind. Apparently there's even a market for those old microwave ones."

"Thanks so much for taking care of it all, Sarah, seriously."

"I'm glad to have done it. You should have seen me; I turned merciless, really."

"Do not tell me that," Lizzie said, half laughing. "I don't want to know." And it was the truth, she didn't. She felt a sludge of panic. "The masks, for Rose Downes? They were put aside?"

"Yes, of course."

"You sure?"

"Yes, of course I'm sure; we put them downstairs," Sarah said, doing little to disguise her irritation. "Along with everything else that we're keeping."

Lizzie nodded, but she was having that familiar sinking feeling, without edges or borders, that she had lost something again. She had written Rose that postcard, and she had never heard back. "You know, maybe I'll just go up there and check things out. The sale doesn't start for another hour, right?"

"That," Sarah said, "is a terrible idea. Everything is fine. And Perkins said owners should stay away."

"I'll go in and out. I just need to make sure."

Sarah shook her head and pulled her hair back, tying it up in a knot in one clean sweep, such a familiar gesture, Lizzie felt her stomach contract. "Because no one else can do it right but you."

"That's not true," Lizzie said, but she could barely get the words out. Their mother used to do that with her hair, in the days before she got sick. Lynn would pick them up from school in her banged-up Dodge, the radio turned up too loud, and she would be lighting a cigarette in one moment and tying her hair up in the next, her skinny freckled arms in motion, yelling at the girls to sit down, sit down and stop arguing! Lizzie saw it so clearly: the sticky black vinyl interior, the brown-orangy shine of her mother's lipstick, Sarah's tiny perfect feet.

"It would be so much easier if you simply admitted how controlling you are," Sarah was saying. "If you just acknowledged it, it would be much easier to take."

Lizzie heard her sister, but her words echoed like faraway street noise, worlds away.

HER FATHER'S SHORT DRIVEWAY WAS thick with cars. A string of bright blue flags stamped with *Westside* snapped in the wind. Inside, the rugs were already gone, as were the Barcelona chairs and the leather couch and the mahogany side tables. The air carried a slight candied smell. There was space galore, great empty pockets, yet the house looked smaller, not her own.

Come back! her father used to call her to say in college. *Come back.* But once she left, she left; she never lived here for more than a few weeks again. Sophomore year, her boyfriend at the time, an econ major from Montreal with a penchant for pot, landed a summer job in the William Morris mailroom. "We should spend the summer in L.A. together," he'd said. "I can't believe you're from there and actually choose to live here." *It's too much*, she'd said, describing the artwork, the glass-and-steel house cantilevered over the canyon, Joseph's cars. "He has more than one?" he had said. She'd simply sighed.

Now a slight guy with thick sideburns in a Westside Estate Sales T-shirt approached her. "Can I help you find anything?"

"I'm looking for Miller Perkins," Lizzie said. "I'm Lizzie Goldstein. This was my house." And it was only then that she realized she was shaking.

"Oh," he said, his face more alert. "He's downstairs. I'll get him for you."

"Actually, I want to find something down there—"

"No, no, please." He touched her forearm, a light touch, but clear enough. "Let me." A braided velvet rope cordoned off the stairs. He ducked beneath it, disappeared down the stairs.

Lizzie waited. She had talked to Miller Perkins on the phone a week earlier, but she began to nurse an odd, dislocated feeling that he wouldn't appear. Maybe the estate sale was a ruse—she and Sarah wouldn't see a cent. She watched a squat woman inspect a trio of sea-green metal canisters: *Flour, Coffee,* and *Sugar,* each stamped in a skinny midcentury font. She remembered that her father had brought them home from a flea market in Pasadena years ago, and filled them with the flotsam from his desk. "The veneer of organization," he would say as he lobbed another uncapped pen into the flour can. "It's all that matters."

She had always liked those canisters. She should have claimed them. She could picture them on the shelf above the stove in her kitchen, or in her bathroom, maybe, one holding makeup, the other a jumble of hairbands.

Near her was a sturdy oak jewelry case, courtesy of Westside Estate Sales, inside of which was a cache of cuff links and a Hamilton watch that Joseph had worn for a time years earlier. Her father's Rolex was squirreled away in her nightstand back in New York. Wasn't it? A man with a bulbous nose tried on the Hamilton and she stifled an urge to grab that too.

The day remained cloudy, but a steely light streamed through the enormous windows. Lizzie watched a little girl squirm and dance.

A lithe woman in a sundress grabbed the girl's hand, hissing, "Not here, Zoe!"

The mother returned to shopping. The girl made her way to the windows. She gazed down into the mouth of the canyon, pressing her palms against the glass. Lizzie had done the same thing when she was younger. She remembered pressing hard, testing the strength of the glass, testing herself, when all the light and airiness flooding this house only seemed to add insult to the fact that such a world could exist when her mother had been taken from her. She had been terrible to her father then. And now he was gone too.

Lizzie returned to the kitchen canisters that the short woman had left behind. She picked up the sugar can and slipped it into her leather shoulder bag. Her bag was big, but not that big. The leather bulged with effort.

"Is that you, Ms. Goldstein? Miller Perkins, at your service." A short man in a flash of color headed up the steps, hand extended, an exuberant smile on his broad face. He wore a navy vest with big silver buttons, a lime-colored shirt, bejeweled rings on numerous fingers. "I am delighted to meet you, of course, but—" His voice was silky, Southern smooth. He wagged a playful finger. "*What* are you doing here? Didn't I tell you and your sister to stay far, far away?"

"Yes, I know, I'm sorry. But a pair of masks is supposed to go to a friend of my father's, and I wanted to make sure they weren't inadvertently sold."

"Oh, my dear, you're worried. Of course, you're concerned. But you know you shouldn't be." He steered her by the elbow, away from the others. He had a surprisingly strong grip. "The masks are downstairs, sequestered away, as we had agreed. I myself have been keeping a careful eye. I *can* handle things. You know, I've been doing this for more than twenty years."

"I'm sorry. I just wanted to check. It looks like it's going well."

"Oh, it is, it is! It reminds me of the Thomas sale, last year. Did I tell you about it? Frank Thomas, one of Disney's most renowned an-

imators? Really, I was so honored to be a part of it. I was just telling
Max—"

"Max?" Lizzie asked. "Max is here?"

"Yes, yes, he's downstairs. Didn't you know? He too wanted to
keep an eye. We could have a tea party with the principals at this
sale!" Miller gave a shot of sharp laughter. "I can take you downstairs,
if you'd like. I prefer to wait until everything is over, but if you'd like
to see what's sold, we can go over inventory. Perhaps something to
drink? I have some sparkling water, my secret stash of Pellegrino."

"Oh no, that's not necessary," Lizzie said. The faster he spoke,
the more tired she felt. Maybe she should go downstairs, lie down
on the sleeper couch in her old room, close her eyes for a while.
(Was the couch still there?) She watched a Perkins employee bang
Joseph's exercise bike up the stairs. "I'm sorry for barging in like
this."

"No, do not be silly! This is your house; these are *your* things. I
take my stewardship very seriously." He patted her bag and lowered
his voice. "And you know, you can always change your mind."

She blinked. "I'm sorry?"

He leaned in conspiratorially. "The canisters." He gave her bag
a firm tap. "Would you like the whole set? They're yours, after all. I
would hate for you to feel as if you were reduced to the role of petty
thief."

"Oh." She felt her face redden. "This? It's just—"

"Please, there is *no* need to explain." Perkins flashed her a well-
practiced grin. "I'm going to get back to it. I'll give you a call later, if
you're not still here!"

"Okay," she said. She felt less embarrassed than deflated. She
didn't want the sugar canister after all.

Perkins headed down the stairs and squeezed past the employee
with the exercise bike. He took care not to come into contact with his
employee or the customer trailing him, a rangy man in fraying jeans
and orange flip-flops who had a tenuous grip on the bike's back wheel.

At the top of the stairs, the man let go of the wheel with a thump. Lizzie felt her heart thump with it.

She knew that man. She knew that head of rich dark curls. She knew that lanky body.

For a fleeting moment, she thought of not saying a word. But how could she not? "Duncan Black," she said, tapping him on the shoulder as if asking for directions.

He gave her a slow smile, then a look of dawning recognition spread across his face. "Lizzie Goldstein? Is that you?"

"Indeed," she said, and she couldn't help but laugh.

"What are you doing here?"

"This is my father's house," she said, oddly confused. Did he really not recognize it? "What are *you* doing here?"

"You know, I thought it might have been the same house, and then I thought, no, it couldn't have been. But I was driving up the hill, and I thought—swear to God, I thought, 'Lizzie Goldstein used to live in a house just like this.' Sometimes, I have the worst memory."

She smiled ruefully, and it was like being back in high school, where a decent memory was a liability, proof that you thought too much, had too much time on your hands. "You just came for the sale?" She gestured at the bike. "A burning need to exercise?"

He flushed slightly, bobbing a bit, he still had that loose fluid way with his limbs. "The bike's for my dad. He's wanted one for months now. I got a great dinette set at a Westside sale in Hollywood last month." He was still attractive, emphatically so, but he also looked worn; his face was sharper than in high school, a fine web of wrinkles fanned off his eyes. He looked as if he'd spent too much time on the beach over the last decade, and she tried to recall what she had heard about him through the years—playing for a band in Ashland? Working for a tech company in the Bay Area? No, no. "My wife thinks it was a terrible idea," he continued. "The table is a beautiful marble and she thinks the kids are going to scratch it up."

Of course. She felt a faint sting, but she smiled and said: "How old are your kids?"

"Five and three. Zoe and Marlon. Zoe's around here somewhere, with my wife." He swiveled around. "Jo," he called loudly. "Jo!"

A couple of heads turned in their direction—none Jo, from what Lizzie could see, and she said, "It's okay." He didn't seem at all self-conscious that other people were looking at him. She remembered that from high school, the principal reason she was drawn to him. Duncan Black was more comfortable in his skin than anyone else she knew.

"No, no. Hold on, she's here, somewhere." He called her name again. The slim woman in a sundress with the blond girl Lizzie had seen earlier now emerged from the hall. "I thought you guys had abandoned me, alone on this mountain," Duncan said.

"No such luck," Jo said. She had a surprisingly deep voice and a delicate face, dark hair, pale skin. Her coloring was not unlike Lizzie's, but she was taller, more graceful.

"This is a friend from high school," said Duncan. "Lizzie Goldstein, this is my wife, Josephine Black."

They shook hands, Josephine smiling easily. The little girl tugged at her mother's dress. "Can't we go? I'm bored."

"Zoe," Duncan said sharply. "Please."

Lizzie stooped down, thinking of how Zoe had played against the windows in the living room. "It's nice to meet you. I knew your father a million years ago, when he wasn't so much older than you."

The girl stared. "So?" she said, then ran off.

"I'm sorry," Jo said. "Manners: we're working on those." She went after her.

"She can be a handful," Duncan said to Lizzie.

"It's okay."

"You don't have kids?"

"No, I don't," Lizzie said, and she blushed. Was it obvious? Was she that awkward with them?

She asked where he was living, he spoke about Culver City, its schools, how he had always wanted to try New York. "It's nice to see you, really," Duncan said. "Maybe we could have you over for dinner one of these days."

"That would be great. We'll figure out a time," Lizzie said. She made a gesticulation, first at her watch, then in the other direction, as if there were this thing, a great unnamable *thing*, that threatened to claim her if she did not leave.

Duncan cracked two of his knuckles, a dull pop. "I just wondered, about your father—Joseph, right?"

Lizzie shook her head, wanting to shake away the question that he couldn't seem to bring himself to ask. "He died," she said. "Two months, nearly three months ago." It felt strange to put a time frame on it. But in nine days, it would be three months. She knew, of course.

"Oh, Lizzie. I thought that might—" His lean handsome face darkened. "But I hoped—I don't know—I'm so sorry."

"Yeah, well," she said, and she felt the tears start up. "It's okay."

He bit his lip. "How?"

"Car accident."

"Jesus, Lizzie." He pulled her into a hug.

"Oh," she said, taken aback. Her head was against his chest, and the pungent smell of his sweat mixed with something sweeter. It had been nearly twenty years since she had last touched him. But his ropy arms felt familiar, her head resting against his chest.

They had first gotten together at the party she had thrown during her senior year of high school. Her father was out of town, a medical conference in Boston. She was supposed to be at Claudia's, and Sarah at a friend's, but Lizzie had taken advantage. This same living room had been dark and loud and roiling, with the sweat of bodies, the sweet smell of pot, the pulse of music, the clink of bottles being opened. Lizzie was floating among her many guests, feeling good, when Duncan finally appeared and, unbelievably, sought her out.

Lizzie was seventeen years old. She couldn't remember a time when she hadn't had a crush on him. Duncan maintained a deadly combination of nonchalance and assurance that should have been patented; he did more looking than talking; he had the pale, elusive gaze of the misunderstood, a fragile, Byronic look that surely translated to depth. (Didn't it?) The air, increasingly choked with smoke and sweat, tasted honeyed. He asked her if she wanted to go outside and her heart darted about like a quicksilvered fish. Out by her father's pool, he plucked a tiny brass pipe from his pocket and they got high, dipping their bare feet in the heated water, the air cool, the sky a band of black. They kissed for the first time, messy, sloppy kisses that left Lizzie breathless and hungry for more. When they finally went back in, Duncan had stood up and offered her a hand, a courtly gesture she never would have expected from him.

She had led him down the stairs and into her bedroom. Even now, twenty years later, she could recall her amazement. He was so beautiful. *Duncan Black,* she yearned to say over and over again. She had wanted him for so long. It didn't feel good. But she was prepared for so much worse. And it was this fact, coupled with the finality of it—her virginity, out the window, spirited away by Duncan Black—that allowed her to feel a certain elation, a pleasure that wasn't at all sexual.

But that elation hadn't lasted. Hours later, she awoke, and her world was never the same.

Now she was sniffling against Duncan's thin T-shirt. This boy who had been her first was now a man, a married man at that. He was rocking her gently. It felt nice. It felt more than nice. She tried to ignore it but she felt a rising heat. She wanted to taste the sweat on his neck. She wanted to taste all of him. Never mind that he had a wife; never mind that that wife and daughter were only feet away. She could unhook Miller Perkins's velvet rope and lead him downstairs. In the name of sympathy and mourning, she could.

After a moment, he pulled back. "Well," he said. "I really am sorry."

"Thank you." She nodded, tried to affect a smile. Had he sensed what she'd been thinking? Was he slightly tempted too?

They exchanged numbers. Lizzie was saying she really would like to see him again, she hoped his father loved the bike, when he asked: "Whatever happened to those paintings? The ones that were stolen the night of the party. It was a Picasso and a Modigliani, right?"

"Soutine," she said. She wished it surprised her that she had to correct him. She looked past him into her father's living room that was emptying of his possessions by the minute. "A Soutine portrait and a Picasso drawing."

"God, remember how the cops were all over everyone? I heard that Cori Carpenter started crying and confessed about the time she bought pot at a Tears for Fears concert. They never turned up, did they?"

Lizzie shook her head.

"Of all the things to steal. You can't fence famous artwork. The paintings are too recognizable. Anyone who knows what they're worth will know that they've been stolen. Well, you can only hope that the fucker who took them had the decency not to shred them."

She was too flustered to speak. Maybe *The Bellhop* was rolled up in an airport locker somewhere, a bank vault in Grenada, hanging on the walls of a garish villa in Dakar or Patagonia. But destroyed?

Duncan, his easy talk of the paintings, her father's empty house: it all felt wrong. For a brief moment, she imagined walking off, leaving Duncan without a word and climbing into her rental car, taking the turns of the hill that she knew so well.

But soon they were hugging again, awkwardly this time. (Why? As if bodily contact, twice in nearly twenty years, might prove to be their downfall?) Soon she was watching him hoist the bike onto his shoulder, press his way out the door.

And then the living room flooded with brightness. Lizzie shielded her eyes. For a second, she didn't know what happened, so quick was the shift—but squinting, she saw that it was just the sun, fisted clouds finally loosening their grip, bathing the room in abundant California light.

She felt a pressure on her arm. A voice, Max's voice, quiet. She hadn't seen him approach, had forgotten he was there. "Let's go. I'm taking you to lunch."

THEY TOOK HIS CAR. DOWN to Santa Monica, to a little Spanish café on Ocean Avenue a few blocks from his office. They didn't talk much. She was glad to have him drive.

The hostess seated them outside on the terrace. The afternoon remained gorgeous, cool but not cold, the sky scrubbed free of clouds. As they looked over the menu, Max told her that a friend of a friend owned the café. He was full of suggestions: sangria, Manchego, the grilled calamari and mushrooms too. Soon he was pouring sangria; he was passing her tiny ceramic plates piled high.

Lizzie ate olive after olive as Max told her about the restaurant's owner. He had been a bond trader, working fifteen-hour days, traveling half the month to meetings in Santiago and Dublin, rarely seeing his family. Then his youngest got sick with Hodgkin's, and the man swore if his kid got better, he would change everything.

"So, the boy got better and the father opted out of the rat race." Lizzie rolled an olive pit between her finger and thumb.

Max gave her a small smile. "His son went into remission, Marco opened the restaurant, and now he works as much as before—making one-tenth of the money."

"That's terrible," she said, laughing, "and completely unsurprising."

"Some habits are pretty deep-seated," he agreed. "At least for Marco."

"I don't know; it's not just him. I mean, who really changes?"

"You believe that?" His tone was easy enough, but his eyes settled on hers.

"Yes," she said, and she found she was serious too. "I do." She was the same as when she had been a kid. The reliable child who stuck

Ellen Umansky

Stouffer's lasagnas in the microwave for herself and Sarah for dinner, who kept track of her sister's orthodontist appointments, who made sure that someone stopped at Vicente for milk in the morning. She was the same girl who followed the rules, who liked having rules, the type of kid who got high and got the munchies for *salad*, of all things. She had a hard time forgiving herself, then and now. ("So you fucked up," Claudia would say with a shrug. "Who hasn't?") Being here in L.A., her father's death, hurtled her back to being seventeen and the one mistake she felt like she could never undo. For years as she ticked off each accomplishment—graduating from a fine college, getting into a top law school, landing an associate position in the appellate department of a reputable firm—she felt like she was trying to prove, to her father and to herself, that that one night didn't define her.

It tired her, this realization. And it made her feel, for reasons she wasn't quite sure she could articulate, lonely. She hung a shrimp by its tail, dragging it through a glistening pool of oil. "You obviously feel differently, though."

Max didn't answer for a moment. "Yes, I do," he finally said. "Partly it's my line of work, and partly it's a question of age. I believe you can make mistakes. Everyone makes mistakes—"

"Of course—"

"But sometimes making such a mistake—an irrevocable mistake, with true repercussions—is what makes you change. You see the way things might have been, and they're not like that, because you messed up. Undeniably. I've seen it with clients. Things that you thought might not be such a big deal, things that you thought you might be able to explain away, loom large. There's nothing you can do about them." He played with the lip of a squat unlit candle in the table's center. "And maybe it's regret like that that fuels change."

"Of course," Lizzie repeated. "But as long as you're not talking about mass murder . . ." It was a lame stab at lightness, and the second she said it, she regretted it. He had defended murderers. He knew about regret.

Or he could be referring to his divorce, the wreckage of his marriage. He had a stepdaughter, Lizzie remembered, a shy little girl she met years ago at Joseph's house, poolside. What was her name? She must be close to college age now, Lizzie thought.

She sipped her sangria. "Sometimes I think I regret too much," she said.

"What do you mean?"

"Well, in some parts of my life, I have a hard time letting go. I wish I could just make a decision and not look back, move on." It was strange to hear herself admit this, and so freely too. Had she ever spoken to Max for more than ten, fifteen minutes at a time?

"Who does?" Max looked at her with his eyes grayer than blue, the color of rushing water.

"Most of the world, apparently." She was thinking of Claudia and her sister when she said this, wishing she could be more like them.

"You don't really believe that, do you? If it's something truly important?"

"No," she said. "I suppose not." He was still watching her, and she hoped what he was seeing did not disappoint him.

She looked past Max, beyond the restaurant patio. Out on the sidewalk, a man in a dirty puffy parka rattled a shopping cart crammed with objects. She spotted a desk lamp, a sofa cushion. The air was growing cooler, the day shifting. Lizzie could see across the street a strip of park lined with prehistoric palms. Beyond it she could make out the rising lift of fog. The water and the sky seemed to commingle, bleeding together in the same implacable color of bone.

"You know, your father used to tell me what a good lawyer you were," Max said. "He was very proud of you."

"Thank you," she said a little too quickly; the mention of her father cracked something open in her. She liked to think Max was right. She could remember the evident pleasure etched across her father's face that warm May day when she graduated from law school.

They stood on the corner of Amsterdam and 116th, among a sea of graduates in shiny blue robes, and he kept grabbing her hand as they tried to catch a cab down to Jean-Georges. She thought of the time they went to the fish market on Wilshire last summer. When it was finally their turn, her father introduced her to the young fishmonger plunging his hand into a vat of raw shrimp. "Ed, this is my daughter, the lawyer from New York," Joseph told him, and Ed looked up and barely muttered hello to Lizzie, but there was no denying the pride in Joseph's voice.

Did her father know how much she adored him? He did, didn't he?

The terrace was nearly empty. An old couple was barely talking, and at a round table sat a trio of young women, lipsticked and bright-eyed. One kept repeating loudly—"So I said, 'just leave your pants on! Leave them on!'"—as her friends hooted and guffawed. How was it possible that all these people were here and her father gone?

"Tell me something else about my dad." Lizzie, her voice shaky, turned back to Max. "Tell me something I don't know." She picked at the Manchego.

"Let's see, a story about Joseph," Max said. "Well, you know how we met."

"My father started coming into your parents' gallery."

"Yes, I was working there during law school, helping my parents who were helping me. It was at the start of your father's collecting frenzy, and he was"—Max paused— "immeasurably proud of his recent endeavors."

"So he offered you some ridiculously low price on a Modigliani sketch," she guessed, "thinking he knew more than you did, and you refused."

"Not quite. He came in carrying a painting that he had found at an estate sale. A Utrillo. He had been very happy with his purchase." Max fell silent for a moment, and gave her a small smile. "And I had the distinct pleasure of telling him it was a forgery."

"Really?" How had she never heard this story before? "He must have hated that," she said, but it pleased her, the thought of this unlikely start to their friendship.

Max grinned. He cupped hands around the fat unlit candle. His fingers were long and slender and tapering. Even the few unruly black hairs that sprang up close to his knuckles seemed elegant. His mouth was generous, his lips full, and Lizzie realized, with the shock of tasting sugar when you expected salt, that she thought he was beautiful. "I can't believe he continued to talk to you," she said, returning to the here and now, trying to brush aside her thoughts.

"Well, it wasn't as if we became such good friends then and there. But he kept coming back into the gallery. I think he was glad somebody caught it before it became a significant embarrassment." His craggy face carried a frank, gentle expression. He dipped the heel of the bread in the speckled oily puddle that was all that remained of the olives. "He grew to trust me enough to buy work from us. We sold him the Soutine."

"*The Bellhop?*" The painting had come from New York; her parents had first seen it together. Lizzie knew this. "But he saw it in New York."

"He did," Max said, nodding. "It had been in a show at the Marlborough on loan from my parents' gallery. He purchased it from them, years later."

Lizzie remembered when her parents first saw the painting. She had been eight years old. Her parents separated six months later, and that evening was etched in her mind, one of the few memories she had of them married. Lizzie was supposed to be asleep when she heard her parents' heated voices rising up the stairs. "Why would I want to own a third-rate sketch from Manet when I can spend the same money and buy something I truly love?" Lynn had said.

"Because it's a fucking Manet! Because he's one of the masters of the art world!" Joseph exploded. "And he's dead, so he's not making any more masterpieces, which means the value is guaranteed to rise."

"Nothing is guaranteed. And it's art. It should be something you love. Like that Soutine."

"Why can't it be love *and* an investment?" A pause. "I'm on your side, you know."

Her mother didn't answer for a long time. Finally she said with a flatness that left Lizzie cold, "Who said anything about sides?"

That was the last Lizzie heard of Soutine until she arrived at her father's house. In those first few awful months in L.A., she would lie on the carpet stomach down and gaze at it. *The Bellhop* was also a stranger in California. It was only paint thrown on a canvas, but the portrait made her feel less alone.

For Rose Downes, there was no such comfort, Lizzie thought. She had lost everything—her home, her parents, her country. It had been weeks since Lizzie had written her. Maybe the address she had found was an old one. She resolved to look again.

Now Lizzie said to Max: "Do you know where your parents got the Soutine?"

"No. Their records were spotty. But I'm sure they had no idea it was stolen during the war. They would have been aghast, like your father was. In those days, people weren't as assiduous about checking the provenance as they are today."

For a moment, neither spoke. Then Max said: "You know your father was very good to my parents." Lizzie nodded, though she hadn't known.

"Especially my father," Max continued. "I can't imagine anyone having been better to my father. When he started getting sick—it was Alzheimer's, but it took us a long time to realize that—the gallery became a mess, but he wouldn't give it up. The more paranoid he got, the more his memory slipped, the more difficult he became. Joseph used to come by, chat with him, listen to the same stories over and over, convince friends of his to buy some pieces. He used to say that my father demented was more interesting than ninety-nine percent of the rest of the world. But really, he saved him. I know he saved me."

Lizzie was nodding hard. This was the father she knew. She kept nodding, as if that alone might stop her tears.

"Oh, I'm sorry—" Max said, as if just now realizing her distress.

"No, no, it's okay. I'm glad you're talking, please keep talking. It's good to hear these stories, you have no idea."

"I think I do," Max said, and he reached across the table and touched her hand. It was a light, evanescent touch. By the time she registered it, he'd lifted his fingers. But she felt jolted by it all the same.

Max cleared his throat. "You know I'm here for you, for you and your sister. If I can help in any way, about anything—please, tell me."

"I know. Thank you." She tried to bat away the tap of disappointment she felt when he said "*for you and your sister.*" What did she expect? He was her father's friend.

Then she felt her phone buzz. She dug it out, and saw a 310 number she didn't recognize. Her sister? Miller Perkins? "Hello?"

"Lizzie? Is this Lizzie Goldstein? It's Rose Downes."

"Rose!" Lizzie exclaimed. "I was just thinking of you."

"You were?" Rose's voice was wary.

"We were talking about the Soutine, Max and I," Lizzie said, then stopped. What could she say? How could she explain? "You got my letter," she settled on saying. "I'm glad you called."

"Yes, you sent it, and I received it. That's the way the postal system works. I'm sorry I didn't get in touch earlier. Are you still in town?"

"Yes, for a few more days."

"Can you meet for a walk tomorrow?"

"I would love that," she said. She felt Max watching her, and sitting outside in the cool dying light of a March afternoon, Rose in her ear, Lizzie was startled to feel a charge of expectation. There was so much she wanted to know.

4

LEEDS, 1940

Acting the part wasn't hard. Rose had all the props: a cup of milky tea that Mary had brought sat untouched on the night table next to Mutti's silk scarf with the birds, numerous woolen blankets under which she lay mummified. "I'm not feeling well," she said from the depths of her bed, only her eyes and nose exposed to the damp air.

"You haven't been feeling well these past three Saturdays," Mrs. Cohen said. She attempted to strike a stern tone, but it came out beseeching. She stood in the doorway of Rose's room, her sharp frame encased in a scratchy brown tweed suit with deep ruby buttons catching what little light there was. "The stitching is fine enough," Rose's mother would say. But it would be the jeweled buttons she would linger over, in a hungry manner Rose told herself she remembered well. *The buttons are nothing*, she wanted to tell Mutti.

Rose bit her bottom lip and didn't answer Mrs. Cohen for several beats. She had been living in the Cohens' house in Leeds for nearly a year now. She didn't like to think about how much time had passed. Here she had turned twelve years old; she had seen the calendar, incredulously, catapult into a new decade altogether. But it had only taken her about a week with the Cohens to realize that silence was her most effective weapon. Finally she said in a thin watery voice, "It's my stomach." And in truth, it was. Her stomach was aflutter, leaping and pirouetting. *Hello!* her insides seemed to be saying. *When are we getting out of here?*

Mrs. Cohen nodded, adjusting the tan feather tucked into the ribbon circling her chocolate-colored velvet hat. (Brown, brown, brown, Rose thought, picturing her mother's blue linen dress, her purple silk wrapper. Why must everything be brown here?) Mrs. Cohen moved closer, looking down at Rose. "It couldn't hurt you to come." Her eyebrows were thinly plucked, sharp like the rest of her.

Rose didn't answer, her gaze falling on the teacup by her side. She detested the milky tea, but the cup was her favorite. The creamy porcelain was etched with a portrait of the young princess Margaret Rose, a garland of flowers framing her face. The handle was chipped, the princess's cheek marred by a smattering of cracks, but she held her neck high, her features fine. Rose felt a kinship with the princess, only a few years younger than herself, with whom she shared a name.

Mrs. Cohen leaned down and, clearing her throat, said: "We're going to the Rosenblatts' for lunch after *shul*. I'll make sure Mary brings you some broth." The cadence of her voice was uncharacteristically soft, her smell clean and lightly sweet. Rose felt a stab of anxiety. She wriggled down, burrowing farther under the sheets. "Thank you," she said. But her words were muffled, and Mrs. Cohen, with an aggrieved sigh and a click of her heels, murmured, "You're a funny one," and took leave of the room.

Within minutes Rose heard Mr. Cohen bellow, "My overcoat, Aida!" Mrs. Cohen's high voice cried, "Ah, Mary, Mr. Cohen's overcoat, please!" She heard the sounds of footsteps in the stone front hall, the creak of the front door opening and closing, and then, finally, mercifully, silence.

She had managed to avoid synagogue for weeks now. The place

gave her the creeps, with its dank smells, its gloomy light, and the Hebrew she didn't understand. From the women's balcony where they sat, Rose watched the men below, huddling under voluminous prayer shawls, bowing and bending like bugs unused to the light. The last time she'd gone, she sat silently next to Mrs. Cohen, who was sitting next to Mrs. Appelbaum, who was gossiping about someone's daughter. Mrs. Cohen tittered in response. The very air in the synagogue was so thick and foreign it seemed nearly unbreathable. Rose thought, longingly, about how her family never went to temple in Vienna. And Gerhard didn't have to go in England either. Once more Rose thought of the unfairness that her brother was lucky enough to live with a boisterous Christian family in Liverpool, while she had been forced to be in Leeds with the Cohens, a childless Orthodox couple who insisted that they wait three hours after beef stew for a slice of buttery cake, who ferreted out any leavened products with a feather before Passover, who swung a chicken over their heads during the Jewish new year, who were the most aggressively un-English family she knew.

THOUGH IT WAS INDISTINCT, ROSE thought she could make out the sounds of Mary's brush attacking the pots in the kitchen sink. Mary took her work seriously, as if she were the true owner of the house and the Cohens long-term tenants whose presence she humored, barely. She wasn't like Bette; she paid little attention to Rose, and when she did, she was dismissive: yet another decorative, questionably useful object that required dusting. But there was something about this lack of attention that made Rose like her all the more.

Rose heard Mary move into the parlor—there was the creak of the floorboards settling under her formidable weight, there were the pings as she ran her rag over the keys of the grand piano. Rose jumped out of bed, wriggling into her pants, pulling a second jumper over her first. She arranged the flat pillows in the center of the bed, pulled the sheet over them, and made a halfhearted attempt to plump them up.

It looked more like a lumpy raincoat than the shape of a girl, but Rose couldn't afford to waste time. Down the rambling Victorian hall, she passed the lavatory, and Mr. and Mrs. Cohen's bedroom, Mrs. Cohen's brown-hued sitting room. ("*England is done up in browns*," she had written to Mutti when she first arrived, and was she ever proud of the observation. "It makes me appreciate the colors of your pretty scarf all the more. The birds on it keep me company.") At the far end, opposite the square window that looked over the garden that had seen better days, Rose pushed open a wooden door without a handle, slipped into the darkness of a tight corridor.

Two baby steps forward, one hand on the dirty brick wall guiding her, reading the mortar like braille. It was cooler in here, the air dank. The steps plunged down. Rose closed her eyes, taking a deep breath and coaxing herself to get moving, *faster, faster!* She knew the servants' staircase well. Mary had been the one to show it to her, saying, "*I go up the front stairs, and so do you.*" But three months ago, after the war began and the char had been dismissed and the cook and gardener too, Rose began to think of the stairs as her own. In this cloistered darkness, everything dropped away: England and Austria, the perplexed looks and sighs of Mrs. Cohen, the letters she received from her parents, and the clamoring silence that took the place of those letters since the war began. Here, as she sank into darkness, the pain in her chest that was her most constant companion—it gave her life contour, even as she tried to ignore it—eased a little. She could be anywhere and everywhere at the same time.

Rose made her way down, her hands scraping against the crumbling wall, skipping the creaky seventh step, knowing to step to the right on the thirteenth to avoid a loose board. At the foot of the stairs, the door leading to the cellar had been propped open, and Rose stooped down to remove the wad of newspaper that she had placed here the day before—she could be a planner, when she needed to be.

She was breathing heavily when she emerged from the cellar to the quiet street, the pavement shiny damp. The sun looked small and discarded, an orangy scrap low on the horizon. But Rose eagerly took it all in. She yanked at a low-lying branch on the giant horse chestnut tree on the corner, making the blossoms dance and shiver, a rain of petals on her skin. She passed the Harveys' house, their Austin Six on blocks in the front yard. A few houses down was the Convoys', whose wrought-iron gate had been largely dismantled, only the far two posts remaining, the rest of the metal given over for the war effort. There on the corner Rose spotted the T of Margaret's back, her shoulders slouching in her dark wool coat, her single fair braid running down her back like a beacon on this gray day.

Rose hurried to her, skipping. "Hallo!" she cried out, expelling the word like a breath.

"Hello." Margaret turned, far more subdued. Her small blue eyes scanned Rose's face. "You're dirty. Look at your hands!"

Rose tried to wipe her palms on her friend's jumper, but Margaret squealed and pulled back. "I'm early. It was easy." Rose did a little jig for Margaret, her arms flailing about, compelled to entertain. Around Margaret, her body had a mind of its own. Back at the Cohens', she would recall her dancing and cringe.

"You're hopeless," Margaret said, but she said it companionably, agreeably. "Come along." Rose was happy to fall in line as Margaret took the lead.

ABOUT A MONTH AFTER ROSE arrived, Mrs. Cohen took her to Woolworth's, or Woolies, as everyone in Leeds called it. Rose was spending most of her time hidden in the darkness of the servants' staircase or beneath the piano in the drawing room. The afternoon when Mrs. Cohen had invited over a pair of sisters around Rose's age, refugees from Germany who had arrived on a train a few months before Rose, did not go well. (The older sister wanted to talk only about hairstyles; the younger sister barely spoke, and all Rose could think about was the unfairness that they had been placed together, while she and Gerhard had been split up. "It's a big expense and responsibility to care for a child," Mutti wrote. "We are very fortunate that two families agreed to take you both in.")

Perhaps a trip to Woolies would prove a useful distraction, Rose heard Mrs. Cohen say one morning to Mr. Cohen as he was nearly out the door. Off to Woolies they went. Rose was examining a display of notebooks, trying to decide what to buy, when a young blond girl peered over from the inkwell section and said, nearly bored: "You want the lined one." As Rose soon would learn, Margaret was six months older, and having lived in Leeds all her life, she seemed to know it all.

They tried to see each other every weekend, Rose skipping synagogue when she could. Today they went to the cinema, and using the sixpence that Mr. Cohen gave to her on Sundays, Rose paid to see *Intermezzo* for the second time. Sitting on the back steps of the post office afterward, digging their hands into the grease-stained bag in which Margaret kept the sourballs and jelly babies that they bought weekly with their ration stamps, Rose found it difficult to care who might walk by and spot her.

"Leslie Howard is the perfect gentleman," Margaret proclaimed. "I'm going to marry someone like him."

"Me too." Rose could picture it. She too would marry an Englishman. He would be tall and fair, with light-colored eyes like Margaret and Gerhard, and even the slightest bit stoop-shouldered like Margaret's father, a doctor, his steps heavy with the gravity of his work.

Margaret said that she had read that in his next film Leslie Howard was going to play a pilot; what could be grander than that?

"Mmm." Rose was focused on breaking a sourball into two. She tried biting it, gnawing on its underside, but nothing was working. The tips of her fingers became sticky and discolored with sugary purple.

"He's very active in the war effort, you know."

Rose nodded. She did know, but she did not want to think about the war effort. Studiously she concentrated on the marbleized fissures in her sourball. The sourball looked so easy to crack, and yet, she was getting nowhere. "What movie is coming next—did you ask Mr. Early?"

Margaret shook her head. "My dad says that it's because of men like Leslie Howard that we're going to get rid of Hitler." She bit off a licorice end, chewing thoughtfully. "He'll be gone, the war will be over, and then you can go home again."

Rose nodded mutely, her throat tightening. *Home.* The very word filled her with such a gust of icy hollowness, one whoosh and her insides were emptied out. "Yes, of course," she finally said, trying to be the good English girl she told herself she was. When she thought about leaving, all she could remember were the reasons she wanted to stay: Margaret and the movies and Woolies and the scrapbook she was making of the royal family.

"Then my brothers will come home," Margaret said. "Can you imagine, the war over?"

"No," Rose said, putting the sticky-wet sourball back into the paper bag. In her mind's eye, she saw her beautiful Mutti, her slender neck bent over the piano keys, intent on practice. She remembered the heavy smell of Papi's leather case and the way he used to let her sit on his lap when she was little and stamp his correspondence. It had been hours since she had thought about her parents. What were they doing now? What would her mother think, if she could see Rose, ignoring the Cohens' rules, stealing off to go to the cinema, laughing with her friend?

Rose stood, unsteady on her feet. "I should get home," she said. All that sugar was unsettling her stomach. "I don't feel so well after all."

WHEN SHE RETURNED TO THE Cohens', she didn't bother climbing up through the cellar, but opened the front door slowly, resigned. There was Mary in the entry hall, her stout body down on her knees, furiously brightening the brass inlay of the umbrella stand. She looked up at Rose, her little blue eyes set deep in her pale moon face, a face that inspired equal amounts of fear and admiration. "Child."

"I went outside," Rose said.

Mary looked at her, but didn't respond. She rubbed the clawed foot of the umbrella stand, and then swatted at it for good measure.

"I shouldn't have."

Mary snorted. "Not my house, not my business."

Rose was feeling too miserable to answer. She felt another twinge in her stomach. Was this God's way of punishing her for skipping out on synagogue, lying to the Cohens? She wished it was Mary's business, she truly did.

"You've got a letter," Mary said. "I've laid it on your bed."

A letter? Rose's stomach flew up to her throat. She hadn't gotten a letter in months. What if it were bad news? After all this time, it could only be bad news. "Oh," she said.

"Go upstairs, read it. Get back into bed." Mary touched the tiny silver cross that nestled in the hollow of her neck. "Or Mrs. Cohen is liable to blame all your nonsense on me, just like everything else."

Rose nodded, swallowed. She pictured the letter upstairs, waiting for her, lying on her tan coverlet—whatever news it contained, it existed, it was not something conjured up by her imagination. She turned to Mary, as if to speak, but no words came out. She wheeled around and tore up the front staircase to the third floor, where she was told she belonged.

IN THE BEGINNING, SHE LIVED for letters. She would ask Mrs. Cohen, by the fire in the drawing room in the morning, from the safety of her perch beneath the piano in the afternoon—how long does it take for a letter to travel from Vienna to Leeds?—so persistently, so often, that Mrs. Cohen threw up her hands, exasperated. "Several days, as I've said many a time before. It takes what it takes, child. What more can I say?"

Rose got through those first dizzying weeks, when she felt as if she were sleepwalking round the clock, when her English was nearly nonexistent, when she was too numb to cry, by imagining what she would write home. From the fat committee ladies who greeted her and Gerhard when they came off the boat in Harwich to Mrs. Cohen, who said to her, "there, there," even when she hadn't been speaking, from the disgusting kippers—and why would anyone ever put milk in tea?—to Mr. Cohen, whose wire spectacles were small and eyes even smaller and whose favorite sweater was a scratchy red cardigan, *the exact red of Herr Soutine's bellhop's uniform,* Rose wrote about it all. She hoped Mutti would be pleased that she remembered the painter's name.

Those first letters she got back, plain pale envelopes filled with tissue-thin purple stationery—a burst of color in this world of browns, a vital heart—these letters written with her father's dark fountain pen in her mother's elegant hand, meant everything to her. *"Ah, my beautiful Rose,"* her mother wrote, *"Papi and I are so glad to hear that you are settling in so nicely. Have you seen any black cats in Leeds yet? Here at home, everyone asks after you and Gerhard. How we all envy your England adventure!"* She went on to tell her how Swibber the butcher had broken his arm and now cut meat in the most awkward manner, and how Oma had moved into the flat too, so they were all cozy and together for the winter. *"Mr. and Mrs. Cohen sound like fine people, and you must remember to show your gratitude and be obedient every day, as I know you will."*

Rose wrote back immediately, told her mother about Margaret and school and the English poetry she was learning. She said Leeds was nothing compared to Vienna; she wrote that she slept with her mother's scarf every night and she couldn't stand the full skirts that were all the rage among the girls.

February brought a deluge of rain, a request from Mrs. Cohen to be called Auntie Aida that Rose pretended she didn't hear, a card from Bette saying she had married a boy from Munich, and a letter from Mutti telling Rose they had moved again. Now she and Papi, along with Oma and Tante Greta and Onkel George, were sharing quarters with the Fleishmans and the Weitzs from downstairs. *"Do you remember the Fleishmans? Their Walter was in Gerhard's form. Mrs. Fleishman is hard to forget. She is a big woman with snapping dark eyes. She used to be a dancer when she was young and is still very vain and particular about nearly everything: her corsets must be washed out twice before wearing; we should not ingest meat during a full moon (as if there were meat to be had) or drink water during our meals as it impedes digestion! Whenever I find her too draining, I remind myself that you and Gerhard would get a great laugh out of her."*

In March, Rose won third place in the annual Tennyson recitation at school. In April, as if to celebrate the lengthening days, she began dreaming in English. The gaps between the letters she wrote home widened. She was so busy in school, she told herself, but she was also venturing forth. Sometimes she would ride the bus alone into town to Schofields on the Headrow. The department store was nowhere near as grand as the Gerngross back home, but she still loved exploring it. In the ladies' department, she would quietly take note of the inventory, thinking, *Mutti would admire that shimmery blouse with the bow. She would despise the checkered skirt.* One time, she wandered into the café and saw ladies in evening gowns and elbow-length gloves sashaying and weaving among the tables. "Bloody fashion show, gets in my way," a waitress whispered to Rose. Then she added: "But it can be quite grand, I will say." *Not as grand as some things I know,* Rose was tempted to say.

June brought a letter from her mother talking about quotas and gardens and admonishments. *"I walked by the walled garden behind the hospital the other day and spied in. It was bursting with color. I could see all the berries—goose, currant, even your favorite, straw.*

"We haven't heard from you in three weeks, my sweet little mausi. Your father and I hope that means you're focusing on your SCHOOL-WORK. Your last description of Mary made me laugh, and made me hungry for more. Is she really as menacing as you say?"

And then, in September, war was declared, and the letters stopped arriving.

MARY WAS WRONG. IT WASN'T a letter but a postcard this time, dated "Sept. 5, '39," more than three months earlier. *"My dearest mausi,"* her mother began, *"please know your Papi and I are well. I fear that with the outbreak of the war we will not be able to write for some time and so I am routing this letter to Cousin Hedy in Holland with the hopes that she can get it to you. We hope to join you and Gerhard before long, but until then, we will be thinking of you constantly and always. You have done all you could. We are very proud of our brave girl."*

Rose lay back on her bed. She clutched the card in her sweaty right palm, and balled up a fistful of Mutti's silky scarf in her left. Her head felt prickly, her eyes achy hot. Her mother was wrong. Rose hadn't done everything that she could. Gerhard had; her brother had bicycled to some of the larger estates in the county, presenting himself at the front door and asking if the household could use a hardworking married couple. Rose was terrified by the prospect, but she promised that she too would ask. Then she had an idea.

"Let's go to your house," she said to Margaret one Saturday after the cinema. "You have the latest *Peg's Paper,* don't you?"

Once there, Rose excused herself to go to the toilet. But instead, she took the stairs down to Margaret's father's study. She knocked, timidly at first, then harder.

"Yes?" The voice sounded exasperated, but Rose couldn't back out now. She opened the door to find Margaret's broad-shouldered father behind his desk. "Margaret is upstairs."

"I know," she said. She dug her fingernails into her palm. "You know my parents are still in Vienna." She flung the words out, her eyes trained on the ocean of papers in front of him. "They would do anything to be here, with us. But they need to be sponsored—"

"Rose," Dr. Bradford said, removing his thin glasses.

"There is so much they could do. My mother," Rose said, trying to imbue the words with confidence and ease, "is a fine cook. The cakes she makes! And my father is a whiz at numbers. His books are impeccable. Might you know of any positions that could be suitable for them?"

"It's an awful situation. Simply horrid."

"Or any positions, suitable or unsuitable. Any positions at all," she said. She feared she sounded desperate, but she *was* desperate. Dr. Bradford knew so many people. He must be able to help.

"It's more complicated than that. But there might be"—he paused—"a possibility. I will ask around."

"Really?" Could this be? She imagined telling Mutti: *I was terrified to talk with him, but then I did.* She felt a smile tugging to lift the corners of her mouth.

"I don't want to say any more, not yet. Don't get your hopes up," he cautioned. "But I will try. Now go on, I have to get back to work."

"Thank you, Dr. Bradford," she said, wild with happiness, and spirited up the stairs to Margaret.

That was the last Rose heard about it. She felt as if Dr. Bradford looked at her differently from then on—there were moments over the next few weeks when she was certain he was about to speak—but a month after she approached him, the war started, and the borders closed for good.

Although there wasn't a tinge of criticism in the words her mother had written, Rose had the most horrible feeling that her mother knew Rose hadn't done all that she could. She sensed that Rose had waited too long to ask Dr. Bradford about sponsorship; why hadn't she asked anyone else? Mutti knew that Rose was impertinent and lied to Mrs. Cohen; she deduced that Rose had secretly gone to church with Margaret last month; she sensed that on the day that war broke out and all the adults at the Cohens' were crowded around the wireless in the drawing room, Rose crouched in the corner away from the others, immobilized by fear, but still she wondered what would happen on her birthday, which was the following week. She was a terrible daughter.

Rose remembered some things from that cold awful night she left Vienna. Walking from the tram with her parents and Gerhard, Mutti in her navy wool coat with the rabbit-fur collar, her face flushed. She wasn't wearing gloves, and neither was Rose, and Mutti gripped Rose's hand in hers, her fingers sweaty despite the chill in the air. Rose could remember her mother chatting about incidental things—a black cat she'd spotted in the neighborhood, Rose's coat that was too big now but was sure to fit snugly next winter if Rose took good care of it. She remembered arriving at the field behind the train station, where the children were supposed to gather.

But Rose did not remember saying good-bye to her parents. She could not remember leaving the field and walking to the train platform. Did she say good-bye in the field? Did they come to the platform with her? What did Mutti say? Rose didn't know. When she thought of that night, her mind snapped shut, leaving a shameful void. Why couldn't she remember?

Her stomach was truly hurting her, fisted and knotted up. She resolved to go to synagogue. She would call Mrs. Cohen Auntie, if she still wanted. Rose would do anything to set things right again.

She felt shivery. The cramps were getting worse. She got up to go to the toilet, and as she was scurrying down the hall, she felt between her legs a small but definite leak. She shifted, and there it was again. A wetness to her underwear, against her inner thigh. She rushed into the bathroom, aghast, slammed the door shut. How could she have had an accident? She was twelve years old. She took care of herself. She hung her head in her hands but she didn't cry. She didn't cry anymore; she wouldn't cry now.

It was only after she had been sitting on the toilet for a minute that she looked down at her underwear. There, instead of a yellowish hue, was a strip of stain winking back up at her, a shock of living, thick red.

All Rose could do was stare. She knew what it was. But knowing didn't help her believe it. Her mind began tumbling: Margaret, a year older at thirteen, hadn't gotten her monthlies yet. Her cousin Kaethe didn't get them until she was nearly fifteen! (Rose remembered the sturdy belt, the thick woolen napkins her cousin paraded in front of her like a prize.) Was this too early? She took her index finger and tentatively touched the rust-colored blood. It smelled dank, earthy. How could she be sure it was her monthlies? How could she know that something wasn't wrong with her?

Panicking, she tore off her wool pants, hopped out of her underwear. Still wearing her thick socks, she examined the damage. Her knickers were woefully stained, and she saw to her horror that a patch of blood had seeped onto her trousers too. Clutching them under the faucet, rubbing the material together, she thought how furious Mrs. Cohen would be if she found out. "We all have to do our part for the war effort," she often declaimed. Their part included using only the allotted pat of butter for tea and not asking for meat or too much soap since they were rationed.

The soap and water were doing little to ameliorate the stain on her pants. Rose feared she was only making it worse. She scrubbed harder, splashing water onto the toes of her thick woolen socks. Finally she stopped. This wouldn't do. She thought for a moment, and began searching the vanity. In the uppermost drawer, she found what she was looking for: scissors.

She sat back down on the toilet, grasped her pants, and was surprised to find that her hand was steady as she cut, then ripped, a tiny hole along the bloodied seam. She would say that she got caught on the gate outside of the Mullroys' house. A tear was much better than blood. A tear was something that was understood.

Rose's head ached and her chest felt both cold and hot at the same time, but she felt better, calmer, as she padded her damp underwear with a wad of toilet paper, put her ripped trousers on. Back in her room, she changed once more, pulling off the ruined knickers in exchange for clean ones. She balled up the dirty ones, looking around her room, hesitating. The pants she could explain away, but her underwear? She needed to get rid of them. But where? She couldn't use the trash or stuff them in the back of a drawer; Mary would surely discover them. But Mary had turned over her mattress just yesterday and given it a good cleaning; she wouldn't be there again for a while. Rose stuffed the product of her shame beneath her mattress.

As Rose was shifting the makeshift napkin between her legs once again, she heard a knock on her door.

"Just a moment—" Rose said, swiveling the pad around.

Another knock. "Please open up." Mrs. Cohen's voice.

"Coming," Rose called, pulling her pants on.

"Rose, now!"

She opened the door to face a shaking, flushed Mrs. Cohen.

"What were you doing?"

"Nothing, I—"

"You seem to have recovered well from this morning," Mrs. Cohen said in a tight voice. "I heard you went out earlier."

"I am sorry," Rose said, sliding away from Mrs. Cohen, onto the edge of the bed.

"You are often sorry, Rose, but that is not the answer."

"Mrs. Cohen, I truly am sorry, truly." Rose lowered her eyes. The room felt warm, murky. Rose thought she could detect the dank traces of her blood in the air. Could Mrs. Cohen smell it too? And what about the postcard? Was it hidden beneath her pillow? She didn't want Mrs. Cohen reading her mother's words, all that Rose sensed from the short card that Mutti couldn't bring herself to say. Mutti's hand had formed the beautiful cursive in black ink, her skin had touched the paper, and Rose couldn't bear for Mrs. Cohen to see it. "I was just getting dressed, and in Vienna," she tried, "at home—"

Pink blotches bloomed on Mrs. Cohen's cheeks. "I know, I know. You do everything differently at home. I am sorry this is not like your home." She turned her head away. "I am trying to do well by you.

Mr. Cohen and I both are trying to do well by you. But you act as if the world were against you, as if *I* were against you."

Rose didn't answer her, and the silence grew thick, ungainly. "I don't mean to," she finally said. But too much time had gone by; the words hung in the air, prickly short.

"Yes. It does seem to be beyond your control." Mrs. Cohen reached over and picked up Mutti's scarf. She examined the wrinkled silky material, casting an eye on the scarf's purple parrots, caught in flight. *Put it down*, Rose pleaded in her head. But she said nothing as Mrs. Cohen pulled on the material, revealing her slender bone-white wrists, hands not much bigger than Rose's own. "This could use a good cleaning," Mrs. Cohen said. "I'll give it to Mary."

"No!" Rose said, and snatched it back, buried her nose in its silkiness. She was convinced the scarf still held traces of Mutti's smell; her mother had packed it herself. Hers were the last hands to touch it, besides Rose's. Who knew what would happen if it were cleaned? But Rose could feel Mrs. Cohen's reproachful gaze on her, and finally she looked up from the scarf. "I'm sorry," she said, and the words felt stuck in her throat. "I like it this way."

"That is *exactly* the type of unacceptable behavior I'm talking about," Mrs. Cohen said. "Some would consider you a very fortunate girl."

"I know I am," Rose said quietly into her lap.

Mrs. Cohen sighed again. "Of course," she said, and then she was gone.

ROSE WOKE UP EARLY THE next morning, determined to do better. A steady rain was pelting the eaves as she squirreled away her makeshift napkins in a bag beneath her bed, went down to the breakfast table, and asked Mrs. Cohen how she could help. Soon she was perched next to Mrs. Cohen in her sitting room, her arms held wide for the skein of navy wool Mrs. Cohen was using to knit scarves for Margaret's brothers in the service.

Not long after the rain stopped and a grainy light speckled the room, Mary appeared. Handing Mrs. Cohen a sheaf of letters that had arrived by post, she announced: "I'd like to take the child for a walk."

Mrs. Cohen looked at Mary. "A walk?"

"A turn in the park."

Mrs. Cohen glanced from the resolute expression on Mary's face to Rose, who, too excited at the possibility, snapped her gaze down. Mrs. Cohen pursed her lips, considering for a moment. Finally she said, "Ah, yes, a turn in the park," as if the idea had occurred to her. "The fresh air might do her some good."

The cool air outside felt like a relief. Then Mary took a right instead of a left at the street lined with horse chestnut trees. Rose became confused. The park was the other direction. They were walking toward town. Mary hadn't spoken a word, but seized Rose's hand and walked at too fast a clip, her bag thumping at her side. Rose struggled to remain apace.

The streets became narrower, the houses smaller. After a bend in the road, they passed a newsagent and a pub with lace curtains. A man clutching a little girl in a camel overcoat by the hand said, "Why, hello, Mary." Mary didn't reply.

"Where are we going?" Rose asked.

"You'll see soon enough," Mary said, not breaking her stride.

Now Rose was growing scared. Mary continued to grip her hand; they walked farther. Maybe she was being kidnapped! Maybe Mary was snatching her away from the Cohens because she couldn't stand that Rose was being raised Jewish! Rose's breath picked up speed. Could that be it? How would she ever alert Gerhard? Could she get word to Margaret? What about her parents? Would they ever know?

And just as Rose was growing misty-eyed about the Cohens—it would be written up in all the papers, they didn't deserve this fate—Mary made an abrupt left, pulling Rose past some scraggly hedges into the tiny back garden, more gravel than grass, of a low-slung brick home.

"Sit." Mary ordered Rose onto a chilly stone bench by a trio of bicycles and answered the unasked question forming in Rose's eyes. "This is where I live."

Rose was too stunned to do anything but comply. Mary removed a small tin bucket from beneath the bench and then opened up her bag, revealing the crumpled paper bag that Rose had placed under her mattress hours earlier. "How did you get that?" Rose asked, astounded, her cheeks spotty and hot.

"Do you have to ask?" Mary snorted. "It's your bag, you take out the remains." She pointed for Rose to place the soiled napkins in the can. "I've got proper napkins for you inside. And I'll get you one of these to keep at the Cohens'. You're to tell me whenever you need to use it."

"Does Mrs. Cohen know?" Rose whispered, too embarrassed to meet Mary's eye.

"Please." Mary snorted again. "You think she notices anything?" She stooped her considerable girth low over the tin bucket, trying to strike a match. It didn't take. The second one sputtered aflame and died out. "This dampness is the devil itself," she said as she cupped her hands and the third caught and cast a weak glow.

As Mary poked inside the bucket with a stick, Rose stole a glimpse at her surroundings. The house was modest, more like a cottage, with gingham curtains lining the windows and a handful of stone, rain-streaked bunnies lining the walkway. She thought she heard the tinny sound of a dance number coming from inside. That didn't seem like the Mary she knew. But maybe she didn't know her, Rose thought, and for the first time in a great while, the realization of not knowing didn't fill her with dread, but rather a quiet, rising expectancy.

Rose couldn't detect any flames, only smoke clouding the can. The air felt cool against her cheek. She pulled her jacket tighter, but she tasted the char in the back of her throat and it warmed her, reminded her of a time long ago, falling asleep in front of the great tiled stove fed by coals—the *kachelofen*, it was called—at her *oma's* house, wanting, more than anything, to stay tucked in the tiny chair by the fire.

As Mary urged the flames on, Rose felt light-headed, heady with the knowledge of a secret that women like Mary carried around with them. She wondered if her mother too burned evidence of her monthlies. Rose couldn't picture it, couldn't see Mutti kneeling over a dirty can like this, couldn't imagine where in their high-ceilinged apartment she would do such a thing.

Then a reckless thought came to her. It didn't matter what her mother did. Rose felt iciness hollow out her insides; it seemed a horrible betrayal. Rose thought of the postcard, she thought of all those letters from her mother written on tissue-thin purple stationery (stored in a biscuit tin with a royal seal in her wardrobe), she saw Mutti putting on a pair of chandelier earrings, tightening her jacket with the rabbit-fur collar the night she left. Rose, turning away from Mary and the bucket and the smoke, thought about how she too was becoming a woman. But she was not becoming her mother. She never would be. This thought filled her with such a strange, sad, tangled mixture.

Would Rose burn her napkins twenty years from now? When she was grown up, when she was already old and married, with kids of her own, was this what she would do? But the questions made the iciness inside gust upward. How could she answer? For so long she told herself that she was going back home. But now?

Her parents would come here, she told herself with renewed resolve. They would all be here. They would make England their home. She was still a stranger, and yet the place and its ways were not unfamiliar. She hadn't wanted to belong here, but here she was.

One day this would all seem like a long time ago—Mary, the Cohens, the strangely damp taste of smoke against her lips, the drumbeat of dislocation, this newer feeling of being on the cusp of something. She would tell Mutti about it. This afternoon would exist as a memory, a story she might tell.

Rose peered over the side of the bucket. The mashed papers were sooty, gone hoary gray with ash and burns, turned into something else entirely.

"It's even harder with proper napkins," Mary muttered, peering into the can. "But this is what we do here in England."

Flush with the possibilities of what was to come, Rose barely registered her words.

5

LOS ANGELES, 2006

ONE MID-OCTOBER AFTERNOON, NEARLY TWO years after Lizzie arrived in L.A., some kids at school noticed a pallid cloud hovering over the ridge. It was thick, but diffuse somehow. It seemed not to move. The air was uncommonly warm and restless, the Santa Anas in full blast.

"It's fog," someone said. It was lunchtime, and the school alley was choked with everyone buying Mountain Dews and Fantas and chips and quesadillas off the taco truck.

"It's smoke." Duncan Black rolled his eyes. He lived in Malibu with his father and considered himself an authority on such things.

"It's past Temescal. It's at Will Rogers."

Another boy was talking about how in the last big fire, his best friend's cousin's house burned down. "He says it was one of the best things that ever happened to him. They stayed in some sweet-ass hotel down on Wilshire, then he got everything new—*everything!*— clothes and skateboards and a new set of Blue Öyster Cult records and even some dumb baseball cards he'd had since he was, like, seven. It was sweet, man. Insurance paid for everything."

No one paid attention. Everyone was looking up at the grayish yellowing cloud, which was unmistakable but not necessarily unusual—it looked more like smog than anything else.

"Where are the flames? You can't see the flames," Cori Carpenter said.

"Dumbfuck, of course you can't see the flames yet. It's not some fucking *movie*," Duncan said with disgust. "Trust me, it's smoke and it's coming this way. We'll be out of school in two hours, tops."

Kids were filling the air with questions—*Is PCH closed down? What about Topanga? How is my mom going to get here?* They were nodding and talking and pushing closer to each other, a moving cloud themselves. All Lizzie could think was *My house, my things.* She thought of her photos and letters and the Mel Gibson collage that Claudia had made her for her fourteenth birthday and her mother's Connecticut College sweatshirt and the old *Mademoiselle* that featured a picture of her mother from the summer Lynn worked there, and *The Bellhop*—oh God, *The Bellhop.* Lizzie was feeling that familiar sickly sensation; nothing was under her control. Where was her father? *No,* she whispered to herself.

It took less time than Duncan had predicted. Within the hour, they were gathered in the school gym, told about mandatory evacuations. They were awaiting parents, awaiting friends, held captive until an adult came to claim them.

When the gym was nearly emptied out, Lizzie remained huddled in a corner, convinced that she was going to spend the night on this spongy flesh-colored floor that emitted a weird gaslike odor. She would never see her house or her family again. Then a distracted-looking Max hurried in, Sarah rushing to keep up with him.

Max had picked Sarah up at her elementary school first. He was taking them back to his house in Venice in his battered VW Bug. Joseph was up at the house packing and "watching things," Max said as he jammed the car key into the ignition, the engine sputtering to life. "He'll meet us soon."

In the backseat Lizzie opened the triangle window, nervously scanning the sky.

As Max drove, he tried to distract them, talking about the old amusement park, the Venice of the West, it was called. One hundred years ago, there were gondolas for the canals and dance halls and arcade games and a huge swimming pool with a mechanical wave machine. Lizzie nodded, though she couldn't picture it. *Just let my father be safe*, she repeated to herself. They got to Max's house and Max convinced her and Sarah to go down to the boardwalk. It was hot and crowded with roller skaters and skateboarders and bodybuilders and people eating *churros* and corn dogs on sticks, people who seemed to have no idea about the fire less than ten miles away. Max bought them ice cream—strawberry in sugar cones—and despite her initial reluctance, Lizzie devoured hers.

It was this taste of cold sweetness that Lizzie distinctly remembered years later, a delicious evanescent treat laced with an unspeakable fear. She remembered Max's small house situated on the edge of the dank canal—his cottage, he called it. She remembered feeling safe in that house—Max ordered pizza and installed Lizzie and Sarah on the couch with multiple blankets despite the day's heat, told them they could watch whatever movies they chose. ("You sure *Godfather II* is okay for Sarah?" "It's fine!") She could recall all this as well as the conviction of her feeling: her house would burn. She would never see her father again.

But when Lizzie woke up the next morning, her father was sitting at Max's tiny metal kitchen table. He was filthy in his old NYU Med sweatshirt, sweat-stained and dirt-streaked, but his eyes were bright. Lizzie could see white in his hair, what she would later learn was ashes.

Joseph hugged her tightly, and Lizzie could smell the smoke and sweat emanating from his clothes, his skin. "The wind," he kept saying, "the wind." The fire had barreled through the mouth of the canyon, edged past Sullivan, and Joseph and his neighbors were ordered out of their houses, off the roofs they were trying to protect by hosing them down. But the wind abruptly changed course, and their houses were spared. Lizzie could remember her father laughing and shaking his head. "I'm a lucky man, Lizzie. I don't know why, but I've always been incredibly lucky."

She remembered Max vividly from that time too. He was younger than her father. Lizzie remembered thinking that he was still old, though, close to forty, she had guessed. She remembered the way the reddish hairs in his beard would catch the light and gleam. He spoke to her like she was a real person, not a kid. And she remembered telling him: "You're very different from my dad."

"Is that so?"

"Yeah," she had said. "You're much quieter."

"I talk," he said, with a sly smile, but then, as if he couldn't help it, he fell silent.

HE WAS A LISTENER THEN and he was a listener now. Because here Lizzie was, back in Max's house, the Venice canal nothing more than a silvery streak out the window, a trick of reflection. Here were his nimble hands, exploring the territory of her body. He was a detailer, that Max, a recorder, a collector; he brought fierce attention to whatever task was at hand, unwrapping the cellophane of a cigarette pack, unwrapping her. Lizzie lay back on his couch and looked up at the wood slicing the living room ceiling, those same thick roughhewn beams that she'd slept beneath on a night more than twenty years earlier when she feared she was once again losing all that mattered. Max had taken care of her. Now he brought the same steadied attention to the tracing of her.

And my God, did it feel good. How in the world could something feel this good? She was dizzied by her desire, under a spell. The only part that made sense was that something that made so little sense was transpiring. She and Max shouldn't be happening. If her father were alive, they *wouldn't* be happening. This, she tried not to dwell on.

She called her senior partner. "I think I need that bereavement leave after all," she said. She told him that her father's estate was a shambles, her sister a wreck. "I need to be here," she said in a gust of prevaricating self-righteousness. "I'm sorry, but I do."

Marc agreed to two weeks. "Thank you," she said. "That's all I need." She thought to herself: *Two weeks, and I'll figure it out.*

But what needed figuring out? She knew, even if she couldn't admit it to herself, even if she hadn't said a word to Max, she wanted to stay here in this delicate bubble, an unreal time that wasn't the past and wasn't the future but a surreal melding of the two.

Her life was like this: during the day, she went for runs in the morning and then read for hours at a time. Max would come home from work, and they would open a bottle of wine and make do with whatever was in the refrigerator, quick cobbled-together meals— pasta and sausage, a frittata with onions and cheese—as if it didn't occur to either one that supermarkets and gourmet shops and dozens of restaurants were just around the corner, provisions theirs for the asking.

While Max cooked, Lizzie asked questions. They both drank. They didn't talk about their shared profession. They rarely spoke about Joseph. Lizzie learned that Max had lived in Australia for a year after college. His mother never tired of telling him that she had wanted a daughter, and barring that, a doctor for a son. Max had been a pudgy kid, looking out at the world from behind thick-lensed glasses. He worried about his ex-stepdaughter, a cool, distant seventeen-year-old named Kendra, whom he tried to see once a month. He was a quiet, relentless competitor, a marathoner who only gave up racing a couple of years ago when his knees gave out. He said he loved going down on her.

They brought glasses of wine to his bed, and she was eager for him to indulge. Max's chest hair had turned mostly white, with some patches migrating to his shoulders. At fifty-five, his stomach was ample, soft, and there was something slightly comical about the way it looked, perched atop his still-muscular runner's legs. But Lizzie couldn't remember ever feeling this hungry for someone's touch. Their time in bed was marked by an urgency, shorn of any niceties, a tumbling down into what felt like her own true hard self. *It won't last*, she told herself. It couldn't.

Could it?

HER FIRST MONDAY, AFTER MAX went to work, she spent the morning examining his prodigious shelves, crowded with art books—Courbet and Ellsworth Kelly and the architecture of the desert—and European histories and biographies and many a volume on the Civil War. She pulled down the doorstopper of *The Power Broker*, which she had always wanted to read, but New York and Robert Moses's machinations felt far away, and after several pages she lost interest, was back inspecting the shelves. Closer to the window, she spotted the creamy spine of *The World of Yesterday*, by Stefan Zweig. Years ago, a boyfriend of hers had thrust the xeroxed pages of a short story of Zweig's into her hands with the fervor of a convert. She could remember little about the story's particulars, only that it took place on an ocean liner and followed two men who played chess. But she had been compelled, she recalled, gripped by a story about a game that she cared little about.

Zweig was Viennese-born and Jewish, like Rose Downes. Lizzie moved to the window seat with coffee and Zweig's memoir in hand. She began to read. Zweig called the period in which he grew up before World War I in Vienna "the golden age of security." Politics took a backseat; theater, music, and literature were revered. Zweig wrote of once passing Gustav Mahler on the street and boasting about it for months. As a student, he took part not in political rallies but in demonstrations that protested the tearing down of the house that Beethoven had died in. Lizzie read about the pleasures of the Viennese coffeehouse, where not only Austrian but also French and English and Italian and American papers and magazines were on offer. This dreamy, intellectual world that Zweig was describing would not hold, Lizzie knew, and she read the nostalgic passages with growing dread.

What happened to Zweig? Lizzie skipped ahead in the book to find out, and read the publisher's note at the end. After Hitler overtook Austria, Zweig had fled, first wending his way to France, then England, then New York, eventually landing in Brazil. Despondent over his exile and the state of the world, he and his wife committed double suicide in 1942.

Lizzie shut the book, shuddering. Zweig had gotten out—he was, in a sense, lucky—and still he had ended his life. And he had killed himself in 1942, before the world knew about the concentration camps, before the full extent of the terror was understood.

But Rose had lived. For decades afterward, however painful it might have been, she had decided to live. Through the window Lizzie saw a snowy egret wade into the shallow waters of the canal, peck at a bobbing yellow something, far too brightly colored to be natural. She stared at the bird but it barely registered.

Then she heard a noise: her phone, vibrating against the glass of Max's coffee table, Sarah calling. Oh God, Lizzie had forgotten all about lunch with her sister.

"SORRY, SORRY," LIZZIE SAID, SLIDING into her seat across from Sarah on the café's patio, her hair still damp from the shower.

Sarah waved off the apologies, kissed her. "It's fine. I ordered myself some courage while I was waiting." She nodded at a frothy, milky glass in front of her.

"Your drink has courage?" Lizzie asked. It felt surreal to be sitting across from her sister now, blithely chatting. Sarah still thought she was staying with Claudia.

"It's called 'courageous.' I don't know if that means it encourages courage. Or contains courage. Either way, it is seriously foul."

A willowy waitress with a buzz cut handed Lizzie a menu. She was wearing a button that said, *What Fulfills Your Heart?* Lizzie scanned

the menu: "pure," "openhearted," "radiant." "I'll get the breakfast ta-
cos," she said, and pointed to the item, unable to bring herself to say
"superb," the dish's name. "And coffee, please."

The waitress nodded stonily. "Anything else?" She gestured at
Sarah with her chin.

"I'm good with my 'courageous,'" Sarah said, smiling sweetly.
"Thank you."

The waitress left. "I hate this place," Sarah said.

"So what are we doing here?" Lizzie said. It had been Sarah's suggestion. When Lizzie had looked up the café online and read that it
had a motto—"stay, acknowledge, be"—she thought: *Of course. This
is exactly what Sarah would choose.*

Sarah shrugged. "Its pretentions are only matched by how good it
is. They hand-hull the nuts for the almond milk. This drink probably
has more nutrients in it than everything else I'll ingest this week."
She downed the remains like a shot.

"Do you need a lot of vitamins these days?" Lizzie said.

Sarah studied her, her eyes narrowing. "Excuse me?"

Lizzie blushed. The words had popped out. "Nothing," she muttered, and she played with her fork.

"You are a liar." Sarah let out a snort. "You've always been an awful
liar. It's like that time when I told Dad I was at Amelia's—"

"You were fourteen! You guys wanted to go to Tijuana. I wasn't a
bad liar; I just wouldn't cover for you."

"Don't change the subject," Sarah said, and she sat up straight, like
the actress she had once wanted to be. She folded her hands, her long
tapering fingers—their mother's, not the stubby ones of their father's
that Lizzie had inherited—on top of each other. She fixed those deep
hazel eyes of hers on her sister. "I know you."

"When I was staying at your place," Lizzie admitted, "I saw something, a prescription bottle, for Clomid—"

"What? You knew about the Clomid? You knew and you didn't
say!"

Lizzie nodded, embarrassed. "I didn't know what to say," she finally said, and that admission felt like a small but essential truth.

"I know. It must have been a surprise. It's not like I talked about wanting kids. I never thought I did." Sarah ducked her head, her dark hair curtaining off her face. "But I don't know—Angela and I kept talking about it, and something just changed. Once it shifted, that was that. I'm excited; I really want this." She looked back up, her fine features settling, growing serious. She reached for her sister's hand. "It scares me, being this excited."

Sarah's fingers were cool to touch. Lizzie understood, she wanted to say. She knew that fear. But it was thrilling too: her sister, a mother. Then she felt something burble up, an unsettling sensation—she was forgetting something. There was something she needed to do.

"Dad," Lizzie said to her sister, on the edge of tears. "You should be telling this to Dad."

"I know," Sarah said, squeezed Lizzie's hand, bit her lip. "I was thinking that too."

For a moment, neither of them spoke. Then Lizzie heard herself say: "I have something to tell you too. I haven't been staying with Claudia. I've been with Max."

Lizzie pulled her hand back, reached for her water. She glanced at her sister, but Sarah's open, expectant expression hadn't changed. "Max . . . ? Max Levitan?"

Lizzie nodded, unable to speak. Was Sarah disgusted?

"You and Max, what?" Sarah said, uncomprehending.

"We've been—seeing each other," Lizzie finished. For a wild moment, she thought: *I'll call it off now. I will.*

"Wait, you and Max, together?" Sarah did look truly surprised, her mouth open, her big eyes growing bigger. "How? Wait, forget that," she said, waving off her own question. "I mean, how long has this been going on—since before Dad?"

"God no," Lizzie said, horrified. "No, not long at all. But, it's happening."

"Oh, I didn't mean it like that; I was just—not expecting it. But of course, it's fine; it's great!" Sarah said, recovering. "Not that you're asking for my approval. But it's not all that surprising. I had a crush on him when I was a kid too."

"Well, I didn't," Lizzie said weakly. Her words sounded small, ungenerous, which wasn't what she had intended. She had only meant this: what had happened with Max had surprised her like nothing else. And of course she wanted her sister's approval.

"Sure you did," Sarah said, waving her off. "All our secrets are coming out now, aren't they?"

AFTER MAX LEFT EARLY THE next morning, Lizzie decided to go for a run. She was meeting Rose in the early afternoon but the day seemed too open. She wished she had arranged to meet her earlier. She followed a path alongside the canals, and tried to imagine what it must have looked like a hundred years ago, when the waterways first opened as a resort, with bona fide gondoliers brought in from Italy. But she kept thinking about the first time Joseph had brought her to Max's little house by the water. She couldn't have been older than eleven. It was their second or third trip out to L.A. after Joseph had moved. Lynn was still alive. Max took Lizzie and Sarah for a ride in a canoe while Joseph stayed behind. The canal's water was dark and unimpressive—she remembered plucking out a slimy green soda bottle, its label too worn to identify. The canal smelled of nothing good. She turned to Max: "Why would you defend a murderer?" she asked.

He looked at her. Everyone knew about the Cohen killings. There had been a storm of press coverage, thanks to the family's Hollywood pedigree. (Just the year before, the father, the sole survivor, had won an Oscar for best director.) The son, who had killed his mother and brother, had gotten life imprisonment, not the death penalty, thanks to Max. And she wanted to know: How could he fight for him? It seemed unquestionably wrong.

"Everyone deserves an advocate," Max said. "If I don't do it, who will?" They drifted close to the mossy edge of the canal, and Max let go of the oar, which clattered against the flooring of the boat's aluminum hull, and pushed off with his hand. "Besides, things are often more complicated than they seem."

"He killed his mother and his brother," Lizzie said, unsatisfied. "What's complicated about that?" Still, she could remember how much she liked being in that canoe, rowed by Max, the distinct feeling of being quieted by the boat's rocking.

She ended her run at the boardwalk and crouched down, panting. A shirtless guy, his torso a coil of muscles, was palming away on the bongos. A woman lifting a headless mannequin clad in a G-string came out of a shop. Displays were being set up at rickety stalls with T-shirts and nose rings and candles and Guatemalan woven shirts, a table manned by Lyndon LaRouche supporters. A middle-aged man in bright Lycra wove unsteadily by on his bike and there was something about the shape of his shoulders, the determined thrust of his neck and head that gave Lizzie a chill of recognition. For a moment she thought: *That's my father*. It brought her comfort, how her body was charged to try to find him. *I'm sorry for your loss*, people said to her, and in these not infrequent moments she felt as if her father were not dead but truly lost, able to be found if she searched for him hard enough.

She turned away from the boardwalk, away from the homeless with their rattling carts and the shiny Rollerbladers, all the cacophony of Venice, and looked out over the broad expanse of beach, a dirty pale carpet of sand. The morning was stubbornly overcast, the sky anemic, the ocean a shade darker. Lizzie headed toward the water, watching the waves careen and heave onshore. The wet sand grew firmer beneath her feet. The wind kicked up, ocean spray mingling with her sweat. She sat down, pulled off her sneakers and socks, and gazed out over the grayish-greenish water. Her eyes burned. The day after tomorrow was the twenty-second, exactly three months since he had died. Last month on the twenty-second, she had gone to

Barney Greengrass for an early breakfast and ordered the most expensive sturgeon on the menu. "Dad would have loved that," Sarah said, and it pleased Lizzie to hear Sarah say it. The twenty-second wouldn't always feel so fraught, Lizzie suspected, and the prospect of that dissipation served up its own fresh sadness.

Lizzie found herself saying, "Hey. I miss you, so much. I promise I do." She felt self-conscious, but it was a relief to say it out loud.

She sat for quite a while. When she rose and started for Max's, she saw something she hadn't noticed before: a synagogue next to the lingerie shop—a whitewashed stucco building with sky-blue accenting its windows. THE SHUL ON THE BEACH, a sign read.

She was gazing at it, surprised she had missed it before, when a short, round-faced man in khakis and a baseball cap approached. "Can I help you?" he asked. "Are you Jewish?"

Once or twice a year, a pair of dark-suited young men, looking as if they were twelve, would approach her in Midtown. They would climb out of a van with the words MITZVAH-MOBILE festooned across its side or hurry down the sidewalk and ask her the same question, thrusting Hanukkah candles her way, the ceremonial fronds for the holiday of Sukkot. Lizzie would pick up her pace, ignoring them altogether.

But now she looked down at her sneakers. "My father just died," she said.

"I am so sorry. May his memory be a blessing," the man said. He didn't avert his eyes as some people did when her father's death came up. "I'm the rabbi here. Morning services are about to start. Would you like to say kaddish?"

Lizzie had last attended services with Ben and his family on Yom Kippur a couple of years earlier, an unpleasant hour at his parents' synagogue in the Garment District with the rabbi using his sermon to rail against Palestinians. "I don't know how," she said.

"I'll explain," he said. "You'll try."

Inside, the sanctuary smelled dank. It was spare, the white walls unadorned, the back lined with books, a low wooden banister separating the room. The rabbi, the baseball cap off and a crocheted yarmulke affixed in its place, gave her a booklet with transliterations along with a lace head covering and bobby pin, and pointed her to the left side of the room. Lizzie sat down behind two older women, the only people on this side of the room, stunned that she was here. She draped her sweatshirt first over her bare legs, then over her shoulders and short sleeves, uncomfortable either way. On the other side of the low partition were about a dozen men, most old and in suits, a few bushy-haired and T-shirted.

The service began. Most of it was in Hebrew, and although she didn't understand it, she found the sounds comforting. What would her father think of her being here? He had never been much of a synagogue-goer himself. But on Yom Kippur he would fast, and he used to insist that they watch Laurel and Hardy movies together on that day. He probably wouldn't be impressed with this synagogue. "What, you couldn't say kaddish somewhere in Brentwood?" she could hear him saying. But he would not be displeased.

The rabbi was saying something in Hebrew, looking her way. "The Mourner's Kaddish," he said in English, nodding at her. She scrambled to her feet. "*Yitgadal v'yitkadash sh'mei raba,*" she read out loud from the transliteration: *Glory and sanctified be God's name.*

Her heart seized. Her parents were gone. She wanted to shake off that fact, she wanted to escape it; she wanted more than anything for it not to be true.

She went on chanting. She ignored the English translation. She didn't want to know the meaning of the words. It was the sounds that mattered, the sounds that were offering her solace. She was here, standing, for him. She was his daughter, still. A raspy voice had joined her, a male voice—another mourner, she realized.

There were probably fifteen people present in a room that could hold a hundred, but when the others joined in to read the last line in unison, to say amen, it was the first time in months that Lizzie felt the weight of her loss ease a little.

After, the rabbi approached her. "You see? You were able to say it. May God comfort you among the mourners of Zion and Jerusalem, and may your father's memory be a blessing."

It shouldn't have felt like such an achievement and yet it did. "Thank you," she managed.

BY THE TIME SHE GOT back to Max's, she was running behind. She had been looking forward to seeing Rose all week. Now she would be late. She showered quickly and downed a yogurt and got in her rental car. They were meeting at the small park tucked behind Wilshire in the shadow of the La Brea Tar Pits. It had been Rose's suggestion; she lived nearby. "First the May Company moved out and then Bullock's too," Rose had said to her on the phone. "Now it's just me and the dinosaurs."

Lizzie made surprisingly good time from Venice to mid-Wilshire, and made it to the meeting spot about five minutes late.

Rose was waiting. She wore a long tailored white shirt, a chunky amber necklace, looking more chic and younger than Lizzie had re-membered. "Shall we?" she said. There was a note of imperiousness in her tone. Without waiting for an answer, she began down the path at the park's edge. Lizzie scurried after her.

"Sorry I'm late," Lizzie said as she hurried. "Traffic." Rose's fast pace surprised Lizzie. She was tiny, a good several inches shorter than Lizzie herself.

Rose didn't respond. When she finally spoke, her tone was softer. "I try to walk every day. After I retired from the school, I was driving Thomas, my husband, crazy, moping around the house—a common enough story—and these walks, they're such a small thing, but they saved me." A thin, rolled-up circular sat in the middle of the path; she kicked it out of her way.

"You're married?" Lizzie asked. She didn't know why it hadn't occurred to her that Rose might be.

"I was, for a long time," Rose said. "More than fifty years. But Thomas died nearly two years ago."

"Oh, I'm sorry," Lizzie said as her image of Rose shifted again: she had been married for more than half a century; she was a woman who had also experienced a big loss.

Rose gave her a curt nod.

"Do you have any other family, kids nearby?" Lizzie asked.

"No," Rose said. "No kids—nearby or elsewhere."

"I'm sorry," Lizzie said. "I don't know why I asked that." She hated it when people made assumptions about her. She had only meant— she was thinking of how difficult it must be to lose someone after all that time—she only hoped Rose wasn't alone.

"It's fine. Not everyone is made to have kids."

"Yes," Lizzie said, still feeling chastened but slightly relieved. "Absolutely." Maybe she was one of those people.

"We were very happy together, just the two of us, Thomas and I," Rose said plainly. She was walking briskly when she said it, didn't look at Lizzie.

"That's wonderful to hear."

"Are you married?"

"No," Lizzie said. "Not married, no kids." She tried to say it airily, but even she could hear her plaintive undertone.

"How old are you?"

"Thirty-seven."

"Still young yet," Rose said.

Lizzie gave a half smile. She did the math in her head all the time: *If it works out,* she might think on a promising first date, *then I could get pregnant in the next year.* Or even if it didn't work out. She had been thinking this with Max. *Would it be so bad if I just got pregnant?*

"You have no idea if you're going to get married," Rose said. "But the world is teeming with all that we don't know. It doesn't mean that you won't."

"True enough," Lizzie said. She was relieved that Rose didn't start naming random single men—the nephew of her mah-jongg partner, that chatty dentist who was quite attractive—that she could set Lizzie up with. Even Claudia—Claudia!—who had been involved in a ménage with her married landlords postcollege, who used to flit from partner to partner like the sun might not rise tomorrow—was now married and talked to her as if she were doing something wrong. "Maybe you need to be a little more open," she had said after Lizzie called to chat after a disastrous blind date. *More open?* Lizzie had just gone out with her friend's mother's oncologist. ("He's *very* sensitive and empathetic," her friend had said. *And arrogant,* Lizzie thought within minutes of meeting him. *And most likely gay.*) Not open? What was Claudia talking about?

At the corner, Rose turned down a smaller, residential street. They passed modest stucco Spanish-style houses built close together, yellowing pocket-sized lawns. The sidewalk was empty of people. Was one of these houses Rose's? Lizzie could imagine passing it, and Rose not saying a word.

"So you used to be a teacher?" Lizzie asked.

Rose nodded. "English, junior high school English, for more than thirty years. Much of that time at Eastgate, when it was still all girls. Such a mistake to merge with Wilton. Come," she said, and they crossed the wide stretch of Third Street, cars flying past.

Ah, Eastgate. Lizzie smiled in recognition. Of course. The illustrious school Joseph had hoped she would attend, but there were few spots the year they moved and Lizzie didn't get in. The high school she went to was more progressive ("ragtag," Joseph had called it). "I went to Avenues."

"Now, that makes sense."

Was that a touch of sarcasm in her voice? "What does *that* mean?" Lizzie asked.

"Nothing," Rose said. "I only meant: you seem more, I don't know, artistically inclined."

"Please, I was the least artsy person there," Lizzie said. She added: "Lawyer," with a gesture toward her chest with her open palm.

"So I heard from your father," Rose said. "Wise."

"I don't know about that," Lizzie said, although she continued to love her work, the precision of the law. But she was thinking of all the books she had been reading at Max's—it had been years since she had read that much. "I always loved English class, and reading in particular," she said to Rose. "It must have been fun to teach."

"I don't know if *fun* is the word I'd use, and reading is the least of it. But it was a wonderful career."

"I was reading a book yesterday that you probably know. By Stefan Zweig," Lizzie said.

"Of course."

"That chess story of his—"

"*The Royal Game.*"

"It's wonderful, don't you think?" Lizzie said. "Yesterday, I read a lot of *The World of Yesterday*. The way he describes living in Vienna before the wars—"

"Actually, I'm not a fan," Rose said. "Zweig's writing is too mannered, too sentimental, especially in *The World of Yesterday*. Not everything was so wonderful before the wars as he claims it to be."

"Oh," Lizzie said, deflated. Sentimental? "I see what you mean; it felt nostalgic, but I kept imagining him fleeing Vienna, being forced to move from one place to the other, then down in Brazil . . ." She trailed off, feeling self-conscious. Had she offended Rose?

"And that double suicide," Rose was now saying. "I am sorry, but suicide is always a coward's way out. Such a selfish act."

Lizzie nodded, reluctant to argue. But what if a person were gravely ill, with no hope of living? What if she were truly suffering?

"I had a cousin, my father's first cousin, although he wasn't all that much older than I, who took pills when he was basically still a child," Rose was saying. "Eighteen, nineteen. A brilliant, sensitive boy. There were rumors that he was gay, though no one called it that. His mother never got over his death, of course. She had an opportunity early on to get to France, but she wouldn't leave Vienna, said she would wait until the family could all go together. Everyone said it was because she wouldn't leave her son's grave."

"That's awful," Lizzie said. "I'm so sorry." Her mother was buried in Westchester, in a large Jewish cemetery that stretched over a series of gentle hills. She hated how far away she was from it when she moved to L.A., hated thinking of how barren the grave would look in winter. "I'll take care of it," her grandmother had told Lizzie without specifying what she was referring to, but Lizzie knew exactly. "How old were you when you left?" she asked Rose.

"Eleven."

"It must have been so hard." When Lizzie was eleven, her mother was newly sick. A revolving mix of sitters—it was hard to distinguish them apart, they turned over so often—picked up Lizzie and Sarah from school, took them to skating and ballet lessons. They were often late. Once, one never showed. After waiting more than an hour and calling home and getting no answer, Lizzie caught a ride with an older male cousin of a classmate. She didn't know the guy but he had been waiting around school ("sometimes I help out with soccer practice," he said) and he offered. Her mother went ballistic when she found out. Then her grandmother moved in. "For the time being," Lynn had said.

"My brother and I were put on a train, together, to England in the winter of 1939," Rose was saying. "After the Anschluss, after Austria was annexed by Germany. I should like to say that Austria was invaded, but it was decidedly not."

The slight wind felt welcome against Lizzie's warm face. She had read about those trains, seen a documentary on PBS about them, maybe. Trains filled with Jewish children, ferrying them out of Nazi-occupied Europe. "Kindertransports," she said.

"Yes," Rose said, "that's what they're called now. At the time, there was no name for it. They were just trains that we were put on."

"Of course," Lizzie said. Rose had said this nonchalantly, but Lizzie felt as if she had blundered.

"I'm not blaming you," Rose said with little hesitation, her fingers at her necklace's amber beads. "You didn't name them."

Lizzie let out a nervous burst—part cough, part choked laughter. "No, I certainly did not," she said, and realizing that Rose might take her laughter the wrong way, she added: "I'm sorry; I know it's not funny."

"That's quite all right. You can be funny." Rose did not seem thrown by Lizzie's unease. Disagreement seemed to enliven her. The wind ruffled the loose white hairs haloing her sharp, finely lined face. There was something striking about her, not one thing in particular, but the way she carried herself, the sum of her parts. "You do remind me of your father, you know."

"I do?"

"Yes, you're quieter than he was, more controlled—"

"Controll*ing*, he'd say."

"But just as smart, just as interested in the world," Rose continued. "And curious about others around you."

"Thank you," Lizzie said. "That's nice to hear." It was more than nice. "I bet it would make him happy that we were together. And talking about him—he would *love* that we were talking about him."

"Yes, exactly." Then Rose added: "I don't know why he didn't tell you about me. He spoke about you and your sister all the time. He told me that he wanted us to meet."

"I don't understand it either," Lizzie said, but she had her guesses. Neither she nor her father liked talking about the stolen painting; it had been such a painful time. She liked to think that Joseph didn't tell her about Rose because he wanted to spare her the reminder. But she feared there was a darker impulse at work: he hadn't mentioned Rose because despite everything, Joseph still blamed Lizzie.

Rose reached the corner before Lizzie. There she gazed over the intersection, hands on her hips as if surveying hostile territory. "We'll turn here," she called over her shoulder, and waited for Lizzie to catch up. "Though I was touched that he left me the masks."

"He must have known how much you admired them."

"No, not really. I've only seen them once, at his house, many years ago, when we first met. But I think it was a nod to the Soutine. African art was all the rage in Paris at the time Soutine was painting. He and his contemporaries turned to African art for inspiration. Obviously it's clearer with Modigliani, but it was true for Soutine all the same."

"I can't help but wonder if my father left you the masks because he couldn't give you the Soutine back." It was hard for Lizzie to say but it was, after all, the truth.

"Something like that," Rose said. Now she was the one looking away.

They walked on in silence. They were passing a large brick apartment building with a colonnaded front, unusual in this neighborhood of small, one-story houses, when Rose said, "Do you know what aggrieves me? This apartment building. It offends my sensibilities, and it has since it was built. Why the columns? If you're doing something in brick, leave it brick. If you want to go rococo, then by all means do that. But the two together, in this instance especially, do not work. It's like crossing a giraffe with a monkey. Why try to be something that you're not?"

Lizzie started to laugh. *They would be friends*, she thought. They would be.

"I am serious," Rose said.

"I know you are," Lizzie assured her. She imagined standing in Max's kitchen tonight, glass of wine in hand, telling him, *She's not like anyone else I know.*

"I'll tell you what I want right now," Rose said. They were nearly back at Third Street, back where they started. "Coffee. How does that strike you?"

"Like a seriously good plan," Lizzie said.

THE CAFÉ WAS A CONFECTIONER'S fading dream. Pink vinyl booths, pink cushions, heart-shape–backed chairs, scalloped wainscoting on the walls, a countertop made out of some fake substance that didn't look like marble but didn't look unlike it either. "It's been this way for decades," Rose told Lizzie, "ever since Thomas and I moved into the neighborhood. If they ever renovate, I will take my business elsewhere."

The restaurant was nearly empty, a few metal chairs upturned and resting on tables. They slid into a booth up front. "The pink is altogether too much, I know," Rose said. "But there's always a seat and the coffee is hot and still less than a dollar, as it should be."

"I love it," Lizzie said. It reminded her of Café Edison around the corner from her old firm, where on those rare days when she actually had time to leave her desk, she would go and order a bowl of matzo ball soup and eat it slowly, imagining the soup dissolving the hardened knot that had taken up residence beneath her rib cage. "You okay?" she remembered a waitress once asking her as she gave her the bill. "I'm fine," Lizzie had said, handing over a crisp twenty, winding her scarf around her neck, thinking of a citation she forgot to include on the draft of the brief; she'd add it once she got back to her desk. The waitress gave her an inquiring look as she took the money in her palm. "You're crying," she had said.

Now the waitress brought two coffees, and Lizzie tipped in milk and sugar.

"You know what you can do for me?" Rose asked.

"Name it," Lizzie said, stirring.

"I'd like to see the reports from the investigator your father hired years ago."

"The investigator?"

"The one he hired after the paintings were stolen."

Lizzie didn't remember hearing of an investigator. Was this something else Joseph hadn't told her? "I'll look for them," she said. "What was his name?"

"You know," Rose said after a pause. "I can't recall. This is what happens now. I hate that this happens."

"I'm sure it won't be hard to find," Lizzie said. "If I can't come across it, I'm sure Max will know."

"Max?"

"My father's friend," Lizzie said, nodding forcibly. "He's the executor of the estate."

"Ah, yes," Rose said. "Max. I've heard of him. Another thing I forgot." Her hands were wrapped around the coffee mug. Her nails were manicured, painted a lovely taupe color, and her fingers were short, stubby, not unlike Lizzie's own. She wore a gold wedding band on her left hand. "It's good to have someone helping you," Rose said. "It's good to have someone like that."

"It is," Lizzie said, and she heard her voice carry. The place was cavernous. Past Rose, a lone man was reading the paper at the lunch counter, his plate of eggs untouched. Lizzie did not want to talk about Max. Toward the back, a busboy filled saltshakers from a pitcher. Were they the only other customers here? The emptiness made her lean into Rose, made everything seem more intimate. "You said your mother bought the Soutine in Paris. At a gallery? From Soutine himself?"

"A gallery. My father had business in Paris—he was an importer, and he bought clocks, I think, in France—my mother rarely traveled with him, but she did on that trip, and she spotted the Soutine. It wasn't all that long after Dr. Albert Barnes, who was on a buying spree for the collection he would eventually amass for his Barnes Foundation, outside of Philadelphia, bought a large number of Soutines. That purchase made Soutine's career."

Lizzie nodded. She had taken a trip down to Philadelphia to the Barnes Foundation when she was in college, not long after *The Bellhop* was stolen. She had gazed at the other Soutine portraits—a baker's boy dressed in white, a thin, heavily browed man in a sea of blue—knowing that she wouldn't see *The Bellhop*, wishing for it to appear nevertheless. She asked: "After you left Vienna, what happened?"

"Our apartment was seized—my parents were still living there at the time. My brother and I only learned this after the war, from friends of theirs. Our parents were writing us daily at the time and never said a word. The Nazis took everything of value from the apartment, and there was a lot: jewelry and paintings and knickknacks, my mother's furs, the silver service. *The Bellhop* too, of course."

Lizzie was nodding, thinking of when *The Bellhop* was stolen from her house. To think that everything had been taken from Rose's family, every last possession of value, and how possessions were the least of what Rose had lost. "I'm so sorry," Lizzie said.

"My parents were ordered to Theresienstadt," Rose continued as if Lizzie hadn't spoken. "That's where I thought they were through the war. But we never learned—anything more."

"I'm so sorry," Lizzie repeated, wishing there were something else she could say. The clatter from the kitchen sounded. And then stupidly—Lizzie would later think, here was the moment where she should have stopped talking: "Did you ever file a claim against the Austrian government? You know you can, right?"

"I do know," Rose said. "And no."

"I could help, if you needed it."

"I don't want their money."

"But it's not theirs, really," Lizzie said. "It's compensation for what's rightfully your family's."

"Please," Rose snapped. "Let me be clear: I don't want that money. It's blood money. It makes what happened about property, and it most certainly is not. Besides, I'm not the victim here; my parents are."

"Of course—" Lizzie said in retreat. It was not hers to decide. Why hadn't she stopped talking?

"I am not a victim," Rose repeated, her voice emphatic. "I don't need anyone to feel sorry for me. Do you understand? I don't want their money."

Lizzie nodded. Later recalling the moment with a sting of embarrassment, she would think: *I just thought I could help.* "I do understand," she said, though *understand* was not exactly the right word. "It's none of my business. It's unimaginable, what happened. Of course you're handling it as you see fit."

"It might seem unimaginable, but it did happen," Rose said.

"I know," Lizzie said, miserable.

Rose downed her coffee. When she spoke again, her voice was firm. "I'm sorry. This is my problem, not yours. Let's not talk about the war or *The Bellhop* or what Austria might owe me. I'll tell you what I do want to talk about: your father."

"My father?" Lizzie said.

"He was a good friend. I bet he was a better father."

"Well, I don't know about that," Lizzie said immediately. "But he was a great father." *The best,* she could hear him saying in her mind. *Why can't you say I'm the best? Why can't you be unabashed, wholly enthusiastic for once?* She shook her head, thinking. "Did he ever take you to dim sum?" she finally asked.

"No."

"He used to take us all the time. My favorite was this place downtown, four flights up, no elevator—with sticky noodles and lotus leaves and purple taro and fried chicken feet—so many new weird foods, it terrified my sister. He could be a pain in the ass about it. 'Just try,' he'd say." It made her happy to recall. "The waiter would tally up the check at the end by counting the number of plates on the table, and my dad used to joke that they should hide plates under the table to lower the bill. There was that time he flew us up to San Francisco for the day—via charter plane—just to try out a dim sum place that a patient of his swore was the best."

"He chartered a plane just for the family?"

"Yes, I know," Lizzie said, reddening. "It was too much." She wished she had left that detail out. "But it wasn't long after we moved to L.A., and in retrospect, I think he was trying to impress us. Our mother had just died. I did not want to be living with him. I think he was trying to make us happy."

"You were fortunate to have him."

"Very," Lizzie agreed. She began stacking sugar packets atop each other, thinking: it had been so hard, but she and Sarah were lucky. Once Rose left Vienna, she was alone.

"So what happened on that trip up to San Francisco for dim sum?" Rose asked. "Did he impress you after all?"

"Not exactly. The flight was bumpy and loud—it was a tiny plane, and it was nerve-racking. And then it got worse when we arrived. Sarah complained of stomach pains, and we spent the first part of the day in the lobby of a Union Square hotel where she locked herself in a bathroom stall. Finally my father insisted we take her to the doctor. So we ended up going to the emergency room in San Francisco, and they checked her out. Turned out that she was just—well, seriously constipated."

"Oh my."

"Yes," Lizzie said with a chortle, shaking her head. "It was a disaster. But he tried. He tried a lot. And I didn't give him credit for it."

"He knew," Rose said.

"I'm not so sure." The sugar packets had become an unwieldy tower. "So he talked about us?"

"He did. He talked about you a lot. He used to say you were like him, you know. He told me that once. 'Determined,' he called you."

Lizzie so wanted this to be true. She gave an odd, contorted smile. "That was code for *'pain in the ass.'*"

"I don't think so," Rose said soberly.

The waitress approached, asked if they needed anything else. Lizzie, following Rose's example, shook her head. The waitress slid the bill on the table. Lizzie reached for it, but Rose was faster. "Please, do not insult me," Rose said. "This is on me."

"Fine," Lizzie said. "This time. Thank you. I wish . . ." She trailed off, that sibilant sound—*sshh*—lingering. There were so many things she wished for. "I wish my father had told me about you."

Rose took bills out of her long zippered wallet. "You know what? I don't."

"You don't?"

"No." And Rose smiled here, as if she knew she was about to bestow a treat. "I'll tell you why," she said as she reached across the littered Formica table and took Lizzie's hand. "Because meeting this way, this has been such a pleasure."

6

LONDON, 1945

AMID THE GIDDY CAROUSING ON that warm May night, Rose and Margaret picked their way through the packed streets, Union Jacks fluttering, bunting spilling out of windows, bonfires ringed by children and adults dancing, faces pink and slick with perspiration. Now and again fireworks shot up; a Roman candle whizzed through the air. They passed a piano that had been dragged out onto the sidewalk, draped with people singing "Roll Out the Barrel." A stranger thrust a glass of lemonade and a slice of apple cake into Rose's hands.

It took Rose several beats to realize why it was so bright, to understand that the blackout curtains had been yanked away, and several more minutes before it occurred to her: she had never seen London lit up at night before.

All the light was unquestionably beautiful. And yet it made Rose feel off-kilter. It illuminated things better left in the shadows: a gaping pile of rubble where a trio of terraced houses had once stood, the dinginess of her thin white cotton dress (despite the red, white, and blue ribbons that Margaret had braided around her waist tonight, and her own too). The light couldn't do anything about that smell, the taste of dust in the back of her throat that she couldn't manage to swallow away.

But none of this mattered. She would see her parents soon. This knowledge was like a strand of silk thread that they used in the factory: barely visible, yet material you could rely on. She would go home tonight and write to her parents. She had an address through the Red Cross. They would surely receive letters now. They would come to England—she would be seeing them soon.

How long would it take? Two weeks, a month? Longer? What would that be like, seeing them again? That last night, on the way to the train station, Mutti wearing her navy wool coat with the rabbit-fur collar, her hands sweaty despite the winter chill; Papi, telling her not to worry, she shouldn't worry, Gerhard would watch out for her. Rose had been eleven then. Now she was nearly eighteen. It had been almost half her life since she had seen them. Would she recognize them? Would they know her?

It was over. All the waiting, over. She grabbed Margaret's hand and jumped up and down, as she used to do when they were kids. "Come *on*. What are we waiting for?"

Margaret's mouth, reddened by beetroot juice, widened into a smile. She had only two inches on Rose but seemed taller, more comfortable in her enviably curvaceous body. "Since when are you in a hurry for anything?" she said, but she picked up speed. They cut through the thicket of revelers. "To Trafalgar we go! We are celebrating—finally!"

Finally was the only word to describe it. The night before, a thunderous rainstorm had woken Rose up. Her body was primed for that shuddering sound, the vibrations that meant a rocket. She looked over at Margaret's sleeping form in her own narrow bed, thinking she had to wake her up, they had to rush down into the shelter. But then she remembered: the war was over.

Trafalgar Square was raucous and crammed with people banging on dustbin lids and singing, bodies pressing up against each other—

Rose barely cleared five feet, so her view was of shoulders and chins, the backs of heads, arms swinging, jostling. "There's Fred!" Margaret yelled, though they were standing right next to each other. "Fred!"

It took Rose a moment to remember who Fred was. Yes, the lumbering American MP that Margaret had met at the Rainbow Corner a few weeks ago. With Margaret these days, there was always a boy. None lasted. (You wouldn't know from the way she went on and on about them that she was one of only a handful of women in her first year at the London School of Economics.) Margaret slipped off to Rose's left, the crowd swallowing her up. Rose tried to follow, but she no longer could see Margaret, and she didn't see Fred. A serviceman shimmied up a lamppost, whirling off his jacket. A girl in a yellow dress clambered up to the fountain with two officers and danced between them.

Rose stepped back, her ankle hitting something hard. It was only then that she realized she was standing at the bottom of the marble steps leading up to the National Gallery. Floodlights blazed, casting the building in an amber glow.

In the eight months that Rose had lived in London, she had been inside the National Gallery once, the same week she had moved, after Margaret had offered to share her London room and enabling Rose to leave the Cohens'. Margaret was registering for classes at LSE and Rose—well, she was supposed to be looking for a job. "Perhaps you can tutor," Margaret had offered, not unkindly. "You can tutor *and* go to school."

"We'll see," Rose had responded, not wanting to spoil the pretense. They both knew she needed a dependable paycheck that tutoring wouldn't offer. But first Rose had come to the National Gallery and queued up. She had heard all about Myra Hess's lunchtime concerts—in the papers, and on the wireless—a friend of the Cohens' had attended one and said it was too wonderful to describe.

It took nearly two hours to get to the entrance, where she dropped her shilling into the box and stepped inside. The walls looked so strange with all those empty frames, no art inside (with the exception of the picture of the month, the gallery's collection was squirreled away in a wartime hiding spot—where exactly, no one knew). Rose bought a raisin-and-honey sandwich from Lady Gater's canteen and ate it at the counter, quickly and quietly, as if someone might spot her and tell her to leave. But no one said a word and she made her way into the packed area beneath the gallery's glass dome, and when she realized that all the seats were taken, she stood along the side and Miss Hess came out—smaller and rounder than Rose would have thought—and she played Bach with such ferocity and perfection that all Rose could think was, *I will tell Mutti all about it. One day I will bring her here.*

Now here was Margaret, pulling her hand, her face shiny, her blond hair still neatly gathered in its roll at her neck and a big man in uniform at her side. They pulled her into a line of people dancing, Rose behind Margaret behind Fred, who wasn't lumbering but graceful on his feet. Another American soldier, a handsome navy man in spite of his odd cap and tie, took his place behind her. It was easy to move, *shuffle shuffle shuffle, kick, kick,* to be pulled along—and she liked being a small part of a larger something. Rose marched, *one-two-three, kick, kick. The war is gone,* she thought. *Kick, kick . . .* she thrust out her legs, one after the other, exhilarated: *no more war.* Her hands slipped down Margaret's waist.

"Help," the navy man behind her said. He nearly shouted to make himself heard.

"Excuse me?"

He gripped his hands on her waist. "My dancing. I need guidance." He swiveled her around. She was right; he was handsome, tall with bright eyes.

"Hardly."

He repositioned his hands on her waist. "But I can think of more fun things than this dancing."

"Now I know you're not in your right mind." Rose tried to say it tartly, but it didn't come out that way. She turned back, hurried to catch up with the line, concentrated on Margaret's backside, the slight way she was swiveling her hips to and fro.

He tottered, grasped at her waist. "Come *on*," he said, and he pulled her off the line. "I'm Paul."

"Rose."

"I'm going home soon."

"Everyone is coming home to me." She liked saying that out loud. The more she said it, the more deeply she believed it. She'd gotten her last letter from Gerhard about a month ago, when his troop was on the outskirts of Berlin. It won't be long, he had said.

"I'm going back home to Maryland, to work with my father." He leaned close, played with the ribbon hanging from her dress.

Her heart sped up. He was so good-looking. She didn't know where in America Maryland was—America was America—and she didn't ask. She thought of the silk factory on Tottenham Court Road. Rose hoped to quit before long. Her parents would be horrified to learn that she had been working in a parachute factory—Mutti especially—but she would show them the hard-earned money she'd saved. She earned five pounds a week; that wasn't nothing. "It was all worth it," she would say.

"You're beautiful," Paul was saying now. He pulled off his cap, nuzzled her neck, his mouth languorous.

She stiffened. "I'm not," she murmured, but she didn't move. Except for a chaste awkward kiss by Phillip Trumbell, a friend of Margaret's second-oldest brother, no one had ever touched her before. And certainly not like this. Was this the way it happened? Rose looked around, her heart careening this way and that, but no one seemed to be paying them any mind.

She tried pulling his head up to meet her lips, but his mouth was exploring her neck, her ear. She felt his tongue darting about. "No, not here," she whispered, but he didn't seem to hear. Tentatively she tried kissing him back, dropping a quick succession of pecks on the top of his head, her palms cupping his ears. They felt delicate, strangely separate from the rest of him.

But the more she tried to slow down, the more he sped up. He leaned over, clutched at her waist. His hands moved up.

"No," she said, but the word was like a gelatinous thickening in her throat. "Paul." That was his name, wasn't it? She tried coaxing him up. She wanted him, but not this, not all of this.

"What?" He breathed out the word, the sound stretching thin, but his hands became all the surer. Before she knew it, he had lifted the hem of her dress and grabbed her backside as if it were simply his for the taking.

"No. Please," she said—she could only manage that. She tried to push him off, but it was no use. Now he was pressing her up against something—a wall? He was so much larger. She went flat with fear. For a moment, she couldn't hear a sound. It reminded her of the dreadful silence that punctuated her past year in London, the envelope of quiet before the *chug chug* and the awful splintering that sounded like a motor spinning out of control, and then a deafening rattle. It happened in seconds. Silence and then the unearthly noise: a rocket, exploding.

But Paul had pulled away. "I'm not going to make you," he said, disgusted.

Rose felt even shakier, more muddled. "I'm sorry," she said. It would be years before she wondered why she was the one who apologized.

She didn't look for Margaret. She kept her head down, hurrying through the throngs, through the relative darkness of Lincoln's Inn Fields. There were celebrators there too, whooping it up and setting off firecrackers, but fewer of them, and no one seemed to register her. She was grateful for that, for the darkness that engulfed her.

When she got home, she drew a bath (lukewarm and no more than the requisite five inches—it comforted her tonight to follow the rules). The water didn't cover her stomach or her breasts, but she lay there a long time. Finally she climbed out, her limbs heavy. What had she been doing out? She needed to write to her parents.

AFTER THE TWO-DAY NATIONAL HOLIDAY that Churchill declared in honor of victory, Rose put on her overalls and pulled her hair back and returned to the factory, which remained open. ("'Course," said Mrs. Lloyd as she took a drag on her cigarette. "Who do you think is sewing the parachutes for the Pacific?") Just as she'd been doing for months, Rose took her seat on her stool, stared at the bright white silk under the lights, and guided the material through the machine. Big-band music on the BBC poured from the loudspeakers, but it was no match for the voracious clatter of the jittering machines. It was hard to focus, and Rose needed to focus (there had been awful accidents; girls' hair got caught in the wheels). But all Rose could think about was where she would go at half past four when she clocked out and her day would truly begin.

She usually went to the Bloomsbury House first, that massive stone building in the West End that she felt a kinship to long before she set foot in it. Bloomsbury House was not a house at all but a multifloored administrative building that held a number of Jewish refugee organizations. Bloomsbury House was the place that brought her to England.

The actual offices were of little interest to her now. There were lists on the walls. There were names. Typed up on thin onionskin paper, tacked up in the crowded halls, the lists were not dated or alphabetized. There were so many names sounding achingly familiar to Rose—Solomon, Karl, Eva, Trude, Lore, Kurt; Singer, Weinstein, Porges, Schwartz. These were Jewish names, people she grew up with. The experience of reading the names made her feel vertiginous. She hadn't seen her parents' names. She didn't recognize anyone on the wall. But there were new lists going up all the time, and this meant that every viewing, every new day, held a flush of promise.

After Bloomsbury House, Rose visited the Red Cross. In the

crowded hallways of the summer of 1945, people talked: Did you try the World Jewish Congress? Did you hear that the American army has its own lists up at Rainbow Corner? The Jewish newspapers—the *Jewish Chronicle*, the *Tribune*—ran columns of names in their back pages. People were being found. New names were going up every day.

It was a laborious, imperfect process, and the people who crammed into these offices alongside Rose were not quiet about their complaints. But Rose for one was grateful for the queues, for the maddening slowness of information trickling out. Shadows meant that there were still facts that had yet to be unearthed. Uncertainty, by its definition, included a thin, silvery shot of hope.

She had heard, of course. Horrible, unspeakable things. Buchenwald was the first camp she had learned about, back in April, when Allied troops were closing in on Berlin and Stalin was taking no mercy. Even before VE Day, there had been reports. She knew: at some point the lists of survivors that she studied so vigilantly would be replaced by lists of the dead. But that hadn't happened yet. For now, there were still survivors. She continued looking.

London in the summer of 1945 was heavy with grime and rubble and shrouded in bad smells—burning newspaper and old frying oil and urine. The lights that so struck Rose on VE Day now flickered—in shops, the underground, the factory. Outages were common. Rations were still in effect. But for some illogical, unnamable reason, Rose felt hopeful. She had purpose. She would ride the Tube after leaving Tottenham Court Road on her way to look at the lists, holding a pole with one hand, the other clutching a fat novel of Margaret's that she felt too impatient to read, the light dim (or sometimes out altogether, when someone pilfered the bulbs from behind the seats). But she felt as if something still *might* change. It was a time when fear and frustration and doubt still commingled with the slightest leavening, the most tenuous and fragile hope, of possibility, that all this might one day recede safely into the past.

How strange it would be if her parents did indeed walk through the door. What would Mutti think of her little girl who was now grown up? Would they recognize each other? What would they talk about? Would Mutti tell her that she needed to wear a coat or who to date, or yes, she was right, *It's That Man Again* was a truly awful show?

She kept searching.

"I DON'T KNOW WHY YOU'RE not coming out." This from Margaret as she sat on the edge of her bed, clad in her robe, legs stretched before her. She was applying a sponge to her calves, dabbing gravy browning to her legs, changing their color from pale to tanned. "I have twenty quid from my father! Tomorrow it will be gone."

Rose shook her head. "You know I can't. I have to be up early."

"You work too hard." Margaret pressed a thumb against her calf and inspected it. "I wish you didn't have to work so hard."

Rose shrugged. "It's fine." She gestured with her chin at Margaret's legs. "I don't know why you bother with that."

"I don't either," Margaret muttered, head down as she blew on her legs. "Takes too bloody long to dry." Then she looked up, her eyes fixed on her friend. "It doesn't have to be this way," she said, and Rose knew they were no longer talking about the gravy on her legs.

"I need to work. You know that." Rose flushed, and focused her attention on smoothing out the thin coverlet on her bed. Their beds sat side by side, with a thin gully of space in between. There wasn't much else; a chest of drawers pushed up against the wall near Rose's bed, a crate beneath the only window where Margaret kept her schoolbooks.

"I know. It's just that you're so smart," Margaret said, and touched Rose's shoulder. "It's not my business, but I wish you had a job where you could use your smarts."

Rose pulled back. Margaret was right; it wasn't her business. Rose was being churlish, she knew. Margaret was only trying to help. "It's only temporary. And there are loads of smart girls on the floor with me," she said. Rose was taking care of herself. When Mutti and Papi arrived, they would need as much money as she could offer. But she knew it wasn't so simple; she wasn't proud to don those overalls every day and stitch together pieces of silk for hours at a time. She feared Mutti's disapprobation when she learned that her daughter worked in a factory. *But you have to understand*, Rose wanted to tell Mutti and Margaret both. She was doing what she could. Of course she was capable of more.

"I know," Margaret said. "I know it's temporary. But I was thinking: What about asking the Cohens again?" She took a thick pencil from atop the shared bureau and sat next to Rose. "Just think: if they relented, you could work part-time, make money, and go to school."

It frustrated Rose to hear Margaret articulate this scenario, as if anything were that simple to attain. She couldn't ask the Cohens. They did not owe her. Rose glanced at the mushroom-colored window curtain that looked like it could fall down at any moment. The room was too small, Margaret, with all her good intentions, too close. "But they're not relenting," she said. "And I won't ask them again."

"They care so much about you, Rose. I know you don't always feel it, but they do." Margaret leaned in. "I know they told you they would only help with nursing. But if you went up for a visit, and truly explained to Mr. Cohen, I don't believe he wouldn't help. It's worth a try."

Rose shook her head. "I can't," she said. Mrs. Cohen had been emphatic. Nursing was a practical profession, a noble one. And if she didn't want to do that? Well, when she was eighteen she was expected to join the ATS. "You should be grateful," Mrs. Cohen had said. "This is the best way to pay back your country."

"All right," Margaret said. "It was only a suggestion." Rose could tell she wanted to say more, but Margaret took the pencil and began drawing a thin dark line from the back of her left ankle up her calf, imitating the seams of the stockings that neither of them could afford.

Perhaps Margaret was right. Perhaps Mr. Cohen would acquiesce. Every month, she got an envelope from him with two crinkled pound notes inside—not that much more than he used to give her as pocket money when she was twelve. And yet, every month the envelope arrived. "For Rose," he wrote in his spidery handwriting, nothing else. That card never failed to deliver a pang. She kept Mr. Cohen's money in a separate envelope and used it to buy small purchases, one more unnecessary than the next—black currants that she spotted in October in a shop in Notting Hill, a slim leather volume of Hopkins's poetry, a tin of marzipan from Selfridges that she ate furtively, not sharing with Margaret, the almond taste taking her back to her family's flat on Liechtensteinstrasse.

"Thank you for suggesting it," Rose said as politely and with as much dignity as she could muster. "But you have to understand, it's different for me." Besides, she couldn't change course, not now. How could she make any decisions until she heard from them?

ONE THURSDAY IN LATE NOVEMBER, nearing clock-out time, a white-coated inspector stopped in front of Sylvia, a small, serious girl from Prague who sat next to Rose and was deft with the massive spools of thread. It was then that Rose realized Sylvia had stopped working. "That's the second needle you've broken this week, Miss Strauss," the inspector said. "It's coming out of your wages."

Sylvia nodded. "It won't happen again, sir."

He strode off, and Rose leaned over. "You all right?"

Sylvia nodded, turning back to her buzzing machine with renewed intent.

"She cut her finger the other day," said Mrs. Lloyd, Rose's other neighbor. "It's swollen up to something awful. It's got septic." Mrs. Lloyd's husband, as she often reminded them, had been a pharmacist before the war.

Rose glanced back at Sylvia and saw that she kept her small left hand in her lap. "She has to go to hospital. She shouldn't be here," Rose said. "Come, Sylvia; let me see." But Sylvia didn't move.

"Infection or no, she's relying on this week's wages," Mrs. Lloyd said. "She's not going anywhere."

"I got back my letter," Sylvia said. She did not look at Rose as she spoke. "It says they were deported."

"Which letter?" Rose asked, but she knew.

"My parents. It came back. On the back it says 'deported to Auschwitz.' And there is a date, the tenth of November 1944."

Rose nodded dumbly. She had never spoken to Sylvia about her parents. They hadn't talked about their families at all. Rose realized she held a hand over her mouth. It felt essential to do so, to keep all that was loose inside of her contained.

"But there are so many people in those DP camps," Sylvia said, "They couldn't have registered them all yet."

"That is right, that is absolutely right," Rose said with a conviction that she did not feel.

IT WAS COLD BY THE time Rose made it to the flat on Catton Street that night. The two sweaters she wore under her overcoat did little to keep out the bitterness. Daylight was long gone, though it was a clear night, the half-moon just clearing the tops of the worn brick apartment buildings across the road. Soon it would be December, the first holiday season after the war.

She was rummaging for her key when she registered an officer in uniform, standing past the laundry on the corner, smoking against the peeling trunk of the plane tree. She paid him little mind. Then she heard: "Why, *mausi*. You're not going to say hello?"

She screamed.

AFTER SIX MONTHS STATIONED IN Minden, Germany, Gerhard had been granted a leave. He had five days in London, and he had just dropped off his bags with Charles, the brother from the family he had lived with up north. "I came straight here," he told her as she led him up the three dank flights to the flat, put the kettle on in the kitchen nook, and pulled down the tin of biscuits that she thankfully had not finished.

"You should have written—or called. But am I happy to see you," she said. "Would you like biscuits? Or, I have a tin of corned beef somewhere. I could fix you a sandwich. Or an egg? Margaret has an egg and I'm sure she won't mind us using it on this fine occasion. Or what am I thinking? Perhaps you want to shower?"

"*Mausi*, stop. Would you, please? I'm fine." He said it with such recognizable, familiar brotherly annoyance that it made her want to nail him to the spot, never let him go.

She squeezed his arm, moved to pour the kettle. Had his eyes always been that vivid shade of blue? They were the same color as the birds on Mutti's scarf.

"I'm a lieutenant now," he said with a wry little grin.

"A lieutenant? That's wonderful. You must be important." Rose handed him a cup.

"Not really. They need translators."

"Really? And how is your German?" Rose asked in English. They always spoke in English now. Papi was going to be appalled by how little she remembered, her vocabulary stuck back in grammar school.

"*In Ordnung*," he said. *Okay*. That she remembered. "They are desperate to get things in order," he said. They were perched side by side at the foot of her bed, balancing cups on their knees. "Little chance of that happening anytime soon. It's a mess over there. Bloody Jerries. They deserve every last bit of horror that comes their way." He sipped his tea, took another mouthful of the biscuit with evident pleasure. "These are delicious."

"They're stale," Rose said. "Now I know how they treat you." She took a sip of her own tea. It was tepid, and she suspected it had never been warm. "Have you found out anything new? Everything is so slow here—I haven't been able to learn anything." She stirred her tea as she said this, her eyes fixed on the metal spoon, the way it looked bent beneath the surface of the hot liquid, another trick of the eye. If she couldn't find Mutti and Papi, maybe she could find someone who knew what had happened. She had started looking for the Fleishmans, the family that had lived with her parents for a time after she and Gerhard had left. She had tried to find Bette too, had written to the last address she had for her in Munich, but nothing. "I know what you said in your letters, but you've found nothing on Mutti and Papi since then?"

Gerhard shook his head. "There's another Jewish lieutenant originally from Freiberg, and we have a system set up to check the DP lists—nothing." He looked at her steadily. "But I was in Vienna."

She was sure she hadn't heard him right. Vienna? Their city? "When?" she finally made out.

He lit a cigarette. "About two, nearly three weeks ago. We had been told that we would be interviewing officials." Without asking, he lit another and handed it to her. She took it gratefully, and brought over Margaret's ashtray from the windowsill. "You know, men real close to the top. They needed a team of us, they said. I was boiling over for it, gunning for it—but it wasn't at all like I thought. They were just small-timers. One was a mayor of a small village called Fiestel, and yessed me about everything—'Did you know the butcher, a Jewish man called Weiss? Did you work with so-so, who was a Nazi official?' Yes, yes, yes, he said. It turned out that he had a sick wife. He would have agreed to anything to get back home to her." Gerhard paused. "I hated him for that too."

Rose was listening, she was trying to understand, but she didn't think she did. What did a Nazi's sick wife have to do with anything? She sucked in smoke. "What did the apartment look like? Is it all right? Did you go inside?"

"I didn't go to the apartment."

"You didn't go to the house?"

"I was there for so little time, and working for all of it. We were quartered outside of town. You don't understand; it was so strange, being there, like this"—he gestured down to his uniform—"with all the other men. It didn't feel like a city I knew, let alone where I grew up."

"But it would have been different if you had gone to our street," Rose said, as if she could still convince him to change course. How could he be there and not go? What if their parents had been there? What if someone had talked to them?

Gerhard was shaking his head. He jammed the tip of his cigarette into the ashtray. "You don't know what it was like," he said. "It is not the same. It's just another bombed-out city."

"That can't be true."

"It is. The opera house burned down. The Burgtheater too, and the roof on St. Stephen's Cathedral collapsed—damaged by a fire that had been lit by looters, Austrians"—he shook his head—"not our men. It is not the same place. That city is gone."

"But Mutti and Papi," Rose willed herself to say, battling the terrible emptiness inside. "They could go back there, somehow."

"No, Rose." He stubbed out his cigarette. "I don't think so."

"You don't know. You can't be sure." She could barely get the words out, her throat so tight, the pressure behind her eyes spiky hot.

"I do," Gerhard said with roughness. "I'm afraid that I am. In Minden, where we're stationed, the town was destroyed—the town hall, the cathedral, all bombed. But people are coming back. One day, we were handing out blankets, and I met these boys, Jewish boys, two brothers, Samuel and Martin, and a friend of theirs, Oskar. They had been in Birkenau together, and they came back because Oskar's father had owned a house outside of Minden—there had been Jews there since the thirteenth century. They didn't know where else to go—"

"You see," Rose said, "that's what I mean. *Of course* they went back to where they're from; that's what people do—"

He put his hand on hers. "Would you let me finish, please? God, you are like Mutti. Always have to have it your way."

The mention of their mother, the pressure of his hand, stunned Rose into silence.

"I'm telling you, the way they looked, the stories they told . . ." Gerhard's voice trailed off. "They're not coming back," he finally said.

"You don't know that," she cried. All she wanted was for him to be wrong. "You don't know that at all."

"I didn't want to know it. I never wanted to know anything like this. But I do," he said, shaking his head. "They're not coming back, Rose." He stood, walking his cup to the tiny sink, twisting on the water.

"Gerhard, please," she said, and she grabbed his arm to stop him. Washing up? *Now?*

He pulled her into a hug. *"Mausi,* we're here. We're still here," he kept saying into her hair.

THAT NIGHT, SHE WALKED. SHE walked away from Holborn and her room on Catton Street, away from Soho, where she knew Margaret was meeting friends, and Clerkenwell, where Gerhard was staying with Charles. She walked as if she had a purpose, as if she knew where she was heading.

She didn't bother putting on a jumper beneath her overcoat. Where was she supposed to go? Tonight, next week? Next month? It was unimaginable, the future.

She ended up at the Embankment, at the foot of the Waterloo. The bridge had taken a hit early on in the war, and over the last few years it had been rebuilt—she'd heard that so many women worked on it that it was called the Ladies' Bridge. Here was yet something else that had been devastated and was rising again, and she hated the bridge as surely as if it had stolen something from her.

She took the steps up. She began walking across. The Thames was a carpet of black. Out in the open, the cold rose. The air whipped across her cheeks, her fingertips grew prickly. Lights necklaced the river; there was Westminister aglow, and St. Paul's beyond.

Rose looked away from the vast city lights and down toward the water. It coursed fast, dark silvery movement that she could sense more than see. She felt a thrumming inside of her. Her hands gripped the icy railing.

Her parents were dead. She knew this to be true. But how could there be no evidence? How could she possibly live in a world where there was no proof? And if no one knew about them, what would happen to her? Her life here in England wasn't meant to last. It wasn't meant to be permanent. What would she do now?

Her head felt too heavy for her body, and she wanted to rid herself of this weight, this awful heaviness. Why was it better that she had survived? Rose thought of the soldier from VE night, the way he had touched her, as if she were his for the taking. She wished he had. She wished he had done every unseemly thing he had wanted. Her tears stung her raw cheeks and she thought, no, no, she didn't want him to touch her at all, she didn't want anyone to ever touch her again, she couldn't help her parents, they were dead, she knew that Gerhard was right, but he was so wrong. She and Gerhard didn't deserve to be here. How could they be here, with bodies to enjoy and lives to live?

The water glittered and beckoned, strangely inviting on this brutal night, and even the thought of falling seemed tempting—tumbling, erasure, blackness. But Rose's hands remained curled on the cold railing. She knew she could never do such a thing, even though she hated herself for it. Why did she deserve to live? she asked herself as she walked off the bridge, steadily, quietly, alone.

"YOU'RE ILL," MARGARET CLUCKED AT her the next morning. "You stayed out too late," and Rose did not disagree. Margaret kept the kettle on. Margaret made her cup after cup, and they listened to *It's That Man Again* on the BBC. By the afternoon, Rose was feeling, if not better, then at least more like herself. She got dressed. Gerhard had called on the shared telephone line and asked to meet her for supper at the White Tower in Fitzrovia. It was his last night before the army would claim him again. And who was she to say no?

"The White Tower, it's supposed to be one of the best restaurants around," Margaret said as she helped her get ready, crimping her hair, applying beetroot juice on her lips for color.

"You look quite becoming," Margaret said. Rose considered the phrase. She was nearly eighteen. What was she becoming?

BY THE TIME ROSE REACHED the end of Charlotte Street and hurried inside the White Tower, unspooling her scarf, it took her a beat or two to spot her brother, though the restaurant, with its green walls and red-beaded lampshades, was less than half full. Gerhard was seated with a woman that Rose did not know, a young fair-headed beautiful woman.

"Hello," Rose said, and Gerhard popped up out of his chair, nearly knocked it over.

"Oh, hello!" he said with nervous energy, as if her presence were a surprise. He reached for her, stuck out his hand, laughed again, and clasped her shoulders in an awkward hug. "So nice to see you!"

Rose stared. Why hadn't he told her? Why was he acting so strangely?

"May I introduce you to Isobel. Isobel, this is my sister, Rose." Rose could have sworn Gerhard blushed while saying it.

"Rose," Isobel said, extending a slender hand. "It is ever so nice to meet you. I've heard so much about you."

Rose nodded dumbly. Isobel wore a dark wool skirt and a pink sweater with black silk trim. Her shoulder-length hair was tousled but shiny, a slight messiness that managed to signal expense.

"Do you love Greek food?" Isobel said as they took their seats. "I adore it. Absolutely adore it. We both do." She turned significantly to Gerhard.

"I've never had it before," Rose said truthfully, looking at her brother. *He liked Greek food?*

"Moussaka, that's what you must have," Isobel said. "You simply must."

Rose nodded. Whatever moussaka was, she would have it. The portraits of mustached soldiers, staring grimly down at her from the walls, were no match for the force of Isobel's words.

Isobel said she had grown up in Yorkshire, but didn't speak as if she were from the north. She was an only daughter after a trio of boys. "Even my father—or especially my father—was relieved when I was born." She asked Rose about her flat and Margaret, living in London. She didn't bring up the factory. She smiled easily. She touched Gerhard's hand often.

Rose asked: "How long have you two known each other?"

"About a year," Gerhard said.

"More than a year," Isobel said with unmistakable pride. "Sixteen months, nearly a year and a half."

"I see," Rose said as she forked off some of her dish. Was that aubergine? It was too soggy to identify, too laden in sauce. "Most of the time while Gerhard was away?"

"Yes," Isobel said quickly. "I'm so proud of him. My officer." She laughed, as if she had made a joke.

Rose continued to pick at her dish, saying nothing.

"Gerhard says that you live in Holborn," Isobel said. "How do you like it?"

Rose shrugged. "It's all right."

"She and Margaret are wonderful roommates together," Gerhard said. "I wouldn't be surprised if they lived together for years to come."

"Well, there's a lovely thought," Rose said, shaking her head at Gerhard.

"One of my brothers lived in Holborn for a time. On Macklin. I quite liked it. It has its charms."

"Yes," Rose said. "I suppose it does." She wound a strand of cheese on her fork, drew it through a puddle of tomato sauce.

"If you'll excuse me for a moment," Isobel said, and pushed back her chair. Gerhard jumped up to help her.

As Isobel walked away, Gerhard leaned down to Rose and whispered: "Why are you being so curt with her? Would it kill you to be kind?"

"You could have told me she was coming," Rose said, her eyes remaining on Isobel, watching her navigate between tables to the back of the restaurant.

"I'm sorry," Gerhard was saying. "I was nervous." And that's when Rose realized: Isobel was wearing real stockings. They were perfect, the seams beautifully straight, not a darn in sight. When she saw the real thing, it made her despair. What was the point in trying to imitate them? She could never come close.

"How does she have money for real stockings?" Rose asked.

"What?" Gerhard shrugged uneasily as he sat back down. "She's wearing real stockings?"

Rose shook her head, exasperated. Of course he hadn't noticed. And that's when she understood that Isobel came from significant money, and it was nothing Gerhard would talk about it.

"Who cares about her stockings?" he continued. "She's a wonderful person. You have to give her a chance. Please." He said this with un-Gerhard-like eagerness. "I really like her."

"You never mentioned her before. Not yesterday, not in any of your letters. Why didn't you tell me about her?" How could he like Isobel so much and not tell her? Did he have any idea how alone she felt? How could he not feel the same way?

"I don't know," Gerhard said, and his face grew serious. "I'm sorry for that. I should have." He turned to his plate, chased down the last morsel of moussaka. Only a reddened stain remained. He had polished off his entire plate while Rose hadn't noticed. "It makes me nervous, I suppose. We are very serious. I feel—well, I want to marry her. I'm going to. You'll like her too, you'll see. She's unlike anyone else. And I want to start my life. I'm ready."

Marriage? Now? Already? Gerhard deserved happiness, of course, but all Rose could think was: *Your life? You want to start your life? How do you feel like you have a life? Mutti and Papi—*

But no. There was no finishing the thought.

The beads on the red lampshades shook and shimmered, throwing off dapple and shadow. "I am happy for you," Rose whispered.

7

LOS ANGELES, 2006

ALL ALONE, IN A COUNTRY that wasn't hers. Lizzie was thinking about Rose as she and Max finished dinner on his small brick patio that overlooked the canal. The darkening sky still bore traces of violet, the air turning rapidly from cool to cold. Lizzie always forgot this about L.A., how swiftly temperatures could drop, how quickly conditions could change.

"Do you know the name of the investigator that my dad hired after the paintings were stolen?" Lizzie asked Max as they cleared the table. He carried the plates and platters, she had the glasses.

"No," Max said, and he held the door open for her. "I didn't know he hired one. Why?"

"Rose Downes asked me."

"Ah." Max took the wineglasses from her, heading toward the sink.

"I was going to do those," Lizzie said.

"I've got it." Max said this easily enough, but he made it clear: he would wash them. It was only in the last day or two that she had come to realize that his solicitousness masked a more exacting part of his personality. She watched him wash the delicate glass under the faucet's stream. He did this deftly. She would have taken more time. She knew she could be clumsy. But also: the glasses weren't hers.

"Did you check your father's papers?" he asked.

"No," Lizzie said. "I need to." The thought made her tired. She and Sarah had taken a storage unit after all, moved Joseph's papers there along with some things that Lizzie wanted to ship back to New York eventually—from the intricately carved Chinese set of drawers that she'd always loved and her childhood books (*All-of-a-Kind Family* and *Summer of My German Soldier* and the Trixie Belden mysteries) to her father's medical textbooks and the framed 1930s photograph of the boxer Barney Ross that had hung in the hall outside her father's room for as long as she could remember.

"We should have Rose over for dinner."

"What?" Lizzie said, taken aback. She had heard him. But they hadn't gone out with anyone yet, not Sarah, not Claudia.

"We should have Rose over for dinner," he repeated with a self-effacing smile. "You're spending a lot of time with her; I thought it would be nice."

"It would be," she said, surprised, pleased. She and Ben used to have the dumbest arguments about their friends: he thought Claudia self-involved and dramatic; she found his best friend to be loud and shockingly confident, given the banal things he had to say.

"As far as I'm concerned, the more friends you have out here in L.A., the better," Max said.

Lizzie bit her top lip, less from nerves and more to keep herself from smiling too broadly.

LIZZIE COULD GET USED TO this life. She arrived at the Dish before Claudia, took a spot on a stool at the U-shaped counter. A compact man with smoothed-back graying hair and a trim mustache manned the grill. He nodded at her. "Hickory, no cheese, cream soda," he said gruffly.

"Yes, please. But wait on the burger. My friend should be here any minute." Lizzie loved this place, with its old-fashioned counter and wood-paneled walls. She'd been coming here since she was a kid, continued to stop in whenever she was in town. She loved the charred smells and scraps of conversation and the sputtering sound of fat on the grill. The screen door banged open and shut, customers coming and going.

The grill man nodded again, slid a soda can and a full cup of ice toward her. "Haven't seen you in a while."

"Busy," she only said. He had worked the grill since she was in high school. She was fairly certain he thought she still lived in L.A. She had no desire to correct him.

"You." She heard Claudia's voice behind her.

"Hello, you," Lizzie said, twisting around, kissing her friend. Claudia was wearing a short leather jacket that Lizzie had never seen before and a shirt patterned with tiny roses, looking stylish as usual.

"Hickory, cheese, fries," the grill man said to her in greeting.

"Actually, grilled cheese and fries," Claudia said. "And a slice of banana cream. Thanks."

"Grilled cheese and pie?" Lizzie asked, looking at Claudia. Was it the shirt or were her breasts fuller too? "Is there something you have to tell me?"

Claudia shook her head, her face tightening. "Nope. Got my period yesterday."

"Oh, Claude." Lizzie gave her friend's hand a squeeze. "I'm sorry."

"Yeah, well," Claudia said. "I'm having terrible cramps, and I think the Clomid is making them worse. Pie is the only remedy."

"It will happen, I'm sure it will." Claudia and her husband had been trying for several months now.

"I'm not so sure anymore," Claudia said. "But I'm still trying."

Soon the grill man slid a burger and a grilled cheese nestled in wax paper toward them, a mound of fries on a separate paper plate. "Okay?" he said. They nodded back. The ceiling fans clicked and whirled overhead.

"What's going on with you?" Claudia asked.

"Me? I have turned into a lady who lunches."

"A lady who lunches on burgers and fries," Claudia clarified, biting into her grilled cheese.

"I only meant it's strange, not working. I feel like I'm skipping out on something."

"It's good for you to relax."

"I'm not relaxing."

"My point exactly," Claudia said, her mouth full. "How's Max?"

"Oh," Lizzie said, dragging a french fry through a puddle of ketchup. She felt a smile unbidden, forming on her lips. "He's good." She still couldn't quite believe it. "He's really good."

"Well," Claudia said. "That is good." The grill guy delivered her pie. She pulled it closer to her, forked off a dollop of cream. "Want some?"

Lizzie shook her head. "I'm not a fan," she said. Her father had loved the banana cream. She remembered the first time she'd come here, during that initial year they lived in L.A. She and Joseph had ordered burgers; Sarah, nearly eleven years old then, had announced that she was a vegetarian. She was unhappy with the menu options. Finally she ordered the grilled cheese.

When it showed up, Sarah took a tiny bite, made a face, and then pulled at the hardened cheese along the crust. "It tastes funny," she'd muttered unhappily to Lizzie, who was polishing off her burger.

"Just try to eat some," Lizzie whispered back. Sarah's pickiness had gotten worse after their mother died. "Here," she said, reaching to tear off a bite for herself. "I think it's good." She tried to say it encouragingly, but Sarah shook her head.

"What's wrong?" Joseph said.

"Nothing," Lizzie said.

"I'm asking Sarah," their father said. "Sarah?"

"I don't like the cheese," Sarah said. "It's too cheesy."

"'The cheese is too cheesy?" Joseph repeated. "But it's grilled cheese. That's what it is."

"I'm sorry, Daddy," Sarah said, faltering.

Lizzie turned to her father and tried to catch his eye. So she didn't like it. Couldn't he be nicer about it? Their mother would have been. Sarah was close to tears.

"Fine," he said, but it was clear he didn't mean it, and no one spoke while Lizzie finished her burger and Joseph did too.

"What do you want for dessert?" he asked Lizzie.

"What about Sarah?" Lizzie said.

"She can have dessert when she finishes her sandwich."

"But she's not going to finish it," Lizzie insisted as her sister hung her head.

"It's dessert," Joseph said. "It is not a God-given right."

"That is really mean," Lizzie said. Why couldn't he make Sarah feel better? She was trying. It was just a stupid sandwich.

Joseph ordered a slice of banana cream. "When you're a parent, you'll make the decisions," he said. Infuriated, Lizzie pulled her straw out of its paper encasing, and folded and crinkled the wrapper to make it as small as possible. Her father had no idea what to do with them. Lizzie could probably make better decisions than him. She sucked up droplets of water in her straw, dropped them on the crinkled-up wrapper, and watched it spasm and elongate; for a brief hapless moment, it seemed alive.

"What do you know about being a parent?" Lizzie said.

"What?"

"You know what I mean; you left."

Joseph let out a strange sputter of a laugh. "Do not test me. Do you understand?"

"Yes," she muttered. She shouldn't have said it, but she was not sorry. Her anger had been hardening for months now, ever since she arrived. How much longer could they dance around what they all knew to be true? She and Sarah didn't want to be here, and Joseph wanted them even less.

"Can we please go?" Sarah implored, her eyes enormous, glassy with tears. "Please." She tugged on her sister's sleeve. She sounded younger than her ten years.

Joseph swung back toward the counter. "No," he said. "Not yet. I am finishing my dessert." He bent over his plate.

She despised him, she really did, she couldn't imagine that her mother had ever loved him. Divorcing him had been the smartest thing she ever did. Lizzie had been young but not stupid. Her father working late, never around. Maybe it had been that part-time book-keeper at his office, maybe it had been someone he knew in the city, but he'd had an affair with *someone*. She had distinct memories of her mother from that time, always whispering on the phone, pulling the curled telephone cord taut, behind closed doors. She must have known too.

"If you two want dessert, you can have it," Joseph muttered. "Sarah, a milk shake?"

"Yeah," Sarah said tentatively, the beginnings of a smile forming on her teary face. "Chocolate, please."

"Good," he said, grinning. "A milk shake's got milk. Lizzie?"

She shook her head. "No thank you," she said clearly, seething. So he had changed his mind; now he was a hypocrite who couldn't stand by his convictions. She wanted to hate him. She had to.

"You're missing out," he said tightly. "It really is delicious." And he'd polished off the pie, hadn't left a crumb behind.

"HOW GOOD IS GOOD?" CLAUDIA was saying.

"What? What's good?" Lizzie echoed. It must have been so hard for her father back then. She had only made it harder.

"How good is Max? Maybe stay-in-L.A. good?"

Lizzie smiled sadly. "I don't know."

"Why not?"

"What do you mean? You know: my whole life is in New York." She said this as much for herself as for Claudia. "And this thing with Max—it's only been two weeks."

"So? I knew I would marry Ian the first night we got together."

"That's you. I'm not like that. You know I'm not."

"Okay," Claudia said. "But why wouldn't it work?"

"Oh, come on, there are so many reasons."

Claudia folded her arms across her chest. "Name them."

"Okay, it's not just that he's so much older." Eighteen years, to be exact. Permutations of that number kept running in her head. In five years, he would be sixty. Would she still be attracted to him in a few months, let alone a few years? And that was the superficial side of the equation. No one stayed healthy forever.

"Irrelevant," Claudia was saying.

"Not irrelevant—"

"Okay, but definitely not a deal breaker."

"Okay," Lizzie said. She knew the principal cause for her reluctance, the reason she felt she could not trust herself. Would they be together if she and Max weren't both grieving for her father? Wasn't it an unseemly way to mourn? "He was my dad's best friend," Lizzie said.

"Also not a deal breaker," Claudia said.

"Come on. It's weird," Lizzie said. When would she stop being embarrassed about it?

Claudia shrugged. "I can think of weirder."

"Of course *you* can." She took up the last of the fries. "And you know I want to have kids." It was hard for her to admit, even to Claudia, this elemental desire.

"And do you know that he doesn't? Do you like him? Do you?"

"Yeah," Lizzie said. For all of her caveats and concerns, she *knew*. "Fuck, I really do."

"You should embrace it. For once, you should embrace something. Take it. The Cossacks aren't chasing you."

"That," Lizzie said, "is exactly what I was worried about here on the Westside."

ON WEDNESDAY NIGHT, MAX BROUGHT home a gift for Lizzie, a gorgeous wrap dress in an eye-popping pattern of greens and blacks. "I saw it in the window of a shop on Abbott Kinney, and I thought it would look great on you."

"Wow," Lizzie said. "It's beautiful. Thank you." No man had ever bought her clothing before. When Ben considered her gifts, he often brought her by the store to get her approval beforehand. At the time she said she liked the practicality of it. But this gave her a rush, imagining Max walk into a boutique and imagining her size, picturing her body in the dress.

She tried it on. "It fits perfectly. I knew it would," he said from the edge of the bed. He gestured for her to come to him. Soon he was running his hands along her back. "I thought you could use some new things. You have so few clothes here."

"That I definitely could," she said, leaning in to kiss him. Her wardrobe these days consisted of the few things she had brought with her on what she thought was going to be a quick trip—her good jeans and old boots, a demure A-line skirt that she usually wore to work, packed expressly to wear to the initial meeting she and Sarah had with Max (nearly two weeks ago, she thought with amazement), a couple of tops, a pair of running shorts, along with a few things of her father's—an old Dodger-blue T-shirt that she liked to sleep in, a thin rust-colored V-neck she was convinced he wore the last time he'd visited her in New York. She liked to think that the speckle of discoloration below the V was the result of the grease from their La Caridad meal. "It's funny, but I don't miss my stuff," she said. "Do you ever feel that way, that it's a relief not to be surrounded by your possessions?"

"No." Max gave her a bewildered smile. "I don't."

"Of course not," she said. "Everything here is gorgeous." Even incidental objects in his house—the cloth napkins he used at nearly every meal—seemed uncommonly lovely.

"What's wrong with having nice things?" He said it mock-serious, but there was a touch of defensiveness to his voice that reminded her of her father. When Joseph had first seen her walk-up apartment on 105th Street, he had been appalled and pushed a plan to buy a place in Midtown. An investment, he had said, a two-bedroom, "one bedroom for you and a guest room—I could stay there when I visit. In a doorman building, with an elevator." But she wasn't interested. "I like being close to school," she said, already feeling hemmed in by the prospect of such an arrangement. Joseph let it go, but not before telling Lizzie: *There's nothing shameful in living somewhere nice.*

"I love your things," Lizzie said now as she was thinking: *Max is different.* "I wish I had an eye like you do. I have a hard time spending money on things—well, some things," she qualified, thinking of the $700 Isabel Marant leather skirt she'd bought (on sale!) just before her father died. She had more than enough money. She had gotten used to the numbers on her pay stub. But she still lived like she was in law school, socking the lion's share of her money away. Who knew when she might need it? Who knew when it might all vanish? This thought ballooned, filling her with a queasy sense of unease. "It's just—everything costs."

"Well, of course. But not everything is expensive."

Once again, she heard Joseph in her head. He used to say at the Dish: *If I could have a hickory burger every day, I'd be happy.*

"And I like wanting things," Max was saying as he touched her wrist lightly, the dress's silky sleeve. "I don't believe we're that different."

"You haven't seen my apartment." She made a face, a preemptive gesture, designed to ward off disappointment. She found it hard to think of Max in her apartment, sitting on her IKEA couch, scrounging for paper napkins after they ordered in from Saigon Grill.

"I would love to see it," he said. "But it's hard for me to imagine it, when all I can think of is how fantastic you look in that dress."

Lizzie raised her eyebrows, shook her head. She'd never been good with a compliment. When she was younger, she could remember her grandmother gazing at Sarah, her huge eyes, her enviably straight hair. "That one is such a stunner," her grandmother said to Lynn. Then she saw Lizzie watching. "You'll be pretty too when you grow up," she said, patting her arm.

Max traced Lizzie's jaw with a solemn expression etched on his well-lined face. "You're so beautiful, you know that? It breaks my heart, a little."

"Now, why would that be?" He was being earnest, she could tell, and it made her nervous.

But his seriousness would not be deterred. "I dread the thought of you leaving. You have to know that." He pulled her hands down, gripped them tight, a look of urgency in his eyes.

"Max," she murmured.

He was still pressing her hands against his. "You could move in tomorrow, permanently."

Her stomach coiled up, a contortionist's trick. Did he mean it? He couldn't mean it. "No joking about that," she said, and now she was the one being serious.

"I'm not."

She pushed him back on the bed. She could hear Claudia in her head: *Here it is, yours for the taking.* Her arms up around his neck, fingers inching up the base of his skull; she delighted in the stubbly feel of his shaved head. *I want this,* she thought as she climbed atop him, hiking up the dress, straddling his hips.

"Come meet me for lunch tomorrow; wear this and nothing under," he commanded, his hands tunneling beneath the silky material.

"Tomorrow? I can't," she said, but she was already working her underwear down one leg, following at least part of his instructions.

SHE AND ROSE HAD PLANS to go to the Huntington. The library's immense grounds were glorious, and here in the late-morning sun, miles inland from the foggy shroud of the ocean, everything popped: the faraway red pointy roofs of the Chinese garden's pavilions, the white dogwoods and the bright coral trees blooming with such confidence. Even the craggy snowcapped San Gabriel Mountains looked purple-hued in the distance.

Rose took charge at the entrance desk, showing her driver's license for the senior discount and taking a while to fish out a card for one free admission from her bag. ("I can pay for us," Lizzie had said. But Rose insisted: "It's the principle of the matter.")

"Come. Let's go to the herb garden," Rose said. "Sometimes, with all these sights, it's smells I like to immerse myself in."

The herb garden held little appeal for Lizzie, but Rose was asking—or rather, instructing—and Lizzie was glad to comply. She had a poor sense of smell (*nonexistent*, Ben used to tease her, after he once again fished out moldering cheese from their fridge). She came from a long line of nonsmellers. She could even remember her mother saying, *Consider yourself lucky. It only changed for me when I was pregnant with you and your sister.*

Rose and Lizzie stepped around a gaggle of schoolchildren, two teachers facing a losing battle trying to quiet them. The garden was nearly empty save for a pale thin man being pushed in a wheelchair by a bored-looking attendant. "You know, the woman responsible for much of this estate, Huntington's second wife, was also his aunt, the widow of his uncle," Rose said.

"Is that legal?" Lizzie said, putting her nose to a woolly mint plant. HOREHOUND, a small sign said.

"Biblical, perhaps. And prudent, actually. Think about it: it cuts down on alliances. Your entire estate would stay within the family."

"That's because you wouldn't *have* any new family," Lizzie said. "That can't be good for the genetic pool. Were you and Thomas secretly second cousins or something?" she added teasingly.

"Ah, no; nothing even nominally salacious, I'm afraid. Thomas and I were nothing alike, in terms of our background, our families, our constitution. People always thought that because he was an engineer, he was the practical one, but he was a dreamer and a romantic, and a far far better person than I." She said these last words plainly.

"Come on, I doubt that," Lizzie said. "How many years were you married?"

"Fifty-one, nearly fifty-two."

"A half a century of breakfasts with the same person, a half a century of dinners together," Lizzie said. The monotony sounded appealing.

"Well, sometimes we let each other out for good behavior," Rose said dryly. "But yes, mostly."

"It's amazing that you were together that long," Lizzie said as they rounded a corner. She detected basil—even she could identify the clean, foresty smell.

"Well, you're young yet; I'm sure you'll meet someone. But it *is* luck. I turned Thomas down twice, you know."

"You did?"

"I did," she said slyly, with a gleam in her dark eyes.

"Why? Because you weren't sure?" Lizzie wanted to know. "Because he wasn't Jewish?"

"Not Jewish?" Now Rose looked annoyed. "I didn't care about that. No. I was very young. I had just learned about my parents. And marrying, believing in the future—it didn't feel right."

Rose couldn't have been much older than a child herself when she found out that her parents had been killed. Lizzie's mother's death had detonated her, twenty-five years ago, and Lizzie felt so unmoored now, as a fully formed adult nearly forty, with both parents gone. It was unimaginable to think of what it must have been like for Rose to have lost her parents, her home, her country, forced to take care of herself when she was not yet twenty.

Lizzie could hear the schoolchildren in the distance, shouts and giggles and teacherly admonishments. Rose was looking at a low bed of herbs. TUSSIE-MUSSIES, a sign explained, *small handheld bouquets of scented flowers and herbs that have special meaning for the recipients;* delicate purple borage meant *bluntness,* while the tiny white flowers of sweet alyssum signified *worth beyond beauty.*

"I remember hearing about tussie-mussies from Mrs. Cohen," Rose said, and her voice had regained its cool tones. "They're a romantic Victorian tradition." She stretched out the first syllable of *romantic* with significant arch.

"Mrs. Cohen?" Lizzie ventured.

"The wife in the house I lived in."

"Oh," Lizzie said. Rose had never mentioned where she had lived in England. "Well, they do sound romantic. A bouquet that tells a story."

"That's what she used to say. It's from the Victorians, and the Victorians had manners, they knew how to live. She was quite an old-fashioned lady, I suppose. But if you ask me, people should say what they mean."

Then you'd lose out on a whole lot of intrigue, Lizzie was half tempted to say, but the man in the wheelchair was slumped over, chin at his chest, the attendant pushing his chair talking on her cell, Lizzie didn't feel like joking. "What happened to Mrs. Cohen, the family you lived with?" she asked.

"The Cohens?" Rose looked at Lizzie with surprise, as if she had conjured them out of nowhere. "They're both long gone. Mr. Cohen died of cancer in the fifties, not long after I moved here, and Mrs. Cohen passed away a few years later. They never had children. They were good to me, Mr. Cohen in particular."

"I'm glad to hear that," Lizzie said, and she truly was. It wasn't hard to imagine a horrible story, with many an ugly permutation. Lizzie had read about a pair of Kindertransport siblings who were forced to work as servants in England. They never wrote to their parents to tell them for fear of upsetting them. And what recourse would the parents have had, from so far away?

"He was kind to me, even after I left Leeds. I wish I had been more grateful," Rose said. "When I lived in London, he used to come into town for work, and I—well, I rarely saw him." She paused. "Can you smell that? Lavender, I think."

Lizzie nodded, though she didn't detect it herself. She wanted to hear more about Rose and London and Mr. Cohen, but she didn't dare ask.

Rose straightened. "I wish I had been more generous toward him," she said. "But it wasn't a time in my life where gratitude or kindness came naturally."

"I understand that," Lizzie said. She was in her father's house, a kid again, ignoring Joseph, staring at *The Bellhop*, thinking, *How did I get here?*

"I know you do," Rose said. She stooped to examine a plant with prickly leaves. "Your father loved you very much," she said.

Lizzie felt a chill out in the bright Southern California sun. "Thank you for saying that," she finally said. "I loved him too." She was afraid that if she looked at Rose, she would start crying.

"He knew. He really loved you. I didn't know him all that well, but I know that."

"Thank you," Lizzie said, nodding fast.

"It's the truth," Rose said. "You need to remember." She tucked the loose end beneath the rest of her scarf, and gestured down the brick path. "Shall we?" They picked up the pace in silence. Then Rose spoke: "I heard you were once engaged." She said this as if passing along a small piece of useful news.

"You did?" Lizzie said as heat rose to her cheeks.

"Your father mentioned it. You're surprised."

"A little," Lizzie said. It both gladdened and unnerved her, to think of Joseph talking about her and Ben. "What did he say?"

"Only that you had been engaged and that you had ended it."

Rose spoke the words so evenly that Lizzie became convinced she meant something else entirely. Did she think Lizzie was the type who couldn't make a commitment? Did Joseph tell her that he thought his daughter was being unrealistic? That was the gist of what he'd said to Lizzie. *Oh,* he said, *I knew things were hard, but I had no idea it was that bad. Are you sure? Because no matter who it is, you'll always have to compromise.*

It hadn't been one of her finer moments; she'd turned it back on him. "Is that what you did with Mom, compromise?" And they were off to the races. *You have no idea what happened with your mother,* he said. *You have no idea what I think about anything!* Lizzie could remember shrieking, fourteen again.

"I do remember him saying that he was glad you had called it off beforehand, glad that you hadn't decided six months after the fact that you'd made a mistake. But he was disappointed."

"He liked Ben," Lizzie said. It was such a simple, innocuous statement, and yet her throat tightened up. "Everyone liked Ben."

"But not everyone was marrying Ben," Rose said pointedly.

Lizzie nodded. She was convinced Ben was going to marry the woman he was with now—once Ben was in, he was *in*. Their mutual friends hadn't told her much: Long Island–bred, Michigan grad who worked in advertising. "She's *organized,*" their friend Jen sniffed, and if that was the worst she could come up with—well, then. Lizzie should be happy for him. She had cheated on him; she had orchestrated their relationship's demise (it had taken her a while to admit that to herself). Even she was impatient with her own regret—and yet she still wondered if she had made an irrevocable mistake. Though, as Claudia had pointed out, it seemed to be the irrevocability that she focused on, and not Ben himself.

"Are you seeing anyone now?" Rose asked.

It was sweltering out here, in the noonday sun. "Well," Lizzie said as she shed her jacket, "no one special. And you?"

Rose shook her head. "No one special either."

Lizzie gave a light smile. They walked on in silence. Then Lizzie said: "Can I ask you a question? You turned Thomas down at first. I know you said it had to do with your parents, but I'm wondering: How did you know?"

"Know what?" Rose said, but she said it with warmth and a distinctly raised brow.

"How did you know that you could be happy with Thomas in the long run?" As she said this, Lizzie thought: *Rose must have met and married Thomas in her twenties.* Lizzie was already fifteen years older, at least. Time was barreling by.

"It's a good question," Rose said. "Honestly, I don't know. Or rather: I wasn't certain. But I wasn't *not* certain either, and that was enough, at some point. I liked him quite a lot. He made me happy— so little then made me happy. But I wasn't certain, not at all. Sometimes you have to jump."

It was, in a sense, standard advice, but coming from Rose, it felt like advice that Lizzie might be able to follow. "I hate jumping," she said. "I loathe heights."

Rose laughed. "Your jump can be from the smallest step. Heights might not be involved at all. And you know, marriage can be quite difficult. Don't let anyone tell you otherwise."

"So I hear," Lizzie said. But her newly married friends didn't like to talk about it—or if they spoke of it, it was to each other, not to her. "Did you ever hear the story of my grandparents?" she asked. Rose shook her head, and Lizzie continued: "Years and years ago—my father must have been in college—my grandparents were having breakfast, and my grandfather, who was a really quiet, taciturn type, said, 'I'm going out for oranges.' He got up, left the table. He never came back. A week later, she got a postcard from him from Florida, which said, 'I'm sorry. The oranges are better here.'"

"My goodness," Rose said. "And that was that?"

"That was that. They never divorced, but they never lived together again," Lizzie said. "So you see: my family does not have the marriage gene."

"Now, that is a cop-out if I've ever heard one."

"What?"

"A cop-out," Rose repeated with impatience. "Blaming circumstances, evading responsibility."

"No, I *know* what 'cop-out' means; I just didn't expect you to use that word."

"Why? Everyone thinks it's slang, but it's 'cop' as in the verb meaning 'to take,' and not as in the police sort of 'cop,' although the two share commonalities."

Lizzie laughed.

"What?" Rose said irritably. "What?"

INSIDE THE AMERICAN WING, THEY admired a small Mary Cassatt painting of a mother and child. (Rose spoke of the composition— "Do you see the diagonals formed by the child's legs?"—while Lizzie noticed that the mother looked so wistful, and wasn't looking at her child at all.) They saw Edward Hoppers and high-kicking dancers carved out of wood and many a landscape. After negotiating the knot of people in front of Gainsborough's *Blue Boy* (he looked so insolent, resplendent in his silvery-blue clothing, so self-satisfied, Lizzie thought), they stopped at the museum's café, and sat in plastic chairs on the shaded patio, overlooking the immense gardens. It was mid-afternoon but Lizzie had skipped lunch. Now she bit into her dry chicken sandwich and said to Rose: "Did your family have a lot of art besides the Soutine?"

"Not really," Rose said. "There were objects galore—vases, music boxes, silver swords that had been my grandfather's, a landscape that I think had been a wedding present. But my parents weren't art collectors. It was strange, the way my mother fell in love with *The Bellhop*. Even now I remember the way she looked at it."

Lizzie nodded. She didn't think it was strange, but Rose's face was veiled in contemplation. She didn't say anything for a moment and neither did Rose. "Do you collect any art?" Lizzie asked timidly.

There was a shift in her look; Rose, returning to herself. She scoffed. "Oh no, I would never spend the kind of dollars on art that you need to."

Lizzie smiled. "So you're not a spender."

"Most definitely not. It used to drive Thomas crazy. 'A yearly trip to Hawaii won't be the end of us,' he'd say, and he was right, but it made me nervous nevertheless."

"Now, *that* I understand," Lizzie said. "We're alike in that way. And unlike my father. You know for my sixteenth birthday he offered to buy me a piece of art. Anything I wanted."

"Anything?"

"Well, he knew I wouldn't have picked anything outrageous. At first I started haunting these galleries on Melrose, and then, one day, I walked into a vintage clothing store, of all places." She remembered the day perfectly. "I saw a photograph from the sixties, a black-and-white shot of two chubby young girls, sisters. One sat on the couch, clutching a doll in one hand and a kitchen knife in the other. It looked like she was about to slice the doll's hair. The other sister sat below her on the floor, staring at the camera, legs spread out, holding a toy grenade. The girls terrified me. And I just knew that my dad would hate it. There was one other obstacle."

"It was thousands of dollars."

Lizzie shook her head. "Nope. It wasn't for sale. But I brought my dad down to the shop anyway." She had declined to tell him the photograph wasn't available. "The shop was dark and cluttered, lots of velvet and mirrors. I brought him in, and he said, 'This is what you want?' and started muttering about Cindy Sherman knockoffs and the overweight girls and tired Appalachia narratives. But he kept staring at it. Finally he said to me, 'I don't like it, but I understand why you do.' He turned to the saleswoman and asked the price. She told him it wasn't for sale, that it was the owner's. And my dad looked at her with a little smile and said, 'Everything has its price.' I remember him saying that so well. He wrote out his name and number and told her that the owner should call. And within a week, the photograph was hanging in my bedroom."

Lizzie remembered feeling astounded by its arrival. How had he done it? What would it be like to never take no for an answer? Joseph paid whatever he paid for it, fought with whomever he fought with, on her behalf.

The embarrassment didn't come until later, though it was the more lasting, saturated feeling, the one that stayed with her, blanketing the episode in her mind, the feeling that fueled her to take down the picture two years later while in college and never put it up again, the one that made this a story she rarely told. She did not want everything to have a price; that wasn't the way she was going to live her life.

Rose stirred her iced tea, squeezed a tiny triangle of lemon. "That doesn't surprise me in the slightest," she said. "He could be persuasive, your father."

"I know. I shrugged off the gift." Lizzie picked at a sliver of pale tomato; it was tasteless, a simulacrum of the real thing. "As if I expected it." Her voice caught. Her sixteenth birthday. A lifetime ago; it didn't matter anymore. But she wished more than anything that she could tell her father how much she appreciated all he did. "I was lucky," she said now. "And I couldn't see it."

"You were a teenager."

"I know, but I could be so nasty to him." It was terrible to recall. Had Joseph thought of it as typical teenage behavior? Was he able to shrug it off? "I don't even know what he spent on it. He shouldn't have been spending money on something I didn't need, especially then."

"What do you mean?" Rose asked. "'Then'?"

Lizzie paused. She hadn't meant to say that; why had she said that? On the other hand, why should she be secretive about it with Rose now? "Just, that's when he was having those problems with his practice. His office manager ripped him off. She was messing with the billing, big-time. She was charging patients the full amount, recording smaller amounts in the books, pocketing the difference. He didn't discover it for months. I don't know all the details, but I do know that he lost a lot of money over it, and that threw everything into a mess. He never liked the business side of things." Lizzie picked at the remnants of her roll—chalky, stale.

"That's terrible," Rose said. "He never said a word to me. We weren't such good friends, but still."

"I don't remember the exact timing. It might have been before you met him. He had stopped buying art then." Lizzie felt herself edging close to the story that was so hard for her to tell. Here, with Rose, she didn't want to stop. "My sister got sick not long after. The night the artwork was stolen, Sarah—"

"I know."

Lizzie nodded, feeling her breath quicken. How much did Rose truly know?

The night of the party, Sarah had been antsy, waiting for a boy she called James P to arrive. James, at seventeen, was two years older than Sarah, a seemingly genial enough (or boring, Lizzie thought to herself) junior who went to a different high school but worked in the same darkroom as Sarah. When he gave her a ride home, she was euphoric for days. A conversation in which he mentioned another girl could send her into a tailspin for a week.

James eventually did show up—Lizzie caught a glimpse of her sister chatting with him in a large cluster—but when Lizzie went downstairs with Duncan, there was Sarah in a heap on the carpet, head down, arms around her knees. "Sarah?" she asked, exasperated. What was it this time?

Her sister lifted her head. She looked pale in the low light, her heavy mascara and liner raccooning her eyes. "I fucking hate him, I can't believe how much I hate him."

"Who?"

"James P. Who else? Did you see that girl he came with, the one with the red hair? That's his girlfriend—his fucking girlfriend! How can he have a girlfriend? How can he do this to me?"

Lizzie got down on the thick creamy carpet and wrapped her arms around her sister. Out of the corner of her eye, she saw Duncan hanging back. What would he think, seeing her mess of a sister? Lizzie tried to tug Sarah up. "You don't know what's going on between them; you don't—"

"Her name is Charlie!" Sarah skirted back from Lizzie. "How ridiculous is that? Carlotta, really—a lame old lady's name. She goes to Eastgate and she's a swimmer and they spend their summers in Europe—"

"Shhh, it's okay." Lizzie saw the desperation etched so plainly on her sister's face, and for a moment, she was afraid.

"No, it's not! It's most definitely *not* okay. James P told me all of this! He's all impressed, he's all, like, proud! I felt so stupid I wanted to die."

"Look, maybe he didn't know how you felt. Maybe he has no idea."

"God, you don't know; you really don't know, do you?" Sarah was weeping now. "I just want to die." She buried her face in her hands, her sobs loud, extravagant.

"Do you think she wants some water?" Duncan asked softly. "Maybe she'd feel better if she drank something."

"No," Sarah had said with disdain. "I do not"—*beat, beat*—"want something"—*beat*—"to drink." She had glared at Duncan. "I want to talk to my sister, okay? I need to talk to my sister."

"Hey," Lizzie said. "He was just trying to help."

"It's okay," Duncan said.

"No, it's not." She was not going to let Sarah fuck this up, not this time. "Just a second," she said to her sister. And to Duncan: "Come."

She led him down the hall as Sarah cried out: "Lizzie!"

"Just a sec!" Lizzie called back to her sister more sharply this time. "Wait for me," she said to Duncan when they reached her room. She kissed him, determined that this moment, her moment, would not slip away.

When she returned, Sarah's crying had slowed. "I'm so sorry, L," she said, hiccuping the words out. Her face remained strained, her pupils enlarged, otherworldly. "I just—I don't know what to do anymore."

Lizzie was tired of all of it, her moods and neediness, her dark beauty and apologies. "You know what? Go to sleep. Or don't. I don't care." Sarah would just take, take, take until there was nothing left of Lizzie. She was newly fifteen, two years older than Lizzie had been when their mother got sick, when Lizzie was heating up dinner for them both, her mother asking her to make sure that Sarah had snacks in her backpack for after school. She did not need a protector anymore.

Sarah's face crumpled. "Lizzie . . ." She could barely get her name out, and covered her mouth with her hands. "Don't say that."

"No, I don't want to hear it. I'm sick of this, okay? You'll be fine in the morning."

And with that, she went to Duncan, left her sister in the hall alone. A few hours later, when Lizzie awoke, Duncan was pressed against the wall, as far away as her twin bed would allow. The house was quiet. She got up, pulled on a T-shirt and underwear, feeling strangely alert. In the hall, a pile of earth-hued bottles and a shiny flattened bag of Doritos greeted her. She found a garbage bag, and began cleaning up.

When she first spotted her sister, it was Sarah's foot that Lizzie noticed. Lizzie had gone into her dad's bedroom, praying that it wasn't a mess, when she remembered thinking matter-of-factly: *That's Sarah's foot.* It was a bare foot, peeking out through the frame of her father's bathroom, not moving.

"Sarah?" Why was her sister lying there with her foot at that weird angle? How could she be sleeping, lying like that? Lizzie's breathing sped up, her heart scuttled about. But she could remember thinking clearly: *This does not make sense.* "Sadie?"

Now Lizzie peered around the corner. Sarah was facedown on the bathroom tile, and there was something about the odd shape of her body—head slumped to the right, legs akimbo—that made Lizzie understand even before she could articulate it, even before she spotted the empty bottle of Valium by her sister's outstretched hand. Lizzie touched her sister, lightly at first, then more aggressively. Sarah didn't move.

The screaming that Lizzie heard—and it was an awful shriek, an inhumane rattling sound—it had come from her. By the time Duncan rushed in, she was cradling her sister's unresponsive body, wiping the saliva that had dripped from her mouth, rocking her. "Please breathe, oh God, please please breathe," she was saying.

It must have taken close to fifteen minutes to reach the ER at St. John's in Duncan's car, fifteen inexorable minutes in which lights must have turned red and cars had to be passed and several miles of Santa Monica streets needed to be traversed. But Lizzie didn't remember any of it. She would remember the soury-sweet smell of vomit, she would remember using her fingers to prop and massage her sister's mouth open, she would remember barely taking in air herself. She would remember the double-wide doors of the emergency room swinging open like a grinning mouth, easing Sarah inside. "I'm her sister, I'm her sister," Lizzie kept saying, as if that would explain everything.

Hours later, after Lizzie had insisted that Duncan go home, a petite doctor in scrubs and orange clogs came out and said that they had talked to Joseph in Boston, pumped Sarah's stomach, and were keeping her under watch. There was nothing more for Lizzie to do. She should go home, get some rest, and come back the next day.

Lizzie hurried out of the emergency room, freshly ashamed, and into a blazing Southern California day. She took a cab home, feeling haggard and more exhausted than she'd ever known. Lying on the couch, she remembered looking up and thinking: *The walls are so dirty. How come I never noticed how dirty they are before?*

That's when it hit her. The Picasso sketch and *The Bellhop*, her *Bellhop*, were gone.

TWO DETECTIVES RESPONDED TO LIZZIE'S phone call: a tall black man with a shadow of a mustache who quietly asked Lizzie about the artwork, and his partner, a ruddy-faced woman with a tight short perm. She was the one who asked Lizzie to make a list of the names of everyone who had been at the party. "It wasn't all that many," Lizzie said warily. "Uh-huh," the female detective said, amused.

There were no signs of a break-in. No clues of any kind. "Whoever took them knew exactly what they were looking for," the male detective said.

The party had provided the perfect cover. Lizzie was haunted by this thought. If she hadn't thrown the party, if there hadn't been so many people, they never would have come inside. It made her skin crawl to imagine someone inside the house, grabbing the painting that she loved, touching all of their things. She had left the door open, and the paintings were the least of it. If she hadn't thrown the party, if she hadn't left Sarah alone to be with Duncan (it disgusted her now, her desire for him; she avoided him at school, ignored the few messages he left on the answering machine), Sarah would have been fine. If Lizzie had only remained with her, done something as easy as sit with her, listened to her tape of *The Queen Is Dead* on repeat or convinced her to watch old episodes of *Who's the Boss?* on VHS, a show that Lizzie thought was stupid but Sarah inexplicably loved; if she had just paid attention to her, taken care of her as she had done so many times in the past, if she hadn't been so fucking stupid and selfish, then her sister wouldn't have done what she did. Lizzie's world would not have imploded.

And she wasn't the only one who felt this way. "A party, Elizabeth, a fucking party?!" her father had screamed at her when he arrived back home from Boston hours after Lizzie had called him from the hospital. "You weren't supposed to be here! Your sister—" He had shaken his head, opened and closed his hands as if he wanted to grip something, but came up empty.

"I'm sorry, Daddy," Lizzie cried, over and over again that first hideous day. But nothing she said made a difference.

"I counted on you. You lied to me! I trusted you. And you lied."

It didn't matter what else she had done in her life, how good a kid she had always been. It was as if this was who she was, selfish and uncaring and a fuckup, every one of her numerous faults on display. She knew it and her father knew it too. The guilt pressed against her and became her most voluble companion. *You were never a good sister,* the voice told her. *Your father knows it and your mother knew it too.* "I'm sorry. I'm so sorry," she said to little avail.

About a week later, her father apologized, telling her: "I had no right to say those things to you. I was out of my mind with worry."

"I know," Lizzie said. It was easier to acquiesce, to simply agree. But she could not stand being here, in her skin. His apology could never take away what they both knew to be the truth: she had been the one to set those awful events in motion.

"I don't think you do," he had said. "It wasn't your fault." She remembered him saying this. They were in the living room, the Lakers game on low. She stood there in agony, watching James Worthy tip the ball with enviable ease into the basket. "You didn't steal the paintings. You didn't take those pills. You need to know that I know that. Come *here.* Please."

He looked so wretched, pleading. Her father was not a pleader. She moved closer. He squeezed her arm. "I'm so sorry you got caught up in this. It was like—a car accident," he said. "And you were a passenger. You had nothing to do with it. Okay?"

"Okay," she said, and she even managed a tight little smile. But she never did believe him.

"They discharged Sarah from the hospital the next day," Lizzie said now to Rose. "She was contrite, so apologetic, kept swearing that she would never do anything like that again. So we brought her home. The doctors basically chalked it up to teenage moodiness and drinking. But the next week she started acting weird again—staying up until two, three in the morning, calling her friends in the middle of the night, asking them to pick her up, not saying where she wanted to go, only that she had to. My father insisted that Sarah had to get another evaluation—I remember call after call, appointment after appointment. He made a big stink, the way only he could." She took a deep breath, remembering.

Sarah would be fine, Lizzie could recall thinking. She had been an intense little kid and was developing into an emotionally volatile teenager; none of this was surprising. Sarah had been hung up on a boy and did something stupid. And now she was being moody and regretful. That's all this was, Lizzie wanted to believe.

But Joseph was convinced there was more, and he was dogged on Sarah's behalf. When Lizzie looked back on that time, she recalled her father installed behind the closed door of his bedroom, his voice rising, needling. It was only then that he sounded like himself. In Lizzie's presence, even after the apology, he rarely spoke. He seemed numbed to everyone around him. She swore she could see him stiffen when she was present. So she tried to be present as little as possible.

"My dad called all these doctors," Lizzie continued. "He eventually got her in to see this child psychiatrist at UCLA, an expert who was doing research into girls and suicide attempts and he had Sarah admitted to the inpatient unit. She spent a few weeks there. It was awful. But she finally got her bipolar diagnosis. They started her on lithium. And finally it was okay."

Lizzie remembered waiting in those red plastic molded chairs in the waiting area at UCLA, not wanting to be called through the excruciatingly heavy locked double doors. When inevitably she and Joseph were, they would find Sarah at the art therapy table, her face heavier, wearing sweats and canvas sneakers without laces. Lizzie hated those un-Sarah-like sweats and sneakers with an abiding fierceness. She would thrust a mess of magazines at her—*Popular*

Photography, People, Seventeen. "Thanks," Sarah would mutter, eyes averted. Lizzie hated everyone there—the competent, omnipresent nurses, the few doctors, the other patients, her sister, her father. She hated them as if hating could actually accomplish something.

"He took care of her," Rose was saying now. "He did everything he could."

"Yeah, he did," Lizzie said, and she bit her lip. She had never needed her father's care like that. Sometimes she wished that she had. "I never gave him enough credit for it. But he did."

LATER THAT NIGHT, LIZZIE LAY next to Max, her foot hooked around his ankle. "Did you know that Huntington was married to his aunt?"

"No," he said. She turned on her side and closed her eyes as he traced the knobby route of her spine. "I did not."

"It just got me thinking. There are stranger beginnings than ours."

"Yes," he said, and he kissed the top of her head. "There are."

She pulled her arms into her chest, curling up. "Maybe we could do this." Her afternoon with Rose had had a strangely buoying effect on her. She thought of Rose telling her that sometimes you have to jump. *This*, she thought, *this is what I want.*

"Maybe we could," he agreed.

She put a hand on his chest, a tangle of matted hairs. It was warm, and she could feel his heart. The steady beat of that thick bloody muscle gave her courage. "The other day, you said you wouldn't mind if I moved in with you," she said. "What if I did?"

"For all intents and purposes, you have."

She shook her head. She could make a joke about it—she could pretend—but no. She meant it, and she wasn't going to feign otherwise. "You know what I mean."

"You wouldn't go back to New York." He said the words slowly. "You'd move here?"

Did she detect a note of incredulity in his voice? Lizzie told herself not to be so sensitive. Give him a chance. "Well, I'd have to go back, for a while anyway: my job, my apartment, everything. But I could come back, network, eventually take the bar. People do move, and I've got family, good friends here. It's not like you're the only one." She tried for a playful tone, but couldn't quite pull it off. "What I want to know is: Would you want me to?"

He didn't answer for a beat. "These past two weeks have meant everything to me," he said, and the meaning hit Lizzie at once. She thought, wildly, *What a fool I am.* "Your dad—"

"No," Lizzie said. "This can't be about him. God, this can't be about him."

"It's just moving so fast—"

"Forget it," Lizzie said. She should have known better. She *did* know better. Why was she trying to change? "I shouldn't have said anything. I'm sorry; I'm not myself these days."

"Please don't apologize," Max said, touching her hair, looking at her when all she wanted to do was escape his gaze. "I care about you so much."

"No," Lizzie said sharply. "Do not." She was done talking. Why was there always so much talking? And with that, she rolled over.

8

LONDON, 1948

CONSIDER IVAN'S WORDS TO ALYOSHA," Professor Hillman was saying. "'I don't want harmony. From love to humanity, I don't want it. I would rather be left with the unavenged suffering.'"

Rose wrote down "unavenged suffering" in her notebook, struck by the phrase. She loved the Russians, and Dostoyevsky in particular.

"Later, Ivan says, 'One reptile will devour another,'" he continued. Rose liked Professor Hillman. He had a plump, kind face that contradicted the stiff striped ties he wore. He was soft-spoken outside of class, seemingly embarrassed if you did as much as say hello, but in class, while lecturing about his beloved Russians, he commanded. She had heard that he had a samovar in his office that he brought out on special occasions for prized students, but although she was doing well in his class, she had never seen it. "What does Dostoyevsky mean by that?" he asked.

Rose, in the front row, shot up her hand. She saw Professor Hillman's eyes register her, then glance away as he scanned the lecture hall. Rose strained her arm higher, but she knew it was hopeless. Half the time he didn't call on her. So she raised her hand often? She knew the answer. Shouldn't that be rewarded? Rose sighed, lowered her arm, and gazed around. The delicate wainscoting of the light blue walls and the ornate marble fireplace that Professor Hillman stood in front of seemed at odds with lecturing. Bombs had demolished a good part of the Bedford College campus during the war, and the university had rented this row of Regent's Park mansions until rebuilding was complete. Rose imagined dances taking place in this ballroom, dances not unlike the ones described in such vivid, blood-quickening detail in the Russian novels she was reading.

"Miss Gissing?" Professor Hillman said. "Why do you suppose Ivan thinks that reptiles will devour each other?"

Eva Gissing sat one row behind Rose. Rose twisted around to see her blush. "I don't know," Eva said. Rose raised her hand again. "I suppose all reptiles devour each other, don't they?"

"I meant in the context of the text, Miss Gissing," Professor Hillman said. "You must return to the text." He nodded at Rose. "Miss Zimmer?"

"Dostoyevsky says that we all have dark, murderous impulses. We all would eat each other if we could. It's prescient, in a sense, as later—well, when the father is murdered. It's the irrational side of us that reigns." Rose didn't need Dostoyevsky to tell her that, but she found his insistence on the ugliness of the human condition comforting. It made her feel, in no small part, understood.

"Indeed," Professor Hillman said. "Part of celebrating the Russian soul is celebrating that darkness. We are now fortunate as Englishmen to have access to these great literary powers. Other writers do no more than play at the feet of the giants that are Tolstoy and Dostoyevsky. For next week, reread the 'Grand Inquisitor' section. And your essays are due next week as well," he finished as the bell rang.

Books and notebooks were scooped up, scarves and coats gathered. When Rose was at the door, Eva caught up with her. "Do not tell me that you've read the entire book," she said with a theatrical exhalation. Eva, like Rose, was small and dark-haired and fair-skinned; but unlike Rose, she was chatty outside of class, tentative in.

"Then I won't," Rose said.

"You know why Dostoyevsky's novel is so bloody long, don't you?"

"Why don't you tell me," Rose said easily enough. It was hard to take Eva seriously, but knowing this made Rose feel more kindly. They headed together down the marble hall, passed a carved depression in the wall where an organ used to reside in the building's grander days.

"Serialization." Eva drew the word out. "If I got paid by the installment, I'd write a long novel too."

"I'm sure you would," Rose said.

"Lore and I are going for coffee," Eva said as they neared the building's entrance. "Come."

"I can't," Rose said, and she injected a note of remorse that she didn't quite feel into her tone. "Too much to do." She gestured down at the load of books she carried.

"You don't have to actually read *everything,*" Eva said, as if reading books in their entirety was a sign of silliness, something a child might do. Rose tightened her grip on her books. It wasn't worth the effort to argue, with Eva especially. She remained astonished and grateful to actually be here at the University of London, doing nothing but studying literature, *reading,* which she would frankly do on her own. She hadn't worked at the silk factory on Tottenham Court for almost two years now and still she would sometimes glance at a clock and think: *It's nearly time for elevenses, the shift half over.*

The girls walked outside. A light drizzle was falling, the sky pebbly gray and vast, the new green leaves budding bright on the thick-waisted plane trees across the street in Regent's Park.

"One of these days you should join us," Eva said. "The coffee is strong, like back home, and there are loads of nice boys there."

"That sounds splendid," Rose said, and she opened her umbrella and shifted her books into her other arm. Students streamed up the paths in sandy-colored mackintoshes, their dark umbrellas unfurling. Rose looked for Harriet. She would be easy to spot, what with the purple scarf she always wore loose around her shoulders. But she didn't see her. She felt dampness at her collar and she sighed, fingered the material beneath the rib of her umbrella. There it was: a tear. "Another time, I'll join you," she said.

Eva had said this before to her—*back home*—and though she knew she was being ungenerous, Rose felt an urge to say, *We don't share the same home*. Eva was from Bavaria. At the onset of the war, she and her parents made it to Basel, and managed to make their way to Spain and then to Lisbon, where they waited it out. They were relatively new to England. The first time Eva and Rose chatted outside of class, Eva spoke to her in German. Rose answered in English. She rarely used her German now. Eva's father had settled in Golders Green, where he taught at a Jewish school. Eva kept inviting Rose over for a Shabbos meal, "or any time at all," she'd say, but Rose kept finding excuses not to go.

Lore, a few years older, came from a town near Prague, and like Rose, she and her brother had come over on a transport. She didn't talk about her parents either. She had lived with a family in Manchester's Cheetham Hill, and then joined the ATS and drove cars for the service during the war. One time early in the year, they had left class together—Eva was sick—and run into a friend of Lore's, a young man named Walter from Berlin. He invited them to tea. Walter was exceedingly tall with a mop of hair, and a great talker. He joked about England's incessant dampness, the lack of meat on the black market, the way his landlady had a habit of coming downstairs in her too-short robe. "Oh! So sorry. I keep *forgetting* there are men in the house," he imitated her with gusto.

"Walter," Lore said with a snort and a hand to his forearm. "You are too much."

Rose smiled faintly. "How do you two know each other?"

"Oh, Lore and I go way back. I was her brother's keeper for a time. We bunked together on the Isle of Man."

"The Isle of Man?" Rose repeated.

"You know," Lore said. "When the men were interned—"

"Less than a year after I arrived," Walter broke in. "I was eighteen, just made the cutoff. Lucky me." He grinned, but Rose wasn't smiling. Now she remembered: the government had rounded up all men from German-speaking countries and held them in an internment camp. Gerhard had been fortunate, on the other side of that cutoff.

"I'm sorry," Rose said.

"Oh, it was fine." Walter waved her off. "The boredom was the worst of it. Such a bloody waste of time. And good thing people are so much clearer now on our loyalties. You know I went for an interview the other day and I was told that I had great ability, but 'so sorry, the firm already has our fill of foreigners. Cool your heels and maybe a spot for your kind will open up soon.'"

"That's awful. And I hear it's gotten worse since last summer." Lore didn't have to explain. The troubles had remained mostly up north, but they had all heard. In Cheetham Hill, where Lore's foster family lived, shop windows were smashed, bricks thrown from cars, the main synagogue vandalized. It was reprisal for the two British sergeants who had been killed in Palestine by Jewish underground fighters. People ascribed the violence in Manchester to a small, bad element—hooligans, they called them. They're not coming to London, everyone said. But Rose thought: *Wasn't this how it began in Germany?*

"It's not happening here," Walter said.

"No?" Rose said, alert, eyes on him, not doubting for a moment that he had surmised what she had been thinking.

"No. England is different. And we're pushy people, or so I'm told." He gave her a shadow of a smile. "We won't let it happen again."

Lore later told Rose: "Walter likes you. He said he wanted to come round again."

"Really?" Rose said, dubious. Didn't he like Lore? He seemed far too confident and attractive to be interested in her. Boys made her more anxious than excited. She had never had anything close to a boyfriend. But maybe things were changing, she thought nervously. She had liked talking to him. Maybe Walter would be the one.

He never came around again, and though she was disappointed, Rose never asked Lore why. It confirmed what she already knew. Rose was at a loss around boys. Sometimes she wondered: What would Mutti have told her? Would she have been more assured, growing up under her wing?

But school was something that Rose understood. In her studies, she excelled.

"I'm off," Rose said now to Eva. She felt droplets collecting on her neck; the drizzle was increasing. The figures hurrying along the paths were no more than smeary dabs. Harriet was nowhere to be found.

"To reread the 'Grand Inquisitor' section," Eva said.

"Yes," Rose said. Eva might be trying to mock her, but here was the trick: Rose didn't care. She felt a small but heady rush; Rose knew what she wanted, and what she wanted was tantalizingly, incredibly hers.

AFTER HER COMMUTE BACK TO South Kensington (two different lines, half a mile's walk), Rose let herself into Mrs. Deering's with her own key. She had begged Margaret not to leave London, she thought it was a big mistake to follow her beau back to Leeds. But if Margaret hadn't left, then Rose would have never ended up at Mrs. Deering's. Her attic room wasn't much to look at, but it had a bed and a gas ring on which she made tea, and a washbasin and, if she craned her neck, a slight view of the walled garden below. She shared a bathroom down the hall. Mrs. Deering wasn't exactly warm, but she was organized and she ran a good house. She rarely saw Mr. Deering, who had been blinded at Dunkirk, and stayed in the two rooms on the parlor floor that he and Mrs. Deering claimed for themselves. Rose liked the seamstress Mrs. Karlkowski on the third floor, who wore bright lipstick and rouge no matter if she didn't leave the house, and most of all she liked Harriet, a clever broad-shouldered blonde from America who was studying science at university and talked less about her family than Rose did. One night, over gin and lemon, she had mentioned a former husband back home outside of Philadelphia. "Technically, he is still my husband. But the things he did," Harriet had said, and stopped.

"What?" Rose breathed.

Harriet shook her head. "He is not a man; only a boy would do such things. I am fortunate that my father finally agreed." She would say no more. "It doesn't matter," she told Rose. "It's in the past. We are very lucky to be on our own." And they clinked glasses, drinking to it.

Rose entered the carpeted hall and walked past the umbrella stand and coat hooks and small curved table that held the communal telephone. Mr. Lewis from the second floor was polishing the banister with fervor.

"Hello, Mr. Lewis," Rose said.

"Oh, hello, Miss Zimmer," he said, and clutched the rag behind his back. "A fine afternoon, isn't it?" A purplish hue bloomed on his thin cheeks.

"Yes," she assured him, taking care not to focus her gaze on him, especially not on the rag she could still partially see. "An absolutely fine afternoon."

Mr. Lewis wasn't supposed to be cleaning the common areas. This everyone knew. But Mr. Lewis, a timid bookkeeper from Wales who so disliked attention that he blushed whenever spoken to, was a firebrand on the topic of cleanliness. He would tiptoe around the house—collecting towels for washing, wiping down the kitchen counter and the telephone with a heady-smelling concoction of disinfectant that he mixed himself. ("Oh no, you cannot rely on store-bought," he would say, shaking his head mournfully.) His cleaning enraged Mrs. Deering, who felt that his dusters and disinfectants were not removing contaminants from her house but adding others that marked his territory.

Now Rose heard a creak, and she and Mr. Lewis both glanced up to see Mrs. Deering making her way down from the second landing. A deep pink flamed across Mr. Lewis's face. "Well, I'm off to the post office," he announced, and scurried away.

"Miss Zimmer," Mrs. Deering said before she reached the floor. "Just the person I wanted to speak with. You are a good tenant."

"And I like living here," Rose interjected, feeling uncertain, as if this were a test.

"I am glad to hear that. But, as I have already informed the other tenants, there will be an increase in rent as of two months from now."

"An increase?" Rose repeated. Gerhard had given her a monthly sum for tuition and board after he had calculated her expenses with precision. There was scant extra.

"You are paying thirty-two shillings weekly. It will be increasing to two pounds."

"Two pounds?" Rose said, aghast. "For my room?"

"Yes, for your room." Mrs. Deering's voice rose indignant too. "Ask around. You will find that's what most rooming houses are charging, or more. What with the housing shortages around here—"

"I cannot afford it." She thought about the leather-bound volume of Gogol's stories on Charing Cross that she had spotted the other day. Twenty-eight pence. She wanted it badly. But she hadn't bought it. If she couldn't afford a book, how could she manage such an increase? She hated to take money from Gerhard in the first place. She couldn't ask him for more.

"I'm sorry, Miss Zimmer. But I am running a business here—it is my home but it is a business, the only business my husband and I now have. And what with all the doctors, and all the medications—" She stopped herself. "Let me know what you decide. But the rent will be increased in two months' time."

"And if I can't pay it?"

Mrs. Deering's voice got softer. "Then you'll have to make other arrangements."

ROSE'S ARMS ACHED BY THE time she made it to Gerhard's in Hampstead. She carried a string bag heavy with three loaves of bread and a fragrant bouquet of purple and white hyacinths that had been a last-minute purchase when she had gotten off the Tube. (She told herself not to think about the fifteen pence that she spent on them.) She walked up Holly Hill, past the white-stoned façade of St. Mary's, the streets much cleaner and quieter than in South Kensington.

When Mrs. Tompkins opened the door to her brother's flat, Rose detected the slight but stubborn odor of new paint. "Miss Zimmer," Mrs. Tompkins greeted Rose. "Mrs. Zimmer is resting in the drawing room."

"No, I am here, I am here," Isobel called as her fair head peeked into view. Her belly was straining against the ribbon that held her silk wrapper closed. Still she managed to look beautiful, her tousled hair shiny, her full lips fuller. "Hyacinths?" she exclaimed. "Oh, Rose, they are too lovely."

"I saw them and decided you must have them," Rose said, and promptly reddened.

"They are positively gorgeous, and perhaps they'll cut that awful new paint smell. It is horrid, isn't it?"

"I barely smell it."

"Oh, you're a liar," Isobel said with a laugh. "I love you but you are a terrible liar."

"Ma'am, let me put these lovelies into water," Mrs. Tompkins said. "Miss Zimmer, I'll take your things as well."

"Thank you, Mrs. Tompkins, and I picked up some loaves as well," Rose said, wriggling out of her coat, handing the string bag over.

"You must stop going to the bakery and standing in that queue for us," Isobel protested. "It is wholly unnecessary."

"You say that every week," Rose said.

"And every week it is true. Come. Let's go into the drawing room."

"How are you feeling? You look bigger than you did last week. Lovely," Rose said, catching herself, "you look lovely."

"Oh, I'm fine," Isobel said dismissively. "Quite fine. No problems at all." And she did look more than fine. No one Rose knew had had children yet, but Isobel looked as if her pregnancy was only one of her many activities. She could fit childbirth in while moving to a new flat while planning a dinner party while arguing that yes, the summer Olympics would be a boon for London.

The late-afternoon light filtered in through the bay windows, and it created honey-colored pools on the maple floorboards. "Look at this." Isobel gestured to a chair by the fireplace. "What do you think of it?"

"Is it new?" Rose said, hesitating. The chair was made of pale wood, austere but sinuous too. The wood bent this way and that. How did it do that and not break? It looked like nothing she wanted to sit in.

"Yes, I bought it the other day. It was designed by a husband-and-wife team who teach at Croydon. Isn't it wonderfully fresh?"

"Wonderfully fresh and wholly uncomfortable," Gerhard called as he came in. He carried a cigarette case in one hand and wore a crisp brown suit. Rose look down at her own skirt and noticed with renewed consternation the wrinkles she'd shrugged off when she pulled it on this morning.

Isobel sighed. "No one is asking you."

"Rose is sensible. She will agree with me." He leaned in and gave his sister a brush on the cheek. "Right, *mausi?*" Rose thought her brother looked bigger—broader in the shoulders, more imperious. But perhaps it was the fine wool suit, perhaps it was impending fatherhood.

"Are you saying I'm insensible?" Isobel asked. "Never mind, I don't care if you think I am." In fact, Rose thought Isobel probably preferred Gerhard to think of her that way. "Come here, Rose." She patted the cushion beside her. "Come talk to me. Sit here: it's a highly comfortable, old-fashioned settee, with tea rose fabric and all. Your brother's favorite." Gerhard snorted, and she continued: "Exams are soon, aren't they? How are you faring?"

"They are. I'm doing all right. It should be all right. I like my Russian literature class," she said with what she hoped was a confident, easy, Isobel-like air. "We're reading Dostoyevsky."

"Dostoyevsky?" Isobel said, twisting to puff up the pillow behind her back, frowning as she did so.

"Yes, *The Brothers Karamazov*."

"Oh yes," Isobel said. "Are you reading Miss Garnett's translation? An astonishing woman. Do you know that she learned Russian when she was confined to bed during a difficult pregnancy? And then she had the child, left him with her husband, and went to Russia for several months—"

"Don't get any ideas," Gerhard said.

Isobel shook her head at him. "She met Tolstoy and stayed with him at his dacha. Then she came back to England and spent decades translating the Russians. I met her once, in Kent, not long before she died. She wasn't well, she was on crutches then, but we had a great chat about Newnham."

"Hold on," Gerhard said. "Did you meet her through that White Russian of yours?"

Isobel sighed. "He was *not* a White Russian. He was a nobleman with the heart of a revolutionary."

"Who preyed on young, idealistic English girls," Gerhard said.

"There was no preying to be had," Isobel said. "But your jealousy is quite sweet, really." She laid a hand on his forearm, cocked her head at Rose. "Pay your brother no mind. It was quite an honor to meet Miss Garnett. Without her, we would not have access to those great Slavic minds."

"Yes," Rose said, still feeling confused. Her sister-in-law had met Constance Garnett, the great translator of Tolstoy and Dostoyevsky? She had read the Russians too? Was there nothing she couldn't do?

Isobel, Rose was sure, would be trotting out unexpected facts about herself well into her eighties.

"I'm so very glad you're enjoying your classes. Everyone should have an education. Particularly women—"

"'Particularly'?" Gerhard asked, opening his cigarette case, taking an ashtray from the mantel.

"Especially," Isobel said. "Especially women. And especially you, Rose. It's criminal to think that you of all people wouldn't have an education."

"I'm grateful to you," Rose said quickly. "To you and Gerhard. I am so grateful."

Isobel waved her off. "Oh, the thought that you would still be in a factory; what a waste, what an absolute waste!"

"People do have to work in factories, Isobel," Gerhard said as he drew in smoke. "That is how things are made. I should only be so fortunate—if the business takes off, then we too shall have a factory." Gerhard had opened a greeting-card business with Isobel's sister's husband in the past year. Sales were brisk, the cheerful, preprinted cards far more popular than Rose would have ever guessed, but a factory?

And yet, look at him, resplendent in his Savile Row suit with his gold cigarette case. "My brother, the industrialist," she had described him to Harriet with more than a little vinegary bite. But certain facts were unassailable: Gerhard had achieved. What she had deemed as his foolish outsized optimism had fueled his success, transformed his daily existence. Yes, he had gotten his start by marrying Isobel, but he had also prospered. He never again would have to fret whether he could spend the money to purchase a book; he never would worry about a rent increase. Oh, how she yearned, in that particular moment, to be more like him. What would it be like, to feel as if success, not the past, lurked around the corner? Sometimes Rose imagined talking to Gerhard, really talking to him, alone, and he would reveal himself: *The dreams I have*, he would say. *You have no idea.*

"Well, yes, people do work in factories," Isobel was saying. "But your sister doesn't. You don't."

"I would if I needed to," he said roughly. And if it hadn't been for Isobel and her money, he easily might have.

"Oh, Gerhard, really," Isobel said with a slight toss of the head. "We are not going down that road, please."

"And which road—"

"I have something to ask," Rose interjected, more out of a desire to stop them than any thought-out plan.

"Of course," Isobel said, but she was still scrutinizing Gerhard as she said it. Then she swiveled back to Rose. "Yes?"

"Well . . ." Rose hesitated. Could she ask Mr. Cohen for the extra money? Margaret? "My landlady told me that the cost of my room is going up," she confessed. "I'm afraid I'm going to need more money for the rent."

"How much more?" Gerhard asked with a bluntness that Rose wished surprised her.

"It doesn't matter," Isobel said.

"Isobel, please—"

"Twenty shillings more weekly," Rose answered, undercutting the figure by ten—too ashamed to say the full amount. She could make up the difference out of her pocket money; she was certain she could.

"That's quite a jump," Gerhard said.

"I know," Rose said wretchedly. "That's what I told her."

"For God's sakes, Gerhard," Isobel said. "Of course we'll give her the money."

"That's not the point. We—and she—should know the details. Perhaps Deering is taking advantage of her. Also, we do have an abundance of room here. And with the baby on the way, she could be useful—"

"Me? With the baby?" The words fell out of Rose's mouth, she didn't have time to scrub them free of her distaste.

"I'm not saying you should," Gerhard said, "only that we should discuss it as a possibility."

"You don't have to," Isobel said quickly.

"No, it's just that—you're so far from school—"

"Not that much farther than South Kensington," Gerhard pointed out.

"Gerhard," Isobel chided.

"What?"

Rose could barely hear them. This was what she had been afraid of from the moment they offered to pay her expenses. She wasn't herself on these weekly visits. The thought of living here made it difficult to breathe. Maybe it wasn't absurd to ask Mr. Cohen for the money. Mrs. Cohen still made it clear that she thought literature an impractical pursuit for a girl like Rose, but several months ago, Mr. Cohen had come to London on business and he called on her. She hadn't seen him in well over a year. The last time he had been in town, she was still employed by the factory, and she avoided him. He knew where she worked but that didn't mean that she had to talk about it. Rose was grateful that the Cohens had taken care of her, resentful that she needed such care. Often there was an air of stiffness to their conversations. But this time proved different. Mr. Cohen waxed nostalgic about reading Kipling and Tennyson during his own school days. "You've turned into quite the young lady," he said as he shook her hand upon leaving. He undoubtedly approved of her studies. She could ask him for a temporary loan to carry her for a few months. Rose could get a job, something part-time, so she could continue at school. She would figure out a way if need be.

"It's—how much is the increase?" Isobel asked.

Rose hesitated. "Thirty shillings more a week," she eventually said.

"You said twenty before," Gerhard said.

"I made a mistake," Rose said, appealing to her brother. He had to understand how difficult this was for her. "It's thirty."

Isobel said: "That's less than fifty pounds yearly. You know, my family doesn't have so much money . . ." Rose gaped at her, baffled. Isobel had more money than anyone she had ever met. ". . . But we have enough. We certainly have more than enough for you not to worry about such things."

"Thank you," Rose managed. Thank God. "Thank you, Isobel."

"We are glad to help," Isobel said, and she stood up, leaned her heavy frame against Gerhard. Rose watched them, relieved. She was always surprised to see how much shorter Isobel was than Gerhard, and she wasn't more than a few inches taller than Rose herself. "I want you to think of it as your money too."

Rose nodded. "Of course," she murmured. But that was like imagining a London without the war ever happening: such an exquisite thought, but altogether impossible.

"MISS ZIMMER," PROFESSOR HILLMAN SAID. HE gestured toward the seat close to the door with his chin. He had a pronounced chin, Rose thought now; she had never noticed it before. She tried to focus on this detail and his receding hair, and not the fact that she had been called in to speak with him. She had thought her paper on *The Brothers Karamazov* was all right. Was it her best? No. But she hadn't been sleeping well. It was difficult to concentrate. Although Isobel said they would cover the difference in her rent, Rose still feared that it wouldn't happen, that her brother would become even more attracted to his idea that she move in with them. Isobel—and indeed her brother—had given Rose no reason to believe this. Still she worried.

Professor Hillman's office was tiny, the bookshelves hulking. There was no samovar. Rose positioned herself at the edge of the chair, kept her moist hands folded in her lap. It was hot in here; she had an urge to pull at the collar of her jumper, allow in more air, but she didn't dare.

"Your paper was intriguing, but undisciplined, for you. I thought your structural point on how Dostoyevsky was playing with time, flattening it in the first half of the book, was well taken. And more than that, original."

"Thank you," Rose said, for that was a compliment mixed into the criticism, wasn't it? It was exceedingly difficult to think straight.

"But it wasn't carried forth throughout the essay. You dropped it quite suddenly, as if you forgot about it. And I expected you to touch more on the theme of suffering you had discussed in class."

"Oh," she said, and she could not look at him. He was right. She too had thought about the notion of unavenged suffering, but when she thought of exploring it, truly articulating what she thought Dostoyevsky meant by it, she felt overcome, panicky with emotion. There was only so much she could say on the subject. Now she simply felt ashamed. She hadn't wanted to do the hard work that university required. Professor Hillman was right. It was a shoddy paper, and it was all she could do not to leap across the desk and grab it and tear it up into minuscule pieces.

"You are a clever girl, Miss Zimmer," he said. "I am telling you this precisely because you are clever. This paper is acceptable. If another student had written it, it might be quite fine. But you can do better. I've seen you do better."

"I understand, Professor Hillman," she said, and even she could hear the quiver in her voice. He was saying something kind, but how could she believe him? She had a hard time believing people, trusting the most basic of facts.

"I called you here for another reason too. Have you thought about your plans after you obtain your degree?"

She shook her head. Of course she had, but only hazily. A job in publishing, perhaps, or a position at the Home Office. These were things she had to consider, she knew—Gerhard and Isobel would not fund her indefinitely, nor would she want them to. But it unnerved her, to think of a time after school, when she would have to get a job again, when she would have someone tell her what to do.

"I hope you will consider teaching. You would make a fine teacher."

"What?" It was something she scarcely allowed herself to imagine, too heady was the possibility. Teaching! "You think I would?"

"Yes, I most certainly do." He reached for a thick catalog on his desk. "It takes work. You must earn an additional certificate through the education department, but you are up to the task. Certainly for secondary school—and there is still a great need, after the war—but I could see you, if you continued on this path, continuing your studies and remaining at a university level too. Not many women have the fortitude, but I believe you do."

"Thank you, Professor Hillman," Rose said, and couldn't help flashing him a pleased grin. To be a teacher would be an honor and responsibility. It would give her security, a clear career path. She feared she wouldn't be up for the task; she would work harder than ever to make it so.

But doubt crept in: Would Mutti have seen it this way? She respected teachers to be sure, but a career? She would want Rose to get married, have a family of her own. This was what mattered most to her. At twenty-one years old, Rose knew she should already be thinking of these things. But she felt so much older than her years, and sometimes she wondered if, after everything she had been through, meeting a boy was a step she had inadvertently bypassed, something that she was simply not destined to do.

"I appreciate all your guidance," Rose said, more muted this time. "Thank you."

Professor Hillman held out his hand and grasped hers with a firm shake that surprised her. "It is I who am honored to teach you."

"YOU'RE QUIET TODAY," ISOBEL SAID to Rose as they neared the end of Sunday dinner.

"I'm tired," Rose said, and it was the truth. She had stayed up late reading the night before. It had been four days since she had met with Professor Hillman, and every night she stayed up hours past the other residents at Mrs. Deering's, poring over her books. She wouldn't let Professor Hillman down again.

"Well, I read the most amazing item in the paper today," Isobel said. "I've told you that when Grandpapa was in Sydney, he had a partner, haven't I?"

"Perhaps," Gerhard said with a little smile directed at his sister. "But the details on Grandpapa's concerns have always been mysterious to me."

Rose couldn't manage a smile back. She forked off another morsel of Mrs. Tompkins's roast. Rose knew that Isobel's grandfather had gone to Australia as a young man and bought dozens of properties. The investments had paid off handsomely and provided the foundation from which Isobel's large family had drawn for decades.

"Yes, well, Grandpapa's ways were mysterious to all of us," Isobel said. "But his partner was a man called Henry Cooper, and Mr. Cooper's family and ours remained close. His grandson Douglas Cooper and I spent summers together in Wales, and he was at Trinity while I was at Newnham. Then he went off to the Sorbonne and Freiburg— and when he returned, he opened an art gallery. He always had such a critical eye. He could be a bit of a rogue, but my parents adored him. In fact, when I came home and announced to my parents that I was besotted with your brother and they were not at all pleased, they trotted out Douglas's name."

"Your father should have known better than to raise objections about a foreigner to you," Gerhard said, raising an eyebrow, dabbing a corner of his mouth with his napkin. Had Isobel ever liked an Englishman? Last year, when she was reading Browning, Isobel told her about a northern Italian boy she had met during a sojourn to Lake Como. "He came from a banking family," Rose remembered Isobel saying, "but he had the soul of an artist." Her brother, Rose thought, was Isobel's perfect match: a foreigner, which of course pleased her, and a man who seemed English to the core for her parents.

"Mrs. Tompkins," Gerhard now called. When the housekeeper emerged, he said: "Delicious, as usual. My whiskey now, please." He turned back to Isobel. "But why were you not enticed by the estimable Mr. Cooper?"

"So many reasons," Isobel said. "Foremost I was not available, but had I been, Douglas Cooper does not like the female persuasion."

"Ah," Gerhard said. "And why are we speaking of him now?"

"Well, I knew from Mama that Douglas was in Europe, but what I did not know was that he became a British officer specializing in art. Tracking down lost art from the war. Douglas Cooper, can you imagine that? In a position of importance and authority!"

"What do you mean?" Rose asked, suddenly alert. "Lost art?"

"That's what the item in the paper today was about. During the war, so many things went missing—'looted' is the better term, of course. And apparently Douglas Cooper was sent to Switzerland a few years ago, and in just a few weeks he was able to turn up dozens of pictures and valuables that had been stolen from their rightful owners and sold by the Nazis—many to people who claimed, cravenly, that they had absolutely no idea what the Nazis were doing. The paper called him a British hero. Douglas Cooper! I tell you. I never would have guessed it. Thoroughly astounding."

"That does sound astounding," Rose said. Gerhard was sipping his whiskey, leaning back in his chair. Was he not going to say anything? His ice cubes clinked, he drained his glass, silent.

Isobel was still speaking. "How amazing: to find a canvas that had been missing for more than five years. The paper said that France has set up a commission to find the art too, and all that they do find they store in the Jeu de Paume until they find the owners. Has either of you ever been there? Oh, Gerhard, we must go one day. It's such a lovely little museum, right on the edge of the Tuileries."

Rose heard Isobel but her particular words did not register, because she felt a flare of possibility. *Everything was gone*, Gerhard had told her, *Vienna was not the same*. Perhaps, just perhaps, he wasn't right.

Now Isobel was talking about the Rothschilds, and how the patriarch of the family, now living in Toronto, had tracked down his Vermeer, which had been sold to a dealer in Lucerne. A woman had gone into an antique shop here in Knightsbridge and spotted her mother's Limoges sixty-piece dinner service, hand-painted with her family's initials.

"You know, Isobel," Rose started to say, her heart resounding, "our family owned some pictures. One in particular that our mother loved very much. By a painter named Chaim Soutine."

"But we aren't Rothschilds, and that's not a valuable painting," Gerhard said.

"Why does that matter?" Rose retorted.

"Really, Gerhard," Isobel said. "There might be something we could do. Why would you not tell me such a thing?"

"It's in the past," Gerhard said. "So many things, they're in the past."

"But that doesn't mean they have to remain there." Isobel said this firmly, but Rose wasn't sure she heard her correctly. She felt a quickening, a fluttering rise. In her mind's eye, she saw the red of the Bellhop's jacket, the thickened paint strokes, she saw her mother, seeing those things.

"Could you write to Douglas for us? Could you ask him about the Soutine?"

"Why, it's not a question. Of course I will."

"It's a waste of time," Gerhard said. "You don't know." His voice deepened, but the words sounded brittle. He grabbed his glass and stalked out of the room.

Her brother's anger only fueled Rose's certainty. Isobel poured herself water and spoke: "You shouldn't mind him. But I suppose you know that better than I."

"I don't mind at all," Rose said. She was somewhere else entirely. It was *The Bellhop* she was thinking of, those dark eyes that gave nothing away. *I will find you*, she thought. And for the first time in years, she felt as if it were a promise she had a chance of keeping.

9

LOS ANGELES, 2006

LIZZIE HADN'T ASKED ROSE FOR her approval. She told herself that she didn't need it. She was gathering facts. What was the harm in being informed?

Plenty, she could hear Rose retort. But Rose was full of protestations. She couldn't always mean them. This was what Lizzie thought as she read online about the 1999 Washington Conference on Nazi-Confiscated Art and the Holocaust Art Restitution Project and the Conference on Jewish Material Claims Against Germany. It was easy to pretend, as she kept scrolling, that *The Bellhop* was like the other artwork in question, languishing in a private collection or a museum somewhere, its provenance suspicious and light on details. But *The Bellhop* wasn't missing because of the Nazis. Lizzie imagined Rose saying, *That's precisely why you want to know about restitution: so you can forget that night.* Still she kept searching.

On a Harvard law school syllabus, she read the language that the Nazis had used to codify the seizure of artwork. They had gone to the trouble to make it legal. The law, established in 1938, stated that "products of degenerate art that have been secured in museums or in collections open to the public . . . may be appropriated by the

Reich without compensation." Lizzie read about New York's 1963 *Menzel v. List* case that had established the demand and refusal rule, which stated that the limitations period begins once the owner makes a demand for the return of the property in question. She read about battles over Monets and Matisses, the stonewalling by prominent museums that insisted there was no plundered artwork hanging on their walls; she read many a reference to Klimt's *Portrait of Adele Bloch-Bauer.*

"The prospect of attempting to claim seized art is daunting, arduous, expensive, and byzantine at best," an attorney by the name of Michael Ciparelli was quoted as saying in one news account. His name sounded familiar. She looked him up. He was an expert in the field of art restitution, and she saw that he had been an associate at Paul, Weiss years earlier, as had her boss. Perhaps Marc could put her in touch. *What's he going to tell you?* She could imagine Rose scoffing. *We don't know where* The Bellhop *is. How can it be claimed?*

I don't know, Lizzie told Rose in her head. *That's why I'm going to ask.*

NONE OF THIS SHE TOLD Rose that afternoon. The plan had been for another walk. But after they left Rose's apartment in the late afternoon, the wind kicked up—it was cooler than either Rose or Lizzie had expected—and the streets felt emptied out, desolate. "I could use some coffee," Lizzie offered, but as they headed to the café, Rose looked at her watch: "Corman!" she declared happily.

Corman apparently meant Roger Corman, which apparently also meant the Los Angeles County Museum of Art. The nearby museum was hosting a retrospective of the director's work ("He's that B-movie guy, right?" Lizzie said, and Rose threw her such a look of disdain. "If that's the way you want to think of one of the most influential directors and producers of the twentieth century, then so be it.") This week his Edgar Allan Poe adaptations were being featured,

Rose explained as she led Lizzie the several blocks to the museum, with more alacrity to her step than she'd had moments before.

They made it with fifteen minutes to spare, and they had their pick of seats in the small screening room. Soon they were watching *Tomb of Ligeia*. It was a hot, gothic, campy affair: a loner of a man (Vincent Price, looking younger than Lizzie had ever seen him) obsessed with his dead first wife, a crumbling abbey, a deranged black cat, hints of necrophilia. The plot was overstuffed but Price hammed it up, and the scenes filmed outside in the English countryside were gorgeous. It seemed to be more concerned with romantic obsession than an attempt to frighten, and it reminded Lizzie of *Jane Eyre* and *The Woman in White*, two books she loved. ("The script is by Robert Towne, who also wrote *Chinatown*," Rose leaned over to whisper.)

As Vincent Price was fighting with the spirit of his first wife, who now took the form of a cat, Lizzie felt her phone buzz. She looked down to see a text from Max ("Miss you," it said. "See you for dinner?"). She turned back with renewed determination to the screen.

The film ended a little after six P.M. It was already dark when they left the theater, Lizzie's thin jacket no match for the dropping temperature. They headed back to Rose's apartment, where Lizzie's car was parked.

"What did you think?" Rose asked.

"It was fun," Lizzie said. "Vincent Price especially."

"You know Robert Towne didn't want to use him. He thought he was too old. But Corman insisted. He made Price wear a wig and layered on the makeup."

"See, there are solutions to everything."

"I would say that it's essential to stick to your guns."

Lizzie laughed; she read it that way too.

"Food. Shall we order in for dinner?"

"Yes," Lizzie said. "Please." She still hadn't answered Max's text. She'd gone to the bathroom, started to peck out a response, then stopped.

Earlier that morning, she had pretended to be asleep when he left, keeping her eyes faux-shut when he brushed his lips across her forehead. After he'd gone, she got up and headed out with her laptop, spent the morning at a nearby café. She came across a long thread in her work e-mail about the Clarke appeal. Kathleen, the associate, reported to Marc that Clarke had complained in a call that they were being too deferential to the lower court in the brief. ("They're wrong; that's what the appeal is based on. Why fuck around?" Kathleen reported Clarke as saying.) But that would be a mistake, Lizzie thought, and she wrote both Kathleen and Marc, furiously tapping out her response. A few minutes later, she sent Marc a separate e-mail about Michael Ciparelli, the lawyer who specialized in restitution cases. "Of course I know him," Marc wrote back. "Sharp, smart. I'll put you two in touch." Lizzie felt a flash of pleasure. Maybe Rose would listen to Ciparelli, if not her.

Now Rose was talking about the dearth of decent Chinese food in her neighborhood as they rounded the corner and reached her building, a stucco four-story fronted by a shallow rectangle of yellowing grass and a forlorn palm tree. A man stood on the steps of the concrete walkway. "Rose! There you are!" He took the stairs purposefully. He was a bear of an older man, clad in a dark blazer and jeans. "I was beginning to worry."

"You were?" Rose said, sounding annoyed. "Why?"

"Porter's—for dinner." He reached Rose and kissed her on the cheek. He dwarfed her. "Don't tell me you forgot." He had a deep, authoritative voice; it assumed people paid attention.

"So then I won't," Rose said. Lizzie was watching and listening to all of this, taking in Rose's irritated tone, the man's clear affection for her. Who was he? She had a sense but she didn't dare ask.

"Come on," he said, head to the side, but he didn't seem annoyed. "Aren't you hungry? I for one am famished." He turned to Lizzie. "I don't believe we've met; I'm Bob Fisher." He gripped her hand in greeting.

"I'm sorry," Rose said. "Lizzie and I were at the movies. Lizzie is the daughter of an old friend of mine. And Bob is—a new friend of mine."

"Not all that new," Bob said.

Rose shrugged.

Lizzie wanted to catch Rose's eye and raise an eyebrow, knowing she would be furious if she did. Rose had a boyfriend!

"Lizzie and I were just talking about dinner; she'll join us," Rose said.

"For dinner?" Bob said. He looked at Rose, then to Lizzie, then back at Rose again.

"No, no," Lizzie said. She wasn't going to intrude. "I'm fine."

"I know you're fine," Rose said. "But you're coming. Do not tell me you have plans. You didn't have them five minutes ago." She turned to Bob. "I took her to a horror movie—the least I can do is feed her."

Bob gave Lizzie a declarative nod. "Of course, join us. I hope the film wasn't too bad; Rose is always trying to drag me to the worst movies." He reached for Rose's hand, grinning.

"It was *Corman*," Rose muttered, but she allowed him to take her hand.

Watching them together, Lizzie felt a quick joyful current. "She does have very particular taste," she said to Bob. "And thank you, I will come."

"Oh, please, what's wrong with my taste?" Rose asked, but Bob was already on his phone calling the restaurant to change the reservation, and Lizzie was texting Max back. "I'm so sorry; I won't be back for dinner," she typed with a strange shot of giddiness. "But I won't be back late." And for the first time that day she truly missed him.

THREE PEOPLE, TWO CARS, LESS than half a mile's drive. In no time at all, Lizzie pulled up at Porter's on La Cienega, Bob and Rose behind her in Bob's boat of an old Mercedes. The steak house was more Austrian ski lodge than L.A.: darkly but invitingly lit, wood beams crisscrossing the high ceiling, wide-mouthed fireplace crackling, leather-bound books for menus.

"They have boar here, and it is delicious," Bob told Lizzie as they were ushered into a leather booth.

"I am not ordering boar," Rose said, nose to menu.

"You don't have to, but it is an option."

"I like options," Lizzie said.

Bob suggested manhattans, he highly recommended the strip steak and creamed corn too. Lizzie took him up on all of it. Rose stuck with water while Lizzie was soon draining her drink and eating a warm roll and oysters (when had Bob ordered those?). And then the steaks arrived—charred at the edges, tender, delicious.

Bob was talking and talking—about being a salesman for a medical equipment company ("He's being modest," Rose added. "He's a salesman and a vice president.") and his boat that he liked to sail out to Catalina. "Have you ever seen the wild pigs out there?" he said. "They'll eat anything, including each other." He asked her about living in New York and how she decided to go into appellate work (he knew what appellate law was; not everyone did). And after ordering a bottle of Merlot, he said: "Here's the thing you need to know about me—and Rose is coming to terms with it—I am a Springsteen fanatic."

"Okay," Lizzie said. She waited. Was there more to it than that?

"What do you think about Bruce?" He was looking at her with such intent, nearly grimacing.

"I think he's fine. I like him fine." The truth was, Lizzie didn't have a strong opinion about Bruce Springsteen. On the musical front, she was a hanger-on, usually decades behind the times.

"I would respect you more if you hated him," Bob said.

"Oh, please," Rose began. "Do not start."

"Why? You hate Springsteen, and I adore you," Bob said. He leaned over, his enormous face intent on Lizzie's. "I've seen him dozens of times. God, Staples Center, 1999, the reunion tour: Those opening cords of 'Jungleland.' And the Big Man on the sax, and then Bruce yelling, 'Is there anyone alive out there?' And it's a good question, don't you think? It's the most important question we should be asking, all the time: Is there anyone alive out there?"

Lizzie was already woozy but she took a long pull on her wine. "You're right," she said. In the middle of the clinking glasses and clatter of dishes and conversation and smoky smells and rush of waiters and all of the rich abundance, gustatory and material, it felt like a striking, profound question. All she could think of were her parents: her father, dead in a nanosecond, her mother's agonizing demise encircling her childhood. *Is anyone alive out there?* Was she? "I should see Springsteen in concert," she said, and her voice turned hoarse with emotion. "I will."

A slow smile flitted across Bob's face. "I know you will," he said with a gravelly satisfaction. "And you will not regret it." He stood, wiped the corner of his mouth with the napkin with a surprisingly delicate gesture. "Now, ladies, if you'll excuse me a moment." He wove past the other tables and the fireplace and disappeared from view.

"Why the Springsteen obsession," Rose said. "I do not know."

Lizzie leaned across the table, touched Rose's wrist. "I love him," she proclaimed. "I do."

Was Rose blushing? "He can be a handful, but I am fond of him," she admitted.

"He is besotted with you," Lizzie said. "As well he should be."

"Yes, well," Rose said. "I'll tell you what I'm besotted with—these rolls." She broke one in half, spread on a thin layer of butter. "It seems easy to do a nice hot roll, but it isn't, and it shouldn't be overlooked; it should be taken seriously and celebrated."

"I'll celebrate that," Lizzie said as Bob returned. The waiter came by and offered more wine, which Lizzie gladly accepted, despite what she suspected was a look of disapproval from Rose.

"Remind me how you two know each other?" Bob said.

"Lizzie's father was the one who owned my family's painting."

"Oh yes. The one that was stolen from the house. The painting by—what's his name?"

"Soutine," Lizzie and Rose said nearly in unison. Lizzie blushed.

"Chaim Soutine," Rose amended. "You would find him interesting. If not as a painter, then as a person. He was a character, a hypochondriac who lived in fear of going bald. He loved his friend Modigliani and the Old Masters like Rembrandt." Rose hadn't told Bob about Soutine before? For a moment, this surprised Lizzie, then she thought: *Who did she talk about Soutine with?*

"And boxing," Rose continued. "Apparently Soutine used to say that if he hadn't been an artist, he would have liked to be a boxer. The writer Henry Miller was his neighbor for a time and they used to go to matches together."

"Really?" Lizzie said. She didn't know that Henry Miller had lived nearby. What else did she not know? Her head was so fuzzy. "You like boxing?" she said to Bob.

"I do. I used to box myself, years ago. I know what people think of it, but they're wrong. It actually taught me to be more patient. I learned that if you swing at an opponent's face, he'll hit right back. It taught me to hold back a bit, to be more controlled."

When the waiter came over with dessert menus, Bob told him: "We'll have the chocolate cake. One slice, three forks."

"We will?" Rose said.

"It's the only thing to get here," Bob said. "Hot molten chocolate cake. It's delicious." Lizzie was already so full, but when did she ever say no to a few tastes of sweetness? "So the detectives never came across any clues?" Bob added.

"No," Rose said.

"There were no signs of a break-in," Lizzie said. "It happened during a party—a party I threw." She managed to say this in a steady voice.

"And they don't think one of the guests took it."

"In the beginning, yes, they thought it might have been a prank, but the artwork—there was a Picasso drawing too—they were the only two things taken. Whoever stole them knew exactly what they were looking for. And all my friends were in high school. None of them knew anything about art."

"That must have been terrible," Bob said. "Being there at the time, knowing that it happened."

"Yeah," Lizzie said. "It sucked."

"'Sucked'?" Rose repeated.

Lizzie blushed. "You know what I mean," she muttered. "It was horrible."

The waiter delivered the cake with a flourish, placing it in the center of the table—round and dark and dusted with powdered sugar. Bob cut into it, and melted chocolate oozed out, darkening the plate. "Delicious," he said. "Have some." When neither Rose nor Lizzie reached for it, he added, "The detectives must have talked to everyone, including your father."

"Yeah, they did," Lizzie said. "He was in Boston when it happened."

"Oh," Bob said, and he gave the one syllable force. His forearms were planted on the edge of the table, and Lizzie was struck by how large his hands were—boxer's hands. "And the paintings were insured, weren't they?"

"Of course," Rose said. "Why?"

"I just wonder how much they were insured for, how much they were worth at the time. The art market is famously volatile. It's interesting."

"How do you know about the volatility of the art market?" Rose's voice was sharp. "And nothing is just *interesting*. Things are upsetting or wonderful, stupid or delightful, charming or beautiful or terrible. What do you mean, 'interesting'?"

A flicker of uncertainty crossed Bob's face. Lizzie saw it, a sudden shift. "I used to have a neighbor who worked as an investigator for an insurance company," Bob said. "He was always talking about the fraudulent claims he uncovered."

"No," Rose said. "Do not. Joseph wanted to get them back. That's it, end of story."

Lizzie felt caught behind a thick distorting pane of glass. What was Bob saying? Rose was sitting up straight, her body tight with anger.

"You're right, I'm sorry," Bob said.

"Of course I'm right. He worked for years to get them back. Do you want to accuse a dead man of anything else, while his daughter is sitting here?"

"I don't understand," Lizzie said.

"I'm sorry," Bob said softly, turning to her. "I'm sure the police cleared it up. I don't know why I said that."

"It's okay," Lizzie stammered. Nothing was making sense. Bob was suggesting—what? That her father had something to do with the stolen paintings?

"No, it is not *okay*." Rose was livid. "How dare you?" She grabbed her blazer, fumbled putting it on. "Who do you think you are, saying such things to us? Impugning my friend like that—a dead man who cannot defend himself. Come, Lizzie, we're going."

"No, Rose; wait, please," Bob said, reaching for her. "It was stupid; I didn't mean it."

But Rose shook him off. "Let's go."

"I'm sorry," Lizzie said to Bob.

"Why are *you* apologizing?" Rose cried.

"You can't leave me here alone," Bob said. "There's still cake." He tried to laugh.

"It looks," Rose snapped, "like a pile of shit."

LIZZIE, BEHIND THE WHEEL OF her car, was shocked into sobriety as surely as if she'd downed a pint of burned coffee. Rose sat beside her, fuming. "I am absolutely appalled. The nerve to suggest such a thing. Your father hired an investigator at his own expense when the police turned up nothing. Years! Decades! All on your father's dime."

"I know," Lizzie said. "I know." A strand of hair fell across her cheek; for a moment, nothing had ever felt more irritating. She yanked at it, clutched the steering wheel with the other hand.

"Bob gets these ideas in his head and he just says them—he'll say anything that comes to mind. He is seventy-three years old and he has absolutely no idea how to behave. I am sorry."

"It's okay."

"It's not."

"It is." Lizzie rolled down her window. "Please."

"It's rather cold, don't you think?" Rose said. "Do you need the window open?"

"I do, yes," Lizzie said. "The fresh air is helping me, sorry." She turned on the heat.

Within minutes, Lizzie had pulled up in front of Rose's building. "You know, I bet my father would find it kind of funny," she said as Rose unbuckled her seat belt.

"What? No."

Lizzie was too worn out to explain. She only meant that her father wasn't easily insulted. He was more confident, more certain of himself than anyone else she knew. She would call Sarah; she would tell her the story. She could hear her sister's response: *Oh, please*, she'd snort. *As if the police didn't consider that on day one.*

"Let's talk tomorrow," Rose said, and gave Lizzie a stern nod. *Chin up*, Lizzie felt she was saying. She nodded in return.

Leaving Rose's, she turned onto Fairfax, heading back toward Venice. After a few blocks, she pulled over and called her sister, who picked up right away.

"The strangest thing happened tonight. I was having dinner with Rose," Lizzie began.

"Yeah?" Sarah asked.

Lizzie hesitated. Why would she tell her the story? What did she think Sarah would say? She remembered that first night in the hospital, the V of Sarah's thin gown puckering, the fluorescent light giving her skin a greenish cast, tubes snaking up from her hand taped to a pole; she heard the clicks and whirls of machines. It had only happened that once. Sarah had been stable for years and years now.

Still. Lizzie took a deep breath. She loved her sister. And the story she was thinking of telling now felt like a burden. "Rose has a boyfriend," she said.

"So? That's the strange thing?"

"Yeah," Lizzie said. "I had no idea she was seeing someone."

"Why shouldn't she?" Sarah said. "Because she's older? Sometimes you suffer from a lack of imagination."

"That's the truth," Lizzie said, trying to blink away all that couldn't be forgotten.

10

LONDON, 1950

ROSE DIDN'T KNOW WHY SHE had settled on this particular antique shop, only that she had. For the past two months, the shop off Old Bond Street was the only one she visited. The smells of dampness and benign neglect made it seem more approachable than its price tags might suggest. Its poor lighting allowed her to examine merchandise in relative seclusion. But those weren't the only reasons; so many of London's shops were dimly lit and dusty. There was something about the heaviness of its furniture—much of it black oak, chairs covered in velvet, chaise longues formidable as stone—the knickknacks, the oil paintings in their ornate frames, and the trove of porcelain vases. Walking into the shop gave her a strange, unsettling sensation. It reminded her of home.

Today the salesgirl was busy helping a flaxen-headed boy who seemed to be far too young to be contemplating the brooch before him. It took Rose's eyes a few minutes to adjust to the light. She saw a large bronze peacock flecked with mottled green and purple that hadn't been there the week before. She gave a marble chessboard and a jewel-encrusted cigarette case little more than a quick, practiced glance.

Rose had no intention of making a purchase. She finally had landed a position—as a secretary, not exactly the teaching job she had been searching for since getting her degree, not exactly well paying, but it was a position nevertheless. She paid her rent, she covered her expenses, and then: well, there was little left. Still, she was glad to be on her own, no longer taking money from Gerhard and Isobel. After she had started working for Mr. Marks, Rose found an apartment in Belsize, a tiny two-room flat at the top of a perilously uneven staircase. The halls smelled like wet wool and she regularly heard the shriek of the baby next door, but the place was all hers. She had a minuscule breakfast table that she was able to situate beneath a small but perfectly suitable window, and an old pair of club chairs that Gerhard and Isobel had given her when they redecorated. It was in one of the armchairs that she would have her tea, balancing a cup and saucer on her knee, even if she was alone, as was most often the case. (Last week her tea offerings vastly improved when she received a small box from Leeds containing a tin of chocolate biscuits, a collection of jellies, and, most wondrously, a small crock containing four eggs nestled in straw. "From the Cohens," the card said, but Rose immediately recognized Mary's hand.) What Rose had these days was a surfeit of time, as Gerhard pointed out far too often. For the past month, as the days shortened and edged closer to winter, she had been drawn to this shop week after week, as surely and as inexplicably as the queues that still crisscrossed the city, nearly five years after the war.

Isobel had been true to her word. She had written her childhood friend Douglas Cooper, and he in turn had guided them. Austria had enacted laws on restitution at the end of the war, the so-called Rückstellungsgesetz, which said that all victims were entitled to list and report the loss of property. Gerhard and Rose wrote to the Austrian Federal Monuments Office with a record of all the valuables they could recall from their parents' home. Months went by, then a year; finally they received word: no matches. The Austrian government was holding thousands of seized artworks in collecting points throughout the country: in a monastery in Mauerbach, in salt mines near Salzburg, storage rooms in the Finance Ministry in Vienna it-self. "There are lists," Douglas had written, thousands upon thou-sands of items on those lists. "The Austrian government claims the work is heirless; they say they are working on returning what can be returned. They are not releasing the lists." But Douglas had seen some, and there were no Soutines, nothing that fit *The Bellhop*'s de-scription.

"But they could be wrong," Rose said.

Isobel sighed. "They probably are," she said. "Unconscionable—ignorant, murderous Krauts."

"Isobel," chided Gerhard.

"What? They are."

Douglas told Isobel of a lawyer, a Franz Rudolf Bienenfeld, a Jew-ish emigré from Vienna, who worked on such issues in London. They met with him. He was a small middle-aged man in a well-cut suit. "There are possibilities," he said. "We could apply for restitution for interrupted schooling. For both of you."

"No," Rose and Gerhard said. On this they agreed.

"They can keep their money," Gerhard said, arms folded over his chest.

"I want my mother's painting," Rose said.

Bienenfeld's eyes squinted behind round wire spectacles. "It is owed to you," he said. "It is not their money."

"I don't want it," Gerhard said. Rose stole a glance at her brother. It wasn't as if she weren't tempted. But the notion of filing a claim felt like acquiescing. She imagined it displeasing both her parents. So she said nothing at all.

Rose continued to look. The trick was not to narrow one's focus. Expectations couldn't be tamped down entirely—that wasn't realis-tic, and Rose was, if anything, a realist (even within this fool's errand). But it was a nameless, shimmery expectation, so light and gossamer thin that it existed as sensation only. She thought about searching when she was taking dictation for Mr. Marks. It was on her mind when Mr. Cohen wrote to her to say that he would be in town on Saturday and was she available to meet for tea? "I'm busy," she wrote back, thinking of the shop on Old Bond. She thought about looking while swaying in the dim light of the Underground, listening to people grouse about Korea and the National Health Service. I have this, she would think. Searching gave her purpose.

Every item was defined by its negative—the ivory handles on the pair of swords hanging opposite the clocks were too intricate to be the ones her grandfather brought back from Constantinople. The rococo mirror she spotted last month was too small and bright to be her mother's. Now she turned over a midnight-velvet jewelry case, but this had a soft gold clasp, not silver, and its underside wasn't nicked as her grandmother's had been.

She remembered what Isobel had read in the paper: how a former cook of one of the Rothschilds had started a new position and was astounded to see the Vermeer from the *baronne*'s dressing area hanging in her new employer's drawing room. In the past two years, Rose had gathered stories from the papers on her own. A Mrs. Arnold had spotted a set of mother-of-pearl nesting boxes inlaid with her mother's initials in the window of an antique dealer in Paris. Nathan Rosenberg went into a Zurich picture dealer and saw one of his family's eighteenth-century portraits hanging on the wall. These things did happen.

Rose had reached the far wall of the shop, on which a select number of pictures were hung. Within a beat, she had her answer—registered by the drop in her stomach before her mind could articulate why. There were pastoral scenes—a brook, a picnicking group—and pictures of horses galloping and boys diving. But no portraits.

"That horse couldn't win a pigs' race, I tell you." The fair-haired salesgirl was standing beside Rose, contemplating a picture with her narrow blue eyes.

"I'm sorry?" Rose asked. She was trying to remember when she had last come in: last week or the week before? Had the landscapes been here? Maybe they hadn't gotten any new paintings in. She should inquire, but she didn't like to ask questions.

"I'm telling you, look at his legs, yeah? Too short and stocky, out of proportion."

Rose looked. "Yes," she admitted. She hadn't noticed. She had barely registered the horses at all.

"I'm Julie," the salesgirl said, extending a hand, her small features composed into a genuine smile. Rose had been in the shop enough to know that she smiled often. Even so, Rose was taken aback. She didn't expect a smile from her—or from most people, really.

"Rose," she said, and took the girl's cool hand.

"Nice to finally make your acquaintance," Julie said. "I told Mr. Bradshaw the picture was no good but he didn't care. If he could, he'd turn the entire shop into an equestrian palace. What are you looking for? I know it's something in particular. You'd think I would know by now, but I haven't a clue."

"Nothing," Rose said, blushing. Clearly a lie. Embarrassed, she shifted her gaze to the chess set. It was made out of two different shades of marble, one honey-colored, one dark. Someone had spent a good deal of time carving it. Papi had played chess, hadn't he? Did he have a chessboard? She couldn't remember.

"If you tell me," Julie said, "I could keep an eye for you."

"I appreciate it, I do, but I'm simply looking." Rose tried to smile but it felt forced, nothing like the genuine warmth on the salesgirl's face. "I should get going."

In the front of the shop, the boy was still contemplating jewelry. As Rose tried to brush past him, he spoke: "Sorry, but may I ask you a question? I'm buying something for my mum. But I don't know which." He pointed at two brooches on the counter. Rose registered that the boy had dark, liquid eyes, just like Dirk Bogarde, that movie star that Margaret used to go on about, a similar Brylcreemed wave to his straw-colored hair. "I don't know anything about these things," he confessed. "But she's dark-haired, like you, with a similar complexion."

"You should try them on!" Julie said with enthusiasm, now beside them.

What? Rose almost scolded her on behalf of Mr. Bradshaw. She almost said, *I'm not the buying type. He isn't either. Can't you see?* It was exhausting, Rose thought, all that people couldn't see, right in front of their faces. "So sorry, I can't," she said, but nevertheless she lingered.

"I'll take this one," he said, and pointed with authority to a sterling brooch in the form of a sunburst, tiny red stones winking at its center. Looking at him up close, his thin face, the set of his jaw, she realized that he wasn't a boy at all.

"So lovely!" Julie said. "That was my choice too." She wrote out a ticket, copied the number into a ledger, then took the pin and wrapped it in a dark cloth with a purple ribbon—wrapping that looked more sumptuous than the jewelry itself. "What a good son. My first sale of the day and a lovely story at that! You would think this would make Mr. Bradshaw very happy. But he'll say something like: 'I don't know the point in making more money. It'll all go to Atlee's government men anyway.' Just you wait."

"All right," the boy said as he slipped the small package, the velvet now twice covered in butcher paper, into his pocket. "We will." He directed a shy smile at Rose. He had a long but friendly face, with a sharp nose, not unlike hers. His eyes were not dark brown as she had first thought, but a lovely striated green. "We will."

Wordlessly, she followed him outside. The air was warmer than she had thought. The rain had ceased. They passed an elegant but worn town house, its façade pocked with shrapnel. At the corner, they slowed. The sun hovered low in the pale afternoon sky. The light above the chemist's shop flickered.

"I don't know why I bought it," he said.

"You're a good son," Rose said. She was only repeating the words that Julie had said, but they seemed hollow leaving her mouth, nearly querulous. *Try to be nice*, she told herself. Why was it so hard to be nice? She imagined the room in which such a gift would be offered. She saw a tea trolley in a richly appointed drawing room, a platinum bowl filled with delphiniums.

"I'm not," he said, and he let out a low mangled laugh. "But she always wanted one. And now she's sick. She's dying."

"Oh," Rose said, less a word than an exhalation. The flickering chemist light caught a wave of his blond hair, and for a moment his curl turned silver. She saw a darkened spot of stubble along his jawline that he had missed shaving. He was skinny and slight, not more than a few inches taller than she. And whatever she had thought was so young about him before dissolved in the face of his proximity. "That's very kind of you," she said.

He thrust his hands in his pockets—his mackintosh was too big on him, its sleeves spoiled and loose with unraveling threads. "I don't feel kind. I'm Thomas."

For once she didn't hesitate. "Rose," she said, and her name seemed to glide out of her mouth.

Thomas smiled. "Do you want to walk, Rose?"

It felt too improbable to be real. "Yes," she breathed.

"IT'S RAINING AGAIN." EVA SIGHED. "I *cannot* believe it's raining again." She had grown fleshier in the years since they had studied together at university, and now her sighs were voluble, full like the rest of her. "When I first came here, I thought it was nonsense—it can't truly rain *all* the time—but no, it does. It's England, and it rains." She leaned against Rose's desk and admired her left hand, on which a tiny diamond caught light. "Edgar says New York isn't nearly as gloomy."

"Is that so?" Rose murmured. She knew far too much about Edgar, Eva's USAF officer, for someone she had never met. She had been typing up letters all morning, and now she was supposed to finish hand-copying the long list of suppliers to another list, but she had hardly made a dent. "I don't mind the rain. It's bracing, natural." This, despite the fact that she feared the rain would mar her blouse when she stepped outside for lunch. She was wearing her best one today, her navy silk, purchased six months ago when she was offered this position, a job she had learned about because of Eva, whose mother had a cousin who knew Mr. Marks. Everyone in the office was an immigrant, including Mr. Marks himself. (He liked to hire his own, he said.) "Perhaps it takes some getting used to. You've been here, what? Five years?"

"Just under," Eva said with a smile.

"I've lived here for more than ten years, nearly half my life. I'm practically English."

"You?" Eva looked amused.

"Yes, me. I'm more English than most English people." Rose prided herself on her degree in English literature and her diction scrubbed free of any German. She was grateful for her ration books, for the fact that there were rations to be had, and she liked watching *Kaleidoscope* and relished the smells emanating from the cafés along Haverstock Hill and taking turns in Belsize Park.

Eva laughed. "That's the problem. No one English tries so hard."

Rose cringed, and Eva's words reverberated, as much as she tried to swat them away. Did she try too hard?

Soon it was half past twelve, lunchtime. Mr. Marks was yelling again. His girl was out but Rose suspected he left his door open on purpose; he wanted the office to hear every word. "Do not tell me that we'll cross that bridge when we come to it. I am so tired of hearing that phrase. Let me buy the casings now!" He slammed the phone down. "*Schwachkopf.* Stupid bridge crossers."

Rose had finally finished the forms and was straightening her desk—she worked hard, she was no bridge crosser—when Eva appeared. "Come now, Claire and I are off to look at all we can't buy at Derry and Toms."

"I can't," Rose said. "I promised my sister-in-law I'd pick things up for Sunday supper."

"Oh, Rose. How will you ever meet a chap in a grocery queue?"

"She's eight months' pregnant. And I am interested in things well beyond chaps," Rose said as briskly as she could manage.

"Of course you are," Eva murmured, and freed a few of her abundant curls from under her wool collar. Rose watched her file out of the office and waited a few crucial minutes, telling herself not to rush. Then she took her coat and went outside.

Near the newsstand, Thomas's face lit up when he spotted Rose. "I've been waiting," he announced with mock seriousness, "four and a half minutes. Four and a half minutes is too long for Miss Rose Zimmer to appear again in my life."

"Hush," she said, laughing, looking around. It had been a little more than a month since they had first met. She still found it shocking that he rang when he said he would, that his interest in her seemed to grow instead of abating. "How was your interview?"

He took her elbow, guiding her past a phone box. She hurried to keep up with him. "You worried someone might think you're with me? Like that coworker of yours that just left?"

"Eva?" Rose looked down the street, trying to spot Eva's full figure, those dark curls that looked wet even when dry. "No."

"The infamous Eva! She turned at the newsstand. Now, why wouldn't you introduce me?"

"I don't know. We're not close."

"But she's a part of your life."

"In the broadest definition of the word. Come now, where are we dining and on what?" She tried to grab the paper parcel from him, but he held tight.

"I'm serious," he said. "I'm serious about you."

She nodded, her eyes averted. It made her anxious, being this serious with Thomas. She felt her face grow slack.

"You know, you tug on your left earlobe when you're nervous." And then, more gently: "Are you nervous? Do I make you nervous?"

Yes, she almost admitted. But her throat felt constricted, hot. "You don't know me," she said, although she knew it wasn't true. But the prospect that he did know her made her feel so vulnerable; where would she go when it fell apart?

Thomas's eyes were on her face—she could feel them. He didn't argue. He didn't seem frightened by what he saw. "Okay, then," he finally said, and his voice was even, as if she had simply suggested toast instead of biscuits for tea. "But perhaps I will get to."

The day was damp but not too cool, the type of overcast afternoon in which it felt that the sun simply needed a little encouragement to shine. They walked to the Embankment, crowded with other dayworkers from Westminster, but managed to find a bench for themselves. Thomas spread his mackintosh and they sat upon it underneath a low clay-colored sky and ate sandwiches that Thomas had made himself. The bread was tough but oozed mayonnaise, the pickles pleasantly sharp, the cheese tasting like a treat.

"Tell me something," Rose said. She was looking at all the boats and ferries crawling up river, an army of them, crowding the water the same oyster hue as the sky. "How is your mother?" A pair of gulls swooped low over a barge.

"She's all right."

"Has the doctor been by?"

He shook his head, and Rose wasn't sure if that meant the doctor hadn't, or if the news was too terrible to convey. He said airlessly: "She's feeling all right."

"I'm glad," she said. She took a bite of her sandwich, concentrated on chewing. She shouldn't have asked. But how could she not? Still, his reticence was something that she, of all people, should understand. When she told him how she'd gotten out of Austria, he nodded, asking, "And your parents?" She only shook her head.

"You didn't tell me about your interview," she said now.

He didn't answer, and for a moment she wondered if she had said something else to upset him, but he leaned down to pull up his trousers, revealing thick, crimson socks. "Do you like them?"

"Your socks? They're very red."

He nodded. "They match my tie, see?" And he pulled back his crumpled suit jacket for confirmation.

"So they do," she said. They were a lovely red, actually, a brilliant vermilion when she least expected it. They were thick and they were heavy, practical despite their rich hue. Her heart scudded and it took her a moment to realize why. They reminded her of *The Bellhop*.

Something welled up inside of her and she tried to swallow it down. It felt like an ambush, the recollection. She spoke: "Were you wearing those for the interview? It seems an awfully bold choice for a junior engineering position."

"Bold, yes; that was my thought." He rummaged in his suit pocket, pulled out his cigarette pack, and offered her one. She took it, and he lit it, cupping it protectively before lighting one for himself. "I thought it would make me stand apart from other candidates."

She took a drag. "And?"

"One of the partners asked me: 'Why are you wearing so much red? Is there a political statement to your choice of color?'"

"What did you say?"

"I said, 'Of course not.' If I had wanted to make such a statement, I would have sewn on a hammer and sickle."

"Thomas! Goodness. You didn't say that, did you?"

"No," he said, leaning forward on the bench, inhaling deeply. "I'm terrible at sewing. But I could have drawn one. Not all engineers are decent draftsman, but I am. Do you know that about me?"

She gave him a little smile, but shook her head nevertheless. "This is not a joke," she said, and handed her cigarette back to him. He stubbed it out on the bench leg. "You know these things aren't jokes. Of course they wondered. Why would you give them any doubt?"

"I didn't give them any doubt. They made their doubt. Bloody Tories. All anyone cares about is the Eton-Harrow match and they act as if a revolution is going on."

"Oh, come now." She brushed the few crumbs off her lap. An old man in a great overcoat was sleeping one bench over, his broad, ravaged face tipped up to the sky. Whatever little warmth or sun was on offer, Rose thought, he was determined to catch it.

"It's five years after the war and it feels like nothing has changed. Everything is still so difficult." Thomas flicked his cigarette filter to the ground.

"I know." All Rose wanted to do was teach, and where was she? Stuck as a secretary for Mr. Marks. But still, she wouldn't complain. "It's getting better," she said.

"We won the war." He let out a sharp laugh. "You would have no idea from the looks of it that we *won*. And now with my mum . . . But it's not just her. I want to leave. I could. An old schoolmate of mine just got a job at Grumman in New York. And Lockheed out in California is hiring loads of engineers too."

"America? You want to go to America?" It was less a question than an echo. She was here, in London, with Thomas. Thomas was talking about leaving. She repeated these basic facts to herself in her head, as if recitation would lead to understanding.

"I don't know," he said, and he squeezed her hand. His fingers were warm, oily from the mayonnaise. "I really don't. But I do want to know this: Would you ever come with me?"

"Come with you?" she repeated. *But I barely know you,* she thought. And yet that was not true. She well knew what was happening. It rattled her, this certainty, this feeling that could be only called happiness. She didn't deserve it. She looked back at the sleeping old man on the neighboring bench, as if he might offer her some hard-won wisdom. But Thomas was trying to catch her eye, Thomas, with his kind expectant face, a face that was equal parts enthusiasm and determination. She liked that face. She trusted it. Him. And she was saying, softly, "Maybe."

He kissed her. "A maybe is nearly a yes."

She laughed. "Maybe," she said again. Together they headed back to Westminster, walking side by side, fingers so lightly entwined that Rose was left not knowing where her hand ended and Thomas's began. She couldn't remember what they talked about, but she would always remember the pulse of happiness she felt, her fingertips abuzz as they brushed against his in the afternoon's mercurial light.

Back at Mr. Marks's office, she spent the afternoon in a trance at her desk, copying more numbers onto more lists, thinking about that *maybe*. Not quite believing that she had meant it, knowing that in fact she had.

Mr. Marks left in a huff around three. Soon afterward, Rose turned to Eva and said, "I'm not feeling well. I think I need to leave."

"Oh, you poor thing. Is it your stomach? Edgar had a touch of upset earlier in the week. Go home and I'll cover for you."

Rose complied. And she felt as if she were still complying, still following someone else's explicit instructions as she went down into the Tube station, got on the train, and held on to the strap and swayed.

She managed to exit at Piccadilly, make her way to Old Bond Street. The pharmacist's sign pulsated like a beacon. Stepping through the antique shop's peeling doorway, she felt soaked with its familiarity, a distinctive relief.

"Hello, you!" said Julie, for of course she was there. "It's not even the weekend!"

"I want to tell you about the picture I'm looking for," Rose said. Julie's eyes widened as Rose spoke of the Bellhop's crimson uniform, tarnished gold buttons, the declarative shape of his thin hands planted firmly on his hips. "It isn't a pretty picture," she added. She tried to describe the thick strokes of paint—the swirls of red and gold and blue, so many colors! She knew she was talking too quickly. She looked down at the glassed-in jewelry counter, the same counter where Thomas had been standing—incredibly, a stranger to her, just a month ago.

As she spoke, as *The Bellhop* took shape by her words, she realized that her fear of talking about the painting had been wrong. She had been afraid that describing it, coming clean, would remind her of its painful absence, dilute her memories. But instead it burnished them. She saw the painting in her parents' room in the flat on Liechtensteinstrasse, its heavy gold frame; she saw her mother playing Chopin on the piano while her father kept trying to persuade her that perhaps they should go somewhere besides Bad Ischl this summer, Gerhard arguing that he was absolutely old enough to go to the UFA by himself for a matinee. Bette rang the bell for dinner, and Rose saw her mother pass by *The Bellhop*, swiping a speck of dust off the frame with her pinkie. All this did not just exist in the hazy firmament of Rose's memory. It had been real. It was.

"It sounds just like a picture Mr. Bradshaw was telling me about," Julie said. "I swear, a hotel worker or a waiter of some kind. He most definitely said expressionistic. *And* valuable. It's not here yet, but he said he'd bring it in tomorrow." As her own words sank in, Julie's tone grew elated. "It does sound like that painting; I knew it! It does!"

Rose looked into the girl's eyes. Could it be? It seemed impossible that *The Bellhop* would be here, in a small shop that she had chosen for reasons she did not understand. And yet. Maybe.

Rose thought of her lunch with Thomas by the river: she saw movement; she felt possibility. She wanted Julie to be right. Every fiber in her body leaped at the possibility. But she also wanted to remain here: no one telling her yes, no one telling her no.

THE FOLLOWING AFTERNOON, SHE RETURNED to the shop. Julie ushered her into the back. A skinny stooped gentleman in an ill-fitting suit stood waiting beside a small drafting table, canvas in hand.

"Mr. Bradshaw, this is Miss Rose Zimmer."

He looked nothing like the debonair antiques dealer she had imagined. She tried not to be disappointed, told herself that it had no bearing on the possibility of *The Bellhop*'s presence. "It's very nice to meet you," she said with renewed vigor. "I adore your shop."

"Why, thank you," he said. "I hear that you're quite excited about a certain portrait that I have here."

"That's right," Rose said as he began to unroll it, her stomach taking root in her throat.

The canvas was only half-visible when she knew. It was thickly painted, like *The Bellhop*, but the coat that the man in this portrait wore was of a darker red, wine-colored. There were no buttons in sight. The background shimmered, a swirl of oceanic blues and greens. The man's face was painstakingly detailed, his pink lips even held the the beginnings of a remote smile.

"Thank you," she managed to say. "But that's not my painting."

"Oh," Julie said, her face falling. "I'm so sorry."

"I'm sorry," Rose said, ludicrously.

"You're certain?" Mr. Bradshaw said.

"Very certain," Rose said. "Quite." She felt unsteady. She wanted to weep. "So sorry," she said as she fled the shop. She would never find *The Bellhop*. It was nowhere to be found.

She began walking, she had no idea where, and her despondency curdled into anger. This was her fault. Why had she pinned her hopes on finding it? Why did she ever think that recovering that stupid, ugly painting would make a difference? She hated that her mother had loved it. She hated that it ever mattered. She passed a deep hole of rubble sandwiched between two standing houses, a burst water pipe still trickling. Past a "Get Your Own Back" war savings banner plastered against a wall, faintly visible in the meager light. She kept moving. Darkness descended. The night was damp.

There were few streetlamps. A lorry rattled past. She thought of that night five years ago, when she had stood at the railing of the Waterloo Bridge, unable to envision a future. Five years had gone by and what had changed? She neared Bethnal Green and she felt so despondent, so unbelievably useless. It was too late for her to be out here at night by herself. She was nowhere where proper girls went by themselves. But she wasn't proper—she had done everything wrong. If she truly had been good, she wouldn't have gotten on that train. She would have done more to get her parents out. They would be here today. It felt like an articulation of everything she had long feared and yet tried to avoid. She bore responsibility. Why did she pretend otherwise?

HARRY WAS A DICTATOR: RUTHLESS, vicious, unrepentant, two years old. Rose was supposed to be keeping an eye on him and his baby brother, in the room that her nephews shared. The boys' nanny was ill. The cook had her day off. Isobel was in the kitchen. Harry kept tossing items into the playpen, dangerously close to his little brother's head—a comb, a rattle, a tin cup. Rose was doing nothing to stop him.

She should, of course. But she didn't have the energy. Or, in truth, the volition. Rose was in a foul mood. She thought: *Harry is a terror but he is a terror that Peter must live with. If I step in then Peter won't fend for himself. If I interfere, how will Peter ever learn?*

Rose had offered to handle supper, but Isobel refused. "I would so much rather be in front of a stove than mind those two horrors," she said with a laugh, though they both knew she wasn't entirely joking.

"Everything all right in there?" Isobel called now.

"Oh yes, fine." Rose took a book of Harry's from atop the bureau and was thumbing through it, a story about a plucky orphan who grew up in his village's parsonage. She looked up from the pages to see baby Peter slowly but determinedly pulling himself up by grabbing the bars of the crib. He weaved, unbalanced, but then—triumphantly—he stood on his own, grinning wildly.

Rose watched Harry take this success in, assessing Peter's presence, his achievement. Harry affixed his gaze on his brother, leaned over the rail of the crib, and slapped his head so hard Peter fell back down with a thump.

"Harry!" Rose yanked her older nephew aside. She scooped Peter up. He didn't seem truly hurt, but he was wailing and blinking furiously. She wheeled around to Harry. "What did you go and do that for?"

Harry stared at her, considering. "I don't know," he said, and he too burst into tears.

Isobel appeared in the doorway. "Harry! What happened?"

"Peter pulled himself up and Harry couldn't stand to see him succeed," Rose explained. "He hit him."

"Has the devil gotten into you?" Isobel slapped Harry's bottom, pushed him on his bed. "Someone needs to knock some sense into *you*! Wait until your father hears this. You stay here. Understand?"

Harry nodded as his face crumpled up, crying.

"Lord help me if this one is a boy too," Isobel said as she rose from the bed.

Rose, still clutching her whimpering nephew, trailed Isobel down the hall. Peter was heavier than he looked, his breath fast and shallow, his rosebud lips warm against her chest. Rose readjusted him in her arms and steadied a hand against the wall covered in a flocked print of tiny gray-green flower buds. Rose had admired the new wallpaper, but today it conspired to make her feel claustrophobic, nothing she desired. In the kitchen she went, with Peter straining in her arms. "I think he wants you."

"He always wants me," Isobel said, not turning around, one hand on her lower back. (She still had a month left to go with her pregnancy; she was already so big. How on earth would her body get bigger?) She handed Rose a bottle from the counter. "And he has to get used to not having me."

Rose nodded, lowered herself into the cane-backed chair, balancing baby, bottle, and herself. She tipped the bottle into his mouth and he sucked at it vigorously.

"Thank you," Isobel said, and the force of her voice couldn't cover up its underlying unsteadiness. Rose looked at her sister-in-law, still beautiful even in her swollen state, her face flushed, her forehead shiny. "Thank you for coming out all this way today to help me," Isobel said. "Truly."

"Of course." Rose had been glad to get Isobel's phone call. Her exhaustion was only trumped by her desire not to be alone.

"I am in no shape for this at all." Isobel's voice cracked a little.

"It's all right," Rose said, wanting to comfort her, uncertain how. Isobel was so rarely rattled. "It's going to be all right. Look, he's asleep." Peter's eyes were closed and he was emitting shallow moaning sounds. She shifted, surprised that he could remain asleep in her arms. She liked his slightly sour smell, the breathy weightiness of him.

"For five minutes, maybe," Isobel said. "And then? I can barely manage to make it to the toilet."

"It'll be all right," Rose repeated again. And it had to be. Three young children did seem an awful lot, but if Isobel couldn't get through motherhood—capable Isobel, who made everything seem stylish and effortlessly smooth—then what chance did anyone ever have? Rose pressed Isobel's damp hand to her own. "I know it will."

Isobel squeezed back. "Thank you. I'm glad one of us is convinced," she said. She heaved herself out of the chair. "How is that new beau of yours? You're bringing him to supper next week?"

"I was planning on it," Rose said, and but today she wasn't sure. She was so tired, and being tired made her feel pessimistic. What was wrong with Thomas? Something had to be wrong with him if he were so unerringly certain about her. "Perhaps we should put it off, until after the baby is born; maybe that would be better."

"No, no," Isobel said. "We cannot wait for that. Who knows what sort of state I'll be in then? And I refuse to wait that long to meet him." She opened the refrigerator. "I still can't get over that we have eggs again. Do you realize it was a decade ago that we could last buy them?" Her voice had regained its brighter tones. "Now, if we could just get sugar—oh, and butter. How I dream of butter. That and sleep are the things of my dreams these days. It's maddening, how boring I've become." She shook her head.

"Please, Isobel, you're one of the least boring people I know," Rose said. "Who else among your friends has talked Russian translations with Constance Garnett?"

Isobel smiled sadly. "I wish I could be reading them and chatting with her now. Three under the age of three. Damn your brother."

As if on cue, Rose heard the door whine open. "Hello," called Gerhard from the hall. He came in, set the string bag on the table, kissed the top of his wife's head. "Did you get the milk?" she asked.

"'Course I did. You asked me to." He cocked an eyebrow at his sister with a half grin, and Rose saw him as he had been when they were kids, her fearless brother who would pull their grandfather's swords from the wall and swoop them through the air, shouting, *This is for the Kaiser!*

Peter had awoken, whimpering. "There, there," Rose whispered, trying to push the nipple back into his mouth. "You want more?" But he batted the bottle away. "Your son is crying for you," she said, holding Peter toward Gerhard.

"Ah, not for me, never for me." But he picked him up and swung him around. "Oh, hello, little man. You're a sweet one, aren't you?" Peter crowed with delight.

"I spoke to Jenny earlier today," Isobel said, easing herself back into the chair. "She and William really are going. This summer."

"Are they, now?" Gerhard said, and he handed Peter to his wife. William was Isobel's eldest brother. Rose knew that Gerhard had asked him to invest in the business early on and William had refused.

They had remained amiably chilly ever since. Gerhard opened up a pack of cigarettes, drew one out, and tapped it against the table.

Isobel brushed her lips across Peter's head. "They've decided upon Toronto. Everyone is leaving, it seems."

"Not everyone," Rose said. Just last week, Margaret had written her that her husband Teddy's brother was moving to Calgary and perhaps they too would follow suit. Thomas had mentioned America, but there were engineering positions in Canada too. Did it matter? The New World was all the same to her: shiny, optimistic. Not England.

Gerhard took his time lighting the cigarette, inhaling with evident pleasure. "We're not. We're doing very well. The business is doing well. Why would we go?"

"We'll be the only ones left."

"That's not true."

"It *might* be true," she said, and took his cigarette from him.

"Why must you be so negative about everything?"

She sucked in smoke, drew her arm over her belly. "I don't know, Gerhard. Why do you think?"

"Perhaps I should go check on Harry," Rose said. "He's awfully quiet."

"I'll come with you," Gerhard said. In the hall, he whispered: "You mustn't mind her."

"I don't," Rose said. "*I* don't mind her at all."

Gerhard exhaled, opening the door to the boys' room. It was strangely silent inside. Harry was . . . where? Then Rose spied him, lying on the rag rug facedown—one leg to his chest, the other splayed out akimbo, arms above, framing his head. Nothing about the position looked comfortable, but he was steadfastly asleep. "He looks so peaceful," she said.

"Probably cried himself to sleep," Gerhard said matter-of-factly. He knelt down and scooped the boy up. Rose was surprised when he didn't wake up, but Gerhard seemed to take it for granted. He sat down next to his son's balled-up sleeping form, patted the plaid coverlet beside him. "How's your new Englishman—is he for God and love and country?"

"Thomas?" she asked, though of course that was who he meant. "He wants to leave too."

"Screw the whole lot of them."

"Indeed." Here, in the moment with her brother, her ally no matter how great their differences, she meant it. "I'm not leaving England."

"Now, that's good to hear." Gerhard leaned back on his elbows against Harry's bedspread. He looked like a giant, Rose thought, a blond English giant. "But you're not really finished with him, are you? I hear you're bringing him to supper next week. I want to meet this man who has captured my sister's heart."

"I don't know," she said. She was so worn out. "Captured my heart is not exactly the way I'd put it."

"I didn't ask how *you* would put it," Gerhard said, and gave her an appraising look. "You're going to marry him. I know it."

"How can you say that?" His certainty rankled her. "You haven't met him. You don't know if you like him, or if he's good for me."

"But you like him," Gerhard said, unfazed. His hand was on Harry's small back. She watched it rise and fall with every breath. They both did.

His calm conviction infuriated her. She had vowed not to say anything to Gerhard, but now the words tumbled out: "I thought I had found Mutti's picture. I thought I had, but I didn't."

"What? What picture?"

"*The Bellhop*, Mutti's *Bellhop*," she said softly.

Gerhard's confusion turned to irritation. She could see it, plain on his broad face. "Why in heaven would you think it was here in England, of all places?"

"It has to be somewhere."

"No, it doesn't. Good Lord, *mausi*, you've been searching for it?"

She didn't answer, and he stood. The mattress shifted with the lessening of weight, and Rose reached out, hand on the bed, steadying herself.

"Why not?" she said, looking down at her chapped hands, nothing like the slender long-fingered hands of her mother. "What's wrong in thinking that we might find something?"

"It's *over*," he said roughly, with sudden force. "That life, it's gone."

She shook her head. She was staring at the bureau, at the leather-bound book of Harry's she'd been reading before, written in a language that she worked so hard to claim as her own, when she repeated: "*Gone?* They didn't vanish. They were stolen. They could be anywhere—houses, basements, museums, collecting points. But they didn't *disappear*."

Gerhard emitted a strange, horrible laugh. "Fine. But they're gone."

Rose shook her head, trying to rid herself of his words. How could he? Didn't he realize how ugly this sounded, what a betrayal it was?

All she wanted was proof. All she knew was this: February 1942, their parents had been sent to Theresienstadt. In January 1945, most of the camp's prisoners were sent east. In May 1945, when the camp was liberated by Russian troops, their parents were not among the survivors. Had they died in the chaos of the brutal winter of '45? Were they shot on the march east? Did they stumble into a ditch somewhere? Were they together at the end? All she wanted was proof of their deaths. She who didn't pray prayed for corroboration.

"Things do not disappear. People don't disappear." She was shocked to hear that she sounded—not *un*calm. She wanted to hit her brother, do him true bodily harm. He had a body; how dare he not recognize what a gift that was. How dare he not feel, as she did, that their parents' paths had been *their* paths. There was no godly reason they had survived and their parents hadn't. Didn't he feel, as she did, like a ghost? "They were killed. Murdered," she said softly. "They did not disappear."

Gerhard looked at her with a gentleness she was startled to recognize as pity. "I know that. You think I don't know that? But it's over. For your sake—and mine—it's enough, Rose. Enough."

"You are wrong, so very wrong," she said, and she was crying openly now. All she could think was, *I need to leave right now.* Because the truth of what he was saying would destroy her. She thought this, and she realized: it already had.

11

LOS ANGELES, 2006

WHY COULDN'T SHE STOP THINKING about it? Why couldn't she let go? Lizzie awoke alone and headachy in Max's lovely, low, king-sized bed. Light was bleeding in along the edges of the heavy curtains; the day had long begun. She was feeling the detritus of last night, the booze and so much food and all that was said. She pulled on the jeans she'd worn yesterday and the first T-shirt she could find, made her way into the kitchen. It took her a moment to realize that Max was seated at the table, already dressed and groomed.

"You came in late last night," Max said.

"Not that late. I was back by ten. You must have fallen asleep early."

He got a mug and went to the carafe to pour, the coffee already made.

"I can do it," Lizzie said. Even she heard the bristle in her voice.

"Sure thing." He made a show of backing off. "If you want."

"Don't," she said, shaking her head. She was too tired.

"Lizzie, I'm sorry."

She focused on her tasks: milk, sugar, stirring. "I really cannot talk about this now."

"Okay," he said. "But we need to, at some point. I mean, I want to."

She glanced at the digital display on the stove. "I need to get going, actually."

"Where?"

She was still so angry at him, she couldn't believe how angry. "Are you surprised that I have places to go?"

"No, not at all. Come on."

She blew into her mug, cooling it down, trying to calm herself down. She took a swallow. "I'm sorry. I'm going to synagogue," she said, though it had only occurred to her in the last few moments to do so.

"You are? Why?"

"I went last week," she said, aware she wasn't answering his question.

"You didn't tell me."

She shrugged. "I went to say kaddish."

"Oh," Max said, and that tiny word seemed to hang in the room, heavying the air. "That's good," he added.

"It made me feel better," Lizzie said, although *better* wasn't quite the right word for it. She thought of that worn bare room, the dankness, the sound of the voices chanting. She remembered the feeling of standing for the prayer. It seemed impossible to rise to her feet, but when she did and saw the few others around the congregation standing too, it felt like a bodily acknowledgment of all that she wanted to forget. Her father was gone. There was no pretending. But she was here. She was his child, and she would endure.

"Well, then you should go again." Max had waited awhile before responding, but he said it firmly. "I want you to know something, though: I've been thinking about what you said yesterday, and I'm sorry."

"Max—" She didn't want to hear explanations, not today.

"No, let me finish." He was wiping off the counter, though to her it looked perfectly clean. "You were right. I care about you so much. I want to try this."

"Wait," Lizzie said. "What?" Had she heard him right? Were they talking about the same thing? "You do?"

"I do." A small smile tugged at the edges of his beautiful mouth and his eyes crinkled. He nodded at her with intent, and she felt a rush of happiness. "Truly," he said. "I was being foolish, but I am not a fool." His voice was scratchy, low near her ear.

"Is that right," she said, and now his lips were grazing her neck and she was laughing a little, amazed. She did not care that he was her father's best friend, she did not care about the age difference. Why did she ever try to deny her feelings? For once she did not doubt herself. She only wanted to be here, with him.

He took her by the hand, led her toward the bedroom. "I can't," she said.

"Sure you can," he said, and he gave her that slow smile that would be the end of her, and soon her synagogue plan was all but forgotten.

AFTERWARD, SHE SAID TO HIM: "Can I ask you a question: Do you still have records from your parents' gallery?"

"Some," he said. "Why?"

"I just wondered; I've been thinking about how *The Bellhop* got here, from Europe. Do you have any idea who your parents bought it from?" Lizzie was out of bed, retrieving her scattered clothes as she spoke. She had wanted to ask Max this for a while, but after last night—well, she wanted to think of something other than what Bob had said.

"No," he said. "Not really. But there's a decent chance they bought it in New York. They purchased a lot of artwork there, in the early years of the gallery, the fifties and sixties, and I do know that they held on to the Soutine for quite a long time."

"Why?"

"They did that sometimes. With lots of pieces," Max said, maddeningly vague.

"You know, I really would love to know who they bought it from," she asked again. She didn't want to be a nudge, but who could she ask, if not him? She pulled her shirt over her head. "Where are these records?"

"I have a few boxes in the garage. But don't hold your breath. They weren't so great on the record-keeping front, especially early on. But I could look."

"Would you, please?" Maybe the answer was right here, in Max's house. Why had she waited so long to ask him? She leaned over, gave him a deep kiss at the edge of the bed.

"You realize that even if we do have a record, it'll only be a name," he said softly into her hair. "That's all it's going to tell you."

"That'll be enough."

"Will it?"

"Yes," she said guardedly. "What do you mean?"

"I just mean—the painting was stolen twenty years ago." He gave a twist of an uneasy smile. "I wish you could put it behind you."

Did he not think that she wanted to? What did he know about that night? She stood, arms across her chest. "I have," she said. "I mostly have. Why would you say that to me?"

"I don't know. I shouldn't have," he said softly. "I know how much you loved the painting. Come here." He pulled her into an embrace. "Forgive me."

She let him, but reluctantly, her arms at her sides. Did he really think there was something wrong with the fact that she couldn't let go? "I'm not the only one with questions," she said, pulling back.

"Yes?" He said it lightly enough, but he tightened his lips and for a moment he looked like no one she knew.

"Last night, I was having dinner with Rose and a friend of hers, and—" She stopped. What was she trying to protect him from? It felt wrong to go on, disloyal to even give rise to the suspicions, but stranger not to. "When the paintings were stolen," she continued, "do you know if the police ever questioned my father?"

"Of course. Many times," he said evenly enough. "Most of the information they had came from him."

"Was ever he considered a suspect?"

"A suspect?" Max said, scooping up his keys, his phone, his money clip from his bureau—the armaments he needed for the day. "A person of interest, sure. He was at first. It's the obvious choice. But that doesn't mean it's the right one. They spoke to him at length, and then they moved on."

"To what?"

He sighed. "I don't know, exactly. They spoke to dozens of people. There were so many possibilities. There still are. Your father, bless him, was not exactly modest about his possessions. He was proud of the art he owned; he told lots of people. And so many people came through your house; think about it. Just those dinner parties alone: guests and friends of guests and the caterer and the waiters and bartenders. All those people in and out. Someone could have been casing it, saw the party, jumped on the opportunity. To say nothing about all those babysitters and drivers you guys had to take you girls around; or more probably, the boyfriend of one of those people, or, most likely, an art thief you did not know at all."

Max was right; there were so many people in Joseph's orbit, any one of them could have done it. But that familiar feeling of unease slid over her. There must have been something she could have done.

"You know what I've learned as a defense attorney?" Max was still talking. "Guilty clients always have an alternative story, but the innocent ones? They never do. They're hard to believe because they don't know who did it. You know why? Because *they didn't do it*. How would they know what happened? An absence of evidence doesn't point anywhere. You know that."

"I know," she allowed, and the sickly feeling was receding, she already felt on more solid ground. "I know; it was just this friend of Rose's, he said it so easily, tossed it out as if it were obvious—"

Max shrugged. "Of course. Twenty years after the fact. Colonel Mustard in the library. What was Rose's reaction?"

Lizzie allowed herself a small smile. "She nearly ripped his head off."

"Ah," Max said. "A woman after my own heart."

WHEN MAX LEFT, LIZZIE NOSED around online. She looked up an old law school classmate, Jonathan Bookman, who she knew had moved to L.A. She saw that his firm had a small appellate department. She was thinking of writing him, to see if he wanted to meet for coffee, when her phone buzzed.

"It's a miracle that I can even call you," Rose said. "My phone has been tied up all morning. Bob: calling and calling."

Bob. His name alone put Lizzie on edge. "What did he say?"

"I don't know," Rose said. "I haven't been inclined to pick up the phone and speak with him."

"You should, you know," Lizzie said, breathing a little more easily.

"In due time. First, I wanted to apologize to you."

"You don't need to." It wasn't Rose's fault, but still, it was reassuring to hear.

"Well, he was my guest. It was my fault that he was there. What he said was unconscionable and presumptuous, not to mention awful. He cannot blithely throw out theories like that." Rose's gravelly voice slowed. "I am sorry. It must have been very painful for you. But I am also calling to ask you a favor," she added after a beat.

ROSE BARELY SAID HELLO TO Lizzie after she opened the door, and climbed on the stepstool in the hall. She stretched to adjust a thick strip of blue painters' tape.

"What are you doing? You're making me nervous," Lizzie said. "Why did you ask me here if you're just doing it yourself?"

"I'm putting up the tape; you're doing the hard work of hanging the masks. I've never fallen yet."

"That," Lizzie said, "is not particularly reassuring."

Soon enough Lizzie was the one climbing up, and before long her father's masks were affixed to the wall. They looked good: the smaller one was a half bird, half reptile made out of a chalky-white wood. The larger one was also carved from wood, but a richer, darker color, and had a more stylized look, with an elongated nose and sidelocks hanging down (*peyot*, Joseph called them) where ears should be. Lizzie had paid little attention to the masks when they had been at her father's house, and was dismissive of them when she had (*Of course the only pieces of non-Western art he has are African masks*, she could remember telling Claudia, *such a cliché*), but now she was struck by their delicate artistry.

Soon Rose made strong coffee that she topped off with cream. She served it in finely etched, pale green porcelain teacups that seemed at odds with the more utilitarian surroundings of her small living room. "Thomas bought them for us," Rose said, even though Lizzie hadn't asked. "They reminded him of home."

"They're beautiful." And they weren't the only beautiful things Lizzie noticed today. Above the club chair where Rose sat hung a framed stretch of silky blue-and-purple material. It featured a lovely pattern of birds, some perched on branches, others swooping through the air, wings outstretched.

"Not that he had china like this at home," Rose was saying. "He didn't come from money."

"Where was Thomas from?"

"Brighton," Rose said. "Do you know it? A seaside town, famous for its pier and promenade. His father worked for years maintaining some of the rides on the palace pier. He could be difficult. By the time I met him, his wife—Thomas's mother—had passed away. He wasn't particularly happy that Thomas was dating a Jewish girl. I remember he was trying to buy something on the black market, a television maybe, and he couldn't get it. He blamed the Jews, of course. Everyone used to say that the Jews—Spivs, they called them—controlled the market. 'You people love your money, don't you?' I remember him telling me the first time we met."

"Wow," Lizzie said. "A real charmer."

"It wasn't all that unusual then, his dislike of Jews. The fact that people get nostalgic for the time after the war amazes me. I love England, but it was a tough time, all around."

"I would have just thought, after the war—" Lizzie didn't finish. How could people blame Jews then, after everything they had been through? It wasn't so long ago, and yet it felt light-years away from the world that she had grown up in. On the Westside, even her non-Jewish friends knew about seders, held forth on their favorite bagels and Woody Allen films. Whatever anti-Semitism there was (and she wasn't naive enough to think there wasn't any), was rarely spoken out loud, at least not directly to her. "So what happened when you got married?" she asked.

"What do you mean?" Rose asked, frowning.

"I just meant—in terms of holidays, that sort of thing," Lizzie said, already wishing she hadn't. "Did you celebrate Jewish stuff, or . . . ?"

"I barely celebrated Jewish holidays with my family in Vienna. Marrying Thomas, a lapsed Anglican, didn't change that. And you?"

"Me?"

"What are your religious beliefs?" There was decided arch in Rose's tone.

"Oh. Well. We were major-holiday Jews: You know, Rosh Hashanah, Yom Kippur, Passover. My father loved the seders. That was about it," Lizzie said. She thought of the synagogue on the Venice boardwalk, the comfort she found there, but she couldn't imagine telling Rose. How could she explain the consolation she felt? *A prayer did that for you?* she could imagine Rose saying.

"Have you gone through his things?" Rose was now asking. "That's one of the hardest parts."

"It was hard. I couldn't—my sister did most of it."

"And he had a lot of stuff," Rose looked at her and there was sympathy in her gaze.

Lizzie took a long pull of her coffee, trying to steady herself. "Yes; we're lucky, though. We have so many great things. He left me a Julius Shulman photograph—do you know his stuff?"

"Shulman! Of course. One of his nieces was a student of mine, years ago. Is it the photograph of the Case Study house?"

Lizzie shook her head. She knew the Case Study house, of course: Shulman's most famous photograph, a nighttime shot of two well-dressed women coolly chatting inside a brightly lit modern house, cantilevered over the dark spread of Los Angeles below. Up until several years ago, you could still buy prints of it, but Joseph hadn't been interested. *Why would I want something that everyone else has?* Lizzie could remember him saying. "No, it's of downtown, the old Department of Water and Power building." Less known but no less gorgeous: a haunting black-and-white photograph of a reflecting pool beside the office building, the sharp lines of downtown reflected in the water, the sky a moody knitted collection of clouds. It reminded Lizzie not of the L.A. that she grew up in, but something more classical, distant. "He bought it years ago, from Shulman himself."

"Really?"

"Yeah." Lizzie smiled, drained her cup. "It's a classic Joseph story. Back in the nineties, he found out from his friend Judy, the woman who owned the gallery where we held the memorial actually, that Shulman liked visitors. And that he would sell prints to anyone who asked. It was Judy's assistant who had told him, a gorgeous young arts student—"

"Oh no, I can see where this is going," Rose said with a touch of a groan.

"Maybe," Lizzie said. "Maybe not. Anyway, this young art student had been to Shulman's house in Laurel Canyon. She said that Shulman liked visitors of all kinds, particularly women, and particularly those who came bearing single-malt scotch. So my dad got the address and showed up at his house, and the old man opened the door, and my dad laid it on thick: 'You're a brilliant photographer,' he said. He gave him the scotch, and Shulman sniffed and said, 'No, it's tequila that I like.' And my dad said, 'You want me to run out and get some? Because I will.' And Shulman waved him off and invited him in and my dad kept praising him, telling him how much he loved his pictures of Neutra's work. 'That guy was a nut-job,' Shulman said. 'But he could build a building.' Shulman must have been charmed because he pulled out a bottle of tequila and the two drank. Shulman had been born in Brooklyn, like my dad, and they talked about that, and the store that my grandparents had owned. It turned out that after Shulman moved to L.A., when he was a boy, his parents ran a general store too, in Boyle Heights, and Shulman used to sell pickles out of barrels to immigrants from Japan and Mexico."

"So at some point, during all this carousing, your father bought the print from Shulman."

"I wouldn't call it *carousing*, but yes, I think it was the second time he went by, my dad said to him, 'You know, Julius, how much I respect you as an artist.' And Shulman said: 'Come now, don't bullshit a bullshitter. Just ask.' So my father did. He asked to buy a print. 'I've got loads lying around here,' Shulman said. 'Take one.' And he did."

"Wait, Joseph didn't pay for the print?"

"No, no," Lizzie reassured her. "Of course he paid for it."

"How much?"

"I'm not sure, exactly," Lizzie said, although that wasn't true. She was growing uncomfortable. The story she had told many times before, her father drinking and charming a famous photographer, seemed to be shifting under Rose's attention.

"Come now. How much?"

"I think it was two hundred for the print."

"It was probably worth ten times that even at the time, if not twenty, at least. He ripped him off. He took advantage of a lonely old man."

Lizzie reddened. She had doubled the amount. "Shulman knew what he was doing. He was famous, even then. He was giving them out, left and right. He *liked* my father," she protested. "Plenty of people visited him and did the same thing."

"Really? That's your excuse?" Rose let out a snort. "Other people behaved poorly? Your father had ulterior motives. It wasn't an original sin, but let's at least acknowledge that."

"I'm only saying," Lizzie said, and stopped. What *was* she saying? She could see what Rose meant, but she also knew that Joseph genuinely liked Shulman, he enjoyed talking to him. It wasn't so simple. "The Getty acquired Shulman's collection before he died. It's worth millions. He did quite well for himself," she said.

"That's not the point and you know it," Rose said, rising. "I need more coffee."

Lizzie got up too. But Rose picked up her cup and commanded: "Stay: I've got it."

If her father were here, he would explain himself, Lizzie thought as she regarded the framed wall-hanging of the birds above the couch. Looking closer, she saw that it was silk, the edges finely stitched, even the birds' feathers painstakingly detailed, elegant. There was discoloration in the lower right corner; it looked like it had been used.

Rose came back, handed Lizzie her cup.

"This is beautiful," Lizzie said to Rose, nodding at the frame.

"It was my mother's," Rose said. "Her favorite scarf."

"Oh," Lizzie said, and she felt an urge to touch Rose's hand, but she held back. "It's beautiful," she repeated. "I'm so glad you have something of hers."

"She gave it to me the night I left. It's one of the only things of hers that I do have."

"Oh," Lizzie said again. It was unbearable, what Rose had gone through, and the pain never stopped, did it? Lizzie thought of all her father's things that she had, her mother's too. Even incidental objects—maybe especially those, like her mother's copy of *Valley of the Dolls* that Lizzie had always wondered if Lynn had kept as a joke—comforted Lizzie through the years. "I wish you had more," she said softly.

"It's gone," Rose said crisply, and Lizzie knew Rose well enough now to know that the sharpness in her tone was only a small part of the story.

"I know you might not want to hear this," Lizzie decided to begin. "But the other day, I realized that I had a connection to a lawyer who is an expert in art restitution."

"Okay."

"Michael Ciparelli. He used to work with my boss, who says he's a good guy and an excellent attorney. I think it's worth talking to him."

"I don't think so."

"Just hear me out. He's hugely connected and has a wealth of expertise in this area. He's been doing this for decades."

"Lizzie, it's not for me," Rose said, and moved to the edge of her chair, sitting taut and straight. "You have to stop trying to convince me."

"But why?" Lizzie asked. She couldn't shake the belief that she could make things better for Rose. "I know that it's not my place, it's your decision, but I feel like there are things that can be done—"

"You're right, it's not your place," Rose snapped. "You don't understand. This didn't happen to you. I don't know how to make you realize that. As sorry as you are, as horrified as you may be, *this did not happen to you*. So, please, stop acting as if it did."

"I know it didn't," Lizzie said quietly. Did Rose really think that she presumed it had? "I never meant to suggest that it did."

But Rose was shaking her head. "I'm friends with a man, a former German professor. A few years ago, his granddaughter took a school trip to the Museum of Tolerance. Like all the students, his granddaughter was given identification when she walked in. The ID was circa World War II, and it featured a child. The girl on her paper happened to have the same last name," she said. "She walked through the interactive exhibits—full of video and buttons you can press. At the end, she and her classmates found out the fate of the children on the papers they carried. My friend's granddaughter learned that the girl on hers had died at Auschwitz. She went home with the paper, showed it to her parents. Her father told his father. 'That was my sister,' my friend said."

"That is awful," Lizzie said. "That is so awful."

"Do you understand? Rose said. "This might be a game to you, but it's not for me. Losing the Soutine was the least of it."

"Of course, I know that." Did Rose really think she thought it was a game? Is that what she thought of her? "I don't think that; I never have. And I know our histories are different. What I went through was nothing compared to you—"

"I do not want to talk about this." Rose tore off each word.

"I'm so sorry." Why had she ever spoken up? If she were Rose, she would despise her too. Maybe she should leave. "I didn't mean to be presumptuous. I'm so sorry," Lizzie said. "I just wish there were something more I could do."

"Do you? Do you really?" Rose said, and dropped her cup back on the coffee table with a clatter. "You say that, but sometimes I wonder. Because there is more you could find out. But you have to want to know."

12

LOS ANGELES, 1958

EASTLAKE SCHOOL WAS HOUSED IN the sprawling Spanish-style former residence of a silent movie star. It was a warm midafternoon in February, the sky cloudless and bright. Rose was walking toward the administrative offices to take a call from Thomas when she heard the rise of giggles, a braiding of voices. "Tennyson," she thought she heard a female voice say.

Then she spotted them. Gathered on the administration steps, a knot of long-limbed girls in uniforms of pale blue pleated skirts and white collared shirts. They were thirteen, fourteen, on the cusp. The burnished coins in their loafers glinted in the sunlight. "Tennyson," she heard again. The speaker was Helen Peale. "You *must* admire him." Helen dropped her usually tentative voice low and guttural. "You have altogether no choice in the *matta*." Her friends giggled again as she turned *matter* into a hammer of a word, losing the *r* entirely.

That was her, Rose thought, stock-still. Helen was imitating her. She stood on the path and watched Helen laugh. She needed a haircut, Rose thought. Her limp brown hair was too thin and those bangs altogether unflattering.

It was then that Helen noticed Rose. "Good afternoon, Mrs. Downes," she stammered.

Rose gave her a curt nod. She continued up the steps of the administration building with deliberation. So Helen Peale was a mimic. Rose could be teased for far worse. Most teachers were. Helen was one of the few boarding students here at Eastgate, an only child whose father traveled constantly for work and whose mother chose to accompany him. She had few friends—even Rose knew this. She was doing what she could to fit in.

And yet Rose still felt a tightening within her chest as surely as if Helen had followed her home and spied on her and Thomas alone in their bedroom.

Nearly three years earlier, they had moved to Los Angeles. Thomas landed a job at Douglas. The aircraft industry was booming, everyone focused on Boeing up north. It was no longer a question of if, but when, and which company would first succeed with a commercial jet. Rose didn't have such employment luck. But one night about two years ago Thomas came home late and said, "I've found you a job, a teaching position."

They stood shoulder to shoulder in their tiny aqua-tiled bathroom. He was brushing his teeth. "A teaching position?" she repeated incredulously.

He spit in the sink, looked at her reflection in the mirror. "Potentially," he amended. "At a very posh school. Someone quit midyear and they're looking to hire immediately."

"How in the world did you hear of it?" Rose had long given up on teaching. In England, there were no positions, nor had she seen any here. She had been circling ads in the paper for secretarial work—had been on a few interviews so far, two for real estate companies, one for advertising—but nothing.

"From Reynolds, who heard it from Douglas's secretary. His daughter goes there. Eastgate. A girls' school near Beverly Hills. It's been there for years. And it's quite the place, apparently: horses, tennis courts, an outdoor and indoor swimming pool."

It sounded like a resort, not a school, Rose was tempted to say, but the possibility of teaching here, in America, even the slight possibility, gave her a thrill. "Are there classrooms too?"

He regarded her image in the mirror. "I believe there are, yes."

"With one or two Jewish teachers at the helm?" She tried to ask this with a lightness that she did not feel.

"That I do not know." He picked an errant hair from the wet sink, dried his hands thoroughly on the towel. "Believe it or not, the faith of the instructors did not come up."

She fixed him with a look. "You know what I mean."

"I do," he said. "I did not ask. Best to simply apply."

There weren't many Jewish teachers on staff among the L.A. private schools, she had heard. (*It wasn't that they refused to hire Jews*, the well-meaning wife of a colleague of Thomas's had told Rose soon after they moved, *it was just that they* didn't *hire them*.) But the world was changing, Thomas liked to say. Not fast enough, Rose thought. Her religious beliefs had not shifted since she had been that unhappy child made more unhappy when the Cohens tried to take her to synagogue and required her to keep the laws of kashrut. But she was all too aware that wasn't the way the world saw her.

"They should seek out Jews. In the nineteenth century, every truly educated soul knew Hebrew," Thomas was saying now.

"Ah, yes, the halcyon days of the nineteenth century," Rose said.

Thomas laughed. "So you'll write Eastgate tomorrow. Tell them that you know Mr. Douglas."

"But I don't know Mr. Douglas."

"Ah, but your husband does. And he told me to tell you to do so." He tapped her backside with affection. "Silly Rosie. Why must you make everything harder on yourself?"

She made a face at Thomas, asserted it wasn't so, but a week later, behind the wheel of her neighbor's Buick (they had barely scraped together the funds for Thomas's clunker of a Chevy, let alone a car for her), Rose wondered if Thomas was right. Did she make everything harder on herself? Her anxiety was mounting: What made her believe she could get a teaching job? She had spent eight months student-teaching at a second-rate vocational school in Croydon six years ago. Her students were sixteen-year-old boys who would have rather eaten their fingernails for supper than recite a sonnet. Why did she ever think she could land a job teaching at an illustrious school in Los Angeles? ("Mr. Douglas told me that Shirley Temple went to Eastgate," Thomas said last night. "You are not helping," she barked at him.)

She took Beverly Glen past Sunset, maneuvering the unfamiliar car up the curving, darkly paved road, past the high hedges that obscured the homes behind them. The lots were big, the houses had to be grand. She was glad in her agitated state not to see them.

The Eastgate parking lot was filled with gleaming Cadillac coupes and Ambassadors with oversized fins. Rose locked the car, and, walking slowly to the main building, passed a gorgeous flowering tree with the most striking bluish-purple blossoms. A jacaranda, she would learn later.

A secretary brought Rose through an arched doorway down to the headmistress's office, Rose's heels making far too much noise against the polished stone. They passed through a corridor lined with framed photographs of Eastgate graduating classes, grave-faced girls dressed in white, clutching single lilies in their hands. Rose realized that Eastgate, for all its luster, was a young school. Forty years at most—laughably short by English standards. Gerhard had recently written her about a construction site down the road from him at which workers had unearthed in the mud a handsome marble bust, shockingly well preserved. It was of a Roman god, and soon it was discovered that the site had been the grounds of a two-thousand-year-old temple. Rose came from a place with true history. She, not Eastgate, embodied tradition.

"Mrs. Downes," said the headmistress as Rose was ushered inside her office. Miss Monroe was a thin, silver-haired woman with a penetrating gaze. "How nice to meet you." Her voice was warm enough but rapid, only a hint of a smile on her remarkably unlined face. She picked up the letter Rose had written. "As you must have heard, we are in a bit of a bind."

"Yes, I heard," Rose said. "Mr. Douglas told my husband, who told me," she clarified.

"Ah, yes," Miss Monroe said. Yes to what? Rose thought in a panic. "A wonderful family, the Douglases." She rubbed her thumb and forefinger of her right hand together—a gesture that seemed to betray her lack of interest in what Rose was saying. "So tell me about your experience. You've recently moved here, isn't that right? From England? And you studied there?"

Rose nodded. "I did. I received two degrees, one in literature and the other a teaching certificate. At the University of London, Bedford College." She spoke rapidly herself. She felt acutely aware that her time was limited. Still, she couldn't help adding. "I don't know if you're aware of Bedford, but it has quite a history; it was the first college for women in Great Britain."

"No, I'm not familiar with it. I know Oxford and Cambridge, of course."

"Of course," Rose echoed. Was she only interested in teachers with degrees from Oxford?

"But I must say I was glad to see that you studied in England. When I was at UCLA, I studied math with a Scottish professor. 'We're too soft in America,' he used to say, and he was not wrong. Here at Eastgate we are rigorous. More so than our brother school down the road, I would say."

"Indeed," Rose said, sensing an opening, "rigor is key. But so is engagement, particularly with younger students. At my last teaching position," she said, and she saw no reason to point out that it was her only teaching position, "I was at a boys' school and they were a rather challenging group of young men, shall we say, so I had to come up with unorthodox assignments to engage them. To trick them into learning, whether they wanted to or not."

"And you did this, how?" Miss Monroe asked, elbow on her desk, chin resting on her hand. For the moment, she seemed legitimately intrigued.

"A number of different methods. I had them write loads of reviews," Rose explained, feeling more confident. "Films they had seen, meals at the pub; one time I assigned them to write a critique of the coach's direction of their football team. That inspired more paragraphs of opinion, more actual writing, than I had seen before." Miss Monroe smiled lightly, perhaps too lightly? "But that didn't mean we steered away from the classics altogether," Rose added hastily. "I took them to see performances, *Tamburlaine the Great* and *Twelfth Night* at the Old Vic. I had them reciting poems weekly. I had a list of words—'the forbidden twenty,' I called it—if any word on that list was misspelled on a quiz or paper, the student received a failing grade. The students thought it draconian, but by the end of the term no one confused the possessive 'its' with the contraction of 'it is.' I don't imagine here that your students need such enticements."

"You would be surprised," Miss Monroe said. "'The forbidden twenty,' I like that. We here at Eastgate place an emphasis on educating our girls on all fronts—how to be strong wives, mothers, citizens in a democracy."

"Of course," Rose said, quickly, "the art of letter writing—"

"But sometimes we do so at the expense of rigor," the headmistress went on. "We could use more of that rigor here." She rose. "I'll introduce you to two of our English teachers, who have some questions for you. But first, may I ask: Downes is your married name?"

"Yes, it is," Rose said. She tried to say this with a smile. The interview had gone well. Hadn't it?

"It's only that your accent is unusual. You weren't born in England, were you?"

"No, I wasn't. I grew up in England," Rose said, considering. "But I was born in Vienna. Perhaps that's what you hear, my German, seeping through."

"During the war, you moved to England?" Miss Monroe's voice wasn't warm, exactly, but there was a newly tentative quality to her words that made Rose conversely feel in control.

"Just before. I'm Jewish," Rose said. "It wasn't safe. My brother and I got out."

"Ah," the headmistress said. "I see. You know, the only time I have been to Europe was in '35, before the war. We spent several days in Munich. It's strange, what you recall. We had gone shopping and we were at a large department store where I was admiring a music box, a beautiful enamel box out of which a silver bird popped. It even flapped its wings, and sang. I was so engrossed in the box that I didn't see several men in brown uniforms appear. They escorted a man out. They were saying—well—anti-Jewish things. It was terrible. A shameful time."

Rose nodded, tense. How many more teachers did Miss Monroe say she must speak with?

"We have a music teacher here, a lovely man, a Mr. Goldstein. Originally from Europe too. He plays the cello. And he plays it so wonderfully, with such a mournful soulfulness; I sometimes find myself wondering where that feeling comes from."

It was too much for Rose, the sympathy, the attention for all the wrong reasons. This woman thought she knew Rose, but she didn't. "It comes from the music," she said, the words out of her mouth before she could consider them.

Miss Monroe looked at Rose in surprise. Rose gazed down at her feet, pinched in pumps she rarely wore. She had spoken rashly. She had botched her one chance.

But here was Miss Monroe, holding out a cool hand and murmuring, "Yes, the music; how right you are." A week later, Rose was hired.

A FEW HOURS AFTER ROSE overheard Helen Peale, Helen entered her classroom uncharacteristically boisterous, chatting with Susan Smith about someone who had been on *Ed Sullivan* the night before. Rose waited for an embarrassed half smile of acknowledgment, a tacit apology of some sort. But nothing. Susan let the door slam shut behind her, and a puff of chalk dust kicked up. Teaching was less about instruction and more about exerting control. "Take out a sheet of paper. We're having a pop quiz," Rose decided to say.

"But we had one last week!" Susan said. "That's not fair, Mrs. Downes."

"That, Susan, is the nature of a pop quiz. You never know when you'll get one," Rose said, still working out what she would test them on.

"Mrs. Downes, I need to go to the bathroom. Can I have a bathroom pass?"

"'*May I* have a bathroom pass,' Linda," she said wearily. "And no, you may not."

More groaning, more litanies of "it's not fair." It was maddening, really, the number of times these well-fed, well-dressed daughters of privilege complained. Helen was quiet, pencil in hand, readied over paper. She gazed at Rose. Was that a hint of challenge in those solemn, dark eyes?

"You're in luck, only one question," Rose said. It came to her in an instant. "We've spent a great deal of time on poetic form. Tell me what form our country's most valuable document is written in."

"Excuse me?" Susan said, openly annoyed. "What document are you talking about?"

"Well, then, it's a two-part question, isn't it? A document that has to do with our country's founding. There is your clue—a big one. And the form it takes is a poetic one."

"We haven't gone over this," came a mutter from the back row. It was Annie, a voluble girl who rarely passed up a chance to complain.

"No, we have not, but you will be in a great deal of trouble if all you can do is parrot back what I've told you." A few minutes passed: several girls, hunched over their desks, wrote down answers; others, including Helen, stared off in the distance. The lack of trying irritated Rose more than anything else. "Helen, please come up here," she said.

Moving slowly, Helen complied. "Write down the first line of our founding document," Rose said.

"I—I don't know what you mean, exactly." Helen blinked, her soft mouth open.

"So you didn't even hazard a guess. You didn't put in any effort."

"Well, that wasn't it—"

"No, I don't want to hear it," Rose said. "Listen: 'We hold | these truths | to be | self-ev | ident.'" She was tired of excuses. She didn't want to hear any. How could it be that she, the foreigner, was the only one who knew this? "I am quoting the Declaration of Independence. I trust you've heard of it?"

A few girls tittered. "Quiet down or you'll come up here too," Rose said. "Helen, please write it."

Helen copied the words in big, flowing letters on the blackboard. She had beautiful penmanship—Rose had to give her that.

"Iambic pentameter, the most popular metrical line in the English language." Rose said, the quiz wholly forgotten. "It helped form the stately prose of this country's founding—our country," she said, though she herself was not yet a citizen. "The least you can do is know it."

FOR THE FIRST TIME IN what felt like weeks, Thomas was to be home for supper. Rose decided to ignore the pile of papers that she had to grade. She stopped at the butcher on Robertson and picked up a roast. They ate it with potatoes and cream and drank red wine and opened the windows, the faint chlorine smell of the courtyard pool that no one ever swam in wafting in. There was something wonderfully dissonant about their heavy meal in contrast to the tropical warmth eddying about. Rose leaned across the crowded linoleum tabletop and deposited a kiss on Thomas's lips. "And what did I do to deserve that?" he asked, delighted.

"You married me. Thank God." It was a sentiment that she thought often, if expressed less. Rose was not given to flights of fancy, but she was convinced if she hadn't gone into that antique shop on Old Bond, if she hadn't been searching for *The Bellhop*, she would still be working for Mr. Marks, still living alone in her tiny Belsize flat, never knowing that she was in fact capable of such happiness.

"Well, Mrs. Downes, it remains my pleasure. Again and again and again." Thomas kissed her back. "I have you and my beautiful new teacups; what more could I want?"

She laughed a little, shook her head. "Is that your way of saying you'd like a cup?"

"Yes, please," he said, and she put the kettle on. The week before, Thomas had a cavity filled, and afterward, he and Rose walked back to the car parked on Beverly Drive. Across the street from Nate 'n Al's, Thomas stopped in front of a tiny antique shop that featured a full suit of armor in the window. "I've always wanted one of those," he said, his words slurry from the Novocain.

"You are not in your right mind," she had said, but it was with affection. Inside the shop they went. And Thomas was oohing and aahing over everything within reach—the armor, a bronze elephant, a silver tea cart—Rose declaring that the drugs had gone to his head, when he spotted the teacups in a glass-fronted case. Even Rose had to admit they were gorgeous, hand-painted a pale green with a spray of yellow and blue flowers, gold leafing on the delicate handle. "They're

Minton," Thomas said, reading the tag. "Bone china, from the late 1800s. My mum always wanted a Minton tea service."

"Let me see," she said, for the tag also listed the price: one hundred and twenty-five dollars for the set. A ludicrous amount of money for six cups, entirely frivolous. Thomas gave Rose such a solemn look—"I want them," he said—that all joking about drugs was pushed aside. She nodded in assent and soon he was writing a check.

"We should use them often," she said now. "That is the only way I can explain away the wild expense." She might tease him now and again, but they reminded him of his mother. She of all people never would have said no to that.

"Ah, Rosie," he said. "Every once in a while we can afford something frivolous. They make me happy. What could we buy you to make you happy?"

"More time," she said as the phone rang.

"Downes residence," Rose answered, holding the receiver, spotted with grease, away from her ear.

"Is this Rose Downes?" a bubbly voice asked.

"To whom am I speaking?"

"Oh, am I glad to talk to you! I called earlier and got no answer, and I thought, 'Poor girl, she must be so busy, so *terribly* busy, and just having moved here and not knowing anyone.' But now here we are, speaking!"

"Yes, we are," Rose managed to say, too confused to dispute this characterization—*newly arrived? Poor girl?* "I'm sorry, who are you?"

"Oh, did I not say? Forgive me! I'm Dotty Epstein, Kurt Epstein's wife, formerly Dotty Gimbel, of the Philadelphia Gimbels, not the New York Gimbels—but the same extended family, those are my cousins." She spoke gaily, rapidly, as if any minute another voice—another friend or another cousin—would join in. "And you *are* Rose Downes, Gerhard Zimmer's sister, are you not?"

"I am," Rose said. "But I'm sorry, I don't know you." *Gerhard? What did Gerhard have to do with this?*

"Did your brother not tell you?"

"Tell me what?"

"Oh, this must be so absolutely bewildering to you!" She said it with such merriment that Rose felt like any objection, even the most clear-eyed of objections, would be taken personally, ruin all her fun. "My husband, Kurt Epstein, and Gerhard went to school together in Vienna. A lifetime ago, *of course*. Is his name familiar to you?"

"What? No." Rose felt an intense need to sit down. She steadied herself against the refrigerator door. Kurt Epstein? Who? The thought of someone from Vienna here in Los Angeles filled her with a strange expectant dread.

"Well, he says he remembers *you*, from when you were a tiny little thing. Anyway Kurt was across the pond for work—he's a filmmaker, you know." Dotty dropped her voice, as if she were bestowing a most delicious secret. "And he was in London and ran into your brother. They hadn't seen each other since they were children, *practically*. When he learned you had *just* moved to L.A.—"

"Two years ago," Rose cut in, "not *just*."

Thomas, scraping food into the trash bin, raised a questioning eyebrow at her. She waved him off, turned away. She couldn't begin to explain.

"We've been here for more than a decade, and we know so many others from Vienna. You must come over. We're in Brentwood. Where are you?"

"Mid-Wilshire," Rose answered, feeling relief that they were in different neighborhoods, a thirty-minute drive from each other.

"Ah, close to Wilshire Boulevard Temple! Lucky for you."

"Yes," Rose said, not sure what she was saying yes to, exactly, but finding it impossible to say no.

"Are you members yet?"

"What? No."

"Well, you must join. I'll introduce you to Rabbi Magnin. He's wonderful and charming and—urbane—not like most rabbis. We go far back, my family and his family knew each other—the retail business, *you know*. But why am I speaking of Rabbi Magnin? I am calling to invite you over this Sunday afternoon. We're having some friends over, fellow expats, for coffee and cake. You'll come over and it will be lovely."

"That does sound lovely," Rose said, "but we can't." She worked to sound regretful.

"Oh," Dotty said. "But you must. Kurt will be terribly disappointed, as will I."

"We cannot, not this week anyhow," Rose said. "But I thank you for the invitation." The more tense she felt, the more prim she acted. She didn't want to be rude, and she was sure that Thomas would tell her she was being silly—*aren't you just the slightest bit curious? Maybe you would recognize him when you saw him.* But whatever curiosity she felt was trumped by her unease. Why did people think that simply because she had been born in a particular city to a particular set of circumstances, she would want to socialize with others who shared those circumstances?

"You'll come another time," Dotty said. "They are wonderful get-togethers, I promise you."

"Yes, another time," Rose said, and soon hung up.

"Who was that?" Thomas asked.

"That," Rose said, "was a force of nature. A woman by the name of Dotty Epstein. She says that her husband, Kurt, might have known my brother back in Vienna."

"Might?" Thomas asked.

"Did," Rose corrected herself, smoothing out a tea towel on the kitchen counter. "He *did* know Gerhard. Apparently they ran into each other in London recently. I don't know why Gerhard didn't mention it to me in his last letter. It's so like him not to mention it."

"So these Epsteins live here in L.A. and invited us over. Why did you say no? We're free this Sunday."

"I don't know," Rose said. She continued to smooth out the towel, folding it into thirds. "I didn't want to."

"Why not? It might be fun."

"I simply didn't want to," she said querulously. Of course Thomas would think that it might be fun, Thomas, who saw the world's ugliness but didn't shirk away from it, managed to come out as an optimist, merely glad to be on the other side. She was not like him. She imagined meeting people from Vienna, being asked which school she had attended, which neighborhood her family had lived in, and though these questions were innocuous enough, the simple possibility of them felt like something hostile. She had been eleven when she left, not a small child, but there was little she remembered. She had one photograph of her family, taken a few summers before she and Gerhard left. They stood on a footbridge over the river in Bad Ischl, her father looking at something outside the frame. Her mother gazed directly at the camera, one hand resting on Gerhard's shoulder (he was nearly her height then) and the other on Rose's small kerchiefed head. Rose was the only one smiling, grinning, really. There were many reasons Rose could hardly look at the picture, but chief among them was this: She didn't recognize that little girl.

Now Rose folded her arms across her chest, trying to bat back her tears. Thomas knew that gesture, and he said, "Oh Rosie," and took her in his arms.

"I'm all right," she said. "I really am." And she was, here with him. He breathed into her hair: "All right, then."

LATER THAT NIGHT, IN BED, when Thomas reached for her, she pulled back. "I'm going to the doctor on Friday to get my new diaphragm—remember?"

"Well, there are certain things we can still do," he said, and bit her bottom lip teasingly. She tasted the smokiness of his scotch. He was small but lithe; they fit each other well.

She closed her eyes. Thomas had always been able to make her feel good. She felt greedy when he touched her, looked forward to her mind quieting.

But now she spoke into his chest: "Thomas. We can't."

"I know. I was only—" and he pulled away, lay on his back. "Did you think I would?" he said to the ceiling. "Like that? After all these years?"

"No," she said. "I don't know. I wanted to be sure."

"Yes," he said flatly. "You can be sure."

They had agreed. Before they got married, they had agreed. Rose had made sure of that. When she told him, when it became finally clear that her *I-can't-have-children* meant, in fact, *I won't have children*, when she tried to explain, she started talking about going to the cinema. She loved movies. She loved so much about them—the immense screen, the velvet seats, the expectant hush as the lights dimmed and the music kicked up. And yet nearly every time she went to the cinema, sat in a crowded darkened movie house filled with strangers, she felt a volley of panic, fought an urge to leave. Why was everyone sitting here, together, so close, so calm? What enabled them to do that? Wouldn't someone somewhere do something terrible?

Thomas had listened. He had let her speak, didn't ask any questions. She loved him for that.

"I feel so fortunate with you," she had said then. "So uncommonly lucky." She felt something spiky lodged in her throat, and try as she might, she couldn't swallow it down. "I'm afraid of ruining it." That was the closest she came to articulating the question that terrified her: How in the world can you protect that which you love?

He knew that too, of course. "But you go to the cinema," he said softly. "You don't avoid it altogether."

She dropped his hand. "I'm not talking about the cinema," she said. They were back in her tiny room in Belsize. She remembered concentrating on the clank of the radiator, trying to focus on that and not Thomas's words.

"Sometimes I think that you think you don't deserve this. But you do," he said. "You have a life. We can have a life together. You have to try."

"I *am* trying. I just don't think I want children. I don't."

"But I think I do," he said, and with that he left. She spent nearly a week catatonic with fear. But he came back. "I love you," he had said.

Now, more than a decade later, she touched her husband, a body that she knew as well as her own. She wanted to climb inside of him, to feel completely surrounded. "I love you," she said now, reaching for him, but Thomas rolled over.

"Love you too," he said. "I have a long day tomorrow," and he clicked off his bedside light. Rose was left alone in the dark, a loneliness all the more acute because she knew she had brought it upon herself.

TWO DAYS LATER, THE RAINS began. A relentless rain, a rain that seemed otherworldly in force. The city was not built for such deluge: Olympic and Pico flooded, rocks tumbled, mudslides ensued. PCH was shut down. Much of this Rose and Thomas read in the paper or saw on the news, grateful for their dry second-floor apartment near Fairfax.

That morning, when Rose left for work, she passed the building's super, Mr. Osaka, in the lobby. "You really driving in this mess, Mrs. Downes?" Mr. Osaka said as she darted through the lobby back out to the uncovered parking lot. The driving rain made a racket on the roofs of the cars, pelted against her umbrella. She could hardly see. Just as she was trying to manage both her umbrella and the key (she and Thomas had bought a used Chevy after she began teaching at Eastgate: "A two-car family," Thomas had said. "Now we're truly Angelenos"), something caught her eye. It was a shadowy something. Discarded piping from one of Mr. Osaka's projects? The piping began to move: a snake, glistening among the deepening puddles, pocked by the raindrops. A moving living snake. It was coppery brown, undulating through the shallow waters with ease.

Rose stared, stiffening. Her back was getting wet, her ankles dampened by rain, but she barely noticed, stunned by fear. She had never seen a live snake before. It wasn't small. She watched it oscillate beneath a neighboring car. Then she ran back through the puddles of the parking lot and into the lobby.

The super was still inside, now atop a stepladder, replacing a light bulb.

"Mr. Osaka, there's a snake out in the parking lot."

"Oh?"

She nodded, breathing audibly. She rubbed her damp cheek with her hand. "Whom shall we call? Who removes snakes in these situations?" She tried to laugh.

"He'll go away on his own. Sometimes they come out in the rain," Mr. Osaka said, shrugging. "Other times heat, the dryness, brings them out."

This was Los Angeles to Rose. A surreal landscape, whether it was the rains, the Santa Anas, the coyotes that roamed the jagged canyons, the brush fires, the cactus flowers that inexplicably bloomed from dust and rock. Even on its many gorgeous days, the beauty of Los Angeles had an underlying hardness. There was nothing soft about it, and she loved this—the city's sharp lines and wild heart even when it tried to disguise them. Los Angeles had made itself. Everything was imported—the water that was pumped in from the north, the palm trees for which the city was celebrated. Everyone and everything here came from somewhere else.

When she managed to drive through the churn that Sunset had become and at last arrived at Eastgate, only five students were in her second-period class, four in her third. By noon, the administration had moved to shut the school for the afternoon. The classroom was chilly, the radiator barely emitting heat, seemingly resentful that it actually had work to do. But Rose decided to stay for the hour to catch up on papers she had to grade, go over lesson plans. She was dreading the drive home.

At two o'clock, ten minutes after sixth period usually began, Rose heard footsteps, a knock at the open door. She looked up to see Helen Peale, clad in a soaked yellow plastic poncho.

"I know I'm late," Helen said.

"Didn't you hear?" Rose asked. "Class is canceled."

"I know," Helen said. She remained in the doorway, the plastic crinkling as she moved, forlorn in bright yellow. "But I'm here at school. So here I am." In the poncho, she looked closer to ten than her fourteen years.

"Well, then," Rose said, sighing. "Take that wet thing off; you're dripping all over my classroom." Helen hung the poncho up, and went to her usual spot, but Rose gestured to the front row. "Come, to Susan's seat. No reason to hide back there. Bring your *Versification* book and turn to page ninety-three."

Helen's expression was solemn as she studied the book. "Robert Frost's 'Fire and Ice.' It is a compact poem, but it is not small," Rose said. "Scholars say that Frost had Dante's *Inferno* in mind when he wrote it."

She asked Helen to read it aloud. The sound of Helen's clear girlish voice reciting Frost's words, the rhythmic patter of rain against the roof, combined to make Rose feel warmer. They were the only two in the classroom; were they the only people left in the building?

"How do you think the world will end?" Helen asked when she finished.

Such a terrible question, but Helen posed it with forthrightness. Rose could remember sitting on her bed in Leeds, waiting for letters that never arrived, thinking, *I am supposed to go to school and study? I am supposed to go to the cinema and enjoy it?* "I have no idea," Rose said.

Helen didn't say anything, and then: "My father died."

"What?"

"My father died." She repeated the words patiently. "Two weeks ago. A boating accident, in Hawaii."

"Oh, Helen, that's awful. I'm so sorry." Rose moved close to the girl, bent down so that she was at eye level. She wished she had known; why hadn't the administration told her? It made her angry that she hadn't been told.

"It's okay," Helen said, chewing on the end of a limp strand of hair, not looking at Rose. "I'm okay. I hadn't seen him in so long anyway."

"Where is your mother?"

"Still in Hawaii. She's staying there for now. She doesn't want to come back. She doesn't want me."

"I'm sure that's not true," Rose insisted, despite what she knew of the family.

Helen shrugged and smiled, the sort of sweet-sad smile that children give adults who lack understanding of the situation, a look that Rose could recall employing herself. "She hasn't come back. And I'm still here."

"Well, I'm here too," Rose said. An absurd thing to say, because where was she but in a chilly classroom with a dusty blackboard and wrinkled likenesses of Dickinson and the Brontës and spelling lists tacked up on the walls? What did she have to offer? *She needs her mother*, Rose thought, infuriated—if she knew anything, she knew this to be true. But here they both were. Rose herself might have been a paltry substitute for what Helen needed, but she hoped in the moment for her presence to be enough.

THAT NIGHT, AT HOME, TWO aerograms awaited Rose. The first, from Mrs. Cohen, contained not unexpected news: Mr. Cohen had passed away two weeks earlier. He had been ill with lung cancer for more than a year. "The funeral was simple, as he would have liked," Mrs. Cohen wrote. "He remembered you fondly, and I hope you will do the same for him."

"I should have gone back," Rose said to Thomas. "I should have seen him more often." Why couldn't she have been kinder, after all he had done?

"He knew how you felt," Thomas said.

"I'm not so sure." With a sigh, she turned to her brother's letter. Gerhard spoke about meeting with distributors in Edinburgh and his hopes that the crocuses in his garden would be blooming before long. "Isobel wants me to tell you she is horrified by what she reads about the South, and Harry wants to know when he can come to California to meet Betty Grable," Gerhard wrote.

"The other day at Kings Cross, I had the most extraordinary experience. I saw a thin middle-aged man staring at me. I kept thinking, why is that old gentleman looking at me?, when he turned and I saw that he was my age—not old at all—and he said my name." Gerhard went on to say what Rose already knew: that Kurt Epstein lives in Los Angeles, that he works in the entertainment industry. "I told him you were there and he immediately asked for your telephone number. He claims to remember you from when we were children. How surreal and wonderful it was to see him again. Like time collapsing on itself. I do hope he calls."

"What does Gerhard say?" Thomas asked.

"He wrote about his garden," Rose said. "He is so focused on his crocuses."

A week later, when Dotty Epstein called, talking about the Sacher torte she made and a well-known actor who would be coming by this Sunday, and how Rose must join them, Rose answered right away. "We will be there," she said, thinking of both Mr. Cohen and Helen Peale.

KURT AND DOTTY'S HOUSE ON Cliffwood looked like a smaller version of the main Eastgate building—Spanish style with red roof tiles, creamy stucco, flowers spilling over the brick walkway. Rose and Thomas headed to the front arched door, nearly twenty minutes late. Traffic had slowed them down, but really Rose's own tardiness was to blame. She had taken longer than usual to get ready, finally settling on a tweed pencil skirt and a cream-colored sweater set.

"I bet not one person here has read Thomas Hardy, except for you," Thomas said, squeezing Rose's hand reassuringly. Just last night he had said to her, *If you don't want to go, you don't have to.*

"You haven't read Hardy."

He grinned. "Exactly."

The door swung open. "Rose Downes! Thomas Downes! Come in, come in!" Dotty Epstein was even bigger and more declarative in person—her voluptuous frame, the colorful pattern of her dress, the large sunglasses in her hand. She gave Rose a noisy kiss on the cheek.

"You look positively darling. What a charming skirt and top." Dotty's tone indicated she thought Rose's outfit sweet in much the same manner that a child wearing bloomers was sweet—charming in its oddity, its essential irrelevance. They passed a blur of rooms—"billiards, study, living room," Dotty said, ticking them off with her well-manicured hand. "Powder room on the left. We are going outside because today is beautiful and I will not be denied."

Rose and Thomas followed Dotty through the sliding glass doors and out into the rich sunshine. Rose hadn't brought her sunglasses—it hadn't occurred to her that they would be outside—and she stood blinking, her eyes adjusting before she could make out in detail the white gazebo situated by the kidney-shaped pool, the water silver in the dazzling light. A dozen or so people milled about, men in light-colored suits and women in bright full-skirted dresses that rustled with the slightest movement.

"Kurt must be around here somewhere," Dotty said. "Kurt?"

A man emerged out of the cool shadow of the gazebo, a tall but narrowly built man in a pale summer suit. When he saw Rose, he clapped his hand to his mouth. "Gerhard's little sister! Is that you?"

"It is indeed," she said. It was odd; he was no one she recognized, but she felt a little woozy at the sight of him. He had thick brows accenting his expressive dark eyes, a chipped front tooth that only seemed to add to his allure. He was handsome, undeniably so, nothing like the few boys she remembered from her Viennese youth.

"Ah, you don't look like your brother—lucky for you—but I swear, I remember your face. I haven't seen you in more than twenty years, but I do remember your face!" He laughed as he said this, grasping her right hand between his two. They were cool, despite the sun.

"I find that hard to believe. I was eleven when I left."

"There are many things that are hard to believe," he said, letting go of her hand. He smiled at her then and there was something intimate about that smile, directed just at her, that made her say: "I'm afraid I don't remember you." She knew she sounded prickly, but she felt the need to defend herself.

"You are forgiven," Kurt said, and laughed again. "The world is a small place after all."

"Kurt, this is Mr. Thomas Downes. He is an engineer at Douglas Aviation." Dotty paused meaningfully. "A top engineer. Working on jet travel."

"Is that so?" Kurt said idly.

"Not *top* engineer," Thomas said, coloring, "not top at all."

"Don't sell yourself short," Dotty declared. "We will have none of that in my house." Rose couldn't remember telling Dotty where Thomas worked, let alone that he was an engineer. How did she find that out? "And my Kurt is an acclaimed screenwriter," Dotty said.

"Acclaimed," Kurt repeated, lifting a bushy eyebrow, "is one way to put it."

"It's my way," Dotty said, and laced her hand with his.

"What films have you written?" Rose asked.

"Have you seen *The Thing?*"

"*The Thing?*" Rose asked, puzzled.

"Yes, the *Thing* movies: *The Thing Escapes*, *The Thing Returns*. Now I'm working on *The Reign of the Thing*. Have you seen any of them?"

Rose shook her head. "I don't believe so, I'm sorry."

"Don't be," he said. "I would be more surprised if you had."

"Why is that? They're witty, *wonderful* films," Dotty said.

"You know, I did see one, years ago," Thomas said. "It was quite entertaining. It truly was. Well done."

"Thank you," Kurt said with a little bow.

"What is the Thing?" Rose asked.

"What do you mean?"

"Is the Thing a person? A monster, a figure of the imagination?"

"We don't know," Kurt said with a wry little smile. "That's why he keeps coming back."

"Now we could talk about the Thing all day, but come now," Dotty said. "Let's get you some food."

Under the gazebo, oh, the sweet abundance: Such an array of desserts—dark chocolate Sacher tortes, as Dotty had promised, and poppy-seed cakes and a platter of almond cookies dusted with sugar and elegant petits fours in the form of tiny purple flowers. There was a large silver coffee urn surrounded by rows of china teacups stacked on top of each other and several pitchers of water accompanied by tall glasses to help wash down the treats just as, Rose unexpectedly remembered, her father liked to do.

Soon Rose was settled on a lounge chair balancing a plate that held a slice of the Sacher torte, and drinking the strong coffee and listening to a composer ("very accomplished," Dotty had ducked down to whisper) talk about the Vienna Opera House and the mournful cries of the coyotes he heard at night from his house in the hills. Thomas was engaged in a conversation with a portly man about air travel while his stunning wife tried not to look bored ("his third," Dotty informed Rose).

"Did you ask your analyst?" Rose heard a mustached man ask Dotty.

"Oh, he would *never* answer," Dotty said.

"That is why I go monthly to Menninger in Kansas," he said. "To have an analyst with such an astute, incredible mind, it is worth journeying."

The composer said to Rose: "Have you been back to Vienna?"

"Me?" She shook her head. "No." After a moment, she asked: "You?"

"No," he said. "Why would I ever go back? It's just as Wilder says: 'The Austrians have managed to convince the world that Beethoven was Austrian and Hitler a German.' You cannot trust them."

"No," she said quietly. "You can't." Rose felt hot in her tweed skirt. Her head hurt. She shouldn't have had that second cup of coffee. She made her way around the pool, toward the house. Inside it was thankfully cool, enveloping. She found the bathroom again, but it was occupied. She waited. A moment later, the door opened and Kurt stepped out.

"Well. Hello." A smile lit his handsome face. He had a hand against the doorframe. "Enjoying yourself?"

"Yes, very, thank you." She gestured at the door. "Excuse me—"

He moved closer. They were neither in the bathroom nor in the hall. "I was hoping to see you alone. You have a look about you. Your eyes—they're beautiful. They remind me of Adele's." His voice was gentle.

Who was Adele? "I'm sorry—" Rose stuttered. Kurt kept his gaze trained on her. She shifted uncomfortably. Thomas must still be outside. She shouldn't be reminding Kurt of anyone.

"It is the most uncanny resemblance," Kurt said. A light smokiness emanated from his clothes. She could have moved past him, but she didn't. "You're lovely like her. Not of this world, like her."

Rose was too stunned to say anything. Finally she murmured: "I have to—I should go."

"Of course." But he leaned in and she didn't move. He grazed his lips across hers. They felt cool and dry. It was quick and then it was over.

"No, don't," she said after the fact.

He looked at her, smiled, shrugged. And then he was gone.

Rose had no idea how long she remained in the bathroom, trying to slow her flailing heart. *It doesn't matter*, she told herself sternly, except that was a lie. She splashed water on her face, once, twice, smoothed her hair, stared at herself in the mirror. Thomas would take one look at her and know. Eventually she walked out. In the hall, she heard: "Rose?"

Dotty was in the kitchen, cutting oranges into quarters and adding them to a glass pitcher with lemons already crowding the bottom. "Sangria," she explained. "It can't be coffee and Sacher torte all the time." Inside, with her hat and sunglasses off, without an audience, she seemed smaller. "I am glad you are here. Was that Kurt you were speaking to in the hall?"

Rose nodded.

"Is he okay?"

"Yes," Rose said quickly. "Of course."

Dotty's hand guided the knife, *chop, chop chop.* "Did you know Adele growing up?"

"Excuse me?" Rose blurted.

"Adele. Did you know her?"

Rose shook her head. Was she too quick to answer? Why would she know her? "Who is she?"

"His wife," Dotty said, funneling sugar into the pitcher, a white snowy path. "His first wife."

"Oh," Rose only said. She wasn't sure she wanted to know the rest.

Dotty stirred the contents of the pitcher. She didn't look up. "They were childhood sweethearts in Vienna. I thought maybe you knew her; I'm certain your brother did. She and Kurt were madly in love. They married, in the camp. They were nineteen. And then she caught pneumonia. Died."

"I didn't realize," Rose said. It was inconceivable. All of these stories were: Kurt's, her parents', so many stories, each ghastly in its own particular way. "That's terrible."

"It is," Dotty said. Only then did she stop mixing. "It is terrible. He yells out in his sleep sometimes: 'Adele, Adele!' He has a Ouija board. I know he tries to reach her. But he won't talk to me about her." She turned back to the sangria, gave it a vigorous stir. "I tell myself it's over, but it's not. When will it be over?"

Rose looked at the pitcher filled with fruit, such a bright, optimistic bounty, and she was back in those bleak days in London after the war. "Dotty," she asked in a voice far gentler than her own, "what can he possibly say?"

MONDAY MORNING, THE HEADMISTRESS'S SECRETARY came to Rose's classroom with a note. "You'll be getting another student for sixth period next week, possibly two. Helen Peale has left."

"What?" Rose could only say dumbly. "When?"

"Her mother came and took her this weekend. Quite right; it's about time."

When her students filed in for second period, Rose took attendance and had to be reminded of the presence of two students, whose names she overlooked. She told the class to take out the *Versification* book. They were reading Frost again today. She had them turn to "The Road Not Taken." Rose couldn't focus. What was the rhyme scheme again?

Elicit and evoke, an old teacher of Rose's used to say. Now she tried; she asked about Frost's intent. Only two hands went up. She called on a chatty girl named Annie. "We should take chances," Annie said. "We shouldn't be frightened by what is less traveled on, what we don't know."

"Don't let the last stanza fool you. Read the poem again. From the top." Rose missed Helen.

Annie did, more hesitant than the first time, and Rose pointed out that Frost called the other path "just as fair," and how both paths had been worn "about the same."

"Frost made it tricky, but the evidence is there. It doesn't matter which road you take; you take one or the other. But you must take one."

"Of course it matters," said Susan Smith. "How can you say that our decisions don't matter?"

"I didn't say that. And that's not what Frost is saying. At the end of the poem, he talks about how he'll tell the story in the future, with a sigh. He is talking about years from then, is he not? When he returns to that moment, when he revisits that decision. You must make decisions with incomplete information, with what you know at hand. That's the way life works. Even if it's paltry."

"No," said Susan. "It's not right."

"Actually, it is," Rose said sharply. It was lost on them, this feeling of darkness. Of course it was. When had they ever felt true discomfort? When had any of them been in a situation with only terrible choices? Escape a war. Leave your parents behind. "That's what the speaker is sighing over, years later. He had to convince himself that one was better. But he had no idea which road to take. This is the lesson. You must pick. Stop your hand-wringing. You must decide." Her voice was louder than it needed to be.

The young faces looked at her. Annie was scared, Susan sullen, resentful. A few others gazed out the window, doodled in their notebooks, paying little attention. But Rose, feeling the white heat of her own anger course through her, did not care. She folded her arms over her chest. "Any questions?"

13

LOS ANGELES, 2006

L IZZIE DIDN'T KNOW HIM BUT she did. Her recognition registered as sensation, a whistle of breath when the door to the forlorn Hollywood coffee shop opened. In came Detective Gilbert Tandy, the same detective who had shown up at her house the morning after the paintings were stolen, twenty years ago.

The small coffee shop was nestled at the far end of a strip mall next to a cell-phone store at the intersection of Sunset and El Centro. Lizzie's booth seat was crisscrossed with electrical tape, the worn carpet sticky in spots. Tandy had suggested meeting there.

The detective was a stocky black man with a wide pleasant face. Lizzie had remembered him as much taller. He had a deliberate walk and wore baggy jeans and a pink short-sleeved collared shirt, attire that made Lizzie feel less panicked. Just minutes ago, before he walked in, she'd stared at the front door, stomach lodged in her throat, thinking: *I can just get up and leave.* But how terrible could it be if he was wearing pink?

"Lizzie Goldstein," she said, rising to her feet and offering a firm hand.

"Of course," he said, sliding in across from her. "I remember you. You look the same."

"Well, that's nice to say, but I hope not," she said. "My hair was huge then."

He didn't crack a smile. "I'm glad you called. And thanks for meeting me out here. You're on the Westside?"

"I'm staying there, yes," she clarified. "I live in New York now."

He nodded, ordered coffee from the passing waiter.

"I can't believe how much this neighborhood has changed," Lizzie said, feeling the need to fill the air. "I just passed Hollywood and Vine and saw condos going up. When I was in high school, I had my car radio stolen a couple blocks from here, on Gower near Melrose. I remember driving around here then and seeing all these women on corners, beautiful women in heels and microskirts leaning into cars, and I remembered thinking: 'They're so friendly, giving directions.'"

"Yes, it's different, at least on the surface," Tandy said. "But expensive condos just mask crimes of another kind."

She nodded, her hands nesting the coffee cup. Of course; he was a detective, he probably saw crime everywhere.

"You said on the phone you wanted to talk," he said.

"I did," she said, and the air felt warmer. "My father died several months ago."

"I heard. I'm sorry."

She nodded. She bunched up her napkin in her lap. "Thank you."

"Did you come across anything?" He asked this gently.

"What?" Lizzie was still looking down at her napkin. Even that little question made her recoil.

"Did you come across anything that seemed unusual, any payments, any correspondence, anything that you were wondering about?"

"What? No." A prickly heat coated her neck. She had been dreading such a question long before Tandy had walked in. But she had been expecting it too—she had initiated this meeting, after all, she had chosen to be here—and that only made her want to reject it more forcibly.

"The artwork is still missing; you know that. It's still an open case."

"Of course I know that."

"May I ask you—" And then: "Why did you call me?"

How could she answer that? No part of her wanted to. What was she doing here? Lizzie looked past him toward the front, where an old man in a beret was trying to get himself settled on a stool at the counter. "You want the cottage cheese, Murray?" the waiter asked. "But of course," she heard the man say.

"So he was a suspect," she heard herself say, eyes still fixed on Murray.

"He was a person of interest—yes. We were very interested in his story."

She swung back toward Tandy. "And what about the private investigator? What did he say?"

"What investigator?"

"The one my father hired."

She felt his eyes on her. "He told you he hired a PI?"

"I heard that he did. To help find the paintings."

"That would surprise me, immensely," he said slowly. He sipped his coffee. "I am highly skeptical that he hired an investigator on his own."

She shook her head, confusion and terror mixing into a new terrible feeling. "I don't understand," she whispered. She wanted so badly not to.

"What I'm telling you," he said, "is what I know: your father did not hire an investigator to look into this case." There was kindness visible on his face, in his steady gaze, but Lizzie felt herself falling, and that kindness registered as an assault.

"You're wrong."

"Look, I'll tell you what I know. In 1986, your father lent the Picasso drawing of the bull and the Soutine *Bellhop* to the San Francisco Museum of Modern Art for a show," he said. "Museums usually insure loaned works under a blanket policy, and no one at the museum appraised the paintings. Goldstein had purchased the Picasso in 1979 at the Phoenix Gallery in New York for a hundred and forty-three thousand dollars. He bought the Soutine three years later from the Levitan Gallery for a little over seventy thousand. In 1986, they were worth about close to a million, combined, but he was allowed to file his own estimate of their value for the museum's insurance purposes: four million. The museum drew up a loan agreement, stating the value provided by Goldstein. And Goldstein took that agreement and got a new insurance policy based on that inflated amount, underwritten by Lloyd's of London and a German company, Nordstern. About a year after that, the art market fell, the work was worth even less, and the painting and the drawing disappeared."

Lizzie was no longer in her body. Someone else was seated in this booth, trying desperately to hold on to that cup of coffee, nodding at the detective, thinking, *It all fits.*

Tandy was still talking. "Goldstein's insurers denied the claim, saying that he had deliberately overvalued the artwork. He sued, alleging bad faith and demanding the four million and then some—he asked for another million in punitive damages."

"My father sued?" How did she not know that?

He gave her a little hard smile. "He did. Rather than risk losing in front of a jury, the insurers backed down. They paid him the full amount."

"You think he set it up."

"I'm telling you the facts as I know them," Tandy said. "And where the facts lead."

"But that's what you think."

He gave the smallest of nods. "Yes."

"So then he destroyed them," she heard herself say coldly, as if she were talking about a stranger, a defendant whose case she'd taken on. "He had to get rid of the evidence."

"I don't know."

"But it only makes sense." That's what she would do, she thought wildly. If she had done something insane like this, she would follow through. "You get rid of them, you destroy the evidence. You can't fucking sell them; everyone's on the lookout, who would buy them? If you're doing something as horrible as this—if you're letting your kid take the fall, you destroy them, don't you?" Her voice had grown shaky. She slid out of the booth, stumbling. What had she been thinking, meeting with this man?

"I'm sorry," he said, his mouth a hard line. "I'm sorry for us all."

"Don't," she said as she flung a ten-dollar bill on the table. "Don't for one moment pretend that we are in this together."

KEEP MOVING. THAT WAS HER instinct, the only thing clear in her mind. She got on the freeway heading east and kept going, flying beneath those immense green signs that announced directions and destinations in what now seemed like a strange, foreign shorthand, not built for human scale. She passed the trickle of the concreted Los Angeles River and the Staples Center and glittery tower of the Bonaventure. The multiple lanes of freeway knotted up, traffic barely moving, and still she urged herself on.

Her mind was caught in an endless loop: her father and *The Bellhop*, *The Bellhop* and her father. She remembered how he had laughed and mussed up her hair when she had asked if the man in the painting was famous. "In our house he is," she remembered him saying.

Did he hire someone? Did he not go to Boston at all?

All those years she had blamed herself. And he let her.

She sped up; she slowed down. No, it wasn't true. Her hands remained tight on the steering wheel, she drove as if she had a plan. She switched the radio off, but within minutes clicked it back on. The silence was worse, shrill.

He had been ripped off by his office manager right before the paintings were stolen. His practice took a beating. And there had been that real estate deal that went bad. He stopped buying art. She knew he had expenses. Hefty ones. But this? Surely this wouldn't have been his solution. There was that time in high school—it must have been before the paintings were stolen, it was definitely before the paintings were stolen—when Joseph had floated the idea of their moving. Friends had gotten a condo off of Olympic. A much smaller place than their house. "It's great!" Joseph had said. "A shared pool and you girls could walk places, even to school. What do you think? Don't you ever get tired of the hill?"

"No," she could remember harrumphing, aggrieved. "I don't."

Her mind sputtered, flayed about. She remembered her first summer as an associate, when she had been doing research and came across a decision from the Second Circuit that seemed to go against the case they were building. She brought it to the senior partner, proud of herself. But the senior associate had thrown the decision back in her face. "What am I supposed to do with this?" Lizzie stammered something about how the facts didn't match the case. "No," the partner said, "you've got it wrong. You *use* the facts. You anticipate how others will use them. They don't use you."

Lizzie passed West Covina and Pomona, the sky giving in to a grayish, almost yellow tint of late afternoon. She dimly registered hunger, her gas meter dipping lower than a quarter of a tank. It was only then that she realized she was heading out into the desert.

She remembered the vastness of the desert from when she was a kid, Joseph's small car careering along the ribbon of concrete, no match for the enormous stretch of sky and the sun-bleached ground and the snow-tipped mountains in the distance that seemed like a trick of the eye. She remembered the wind turbines, a gorgeous man-made orchard of tall sleek slices of metal, spinning, spinning.

But now the city had taken over, the Angeleno sprawl had spread. Now there were endless subdivisions and malls with Outback Steak-houses and Starbucks and Targets and Noah's Bagels. Nothing was the same.

Lizzie drove and she drove and she thought: *It's not true. It can't be. He had money; he did. And even if he had been in trouble, he loved the Soutine. He never would have done something like this. Not to me.*

But the jagged details came careening back: her father's face blotchy, hair matted down with sweat, as if he had flown back from Boston powered by his own vitriol and fear. *A party, a fucking party, Elizabeth?! You lied to me; I trusted you and you lied.* Those weeks of ugly silence: Sarah in the hospital, the two of them in the house, weary, embattled, alone. For years Lizzie's own guilt had impelled her, shaped her.

She was crying now, her hands shaky on the wheel. He had orchestrated this. He had set it up. All those years—all those times she had wished she could go back, undo the damage she had caused. *He* had done this.

Somehow she managed to switch lanes, get off the freeway. She pulled onto the shoulder, glanced at her gas gauge: nearly empty. She was going to stall out here in this no-man's-land of Walmarts and In-N-Outs and Wendy's.

Lizzie twisted around, looking for a station, and it was then that she saw the dinosaurs: two gigantic prehistoric sculptures that commanded the desert, shadowing a low-roofed diner and a gas station too.

Lizzie had forgotten all about the dinosaurs. How could she? She circled the service road that followed the curve of the larger dinosaur's slender neck and took her into the gas station. She got out of the car, her legs unsteady. The warm air was fragrant, a heady scent of flowers and gas and oil-soaked fry. She paid for a tank, downed a bag of oatmeal raisin cookies and a bottle of seltzer. A sign read WORLD'S BIGGEST GIFT SHOP INSIDE A DINOSAUR! She made her way over to the door cut into one of the dinosaurs' tails.

She'd been inside this gift shop before. It was before her mother had died, when her father was working so hard to impress—an antic tap dance of plans and sights and attractions—bumper cars and corn dogs at the Santa Monica Pier! Lunch at a movie studio! Guess jeans and Kork-Ease and satin jackets and anything she and Sarah wanted! Sunbathing in the desert in January—can you do that in New York? Can you?

But this particular outing had not gone well. Neither she nor Sarah would try a date shake at Hadley's Farm (*but they're sweeter than sweet!* Joseph had said) and then there was Sarah's meltdown about the lack of a miniature personalized license plate; they didn't have her name (inexplicably they had *Sara*, but no *Sarah*. "Who cares?" Lizzie could remember saying. There was no *Lizzie* or *Liz* either. "It's not like it goes on a real car"). Their father had tried to tell them about the man who had built the dinosaurs. He had spent years working on them, using concrete and steel left over from the construction of the freeway she had just gotten off. *Everyone thought he was nuts*, she remembered Joseph saying. *But he didn't care.*

She walked in. The gift shop occupied a small dark space, filled with rickety displays of dinosaur kitsch. But the back wall held a different type of attraction: INSTITUTE OF CREATION SCIENCE, a sign read. *Primordial soup to the zoo to you; is evolution true?*

Apparently not, according to the display, which talked about how early humans coexisted with dinosaurs ("just like the one you're standing in!") and how the earth ("in all its splendor and diversity") was created in six days. A painted bust of a Cro-Magnon man, looking like a hirsute Jon Voight, sat next to a sign arguing against Darwin's theories; a clay diorama of Noah's Ark showed two dinosaurs next to a duo of giraffes.

"I don't understand," Lizzie said to the young girl behind the register. "Since when is the gift shop a creationist museum?"

"We're just offering information," the girl said coolly, and returned to her book.

"Well, it's insulting to both scientists *and* dinosaurs," Lizzie said, but she said it as she was nearly out the door, a coward's retort. Outside, she leaned against the dinosaur's tail, pulled out her cell phone.

What was she doing? She felt a heaviness slowing her breath. Still she dialed. "Do you know there's a creationist museum in the dinosaur gift shop?" she said. "A fucking creationist museum—how crazy is that?"

"Lizzie? What are you talking about?" Sarah said. "Where are you?"

Lizzie looked around. In the pale crepuscular light, everything winked and glowed—the nearby Burger King, the dinosaur belly, the cluster of desert city lights in the distance. "I'm in Palm Springs— well, almost in Palm Springs. Remember the giant dinosaur sculptures? I'm there. I'm here; I'm getting gas."

"What are you doing there? Are you with Max?"

Lizzie shook her head. *Max*, she thought. "No," she said.

"What are you doing there?" Sarah repeated, more forcefully this time.

Lizzie shook her head again. "I don't know," she whispered. And then, "I saw the detective. It's a mess." She was crying now. "I'm a mess."

"What detective? What are you talking about?"

Lizzie didn't answer; how could she answer? She gripped her phone close to her ear, suddenly precious, the only thing securing her to this world.

Sarah's voice sounded tinny and far away. But she did not hesitate. "Just stay where you are. I'm coming."

WAS IT MISFORTUNE OR GOOD luck that one of the few rooms available was a luxe villa at the Grove on Palm Canyon Drive—a midweek special, theirs for the night for a mere $600. By the time Sarah arrived, Lizzie was already checked in, ensconced on the big private patio, listening to the hum of the few golf carts still traversing the green, the light clicking of the sprinklers, when her phone rang. Max, she saw. She let it go to voice mail, looking past the sand traps and the fourth hole at the marbleized surface of the craggy mountains in the distance, inured to the bite in the air. She had taken only a cursory glance at the sumptuous king-sized bed, the deep soaking bathtub that could hold a party. *I earned this luxury*, she thought, pulling a bottle of Côtes du Rhône from the minibar, feeling as tender as a bruise. *Every moment of this, I deserve.*

When Sarah rushed out onto the patio, they hugged and hugged, and for once, Lizzie wasn't the first to let go. "Dad did it," she kept saying.

Sarah shook her head. She poured herself a glass of wine and motioned Lizzie to sit beside her. "Tell me."

Lizzie recounted what the detective told her, the free fall in the art market, the fact that the artwork was insured for far more than the current value. She told Sarah about the PI Joseph had supposedly hired and how that wasn't true. She reminded Sarah about the business manager who ripped Joseph off, and the real estate deal that had soured. "It all fits," she said to her sister.

"It doesn't," Sarah said firmly. "I don't believe it."

"I do," Lizzie said. She was worn out, exhausted and depleted, and yet she felt a smooth glide of a sensation that she recognized as truth. "It makes sense. No one broke in, they took the most expensive art and didn't touch anything else. He was stressed about money and then he wasn't. It all makes sense."

"But none of that means he did it. Where is the evidence? Where is the proof? The fact that I can't prove to you that he didn't doesn't mean that he did."

"If you had talked to Detective Tandy—"

"I don't *want* to talk to him."

"I know," Lizzie said softly, miserably. "I know, I'm sorry."

"No, you're not," Sarah said, looking out at the lights spotlighting the fourth hole of the golf course, the ground's bright, unearthly green. "You think the worst of him; you always have."

Lizzie shook her head. "That's not true," she managed.

"Of course it is." Sarah said it so gently Lizzie started to cry. "He tried, you know. It couldn't have been easy, but he tried."

"You think I don't know that?"

"I wonder sometimes. And it's always been about the painting for you. I don't know why you're so hung up on the painting. Why does it matter? He loved you. He loved you, no matter what."

"I know," Lizzie whispered.

"No, he really loved you. Can you imagine?" Sarah said with a volley of insistence. "A single parent of two little girls? His ex-wife dead? He tried his best."

"I know," Lizzie said, and now she was pleading, out into the night, the tiny white lights that necklaced the patio. "But you know, he didn't always try." She looked back at her sister, her pretty face striking even in the low light, a face she knew almost as well as her own. "You were so young when they were still married. But things were tense; he was never around."

"I remember," Sarah said. "I remember more than you think."

"She wanted—I don't know—she wanted more."

"*Please.*" Even in the fuzzy light, Lizzie could see that Sarah's mouth was firm. "Yeah, she wanted more."

"What does that mean?"

Sarah shook her head. "Nothing," she muttered.

A rudimentary fear rose inside of Lizzie. "Come on. What did you mean?"

"Why do you think you know their relationship? How could you possibly know what happened?"

"I was eight years old; I saw things."

"Yeah, well." Sarah reached for her wine. "I remember that time before their divorce pretty well. And I know you think he was the one who had an affair, but he wasn't. It was Mom."

What? No. Lizzie was shaking her head, warding Sarah off. "That's absurd. You were five, six years old. How would you know?"

"I just do." Sarah said it with such finality that for a heart-stopping moment, Lizzie believed her. "I saw something. Someone. There was this guy: tall, bearded. He came by a bunch. You must have been in school. He called me Sarah Sue. One time Mom was supposed to take me to ice-skating lessons and instead we took a drive to his house; it was on a kind of farm, or at least, there were chickens there, and some turkeys too. I remember this drafty, messy kitchen, lots of dirty dishes and pots, a big sink. I asked for something to drink, and Mom made him clean the glass twice before giving it to me. I remember her laughing. And then he filled it up with chocolate milk and it was really good."

Lizzie studied her sister, her disbelief morphing and twisting. "That's it? You had chocolate milk from some hippie and now Mom had an affair?"

"I know what I saw," Sarah said. "My therapist," she said, and stopped. "What?"

"Nothing," Lizzie muttered. Of course this came out in therapy.

"And anyway, that doesn't even matter. I asked Dad."

"You asked Dad?" Lizzie said with unvarnished surprise.

"Yeah. He confirmed it. He said he didn't blame Mom, and I shouldn't either. He said people make mistakes. He said they both had been at fault, that he hadn't been home, and when he was around, he wasn't *really* around."

Lizzie stared at her sister, who was gazing out into the cool desert night. "Why didn't you tell me before?"

Sarah exhaled. "I thought about it; I wanted to. But, I don't know. So then you could think worse of Mom too? She wasn't around to defend herself or explain. It didn't seem right."

Lizzie shook her head. She was thinking of her mother, her beautiful mother, her warm eyes and her crooked half smile and that laugh that had made Lizzie feel more loved than anything else in the world. She was thinking about those afternoons when they would go alone into the city for what Lynn called L time (*just the two of us*) to lunch in Little Italy, where the food wasn't much better than the pizza place in town, but they called Lizzie signorina and they had chocolate chip cannolis and it was only two blocks away from the arcade in China- town where you could put in a dime and watch a live chicken dance in a cage. Lizzie had always thought of those afternoons as their time, together, but maybe they were an escape for her mother, to get out of Westchester, if only for the afternoon. She saw Lynn in her jeans and boots and her suede coat with the big buttons, her hair frizzing this way and that, just a touch of lipstick, astonishingly beautiful and alive, walking in the city she loved, and Lizzie thought: *Of course someone fell for her.*

But when Lizzie thought of how vibrant her mother looked on those afternoons, striding down Canal holding her hand, another, less pleasant memory forced its way in: the errand they ran after their Little Italy lunches. The storefront in Chinatown had windows lined with rows of dusty unmarked glass jars filled with dried purple and blackened herbs. The store smelled something awful, but her mother took no notice. Lynn handed a slip of paper to a short woman at the counter who measured out the herbs, gave them to Lynn in a series of clear-faced envelopes with no explanation. Lynn swiftly paid, depos- ited them in her purse, and took her daughter's hand. "Youth potion," she said, and outside Lizzie gulped down the exhaust-tinged air of Chinatown as if it were the freshest she had ever tasted, too afraid to ask any questions.

Lizzie told herself she didn't want to remember stopping in that shop—it was awful to contemplate; what were those herbs exactly? Had they done more harm than good?—but it wasn't wholly true. Lizzie longed to remember it all.

"It's hard for me to picture her face," she confessed to Sarah. "I mean, I know what she looks like, but I can't see it anymore in my mind."

"I don't know if I ever could."

Lizzie grabbed her sister's hand. Neither spoke for a long time. "It's going to happen with Dad too," Lizzie said.

"Yeah, it will." Now Sarah was the one tightening, holding on. "But we'll be okay."

"I don't know about that," Lizzie said. She could barely get the words out. "I loved them both—so much." How could it be that she would never see them again? How was that possible?

"I know, I know," Sarah murmured. "But you've got me."

"Thank fucking God." Lizzie let out a weird hiccup of a laugh. When had Sarah become such a stalwart, so steady and calm? With one hand, Lizzie wiped away snot and tears, sniffling, unseemly; with the other she gave Sarah's hand a little squeeze.

"I'll tell you what I need," Sarah said, rising. "Food. I bet you this place has everything." She took Lizzie's glass and filled it up, took a swig. "Maybe we need another one of these bottles too."

"Hey," Lizzie said, for it just dawned on her. "You're drinking."

"I am." Sarah met her gaze. "It didn't happen this month."

"Oh," Lizzie said. She had truly thought it would. "Sadie, I'm sorry."

"It's okay. The doctor says we just need to be patient. But I'm not exactly the patient type. We Goldstein girls aren't."

"'We'? I'm so patient and laid-back."

"Ha." Sarah said, and she swatted at Lizzie. "Ha, ha. Ha. What did Max say?"

"Max? About what?"

"About the detective."

"Oh," Lizzie said, and her stomach contracted. The detective, Max. She couldn't handle thinking of either. "I haven't spoken to him."

"Why not?"

"I don't know." That wasn't exactly true. She thought back on the other day, when he was so adamant. "I didn't think it through. I wanted to talk to you."

"Ah. So you ran away." Sarah grinned, which was both irritating and comfortingly familiar. "You ran away like you often do."

"Come on, that's not true," she said, although the second Sarah said it, Lizzie was supplying her own examples: she had run away from Ben; she had fled California and her father; she had hightailed it out of L.A. after meeting with Tandy. She ran away as if leaving the scene of the crime would negate it—which it never did. "Jesus, do you ever let up?" she said with affection. Her sister had driven a hundred miles, just for her.

Sarah shrugged. "Not really," she said, grinning again.

THEY ATE FRIED CALAMARI AND tuna burgers sandwiched in sweet buns and slathered in tarter sauce and all that richness didn't come close to filling Lizzie up. They curled up on the giant bed, flipping through the channels until they found Gene Hackman in *The Conversation* (Sarah: "I always thought he was sexy." "You think a lot of men are sexy," Lizzie said, which made Sarah laugh.) Lizzie called Max, leaving a message on his cell phone, saying, "I'm out with my sister, and I'm drunk. I'm staying with her tonight," which was, at least, part of the truth.

They pulled back the comforter and climbed beneath the sheets, so soft they made Lizzie want to cry. "You're always looking for answers, you think every situation *has* an answer," Sarah said after they turned off the lights. "Maybe there isn't one here; did you ever think that?"

"No," Lizzie murmured honestly. "I didn't." She rested her head on her sister's shoulder. She was so tantalizingly close to sleep. She had a flash of flying back and forth from New York to L.A. when they were kids, Sarah's head damp with sweat as she slept against her, shuttling between their parents' homes, thousands of miles up in the air. They weren't their mother's or their father's then, but each other's. Here was the best thing their parents had ever done.

THE NEXT AFTERNOON, THEY TOOK to the road, and before Lizzie knew it, she was back in Venice. There was Max, swinging the door open before she rooted out her key. "I thought I heard you," he said, leaning in to kiss her. "I just got home a few minutes ago."

In an instant, she was taking in his watchful eyes, the lanky height of him. She felt her heart lurch, a gawky, clumsy step. "You look tired," she said, following him in. If anything, she knew she was the exhausted-looking one. But his eyelids did seem heavier, the lines gullying his mouth sharper, more pronounced. He seemed, if only for a second, not just older but old.

"I stayed up late last night—too late. But I still can't believe I found it," he said with a sly smile.

She looked at him, not comprehending. "Found what?"

"Didn't you get my message?"

She shook her head; she had never listened to the voice mail he left last night.

"The gallery records," Max said, gesturing toward a pair of open boxes by the sofa. A cloth-covered book lay next to the glass bird sculpture and a bottle of scotch on the coffee table. Max picked up the thick book. "I found it on my first try," he said with a melancholic stamp of pride. "See?" He pointed at a swollen page. The entry, written in florid cursive, was divided into columns and filled with numbers looping and dipping across. Lizzie felt dizzy, as if she too were swimming off the page:

> *Chaim Soutine (1893–1943)*
> *The Bellhop*
> *signed "Soutine" (lower right)*
> *oil on canvas*
> *26 1/8 x 20 1/8 in.*
> *Painted c. 1921*

"My parents purchased it on September 12, 1971, for fourteen thousand seven hundred dollars. They bought it from a Jack Mendor.

I went online," Max was saying. "And I found this obit." He handed her a printout. She read: "John ("Jack") Thomas Mendor, of Fair Lawn, N.J., passed away on November 29, 1989, his beloved wife, Maggie (Ingoglia), by his side. A World War II veteran, he proudly served his country during three major battles in the European theater, including Normandy and the Battle of the Bulge. After returning from war, he gained employment at the Joseph Kurzon Electrical Supply Company as a salesman, and worked at the company for twenty-nine years, rising to become an executive. He leaves behind his loving wife and two sisters."

"I'll bet you he bought the painting while he was in Europe during the war," Max said. "Doesn't that make sense? It all fits."

It all fits. That's what Lizzie had told herself when she was speaking to Tandy, that's what she had said to Sarah earlier. "Yeah," she said faintly to Max now. A GI brought *The Bellhop* back to America, to Jersey? An electrical supply salesman?

"I looked up his wife too. She died in 2002. They didn't have any children. I wish there were more to learn," Max said. "But now we at least know who my parents bought it from and how it probably got here."

"Yes, thank you," Lizzie said automatically. "Thank you for going to the trouble for finding this." Her mind was skittering about: a vet grilling in his Jersey backyard, boasting about the painting he had bought for pennies in Europe; *I'm telling you where the facts lead,* Detective Tandy was saying. Lizzie put Mendor's obituary and the gallery book on the coffee table, next to the bottle of scotch. It was open, she saw. "You've been drinking," she said.

"My company while you were gone. I've gotten used to having you around."

She nodded, looking out the window at the strip of muddy canal. "You okay?" he asked.

"I saw the detective yesterday." Her voice sounded hoarse.

"What detective?"

"Gilbert Tandy."

"I don't know who that is. Should I?" There was no look of recognition on his face—his gaze remained steady, maddeningly difficult to read. Could he really not know?

"The detective investigating my father's stolen artwork."

"Oh," he said, and she could have sworn that he pursed his lips. "And how did that come about?"

There was no turning back now. "I called him."

"And? Did you learn anything?" He folded his arms over his chest, but his voice stayed infuriatingly calm.

"He said; he said . . ." The words felt bony, useless; she had to force them out of her throat.

"What?" And there was something—a shadow crossing his face, a crack of hesitation. She hadn't imagined it, and now she felt a terrible fear.

"You have to tell me. Please tell me," she said.

He shook his head.

"I'm asking you, Max," she said, quiet but no less desperate, her heart a knotted collision. "You."

Max tented his hands over his nose and mouth. "He didn't want to," he finally said. "It was just an idea." He was staring beyond her. "He needed money. I told him no, I said it was crazy, but your father—he could be persuasive."

"Persuasive?" Lizzie said with incredulity. That was his explanation? She had lived her entire life with her father's persuasions, his appetites; she had been cowed by them, shaken them off, been defined by them. But she had been a child. *Persuasive* was all it took to convince Max?

"Lizzie—" He reached for her arm, but she wheeled around, bumped against the coffee table; the glass figurine teetered and fell, its delicate beak cracked.

Max bent to pick it up. "You okay?" He tried to touch her, but again she shook him off. What was she doing here? She would drown in the warm sea of Max's explanations.

"You were there that night, weren't you?" she said in an anguished rush.

"No, no, Lizzie, you don't know—"

"No, I don't," and she was crying openly now. "I have no fucking idea. But he let me take the blame. You both did. You let me think it was my fault, all these years."

"Lizzie, please, you don't understand. He never meant for it to be permanent. I've wanted to tell you, I've wanted to say something for so long. It never should have happened; I should have stopped it from happening. It was a mistake, a huge, monumental mistake, and all I've ever wanted to do was make it up to you."

"My God. *That's* what this was about?"

"No, no; I love you, I do. You know that, don't you? I love you, and I'll do anything not to lose you—"

"No," she said. She backed against the bookshelf and slid down, making herself as small as possible. "You have to stop. No more talk." She said this into her knees. "Please."

"Oh, Lizzie." He spoke in a raspy, choked voice. "Oh God." He was sobbing. Making awful sounds, his body shuddering. "You have no idea how sorry I am. If I could take it all back, if there was some way I could go back in time, I would; you don't know what I would give to make this right for you, for all of us."

"You helped him, didn't you?" she heard herself ask.

"I only told him, I only gave him a name. No one was supposed to be there that night, you girls were supposed to be staying with friends—"

"Jesus, I *know that*. Do not tell me that. This had nothing to do with me or that fucking party." She had scrambled to her feet and hurtled the words at him. She had blamed herself for so long. "What happened to the paintings? Tell me. You have to. Where are they now?"

Max shook his head. "Gone," he said softly.

"What do you mean, 'gone'? Did you—get rid of them?" Lizzie saw *The Bellhop* in her mind's eye: his hardened mouth, the glossy dark eyes, the oversized ears, the tilt of his head that seemed like posturing. That first night at her father's after her mother died, she had laid eyes on *The Bellhop* and she had thought that he would keep her safe. But no, she had been foolish, so unbelievably wrong; that was never *The Bellhop's* job. Lizzie was crying, sobbing, as terribly as Max had been. Her father.

"Lizzie, please stop," Max was saying. "Oh God, please." He kissed the side of her neck. *No, no,* she wanted to say. But she was drowning and his lips felt soft and she was desperate to hold on to something. Soon she was doing the only thing she knew to do with Max; she was tugging at his clothes. Soon she was matching his greediness with her own.

LATER, THEY LAY ON HIS Turkish rug, limbs entwined. Lizzie's unhooked bra hanging limply at her chest. Her thighs were cold. Max's pants and boxers were pooled at his ankles.

"He let me take the blame," Lizzie said quietly.

"He never meant to. You have to believe me; that was his biggest regret." Max smoothed back her hair with the palm of his hand, kissed her brow with what struck Lizzie as an unmistakably paternal gesture. "Come," he said, shifting his legs, pulling up his boxers. "Let's go to bed."

Lizzie shook her head. It was like that first night out in California when she was thirteen, when her motherless world was not one she could bear to inhabit. She didn't want anything to do with a reality that insisted, *All this is true.* She couldn't stay. But how could she leave?

14

LOS ANGELES, 1968

NEARLY NOON AND HARRY WAS still sleeping. It was the fourth day after his arrival in Los Angeles. "Maybe he is ill," Rose said to Thomas. Her own stomach had been bothering her of late. "This can't still be jet lag, can it?"

"He isn't sick. He's lazy," Thomas said.

Where had this handsome, dark-eyed man come from? The last time Rose had seen her nephew he was a slightly built fifteen-year old with wispy facial hair and a head that seemed too large for his body. Now Isobel and Gerhard's eldest stood more than six feet tall, with dark curls, a strong jaw, and an olive complexion all his own, confident as only a twenty-year-old could be.

Harry had recently dropped out of the University of London ("I am *not* pleased," Gerhard had said on the phone, and Rose could hear his disapproval surging through the transatlantic crackle). He was here to try his hand at acting, a plan eventually approved by his mother, grudgingly tolerated by his father. But as far as Harry was concerned, there was no trying: "I'm an actor," he'd maintained when Thomas asked him what he'd be doing for money. "I'm going to act." Rose and Thomas had agreed to put him up in their small study for the month. "Then you must promise me you'll kick him out," Gerhard said to Rose. "He needs to learn to take care of himself."

"Oh, we will," Rose said into the phone, and rolled her eyes at her husband. Gerhard and Isobel paid for everything.

SATURDAY MORNING, EDGING PAST TEN. Thomas had to work for a few hours. No sound from Harry. Finally Rose opened the door to the study. Harry's suitcase still lay open and unpacked on the floor. Was that a dirty sock draped on their Smith Corona on the desk? "It is long past time to get up," she said to the figure under the sheets. "What are you going to do when you have auditions?"

"Oh, Auntie." Harry sat up, rubbed his eyes. "I'm acclimating. My body's adjusting—just like the astronauts. You can't rush these things."

"In fact, you can," Rose said. "And you will."

Within the hour, they were on the road. First stop: the Griffith Observatory. They took her Impala, Harry slumped down in the passenger seat, sunglasses on. "You know the '68 model comes in a convertible," he said. "Simply gorgeous. And it's not all that much more money."

She laughed. "How in the world would you know how much money it is?"

"I'm hardworking," he said. She laughed some more. "I am. When I set my mind to something, I most certainly am." He rolled down the window, fiddled with the radio dial. Someone was singing about a beautiful balloon. "God, I adore this place," he said, fingers trailing in the warm air.

At the observatory, Harry bounded about, paying little attention to the magnificent views, all of Los Angeles fanned out below, talking about *Rebel Without a Cause* and soon enough, his hunger. "Absolutely *famished*," is what he said. "Is Schwab's anywhere near here?"

She exhaled. "Schwab's is a tourist trap and Lana Turner wasn't discovered there anyhow. I'll take you somewhere better." They drove back down the hill into Hollywood proper, to Carolina Pines Jr.'s. It was just a diner, nothing fancy about it—but she loved the futuristic swoop of the roof, the large glass windows that looked out onto the bustle of Sunset, the warm cinnamon rolls topped with the perfect amount of icing.

A young copper-haired waitress took their order. Rose asked for a cinnamon roll and a cup of coffee. Harry ordered coffee too, and a steak sandwich. And fries. "Wait," he said as the waitress was turning away. "Can you add a side of chili too?"

She smiled at him, revealing a sweet gap between her top teeth. "'Course," she said.

"Are you certain you'll eat all that?" Rose said. "That's quite a lot."

"That it is. I'm a hungry boy."

Rose shook her head while the waitress laughed, twirled her pencil between thumb and forefinger. "You look familiar," she said. "You've been here before?"

"No," Harry said, and he sat up straight, folded his hands like a schoolboy. "But I'm an actor."

"Really? Maybe I've seen you in something."

"I don't think so. But you will." He said it so seriously; in the moment, Rose nearly believed him.

When the food arrived, Harry tucked in. He ate and he ate, chased the last slivers of onion from his sandwich. After he finished nearly everything on his plate, he tore off some of Rose's cinnamon roll and dunked it into his coffee. Rose watched, astounded. Her brother had always been a careful and appreciative eater, even before the wartime years; her nephew ate as if he might never fill himself up.

Harry drained his cup of coffee, leaned his long torso back. "You were right; that was good. And now?"

"I thought we'd go by the County Museum. It just opened last year." She told him about the plaza out front, the Rembrandt portrait that she admired.

Within the hour, they were heading up the stairs from Wilshire to the museum, Harry taking them two at a time. "Oh, it is lovely," he said. A trio of austere white buildings aproned the plaza, rising up and cutting against the cloudless sky. "When you and Uncle Thomas get sick of me, perhaps I'll pitch a little tent here."

Rose didn't answer. She was staring ahead, shading her eyes. Could the sun be playing tricks on her?

"Auntie?"

Rose was walking toward the museum entrance, feeling light-headed, paying Harry no mind. There was a poster hanging by the entrance, an abstract swirl of a landscape in a blaze of colors—yellows and greens, roiling in movement: CHAIM SOUTINE RETROSPECTIVE, MARCH 3 TO APRIL 18, 1968.

There was such a pounding in Rose's ears. A Soutine exhibit, here? Opening in less than a week? Harry was saying something—she couldn't hear him, she couldn't hear anything—she nodded mutely. He disappeared. And soon Rose was standing alone in front of the admissions desk.

"May I help you?" asked a fleshy woman with glittery cat-eye glasses.

"I'd like to know about the Soutine exhibit," Rose said. Here she stopped. What did she want to know? "Are there portraits in the show?" she finally asked, feeling a profound sense of anticipation and unease.

"I believe so. There are lots of paintings, close to one hundred, I think."

"Is there a list?"

"A list?" The woman behind the desk looked perplexed.

"Of the paintings in the show."

"No. I'm sure someone has one, but we don't have it. We're just volunteers. Come back next week; it's supposed to be terrific."

Rose nodded, made her way to a nearby bench. She was sitting there when Harry emerged from the restroom. "You ready?" he asked. "Let's go see that Rembrandt fellow everyone raves about."

"Actually, I'm not feeling well; let's go home."

SHE DIDN'T TELL THOMAS. WHAT was there to tell? She had known about other exhibits of Soutine's work through the years—significant ones. A show at the Museum of Modern Art a few years before she moved to America, and a show in London at the Tate after she had left. The Barnes Foundation outside of Philadelphia boasted of many Soutines in its collection. She had written to the museums and galleries, requested and received (at no insignificant expense) catalogs of the exhibits, lists of paintings with their provenance included in their collections. *The Bellhop* had never been among them. What were the chances that it would magically resurface now, at a museum a mile away from her home?

Still Rose felt a low-grade nausea, a blanket of queasiness wrapped around her. The day the exhibit opened, she felt worse. She told Thomas she had a stomach bug and called in sick. She went back to sleep, and by the time she woke up again, even Harry was gone. She finished the dishes and made her bed and tidied up the study too, but all this seemed to be staving off the inevitable.

When she arrived at the museum, there were few people in the exhibit's three rooms. Rose's heart resounded so loudly, she felt as if it might crash out of her ribs; she half expected one of the elderly women milling about to hear its beats, look askance, shuffle away. Instead she heard one woman say: "Van Gogh's work is *much* more precise, don't you think?"

Rose looked and looked. Ninety pieces of Soutine's work were gathered here ("the largest ever exhibition of his in this country," the curator noted in an introduction mounted at the show's entrance). She moved past so many—steely faces of waiters, forlorn brides, dizzying landscapes with windswept trees, silvery herrings about to be pierced by forks, skinny, headless, nothing chickens, swaying in front of brick walls.

Then her heart contracted. On a canvas in front of her was a boy in a red thickly swirled uniform. Rose's cheeks flamed hot, her hands went cold. But no, this boy's hands were at his side, not on his hips; his eyes were wider, his face paler and pancaked white. He didn't look as constricted, as sullen, as she remembered *The Bellhop* being. Rose looked at the card. It was called *Page Boy at Maxim's*, painted in 1925. It wasn't hers.

She kept looking. Ghostly sting rays, their faces eerie and yet humanlike, portraits of a baker's boy and a man in blue. Huge sides of raw beef, splayed open, entrails exposed with such furious brushstrokes that Rose had to avert her eyes, nearly mistook the paint for blood.

She reached the end of the show. Her inevitable disappointment overcame her like a warm murkiness, a thickness to the air. Everything slowed. She looked at the last picture. A distorted landscape of a country road beneath a vast swirling sky, a pair of children holding hands—were they siblings?—faces blurry, unclear. *Two Children on a Road*, it was called, painted in 1942.

She knew how Soutine's story ended. By 1942, the painter was living in the French countryside, moving from village to village, trying to avoid detection by the Gestapo. He suffered from ulcers. A particularly ugly bout left him writhing in pain, bleeding. His girlfriend urged him to return to Paris to see a doctor. They took a circuitous route to evade officials. The trip took more than twenty-four hours. By the time Soutine arrived, his condition was dire. He died on the operating table.

Rose's breath felt shallow, not at all sufficient for her body. She shouldn't be here. There was nothing to find. Why did she ever think otherwise?

She hurried back through the exhibit, past a black-and-white photograph of Soutine himself, smoking, taken in profile, handsomer than his self-portraits would suggest.

Then she saw another portrait that she had somehow missed; she slowed down. The painting was of a woman, an elegant, sharp-eyed woman, her dark hair cut in a fashionable bob. She wore a sumptuous red dress, and a fur cloaked her shoulders. The woman's legs were stylishly crossed at her ankles, her fingers lightly touching in her lap. There was a wryness to her gaze that made Rose think she was tolerating the painter, humoring him. She had better places to be. *Portrait of Madame Castaing*, the card said; she was a patron of Soutine's. Rose had seen reproductions of it before. But now, seeing it in person, Rose's skin went icy. There was something in that knowing gaze that Rose recognized. She couldn't shake the thought: it reminded her of her mother.

A great swell of nausea overtook her. Rose hurried out of the museum into the bright California light. She blinked and took in the fresh air, but she felt a bilious heave, a sour, metallic taste curdling in her mouth. She leaned into a nearby bush and vomited what little food was in her body.

"Love, you all right?" She heard a woman with a thick Scottish accent behind her.

"Yes, thank you." She tried to sound convincing. Rose thought of the Scottish woman who used to man the tea counter near her apartment in Belsize, and this reminder of England brought her to the brink of tears. She wiped her mouth on the cotton sleeve of her dress, trying to rid herself of that awful metallic taste.

"Oh, dearie, you most certainly are not." The woman handed Rose a handkerchief, produced a cup of water from who knew where. It tasted deliciously cool and sweet.

"I'm fine," Rose said, "I'm fine." And this little kindness from a stranger made it so.

ROSE WAS ON THE COUCH when Thomas came home that night. "How you feeling?"

"Okay," she said. Thomas studied her. "Not great," she allowed.

"Poor thing." He brushed a kiss against her forehead. "Still the stomach?"

She nodded. "It's nothing. I'll be fine by tomorrow."

"I'm going to put the kettle on; want some?" She shook her head. Speaking made her feel more nauseated. "Where's the boy?" Thomas asked.

"Out."

"May I ask you a question? Has he actually been on any auditions?" He said it lightly, but Rose knew where it was leading.

"I have no idea," she said with considerable effort. She had little interest in monitoring her nephew's whereabouts when she was feeling her best, and absolutely none now.

"I never realized how low the ceilings in our apartment were until he moved in. How long did we say he could stay?"

"A month," she said. "And it's been two weeks. Please don't start." They had the extra room. Harry went to the grocery store for her, he took the bus down to the mechanic's on East Vernon the other day to pick up her car without complaining. She liked having her nephew around. How much of an imposition was he on Thomas?

"I'm not starting." He sat at the edge of the couch, played with the crocheted throw at her feet. "What can I get you? Maybe a scramble? Have you eaten anything all day?"

She shook her head. "I don't want anything." The nausea, which had retreated, had snuck back with force. She despaired that she might remain on the edge of vomiting for a good while. When she called in sick, the school secretary had told her that three girls were out with the stomach flu.

"It's not good for you not to eat," Thomas said.

"I know. In a bit."

"If you feel this rotten tomorrow, you should see the doctor."

"It comes and it goes. There's a virus going around at school. There's no need."

"So he'll confirm it. You always put it off, going to the doctor; then you go, and you feel better."

The thought of going to the doctor made her feel worse. "I was feeling better earlier," she decided to say. "I went to the County."

"Museum? When you were feeling this ill?"

"I was feeling better then. There was an exhibit." She paused, looking up at the ceiling. "A Soutine exhibit." She pulled the blanket off, swung her legs over, sat up. It took significant effort. She walked to the sink, slowly.

"I'm confused. An exhibit of his paintings opened? How did you know?"

"I saw something. In the paper."

"Why didn't you tell me? I would have gone with you."

"I know." She filled a glass. Tepid water. Maybe that would calm the upset. She shook her head, took a sip. "*The Bellhop* wasn't there. Of course."

"I'm sorry," Thomas said with a hand to her shoulder. Gingerly she walked off, made her way back to the couch, water in hand. It made him nervous when she spoke about the Soutine. Thomas knew that the missing painting, and all it represented, made her unhappy, and he knew he couldn't fix it. Rose understood that he wished more than anything that he could, but he couldn't. It was Thomas's frustration that he couldn't make her feel better, Rose had long decided, that wedged between them, and not her past itself.

She reached the couch. She felt as if she were moving through sludge.

Thomas came over. "Are you okay?"

"No," she said to the ceiling. "I am not. I feel awful. On many levels."

"I'm sorry," he said. "It must have been disappointing."

"It was. And it was strange. Awful and strange."

"I wish I could have been there with you."

"I know, but it doesn't matter."

"Don't say that. It does matter—to me, at least. And I hope to you."

She nodded, took his hand. She held it, felt the rise of his knuckles, bone, the pulsating warmth of his skin.

"You do things on your own," Thomas said. "But then you're upset that you're on your own."

"I know," she said, feeling worse than before. "But not today. Please. No lecturing, not now." She stood, uncertain.

"What?" Thomas said.

"I have to—" She pushed past him, nausea overtaking her.

BY THE TIME ROSE GOT out of bed the next day, Thomas was long gone. He had left a note by her bedside: "You have an appointment with Dr. Cohen at three o'clock. No skipping it."

Rose pulled on her bathrobe, went into the kitchen. Harry was there, in jeans and a flannel shirt, long legs stretched out beneath the breakfast table, a copy of *Variety* along with a crumbled pack of cigarettes on the table, spooning peanut butter out of the jar into his mouth. He sprang up when she entered. "Hello, Auntie."

Rose motioned for him to sit, turned on the kettle. "You're up early."

"Yes. Well, you're up late."

She took a spoon from the drawer, took the jar of peanut butter from him, and carved out a generous spoonful. She had awoken with the nausea mostly gone. She was starving.

"Today is my first elocution class," Harry said. "I'm gonna learn to speak like an American." He said this last part with a deliberate twang.

The kettle whistled. Rose poured tea for herself; Harry declined. He reached for the jar of peanut butter, spooned out more. "Peanut butter is a very strange substance, don't you think?" he said. "I remember it from my trip here when I was fifteen. I was repulsed by it—the stickiness, the flavor, all of it. But I was also determined to like it. I thought it would make me American."

Rose let out a rueful laugh, sipped her tea. "I hated it too, when I arrived. But nothing makes you American. One day you wake up, and you simply are. The moment has passed, and you didn't even see it happen."

"I should only be so lucky." Harry pulled a cigarette out of the pack, and only then, while tapping it on the table, said, "Do you mind?" Rose shook her head. He lit it, took a long drag.

"May I have one?" Rose gestured at the pack.

Harry offered it to her. "I didn't know you smoked."

"I don't."

Harry smiled, lit a cigarette for her. She hadn't smoked in years. She had never been a heavy smoker, but she had liked a cigarette at night, after supper. She had quit along with Thomas not long after they moved here. The last time she could remember having a cigarette was at the Ambassador; she and Thomas had gone to celebrate her getting the Eastgate job. In the ballroom's low light, the fake palm trees that fanned the perimeter of the crowded dance floor looked disarmingly real—papier-mâché coconuts and mechanical monkeys climbing the trees, their yellow electric eyes blinking and following her every move. She and Thomas drank and smoked and danced—Thomas was a good dancer, agile on his feet, more graceful than she—and the place felt silly but wonderful too. She had not wanted to leave England, but now that they were settled here, it was difficult to recall the particulars of why.

Rose sucked in smoke, felt the rush go to her head. "Now, why did I ever quit?"

Harry let out a low laugh and tapped off ash into a gold-rimmed ashtray that Rose realized wasn't hers—Harry must have picked it up somewhere. She was about to ask him where when he said: "May I ask you something, Auntie? The other day, when we were at the museum, you got upset."

Rose drew in and held the smoke in her lungs. She tapped the cigarette against the ashtray. This was another reason she had liked smoking: it gave her something to do with her hands. "I wasn't feeling well."

"I know," he said. "But it was more than that, wasn't it? I saw the poster too."

"What?" she asked thickly.

"I saw the poster for the Soutine exhibit. That's what you were looking at, wasn't it?"

"How do you know about that?"

His prominent unlined brow now furrowed. "You mean the Soutine? My dad told me."

"He did?"

"'Course. He told me that your mum had loved the painting and that the painter was well known. He must have told me when I was a little kid. He told me that your flat had lots of beautiful things. That your mother had a good eye."

"Of course," Rose echoed as she ground her cigarette down. She was trying to take all of it in. Her brother, the same one who told her to forget it all, was telling his children about the Soutine? He was proud?

"He doesn't talk about Vienna much, but he'd tell us stories now and again: like how your mother used to ask, 'Are they fine people? Or are they not so fine?' about anyone she would meet. And how frugal your father could be, how he refused to smoke an imported cigar because he thought it was an unnecessary extravagance, instead smoking whatever the government issued."

"'Just like Franz Joseph.'" Rose heard herself quoting her father automatically. She hadn't thought about that in thirty years. She remembered her father smoking, that stale woodsy smell from his study—was that the smell of a cheap cigar? She hadn't remembered her mother's focus on 'fine people,' but she could so easily hear Mutti saying that. What else did Gerhard remember that she did not? They rarely talked about their childhood.

"The painting wasn't at the exhibit, was it?" Harry asked.

She shook her head.

"I'm sorry."

She nodded again. "As am I," she managed to say.

"But you still find yourself looking for it, even when you're not looking."

"Yes," she breathed.

"I do too." His voice was low. "I don't even know what it looks like exactly—but I do too."

Was he truly looking for it? For Gerhard? For himself? Rose couldn't bring herself to ask. The kitchen was warm. She was aware of small noises floating about: the ticking of the electric clock, the wheeze of the ice-maker. She touched Harry's wrist. *Thank you for saying that*, she wanted to say, but she said nothing, afraid the words might have proved her undoing.

THE DOCTOR'S WAITING AREA WAS stifling. Even the ficus in the corner looked dejected. Rose's queasiness had returned. The exam room she was ushered into felt twenty degrees colder. The nurse instructed her to change into a gown and then Rose waited some more. She pulled her knees to her chest. Why such thin gowns? Why didn't they provide something with a little more protection?

Finally Dr. Cohen walked in. "Good afternoon, Mrs. Downes! I haven't seen you in a while. Too good for me these days?" Dr. Cohen sported a thick, snowy-white mustache and a jovial demeanor. While she complained about his style to Thomas—she half expected him to say one day, *Hello, Mrs. Downes, I'm here to tell you that you have shingles!*—she found him surprisingly reassuring. *It could be worse*, he was fond of telling her, and most of the time, she had to agree.

He took her temperature, asked her if she was still teaching at Eastgate, checked her throat, ears, and nose, pronounced all normal. Then he examined her abdomen, pressing down with his thumb and forefinger. He asked about her symptoms again, nodding all the while.

"When was your last period, Mrs. Downes?"

It had been some time. She struggled to remember. A month and a half? Maybe longer? It hadn't alarmed her. After all, she was nearly forty-one. "They've been irregular as of late," she said. "I'm not quite sure."

"Well! I believe a blood test is in order. I would not be at all surprised."

"What?" she asked dumbly.

Beneath that great brush of a mustache, Dr. Cohen's mouth turned upward into a grin. "All your symptoms point to a pregnancy. You should make an appointment with your gynecologist."

"No, it can't be," Rose said. "Can't you check? I don't want to see another doctor. It cannot be." She was shivering audibly. "I'm forty."

He sighed. "Mrs. Downes, you have to follow up. It absolutely *can* be," he added without any gaiety or adornment. And it was his serious tone that made her believe him.

SHE TOLD THOMAS THAT SHE had to go back, Dr. Cohen wanted to run some tests. "Tests for what?" Thomas asked, looking concerned.

"Nothing," she said, "it's nothing."

She went to her gynecologist. Four days later, after she returned home from school—Thomas still at work, Harry, who knows where—the nurse called. "Congratulations!" she exclaimed. Rose was nearly three months' pregnant.

"All right, then," she said, though she had no idea why. It was certainly not all right. Pregnant, after all this time? What in the world was she going to do?

She filched a cigarette from Harry's room. Out on their tiny balcony, she perched on the edge of a plastic chair grimy with dirt and lit the cigarette, inhaled deeply. The nicotine enveloped her. Even with the smoke, Rose could still make out the odor of chlorine drifting up from the courtyard. The pool water was a murky grayish green, a scrim of leaves laced the edges. They had taken the apartment in part for the pool, but even when it had been in good condition, they had rarely gone swimming.

She could get rid of it. She knew enough to know that it wasn't the way it used to be. She was friendly with a math teacher at school; Joan was an Isadora Duncan devotee at least fifteen years Rose's junior who was teaching herself German and lived on a diet of nuts and honey. Rose felt certain that Joan would know where to take care of it. Thomas wouldn't need to know.

But how could she not tell him? They almost never spoke of it anymore—his desire for children, her desire not to have them. She had thought and thought about it. She had believed herself to be right. For years she had told herself: not everyone was made to be a mother. It was easier to believe that than reckon with the more pointed question that often came to her at night: How could *she* be a mother? What did she know about taking care?

Whenever she thought about it, Rose felt like a child herself. She was back in the flat in Vienna, watching Mutti, dressed in silk, give her nose a final dusting of powder. The Mutti in the letters that Rose treasured was warmer and chattier than the elegant, distant mother she recalled from her early years. When she considered being a mother, all Rose could think about was the pain of separation, of being left behind.

Rose liked to think that not having children was not a tension in her marriage, but what had begun as a question between them had morphed into a sadness, a particular sadness for both of them, with a presence all its own.

And now? Now she was at sea with no idea of which way to turn. She hadn't wanted this. They hadn't been careful of late, but they had been careful for so long. How could it have happened?

That wasn't the point anymore. What if for all these years, she had been trying to protect herself against something that could not be protected? The growth inside of her felt violent, a disturbance, disrupting everything that she had insisted upon. Nothing was the same. Her body was telling her so. And, perhaps, Rose tried to tell herself with a calm that she did not feel, it was time for her to quiet and listen.

THAT NIGHT, IN THEIR TINY windowless bathroom with the turquoise tiles that Rose had thought about replacing for a decade now, Thomas brushed his teeth methodically, keeping an eye on his watch as he always did, timing himself.

"I have to tell you something," Rose said, looking at her husband's reflection in the mirror.

He held up several fingers—three more seconds—and spit into the sink. "Mmm?"

She had a hand on the edge of the wet sink, leaned on it for support. *Just say the words*, she told herself. "I'm pregnant," she finally said.

He stared, his thin lips whitened by toothpaste, his cheeks drained of color. She would never forget how in that moment he was a stranger. "What?" He said it so sharply that Rose could only hear disappointment.

She swallowed. She wasn't sure she could work up the courage to speak again. "I'm—"

"I heard you," he said. "My God, did I hear you?" He clapped a hand over his mouth. "You're pregnant?"

She nodded, grabbed his wet hands with her own. A sob ripped through her.

"Are you sure?" He was crying now, but also—she was sure of it—laughing. "You're certain?"

She nodded again. "You're happy?"

"I'm delirious." He pulled back, scrutinizing her. "And you? What about you?"

"I'm scared," she said, and she was crying now too.

"Do you—do you want this?"

She gripped him hard—she was that frightened. But she made

herself say the words. "I think I do. I do. But, Thomas, we will be so old; people will think we're the child's grandparents."

He kissed her damp cheeks, one after the other, laughing all the while. "I do not care," he said. "Do you hear me? I do not care at all."

THE NEXT DAY WHILE ROSE was teaching fourth period, a junior came to her classroom. "There's a call for you, Mrs. Downes," she said. Rose hurried to the office. What was wrong? Thomas only called if it was urgent.

But it was her nephew on the line. "I got a callback!" Harry said joyously. "For the doctor role."

"Oh, Harry," she said, irritation mingling with relief. "I was in the middle of teaching. You worried me."

"So sorry, Aunt Rose," he said, not sounding sorry at all, "but I got a callback! They want to see me again. This afternoon." His voice dropped. "But I'm not at all prepared."

"But you are," she told him.

"You don't know that."

"I do. You are only scared because you care so much." She believed this, didn't she?

ON SATURDAY, ROSE RETURNED TO the Soutine exhibit, Thomas and Harry in tow. This time, she felt prepared, happy even, her nausea abated, glad to have her men by her side. Today the gallery rooms were crowded, and Rose elbowed her way to show Harry the *Page Boy at Maxim's*, the portrait in the show that had reminded her of *The Bellhop*.

Harry, attentive, eager, was taken with the still lifes. He kept bounding between them and Rose and Thomas—"that bloody side of beef," he said. "It's unseemly and awful and fantastic." A few minutes later, he came back. "I just read an amazing story in the catalog; did you know that Soutine hauled an actual side of beef up to his studio, and kept buckets of cow's blood by its side and doused it whenever it started to turn gray?"

"I did know that," Rose said. It was an oft-told story about Soutine and she had wondered if it was true. She loved that Harry was taken with it.

"The smell and flies got so bad that the police were called," Harry continued. "And apparently Soutine said, 'What does sanitation matter when compared to the sanctity of art?'" He chortled, and off he went again.

Thomas stayed by Rose's side, a hand on the small of her back, walking where she led them. She pointed out the portraits; she told him that Madame Castaing reminded her of her mother. "She's beautiful," he said. He cast a sideways glance at his wife. "Like you."

She shook her head at him, gave him a grateful smile. The waistband of her dress felt tighter. She could take this one out, but soon she wouldn't be able to wear her regular clothes.

They paused in front of a Soutine self-portrait, his ears and nose exaggeratedly large, his misshapen body adorned in a garish yellow-green jacket. "Now, that is positively monstrous," Thomas said. "Why in the world would someone depict himself that way?"

"He was not a happy man," Rose said.

"That's one way of putting it. But look: there aren't any hands in the portrait. He cut off his own hands. Why would he do that?"

"Apparently hands are hard to paint," Rose said. "And it's probably harder to paint them when you're using them *to* paint."

"Maybe," Thomas said. "But I think it's awful. He needs his hands, and now they're gone."

That wasn't the way Rose thought of it. But standing next to her husband, seeing it through his eyes, she did not disagree.

FOUR DAYS LATER, AS SHE was teaching sixth period, the cramps started. *It's nothing*, she told herself. They continued through the day and intensified on the drive home. But by the time she managed to get up the stairs and inside her apartment, the bleeding had begun. She fought her way to the toilet, doubled over, sweating, terrified. She held on in desperation as her insides knotted up, the pain ballooning. Nothing was anchored, nothing safe. Eventually she forced herself to stand: dark purplish swirls of blood, clots that Rose couldn't bear to look at, filled the bowl. She grabbed towels, staggered to her bedroom—the phone was in the kitchen, miles away—and there Thomas found her two hours later, curled up, soiled towels beneath her.

"It's over," she said to him. "Thomas." She said his name again as she wept. Mutti, this had happened to Mutti too.

"No, it's not," he said. "It can't be." But when they got to Dr. Cohen's that night (he had returned to the office to see them, a kindness she would never forget), he shook his head, confirmed what Rose already knew.

THE HOSPITAL SET IN STUDIO 43 in CBS's Television City was smaller and more makeshift than Rose had envisioned. Harry had landed the part of a newly arrived, mysterious foreign doctor: "No one quite trusts him, but few can resist his charms," he had told them.

"Now that sounds like a stretch," Rose had said. But when she called Gerhard and Isobel, she boasted of how much the producers loved him; three weeks in, the role had already been expanded.

Thomas and Rose watched him stride onto the set—the ceiling a forest of lights and girders and beams and cameras—in his white doctor's coat, then turn his face toward the makeup girl, who sponged on some lurid-looking cream.

"I hope that looks better on camera than it does in person," Rose couldn't help but say.

"Let us hope," Thomas whispered back. And then: "Harry George is an inane name."

Rose shrugged. "The producers didn't like Zimmer," she said. She agreed with Thomas, but it was hard for her to get worked up over the name change. It was hard to get worked up over much these days. The last month she had felt so tired, too tired to object.

"He might actually become something," Thomas whispered.

"I believe he already has."

He smiled, sidled up closer. In her heels, they were about the same height. "You are looking particularly lovely today, Mrs. Downes."

She was wearing one of her favorite dresses today. It was a simple cotton A-line in periwinkle with pearl buttons that flashed against the blue. It fit her well again. Most of her clothes did, a fact that unnerved her, made her slow as she was buttoning up in the morning. "Why, thank you," she said. Her eyes remained on her nephew. He truly was handsome, and though he looked nothing like Gerhard, she saw something familiar in the shape of his mouth, his prominent brow—Papi, she thought now.

She heard Thomas's voice, close to her ear. "I want to try again."

Try again? she nearly asked, but she knew. She couldn't bring herself to answer.

The pregnancy had been a fluke. Rose's gaze remained on her nephew. "It's too late," she said, her voice catching on something nubby in her throat.

"It's not. It happened once. It can happen again. We just need to try." He wove an arm around her waist. "Hard work, I know, but please say you'll try."

She rested her hand on top of his. It *had* happened. And if for a moment she could scrape away the terror and doubt, ignore the constant churn of sadness, she could admit this, if only to herself: she *had* been happy.

Here was Thomas asking; she wanted simply to feel his hand on her, steadying her.

"Yes," she said even if she didn't quite believe it. She turned to him, allowed herself the tiniest of smiles. "Yes, I'll try."

IT HAPPENED AGAIN AND FAST, not three months later. It wasn't like the time before. Rose knew right away. It felt like a thrum, this pregnancy, quieter, but more insistent. By the time Dr. Cohen confirmed it with a due date of September 15 (*three days after Mutti's birthday*, Rose thought but did not say), her stomach already felt swollen, her body readying for action. She was less queasy this time, and that made her nervous; she was vigilant about tracking every twitch and wave of nausea. One night, long after they both had gone to sleep, Rose woke up with a start, convinced that she had felt blood. In the bathroom, she checked and checked. "Everything is fine," Thomas murmured when he found her there, his words blurry with sleep.

"You don't know that," she said with equal parts fury and despair.

She realized she was miscarrying a second time when they were seated in a front booth at Carolina Pines Jr.'s, eating a celebratory breakfast in honor of Thomas's forty-third birthday. As Thomas sped them in their car down Sunset to the doctor's, Rose wincing with every cramp and turn, she thought, *How could Mutti have withstood this? How did she ever keep going?*

They ceased talking about it. They never did stop trying. A year later, as Rose neared her own forty-third birthday, her period was late. She didn't tell Thomas. *Wait*, she cautioned herself, *simply wait*. But there was little private joy. When eight weeks later, her period arrived, Rose felt more resignation than sorrow. She had known that her body was broken for decades, even if she couldn't have articulated it before. There was relief in acknowledging what she was, if only to herself. She could remember sensing it when she lived alone in London after the war. *Ghosts can't give birth*, she thought.

Ludicrous, Thomas would say. *You are here, living. You are simply afraid.*

But she never did give him the chance to respond.

15

LOS ANGELES, 2008

Are you sure you're up for this?" Sarah whispered to Lizzie.

"Of course," Lizzie said, lowering her voice to match her sister's.

"He fell asleep in the car on the way over," Sarah said as she wheeled the stroller into Lizzie's apartment. "By some miracle, I was able to transfer him. If you're lucky, he'll sleep for a couple of hours." Oscar was ten months old, a grave-faced child with a scattered patchwork of pale downy hair. For the first few months of his life, Lizzie privately thought he looked like a tiny old Southern senator in baby garb. But now his body was filling out, and when he laughed, often unexpectedly, she felt like she caught a glimpse of the boy he was becoming.

"There are more diapers and wipes than you'll ever need," Sarah said, unclipping the bag from the stroller. "A bib, a couple of binkies, his bottle. I stuck in two changes of clothes, just in case. He has a slight runny nose; he seemed fine, but he might drink more milk because of it. Just heat up half at a time; my supply is getting low."

"Got it," Lizzie said with what she hoped was a confident expression. She had taken care of Oscar before, but never for this long. "It's going to be fine."

"I know; thank you so much. And it's good training for you, right? If you're unsure of anything, just call. If I have to step out of the event, it's not a big deal. Angela's got a few procedures today, so she'll be harder to reach."

"I've got it. You're coming back in a few hours, right? He's not staying for the month."

"You never know," Sarah said. "If I get a taste of freedom, I might run off." She leaned down, kissed her son's sleeping head. "I would never do that, monkey," she murmured. She threw her arms around her sister. "Thank you. I'm so so glad you're here." And soon the door clicked behind her.

Lizzie had moved back to L.A. nearly six months earlier. In many ways, it felt longer. After she and Max had ended things, she went back to New York, tried to throw herself into work. But as she elbowed her way down the packed subway steps in the morning, she would find herself picturing the canyon behind her father's house, the steep drops and sun-bleached terrain, and the clusters of poppies in February. When, amazingly enough, they won the Clarke appeal, Marc took her and the other associates out to a boozy, celebratory meal. Lizzie tipped back oysters and glasses of Prosecco, pleased that their strategy had done the job, but she was thinking: *Now what?*

Her mother's birthday passed. Then it was her father's. That summer, Sarah got pregnant. November marked the first anniversary of her father's death, and Lizzie, felled by a mean virus, was glad for an excuse not to leave her apartment for days. Her life felt full of ghosts, her dreams often sharper and more vivid than her waking life. And then Oscar was born and she flew out to meet him, and holding that tiny, wheezing alien being tight against her chest, she thought, *What are you waiting for?*

Miraculously, she quickly landed a job in L.A.: directing a family foundation, of all things. A former client was on the board, and he called her when he heard she was on the hunt for work. *I don't know anything about running a foundation,* she was about to say. But even as she thought it, she was typing the name of the foundation into Google with nervous excitement, and she heard a voice in her head—an undeniable mixture of Claudia's and Rose's—that made her sit up. *Don't run away*, this voice ordered her. *You are stronger than you know.*

Now Lizzie turned to her sleeping nephew, wearing striped shorts that ballooned over his knees. Though he was snugly buckled into his stroller, his head lolled askew. Delicately she tried to straighten it. His head was warm, moist. Snot was encrusted around a nostril. He smelled yeasty sweet. Within a second, his head had toppled back down to the same awkward angle. "Okay, okay," she said. "If that's what you want."

She headed into the second bedroom that she was using as a study, still lined with boxes. She hadn't been inclined to take the apartment until she walked into that second bedroom. It was tiny but overlooked the courtyard and was suffused with sunlight. As she stood, looking down in the courtyard, the Realtor impatient behind her, an unexpected feeling came over Lizzie: *I could be happy here.* The master bedroom was dark, some of the cornflower-blue tiles in the shower were cracked; the common hallway carried a faint mildew smell. It was well within her newly diminished budget, though, and the balcony was big enough to fit a two-person table, and she loved that second bedroom. But it was probably the way it reminded her of Rose's home—the balcony, the stucco, the utilitarian feel—that convinced her most of all.

They hadn't spoken in more than a year. Rose had called Lizzie a few times after that day, but Lizzie, embarrassed, ashamed, hadn't returned her messages. She thought of her all the time, when she was driving down Wilshire and passing the La Brea Tar Pits, when she caught a mention of Roger Corman on the radio. There was a new tearjerker of a Holocaust film about the daughter of a Danish fisherman who tried to ferry Jews across the narrow strait to Sweden during the war. It was hugely popular, despite critical grumbling, and Lizzie knew that Rose would have much to say about it, little good.

She wanted to reach out to her, but the more time went by, the harder it had become. What could she possibly say?

Lizzie went to her laptop and returned a quick e-mail to a board member. When she went back into the living room a few minutes later, Oscar was staring at her from his perch in the stroller. "Oh, you're up," she said. "Hello."

He considered her gravely. Then he began to howl.

"No, no," she said, hurrying to unbuckle him. "No, no, baby." He was screeching and he was squirming—she couldn't believe how much he could squirm. What could possibly have gone wrong so quickly? How did he already know that Sarah was gone? Finally she got him out, plopped him onto the floor. "Maybe you just need a minute."

He eyed her. "Meh," he yelled. But the sound of it wasn't as guttural and intense, and for a moment he fell silent.

Lizzie let out a breath. "You better?" she said, and allowed herself a tentative half smile.

"Meh!" He swatted at the air.

"I'm sorry, no smiling. But I don't know what you want," she said. "What do you want?"

Oscar grunted and crawled on his belly, commando-style, toward a trio of boxes in the corner. He grabbed hold and began to pull himself up.

"No, no," Lizzie said, and swooped him up. He screamed as she carried him into the kitchen. Screamed as she heated his milk. He batted the bottle away. Was he going to scream for the next three hours? Is this what she had signed up for?

"What about a peach?" She grabbed a perfectly ripe one from the bowl, washed it off. He followed her movements with his eyes, too distracted, it seemed, to cry. She sped up, sliced the peach fast. Any minute that ungodly screaming would begin again. The peaches were only a part of the bounty she had purchased yesterday at the Santa Monica Farmers Market. She had been contentedly walking among the stalls alone, tasting samples of pluots and apricots and tiny strawberries grown in Oxnard, still feeling amazed by the gorgeous abundance of produce in February. That's when she saw him.

It's someone who looks like Max, she first thought as she stared at the back of a lanky man in a gingham shirt several paces ahead on his cell phone, standing near the oranges. She still saw versions of her father all the time—men younger than him, men with more facial hair, a man at least six inches taller but with a similar determined step in his walk. She would feel a drop in her stomach, the ground unstable. Was it him? It wasn't him.

But no, this man in the gingham turned and it was decidedly Max, baseball cap visoring his roughly handsome face, sleeves rolled up to reveal his sinewy arms. He was ending his call, looking around; he was chuckling. She ducked near the almonds. He looked tanned, relaxed. Her heart jackhammered. And she simply knew: *He's seeing someone*, she thought.

He inspected a handful of satsumas, paid the cashier, and walked off. The bags didn't seem to weigh him down. Lizzie observed all these details with prickly astonishment, waiting for him to notice her, waiting to hear herself call out his name. *I've never said anything to anyone about the paintings*, she wanted to tell him. But she said nothing, her insides wrenched. Was he leaving? Could she actually let him go? She felt drunkenly off balance, as if one of her legs was heading off without her. The crowd had swallowed him up; for a moment, she strained in the bright sunlight and could see a spot of royal-blue check, a flash of shoulder. And then that too was gone.

Now Lizzie cut tiny pieces of the peach, sticky and dripping. She handed them to Oscar. "Meh," Oscar said crossly, and dropped them on the floor.

"My sentiments exactly," she said. All that sweetness, and she was left wanting too.

Her phone rang, a 213 phone number she didn't recognize. Sarah? She picked up.

"Ms. Goldstein?" the male voice said. "Elizabeth Goldstein?"

"Yeah," Lizzie said. He sounded vaguely familiar. She opened up a bottom drawer filled with Tupperware, and gave two pieces to Oscar to play with.

"This is Detective Tandy. From the LAPD."

Detective Tandy. Her stomach lurched.

"We found the paintings, Ms. Goldstein."

"Excuse me?" she asked, though there had been nothing unclear about his words.

"Your father's artwork. The stolen Soutine and Picasso." She detected a shred of impatience.

"I'm sorry," she said. The paintings? Her mind couldn't take anything in. "You found *The Bellhop?*"

"We found the artwork holed up in the garage of a house in the Valley; Reseda, actually. A ranch house in miserable condition, falling apart."

"Jesus," she said. "The paintings—are they all right?"

"Yeah, unbelievably, they're all right."

She closed her eyes, woozy. Could this really be? Rose; she had to tell Rose. And her sister. She heard something slam and opened her eyes: there was Oscar, banging away happily on the Tupperware lids, drooling. She sank down beside him.

Tandy was still speaking. "No thanks to the person whose care they were in. The house is owned by a Jane Reynolds. The mother of Desdemona Reynolds, the ex-girlfriend of Sean Malone. Do any of those names ring a bell? Did your father ever mention Malone to you?"

Lizzie shook her head. "No," she whispered. Who were these people?

"Sean Malone's a former cop who contracted services to Kruger and Dunn, where Max Levitan worked before he started his own practice. Levitan and your father enlisted Malone to take the paintings—"

A hot viscous sensation heaved up, flooding Lizzie's insides. "You know that?" she asked. "You're sure?"

"Yes," Tandy said, and the single drop of the word sounded gentle. "Malone will testify to it. His girlfriend too; she was privy to conversations. There is significant evidence."

Lizzie nodded, but didn't say more.

"There were disagreements afterward," Tandy continued, his voice warming up. "Malone wanted a larger take, saying he hadn't gotten paid enough for the job, that there were complications."

"The party I threw," Lizzie choked out. Oscar was trying to climb into her lap now, his tiny sticky fingers clawing at her hair.

"Yes. So he held on to the paintings, refusing to turn them over. He wasn't exactly quiet about it. He told his girlfriend, bragged about it. Everyone seemed to know about the goddamn paintings." For a moment, he sounded strangely like Joseph. "Years went by. Desdemona was pushing Malone to get married. Then she caught him screwing her best friend, and she decided that she'd had enough of him. She went to the cops—turned out he was dealing opiates, big-time, in cahoots with a doctor in Woodland Hills. And she told the police all about it, and then said, maybe you'd be interested in some old artwork too? It's a miracle those paintings survived. Desdemona's mother had built an aviary in her garage, metal cages filled with birds—all different kinds—and let me tell you, birds are nasty creatures. Dirty and mean. She had decided to raise the birds as part of her retirement plan—she had some crackpot scheme to breed them."

"And the paintings?" Lizzie broke in. "What about the paintings?"

"The paintings were holed up on a top rack of a shelf, surrounded by that squawking mess, a carpet of bird shit and seeds. I never knew birds smelled that much. They were in metal canisters. Desdemona had told her mother that it was a drawing and a painting of hers from high school; can you believe that? Her mother didn't have a clue that they were worth millions."

"Of course she didn't," Lizzie said, and she felt a strange rush of feeling. Poor Mrs. Reynolds and her birds.

"All the work we had done through the years didn't mean shit," Tandy said, and Lizzie could tell he wished they hadn't found the paintings this way—he viewed it as cheap, lucky—he almost wanted the mystery back. "It's always the girlfriends. They'll turn on a dime."

Lizzie pulled Oscar tighter. She started to cry. Oscar pushed a wet fist into her mouth, rooting around for her teeth. Now she was laughing and crying.

"We'll need you to come in and identify them. You and your sister," Tandy was now saying. "There are details to be worked out, of course; but the important thing is we've got them back."

"We'll be there," Lizzie said.

16

LOS ANGELES, 2008

ROSE REMEMBERED WHEN SHE AND Thomas were waiting, grimly, for the first biopsy report. "We need to prepare ourselves," she recalled him saying. "If it looks like a horse and acts like a horse, it's probably a horse and not a zebra."

"But I want a zebra," she said to him. "I demand a zebra."

By the time the pancreatic cancer was diagnosed, metastases had already taken root in his liver and lungs. He was gone within nine months, an awful, harrowing time. And yet Rose would gladly relive any one of those days to have him again. Nearly fifty years they had been together. She had been uncommonly lucky. When Thomas died, she told herself that it was a gift to have his body at all, a luxury to be able to decide where to bury him, to have a burial, a headstone, a spot of her own choosing, one that she could visit, that would be tended to, not vandalized or ignored.

But she wanted more. After all those years of feeling as if she didn't deserve happiness, that she was snatching bits of goodness wherever she could, that one day she would be punished for surviving—after all of that, she was left wanting, wishing for more.

Getting older meant facing loss, over and over again. Its presence was not limited to one's spouse. People got sick; they suffered; they died. Turn left, turn right; there was a former colleague of Thomas's, murdered in his Laurel Canyon home by a meth addict; Rose's dentist, guffawing at her last cleaning, asking about her summer plans, nearly mute six months later when he told her his seven-year-old had lymphoma; five Amish girls shot and killed in their school by a truck driver; hundreds dead from a heat wave in India.

Rose, of all people, understood that devastations occurred all the time. But that didn't mean you got used to them. Or accepted them. Almost four years after Thomas's death, his plastic reading glasses remained on his nightstand. She still couldn't sleep on his side of the bed. As Rose got older, she was surprised less by tragedies than by the absence of them. Life was fragile—what else was new?

But what to do with an actual astonishing turn, something that presented indisputably good news? "They found *The Bellhop*," Lizzie said on her voice mail, and it took Rose three more vertiginous listens, rewinding and replaying with shaking hands, to come close to understanding.

She called the detective Lizzie cited in her message. He told her about the former cop who had once worked with Joseph's friend Max, how he had been hired by Joseph to steal them. "Not unlike what I had always thought," the detective offered. "The deal went bad from the beginning."

"Can I see it? When can I see the painting?" The details he was telling her were not insignificant, but for now, she only cared about one thing.

"Why don't you come tomorrow afternoon with Ms. Goldstein?" He gave her the address and she repeated it back to him twice, still in disbelief that any of this was happening.

She called Gerhard. "That's not possible," he said.

"But it is," she said, laughing a little. "It's in police custody. Here in Los Angeles. You should come. You need to." If there were ever an instance where he would hop on a plane a day later and fly the more than five thousand miles between them, shouldn't this be it? "I can see it tomorrow, but I will wait if you can come. We can see it together."

He signed. "I can't leave Izzie. And she can't fly."

Then Isobel got on the phone and, lowering her voice, said, "I wish I could be there, but I can't leave your brother. And he simply isn't strong enough for the long flight."

But Harry, who was wrapping up a film in Vancouver, was ready and willing. "I always *knew* it would be found," he declared. "I told you last year, when I read that script involving Modigliani, that it meant something. I had this *feeling*—"

"You were right, Harry, absolutely," Rose said. Even she couldn't deny him his flights of fancy that day.

Harry drove them downtown in Rose's car. As traffic slowed on the 101, Harry kept chatting, about his current director's penchant for multiple takes—"he thinks he's Kubrick but he's not"—his ex-wife's refusal to support their daughter taking a year off from college to teach English in Guatemala. (On this, he sounded very like Isobel: "She's nineteen, for God's sake! Why shouldn't she explore?") At the LAPD's glass tower in the Civic Center, she and Harry passed through security, stepped into a lurching elevator. As she pressed the button for the seventh floor, Harry was still talking: "It is such a crazy story; if only the canvas could talk—"

"Harry, can you please be quiet?"

Out of the elevator, Rose knocked on the door to suite 703, and a short young man opened it. "I'm looking for Detective Tandy," Rose explained.

"Tandy!" he yelled.

Detective Tandy, wearing a brightly colored shirt and no tie, appeared. "It's good to meet you both," he said, and ushered them inside. The large office thrummed with activity: people milling about, odd assortments of furniture—scratched-up file cabinets and desks, a battered refrigerator, green and red tinsel twisted limply above a whiteboard filled with scrawl—"57?" It was a corner space filled with light, but the windows had gone gray with grime.

"Rose," she heard a familiar voice. There was Lizzie near the file cabinet with her sister. It was unquestionably her, but she looked different, Rose thought, her hair longer, spilling past her shoulders. Despite the tailored blazer she was wearing, she looked younger, and for a brief disorienting moment, on the cusp of seeing *The Bellhop*, Rose thought, *Time is going backward.*

"Lizzie," Rose said, and she was pulling Lizzie into a hug.

"Rose," Lizzie said, her voice cracking. Rose felt her limbs stiffen, then undoubtedly loosen. Rose held on tight.

After a moment, Tandy cleared his throat. "It's a small space; I'll take you in two by two."

Lizzie pulled back, wiping her eyes. "You go first," she told Rose.

Tandy led Rose and Harry through the maze of his office into another room guarded by a man in uniform, who handed Tandy latex gloves. He snapped them on. They made his hands look bulbous, fishlike.

Rose and Harry followed him into a tiny, low-lit, windowless space dominated by a large industrial table ensconced in plastic. The air felt thin, stripped of oxygen. Rose grabbed for the edge of the table. "Auntie?" Harry said as he steadied her elbow. For a moment, she thought she might pass out.

There he was, *The Bellhop*, lying unadorned on the table, the boy in red on the flat canvas, just as she remembered, with his gold buttons and strange surly face and stretched-out limbs. It was him, absolutely.

But gazing at him for the first time in more than sixty years, Rose felt a dark expanding swath of fear. The thick swirling redness, his tiny mouth, dark eyes, the way he positioned himself at an angle against the rich background: the boy didn't want to be here. She hadn't remembered that about him. He stared resentfully. He didn't want to be here at all.

Time folded in on itself, snaking, contorting. She saw *The Bellhop* in their Viennese flat, hanging on the wall in her parents' bedroom, Papi complaining about it ("I should be the only man in here"). There was Mutti, at the piano, practicing a spirited Shubert concerto in the drawing room with the red velvet chairs and Herr Schulman by her side, murmuring, *gut, sehr gut,* watching her with hooded eyes. Rose remembered dancing alone in front of *The Bellhop* on New Year's Eve when the lead-pouring went awry and Bette sensed the ugliness of the year ahead. She could hear Gerhard arguing with Mutti and Papi: *The soldiers aren't going to bother me. I'm going to see Ilse. I am.* There they were, gathered around the dark oak dining table beneath the massive brass chandelier, Mutti and Papi and Onkel George and Tante Greta arguing about the wait at the American embassy. Mutti wanted to put their name on all the lists. *We are not going to Argentina,* she could recall Papi saying. *Why not?* Mutti demanded.

Rose remembered when she was younger, Mutti in the cot in the tiny room that was to be the nursery, her cries of pain, the doctor rushing past, Bette cleaning up the blood. Mutti asked for *The Bellhop*—that's what she wanted, not Rose or Gerhard, but *The Bellhop,* by her side.

"Let's go," Rose said to Harry in a gravelly voice she did not recognize.

"But that's it, isn't it?" Harry said. Tandy too was studying her. "That's the painting?"

Rose nodded, turning away from them, eyes back on the canvas. Here it was, after so many years, and all she felt was sorrow. She was an old woman. Her parents, so many people she had loved, had suffered. They were murdered. They had been dead for decades now. *The Bellhop* was paint covering a surface; that was all. "Let's go," she said to Harry, her voice barely above a whisper. She hurried out of the small room, past Lizzie and her sister, waiting beside the door.

"Rose?" she heard Lizzie call. "Rose?"

"I'm sorry," she muttered, head down.

"SHALL WE STOP FOR COFFEE? Is that pink palace of yours still in business?" Harry asked, back behind the wheel of Rose's car.

"No, I want to go home."

He cast a glance at her. "I know that must have been overwhelming, Auntie, after all these years, but—"

"Harry, *please*: I do not want to talk about it."

He nodded. "It is good news, Auntie, unquestionably. After all of these years, you and Dad are getting the painting back!"

"It's not ours anymore," she said, and it was too painful to say anything more. "Technically, it's the insurance company's."

"The lawyers will take care of that," he said. "It's very clear."

She shook her head, slumped in her seat. She and Gerhard had already spoken about it. They would hire a lawyer here in the United States. But hiring a lawyer was the least of it. Cases like this could drag on for years. Rose was so weary, she wasn't sure she had the fight in her. (*Yes, you do*, she could hear Thomas telling her. *Of course you do.*) Why in the world had she cared so much? This was what she had said she wanted for all of those years: *This*? A painting? After the murder of her parents, a painting was what she had focused on?

Even Gerhard had said to her, *Mutti's* Bellhop, *your* Bellhop! You can have it back.

I don't want it, she thought petulantly. The image of *The Bellhop*, lying flat on the table in police custody, made her seize up with shame. It wasn't the painting she had wanted.

HARRY DROVE ROSE BACK HOME and clucked around the apartment, checking, Lord help her, if the milk in the refrigerator had not expired and turning up the heat ("Why is it sixty-five degrees in here? Why are you denying yourself the bloody comforts of the contemporary age?"). "Harry," she said, "I like it this way. I am seventy-nine years old, not ninety-nine. I can still do things for myself."

"It's called concern, Auntie," he said, and leaned down to give her a slide of a kiss. "Shall I order us dinner?"

"Bob is coming over. I'm sorry, but I'd like—"

"No need to explain," he said. "No need to humor your poor, single nephew; I'll eat alone, despondent, in my hotel room."

"Harry," she protested. The notion of Harry despondently alone was ludicrous. But what did she know, really?

"I'm only joking. Have your romantic dinner and I'll be back tomorrow," he said with a grin.

"Thank you," she told him firmly.

After the door closed behind Harry, she called.

"So?" Bob said. "How was it?"

"It was something," she said. "It truly was. I'll tell you all about it later. But about dinner—my nephew wants me to join him, alone." She lowered her voice as if Harry was still nearby. "I'm sorry, but he's only in town until tomorrow, and he's being quite insistent."

"Oh," Bob said with audible disappointment. "I would like to meet him, you know."

"I know," Rose said, and she felt a pulse of regret. Bob was a good man. He wasn't Thomas, but he was a good man. Why was she pushing him away? "After everything today, I just can't tonight," she finished, honest in sentiment if not in fact.

After she got off the phone, she went straight for the kitchen cabinet with the bottle of Ardbeg—Thomas's favorite. She loaded a coffee mug with ice cubes, tipped in a generous measure of the whiskey, and settled into the armchair with her Dick Francis mystery. This was what she needed, she thought. She read and she drank and she nodded off.

THE LIGHTS WERE ABLAZE WHEN Rose awoke, her heart careening, her limbs stiff. Where was she?

It was long dark by the time they had gathered in the field behind the station, the cold air biting. Mutti and Papi and Gerhard and Rose had taken the tram together and walked the last several blocks to the train station. The field was packed with people, children and parents and representatives from the Jewish organization. Dim lights bobbed up and down, flashlights carried by officials providing paltry illumination.

"We need to check in," Papi said. His wool overcoat hung loose on his frame. His face looked haggard in the shadowy light, but he also seemed strangely energized, more talkative than he had been in months. "Where do we do check in?" he asked aloud, before flagging down a representative with a flashlight, who pointed to a thick cluster across the field.

They pressed through the crowds and finally reached a red-faced woman carrying an armload of materials. "Yes," she said, consulting her papers. "Rose Zimmer, you are 163, and Gerhard Zimmer, 171." She thumbed through and pulled out two stiff placards with strings attached. "You must wear these around your neck. Attach the corresponding tags to your luggage. In a little while, we'll walk to the platform in groups. You two are in the same one, group C, 151 to 199."

"They're together," murmured Mutti. "Thank God."

"You can see the posts now with the placards," the red-faced woman continued. "You should make your way to your group soon." She looked past them. "Next," she called.

They moved to the side. Mutti put the placard around Rose's neck, freed her hair from the string. Gerhard put on his own. The string was itchy against Rose's skin. She yanked at it.

"You must leave it," Papi warned. "You don't want it to fall off."

Rose nodded, silent. What would happen if it did fall off? Would anyone know where she was supposed to go? What if she were separated from Gerhard?

Mutti pulled at the shoulders of Rose's plaid coat, inspecting the seams. "This isn't all that big. I hope it'll still fit you in a few months' time."

"That's all we need," Papi said, and Mutti nodded fast.

"Of course," she said. "*Mausi*, I packed my blue scarf with the birds that you like. And Gerhard, there's a diary for you. It's leather-bound, a fine book, and I want you to fill it with lots of details from your English adventure."

"Thank you, Mutti," he said. "I promise I will." Why did he get the diary? What was Rose supposed to do with a scarf? She had always thought it pretty, but on her mother, not herself.

Gerhard looked so mature, so serious, that Rose couldn't help but say: "I would have liked a diary instead. I'm old enough."

"Really? You want one now?" Gerhard said. "When have you ever wanted a diary before?"

"Just because you have one doesn't mean I can't," Rose said.

"Please, children," Mutti said, burying her face against Papi's over-coat.

He barked: "For heaven's sake, not now."

Gerhard was murmuring, "I'm sorry, so sorry," and Rose was sorry too, but she felt chilled into silence. She was terrified of what she might say: *I'm not leaving, I'm not.*

Mutti turned back to Rose, her face mottled and flushed. "I'll send you one tomorrow morning, just like Gerhard's. First thing. How does that sound?"

Rose nodded in assent. Why had she ever asked for it? The hollow feeling in her stomach was expanding by the moment. She couldn't imagine wanting to write anything down.

"It's time," they heard a man call out. "Line up. Please check your number and make sure you are in the correct line." Representatives were waving big signs attached to sticks listing groups of numbers. The numbers swam in the dim light. The four of them, Gerhard carrying his suitcase, Papi carrying Rose's, made their way through to their group.

Their names were checked off again, this time by a man so short that Rose nearly mistook him for a child. Papi handed Rose's suitcase to Gerhard, clapped his son on the back. "Write a letter as soon as you arrive—even before you arrive. And take care of your sister. I am counting on you."

"I will. I promise," Gerhard said. Rose didn't want to hear it. She moved closer to her mother, slid her hand into hers.

"We will take care of each other," Gerhard said, wiggling his eyebrows at his sister, and for the first time that night, Rose felt a slight leavening.

"I only wish they were going to be in the same house," Mutti said.

"It can't be helped," Papi said.

"I know," Mutti said with desperation, "I know."

A ginger-haired girl ahead of them in line clung to her father. She looked about Rose's age. "I won't go," she cried. "I won't." Rose watched her.

"You are very brave," Mutti whispered close to her ear.

"I'm not crying," Rose said. This was a statement of fact. She felt too numb to cry. Mutti and Papi said it should only be a few months, six at most. She knew precisely four words in English: *toilet, day, jam,* and *yes.* How was she supposed to live with a family she didn't know? How would she talk to them? Who would take care of her? What would happen when she got those cramps in her legs at night that only Mutti knew how to make go away? She had seen a picture of the couple she was going to live with, and they looked very stern. They had no children. *But they must be good,* Mutti had said. *For they are taking you in.*

I can't go. I won't, she wanted to cry. But she needed to make Mutti proud. "I *am* glad for your scarf," Rose whispered, flinging herself at her mother's hip. "I truly am."

"I know you are. You are my brave strong girl," Mutti said with unaccustomed fierceness.

All too soon the baby-faced man who headed their line cupped his hands together. "We need to go to the platform. Please, remain orderly." The crowd surged forward as he strode down the line, assessing. "Carry your own suitcase and remain in line!"

Gerhard gave Rose her suitcase, who strained to lift it.

"Why can't he help her? How in the world is she supposed to carry that?" Mutti asked Papi.

"Charlotte," he said. "She has to."

Rose struggled, her arms shaky with effort, but she managed. Her nose stung from the cold; her chest felt hot. As the lines wound through the field and to the platform, Mutti walked beside her in silence, holding her hand. Neither wore gloves. Mutti's fingers were slick with sweat, entwined with her own. "Look," Mutti said, "see the moon?" It was a bright inhospitable shard, emerging through the knitted clouds. "You will see the moon in England, and I will see the same moon here in Vienna. You see? We will not be so far away from each other." Rose gripped her mother's fingers tighter, said nothing. She did not want to think about the moon in England.

All too soon they arrived at the train platform. So many people jostling, so much noise—crying, reaching for each other, weeping. "Don't forget there are cheese sandwiches in both of your rucksacks," Mutti said as a pair of SS men strode past. "And I want to hear that you are working hard on your schoolwork, harder than you would at home. And you must be polite, no matter what. You are good children." A boy tripped, fell onto Rose's suitcase. "What did you do that for?" he cried accusingly, but Papi scooped up Rose—his wiry arms, his smoky smell, his rough cheeks, Papi hugging her so hard that it didn't feel like a hug at all but something more. And yet it wasn't enough; it would never be enough. Then Rose was clinging to Mutti, burrowing her head at her chest, in the warmth of her wool coat, stroking her rabbit-fur collar. "We will see you soon," Mutti promised, her cheeks aflame. "We will see you in no time at all."

This was not good-bye. Rose held on to her mother. She didn't want an English adventure. She didn't care if it was safer. Why were they sending her away?

A mittened hand tunneled into hers. "Rose," Gerhard said as he tugged at her. "We have to get on."

"We will be here, watching the train," Mutti said, pressing her hot cheek against her daughter's, desperately kissing her brow, her lips. "We will not leave."

Blindly Rose followed her brother. They stepped inside the train. The group leader pointed them into a compartment where several children were already gathered, including the ginger-headed girl who had been weeping earlier, now calm, and a pair of older boys, playing a card game. Gerhard moved close to the boys. Rose went to the big window beside the girl.

"I'm Anita," the girl said, tugging at the window. "I'm twelve."

"Rose," Rose said. "Eleven."

"Can you help me, Rose?" And the two of them pushed the window as high open as it would go, letting in a swoop of cold air, and used the leather sash that hung from the ceiling to secure the window into place.

She and Anita leaned out. Rose saw a pair of SS men conferring near the train door on the platform. Anita saw them too. "Soon we'll be leaving them behind," she said. Rose nodded. No more Nazis, this was true. This was good. But where were her parents? She scanned the crowded platform. They had promised that they wouldn't leave. There! She alighted on their worried faces, carved out and distinct from the others. "Mutti, Papi!" At the sound of her voice, they rushed toward her, waving furiously.

"Papa!" Anita called. Her father pushed his way through the knots of people to a spot beneath the train window. Anita leaned out more and her father grasped her hands. "My baby," he moaned.

The engine coughed and began to shudder. It was happening, they were leaving, Rose thought, shocked. They could not be leaving. How could her parents do this? "Mutti! Papi!" she cried.

Lights flooded the platform—Mutti's face was an awful purplish hue. "We are coming." Mutti choked the words out. "We are."

Slowly the train began to move. The crowd along the platform moved with it. Anita's father hurried alongside, held on to her hands. "No, I can't let you go," he moaned. "No."

"Papa," Anita cried.

"No, no." He grasped at her elbows, tugging, yanking. "Papa, no!" she shrieked as he pulled her torso through the window. Suddenly Anita was neither in the train nor out of it. Rose watched in horror as she tumbled onto the platform. Adults rushed over as Anita's father, weeping, hugged her tight. Out the window, Rose leaned, frozen, the air lashing against her face, her neck—*Take me*, she wanted to cry out. *Grab me too!* But the train picked up speed, and the platform and everyone on it—Mutti's contorted face, the heap of Anita—was receding. "No!" Rose cried. She felt pressure on her legs, a tugging at her waist. "Rose!" Gerhard, pulling her back.

"I don't want to go," she cried inside the warmth of the train. Gerhard jammed the window closed as she scooted feral-like to the farthest seat on the bench, away from the others. The train clanked and careered down the tracks and her brother was hugging her and she wanted none of it. "No," she howled as she buried her face against her brother's side.

"I know," Gerhard kept repeating, "I know," as the train chugged west and left everything they cared about behind.

BY THE TIME ROSE WOKE up a second time that day, it was late morning in Los Angeles. It took her longer than usual to get herself dressed. She made an egg scramble—slowly, over a low flame, just as Thomas taught her. She sat down to eat it with buttered toast and coffee, surprised at how hungry she was. She tunneled the food into her mouth automatically, with little pleasure.

The images kept shuttering through her mind: her mother's slick fingers grasping her own, the chaos and pushing on the platform,

Papi's rush of words, that distant chilly moon, Mutti's contorted expression, that poor girl pulled from the train. The memories tumbled forth, unbidden. That night on the platform had split her in two—everything that came afterward felt like an accident, one that she was never wholly present for.

But Rose grasped on to every shred of memory that muscled through. She was still the little girl leaning out that window, and yet she was now at least twice the age her parents had been then. She saw herself on that train, bereft, wanting more than anything not to leave, but she also saw herself standing on that platform as her parents had, her heart wrenched from her body, watching in agony as the train pulled away.

It was after dinnertime in England by the time she dialed. "I spoke to Harry already," Gerhard said, "but I want to hear it from you: Is *The Bellhop* as ugly as I remember it being?"

Rose laughed. It was a relief to hear Gerhard being Gerhard. "I will not lie to you: it is ugly, but beautiful too. Once I saw it, I couldn't stop thinking of things. Do you remember, at the train station, the girl who got pulled out?"

"Of course," Gerhard said, with unmistakable impatience. "That was nothing you can forget."

Alone in her apartment, Rose blushed. "What do you think happened to her?"

"What do you mean? Mutti wrote that the girl was bruised and a little cut up, but basically okay. It was a miracle that she didn't fall to the tracks, die on the spot. Bloody madness, pulling her out like that."

"No," Rose ventured. "I meant—what happened to her during the war? Do you think she survived?"

"Oh," Gerhard said, and sighed. "I don't know, who knows. The odds aren't good." He paused and she wondered if he too was thinking of their parents. "What made you think of that? I haven't thought of it in a very long time."

"I don't know," Rose said, and then: "I had a dream."

"Oh, dreams," Gerhard said. "Did I tell you that Isobel is now keeping a dream notebook? She's on a kombucha kick, she's convinced it's improving her memory. And her eyesight. And keeping cancer at bay. Sometimes I wake up in the middle of the night to see her scribbling away in her notebook."

"I miss Isobel," Rose said with a rush of warmth. "And I miss you too." It was true, and she didn't say it nearly enough.

"We miss you too," he said, and cleared his throat. "I can't imagine what that must have been like, to put your children on that train. I think about it sometimes. And I'm not sure I could have done it—even knowing what I know." He cleared his throat again.

"I know," she said, and it surprised her, how natural this conversation felt. This was the most she and Gerhard had talked about the past in decades. Rose was thinking about all the leaps of faith their parents had to take: that the train would not be detained, the children rounded up by the SS, that they would actually make it across the various borders and onto the boat and across the Channel to England. That once they were there, the families that said they would take care of their children, would in fact do so. Her parents were forced to make an excruciating decision—their children would be better off without them—and devastatingly, they had been right.

"We were fortunate," she said to her brother.

"Very," he agreed.

WHEN THE DOORBELL RANG A few hours later, Rose still felt worn out, jet-lagged, her body at war with itself. She answered it shoeless, expecting Harry. But Lizzie stood at her door, clutching a small cardboard box.

"Cookies," she said solemnly, and thrust the box into Rose's hands. "I thought you might like some."

"I never don't like cookies," Rose said, surprised. "Come in."

"I'm sorry I didn't call," Lizzie said, "But I thought it might be better if I just came by."

"I'm glad you did," Rose said, and led her into the living room. "I'm sorry I ran off yesterday."

"You don't need to apologize."

"Well then. How about some coffee with these cookies?"

"That sounds lovely." Lizzie was wearing a long dark top over dark leggings, curly hair loose over her shoulders. All that darkness conspired to make her pale skin look luminous. Had she always looked this young? Yes, Rose told herself. She was at least forty years younger—another creature entirely. But there was something else at work, Rose decided: she had gained weight. It suited her.

In the kitchen, Rose opened the box: "Linzers!" she exclaimed. "Wonderful."

Lizzie smiled shyly. "There are two kinds, raspberry and black currant."

Rose started the coffeemaker, arranged the cookies on a plate. "You know, we never had Linzer cookies growing up, or if we did, I don't remember them. I only started having them here, in America," she said as she brought the plate back into the living room.

"I'm glad you like them," Lizzie said, and lapsed into silence. Rose broke a cookie into two.

"Delicious," she said after taking a bite. "Sometimes Linzers are too sweet, the filling can overwhelm, but these are done right. Thank you for bringing them."

Lizzie was gazing toward the entry hall, where Joseph's masks still hung. "I'm so sorry, I still can't believe that my father—" She stopped. "He did this."

"He had his reasons," Rose found herself saying. It disturbed her to think of those lunches with Joseph, all those times he had talked to her about the supposed investigator on the case, but after seeing the painting, after all that she remembered . . . well. Things were different now.

"That's bullshit," Lizzie said, her dark eyes fixed on Rose's own, no longer tentative, and Rose heard an echo of Joseph in her tone.

"It's not," Rose said, and she felt this was essential to impart. "I didn't say they were good reasons. I said they were particular to him."

"What does that even mean?" Lizzie said.

"Look, what if I had known that your father had engineered the theft of the painting years ago? If I had gotten it back, that would have meant something, of course. But it wouldn't have meant everything. Not to me." Such a simple truth but it hurt to articulate it. There was nothing she could do to change what had happened.

"I know," Lizzie said, "I *know*." Her voice cracked on the last word. "But it would have meant something to you. You can't tell me it wouldn't."

Rose gave her a short nod. What would be the point in lying? That would help neither of them.

This wisp of an admission seemed to soothe Lizzie. She swiped a few errant cookie crumbs into her napkin, her face calmer. Finally she spoke. "I'm sorry I was out of touch for so long. So many times I thought about calling. But I felt so guilty. I didn't know what to say."

"You don't have to explain," Rose said. "It's not necessary."

"I'm going to help you get *The Bellhop* back," Lizzie said. "The situation with the insurance company is only temporary—"

"I know."

"I've already made phone calls. There's Ciparelli, who I told you about before. But there's also Michael Zalman in New York, who won the Schiele case. And I've heard that Roger Yannata here in L.A. is terrific, tenacious and surprisingly pleasant, at least to his clients—"

"Lizzie, stop."

"I know, you hate talking about this. But this time it's different," Lizzie insisted. "You can't ignore it."

"I'm not ignoring it. My brother and I are handling it. And I'm grateful for your help, truly." She meant it. *The Bellhop*'s reappearance didn't solve everything, but its absence wasn't to blame for everything either.

"I should be the one thanking you," Lizzie said, picked up another cookie. "This might sound strange, but some of the things you said to me last year—they resonated. You have no idea."

"I see," Rose said, because she was beginning to. She studied Lizzie openly now. It wasn't Rose's imagination; Lizzie had gained weight. "So, out with it. How far along are you?"

A speckled pink spread across Lizzie's cheeks. Rose was right, she knew she was. "I'm due in June. I'm just over four months now." Lizzie held her palm to her stomach, smiling an inward but unquestionable smile. "I can't believe you noticed."

"Of course."

"Not *of course*," Lizzie said with frank admiration. "So many people don't—or are too afraid to ask me. But you never miss a thing."

Rose shrugged. "It suits you." It was more than just the changes to her body, it was the way she carried herself, more confident. "You look good."

"Thank you," Lizzie said, and blushed some more.

"You won't be able to be able to hide it for long, you know."

"But I'm not," she said. "I'm not trying to hide a thing."

Of course not. Lizzie had no need to hide anything. Rose caught her breath. She thought back to her miscarriages. What would have happened if they had tried sooner? What would have happened if she simply let herself live? But she could hear Thomas in her head: *There you go again. You did live. You are living.*

Thomas would have liked Lizzie, Rose thought with a strange but unmistakable fierceness. The two of them would have gotten along splendidly. Rose reached across the coffee table and patted Lizzie's hand, a light gesture that did little to reflect the emotions roiling inside her. "A summer baby, how nice," she murmured.

Lizzie held on, her fingers moist. "It's just me. I'm having the baby alone. I have no idea what I'm doing."

"Oh, you're going to do just fine," Rose said, and she stroked her palm. She was certain of it.

"Maybe," Lizzie said, with a half laugh. "I don't know that at all."

"But you do," Rose said, looking at her with steadiness, and she was thinking of Thomas as she said it, trying to channel his generosity. He could calm like no one else she knew. "I know you do."

Lizzie rubbed her eyes with her fists, almost childlike, and then she exhaled sharply. "Okay, then," she said. "If you say so."

"I do," Rose said, remembering: coffee. She went into the kitchen, reached for the delicate green teacups Thomas had loved, and poured. Back in the living room, she handed Lizzie a cup and asked: "Do you know if you're having a boy or girl?"

"I don't know."

"It's too early."

"No, it's not. I've decided not to find out," Lizzie said shyly. "I would have thought I'd want to know, but I decided—so much of this was planned, and you can't know everything."

Rose's hand felt shaky, and she worked to steady her cup on the table. "That's right," she said. She nearly whispered it. "You cannot." Just like that, she was sitting by the Embankment with Thomas when they first met, the meager lunches they had on those overcast spring days when the oyster-colored sky and the water of the Thames seemed to be one and the same. She wasn't dead and she mattered to someone and these plain facts fueled a giddy promise. The possibility alone had been enough.

Rose wished she could tell Thomas what happened on that train. *I wanted to jump too*, she would say. *I wanted my parents to pull me out of the train.*

But you didn't. And they didn't, Thomas would tell her. *And I for one am so very glad.*

"You know," Lizzie said. "I live here now, in Los Angeles. I moved back."

"No, I did not know that." It came out sharply but that wasn't how Rose meant it. "How nice," she added, more softly.

"Maybe I can come over every once in a while," Lizzie said. "Bring the baby when the time comes."

"I would like that. But you should know that I know nothing about babies."

"That makes two of us." Lizzie offered her a small cracked smile.

And perhaps it was just the haze of the afternoon light filtering through the window, but the contour of Lizzie's stomach suddenly seemed more pronounced. Rose tried not to stare. She remembered that feeling. She thought of Mutti, the impossible choice she and Papi had to make, and she wished more than anything that she could have told her she understood.

"These teacups are beautiful," Lizzie observed. "Didn't you tell me they were from Thomas's family?"

"No, he bought them here," Rose said, sipping the coffee that was good and hot. "Not long after we moved. It's a funny little story, actually."

"I want to hear it," Lizzie said.

And Rose began.

AUTHOR'S NOTE

THE LITHUANIAN-BORN CHAIM SOUTINE MOVED to Paris in 1913, where he indeed became friends with Modigliani, and struggled to eke out a living as a painter. In December 1922, Dr. Albert C. Barnes arrived in Europe on an art-buying spree. He saw a painting of Soutine's in a Montparnasse gallery—a portrait of a young pastry chef—and fell in love. He snapped up dozens of works by Soutine, giving the artist much-needed funds and igniting his career.

In the 1920s, Soutine painted numerous portraits of people who often went unnoticed—waiters, cooks, and hotel employees—including several bellhops. The portrait described in *The Fortunate Ones* is an amalgam of Soutine's bellhops, but the owners depicted in the novel are purely fictional.

I first came upon Soutine's work years ago in a wonderful exhibit at the Jewish Museum, and I'm grateful to its curators, Norman Kleeblatt and Kenneth Silver, as well as to Maurice Tuchman and Esti Dunow for their extensive Soutine scholarship.

While this is a work of fiction, a number of books served as key resources and inspiration, including: *Austerity Britain*, by David Kynaston; *London 1945*, by Maureen Waller; *London War Notes*, by Mollie Panter-Downes; *War Factory*, by Inez Holden; *The Tiger in the Attic*, by Edith Milton; *The Rape of Europa*, by Lynn Nicholas. Lore Segal's clear-eyed *Other People's Houses* is both a terrific novel and an invaluable testament. I spent fruitful hours at the Center for Jewish History, and the memoirs and oral histories contained in its archives were indispensable.

Mark Jonathan Harris and Deborah Oppenheimer's vivid documentary, *Into the Arms of Strangers*, and its accompanying volume, opened my eyes the Kindertransport experience and was a crucial reference. I'd like to offer a special thank you to Lory Cahn; her memory of being pulled through the window and off the train has haunted me for years, and I'm grateful to her for sharing it, as I am to all those who told their stories.

ACKNOWLEDGMENTS

This book was many years in the making, and many people were instrumental along the way. Thank you to Al Filreis, Deborah Treisman, and Sarah Burnes for early encouragement. I'm especially grateful to Helen Schulman, who cheered me on from the start.

Thank you to Merrill Feitell, Halle Eaton, Jennifer Cody Epstein, Lizzie Simon, and Sarah Saffian, all of whom read early versions and were full of good advice and unstinting support. I owe an incalculable debt of gratitude to the talented and ever-inspiring Joanna Hershon, who read countless drafts and offered astute suggestions at every turn. Her faith, friendship, and wisdom kept me going; this book would simply not exist without her.

For ideas, advice, and support of all kinds, I'm grateful to David Boyer, Sam Zalutsky, Ed Boland, Sara Pekow, Karen Schwartz, Emily Nussbaum, Hana Schank, Lewis Kruger, Dorian Karchmar, Rebecca Gradinger, Yona McDonough, Cathy Halley, Cassie Mayer, and Ruth and Enrique Gutman. To the Millay Colony of the Arts, where I took the first steps in writing the novel, thank you. I'm lucky to have a coterie of literary-minded cousins, and I'm grateful to Sara Mark, Kate Axelrod, and Sam Axelrod for their suggestions and encouragement, and to Marian Thurm for leading the way. An enormous thank you to Jen Albano, who suggested the title.

I'm deeply indebted to my stellar agent, Lisa Grubka, for her enthusiasm, wise counsel, and unwavering commitment. Kate Nintzel shaped this book and had faith in its potential; I am hugely appreciative of her vision and sharp editorial eye.

To my family, I owe more than I can ever say: my excellent brothers, Eric Umansky and David Umansky; my wonderful parents, Michael Umansky and Sherry Weinman, and Gloria and Allan Spivak, all of whom believed in me from the beginning and unfailingly supported me throughout. I wish more than anything that my mother was here to read these words.

Lastly, especially, to my husband, David Gutman, who encouraged me throughout the long writing of this book, and whose intelligence, humor, and keen sense of character were a boon to this narrative, but more important, to my life. I am forever grateful for his love and partnership. He and our daughters, Lena and Talia, are my greatest pieces of luck and true fortune.

About the author

2 Meet Ellen Umansky

About the book

3 Ellen Umansky Talks
with Joanna Hershon

12 Reading Group Guide

Read on

15 Recommended Resources

Insights,
Interviews
& More . . .

Meet Ellen Umansky

Sam Zalutsky

ELLEN UMANSKY has published fiction and nonfiction in a variety of publications, including the *New York Times, Slate, Salon,* and the short story anthology *Lost Tribe: Jewish Fiction from the Edge.* She has worked in the editorial departments of the *Forward, Tablet,* and *The New Yorker.* She grew up in Los Angeles, and lives in Brooklyn with her husband and two daughters. ❧

2

Ellen Umansky Talks with Joanna Hershon

JOANNA HERSHON is the author of four novels, *Swimming, The Outside of August, The German Bride,* and *A Dual Inheritance.* Visit her website at www.joannahershon.com.

Joanna Hershon: You are one of my dearest friends and trusted editors. I remember the first time you told me about the seeds of this novel, so many years ago. Can you talk a bit about that story and how this novel grew out of it?

Ellen Umansky: As you know, I grew up in L.A. There was an ophthalmologist in our social orbit. He treated my younger brother, and I went to school for a time with his daughters. He was a high roller and collected art. In the early 1990s, his two most valuable paintings, a Picasso canvas and a Monet landscape, were stolen.

Years later, the police tracked them down to an airport locker in Cleveland. It turned out that the doctor had set up the theft, to collect insurance money. I kept thinking about it. Why had he done it? Couldn't he have gotten money some other way? I was also struck by this thought: his inability to destroy the paintings served at least in part to aid his downfall. If he had gotten rid of them, he would have eliminated the evidence. But he couldn't do it, and I remember thinking there was a deeper story there. ▶

Ellen Umansky Talks with Joanna Hershon
(*continued*)

Joanna Hershon: Sense of place is one of your many strengths as a writer. I'm curious about your relationship with Los Angeles and how it inspires you. Did your relationship with the city change during the course of writing the book?

Ellen Umansky: I loved writing about Los Angeles. I moved there from New York when I was six years old. I grew up in a canyon much like the one where I placed Lizzie's house (though mine did not hang off a cliff). We had a pool and a beautiful backyard that overlooked the canyon, and I spent what feels like endless summer days outside (in my case, often getting burned to a crisp while reading).

We went back east regularly to visit family, and as I got older, I felt a strong pull toward New York—even its grittiness was glamorous, as far as I was concerned. I remember being a teenager and grousing about yet another perfectly sunny L.A. day. By the time I graduated high school, I was desperate to leave.

But I don't feel that way now, at all! I love L.A.; I love going back, bringing my kids. I had such fun writing the L.A. scenes, putting my characters in places that I knew so well, and imagining the city in the 1950s and '60s. It's a gorgeous, vital, exasperating city, much more interesting than it is often given credit for. I spent a great deal of time there while writing the book, in my childhood home in the canyon. When I wasn't there I was often thinking of it, trying to capture it in my writing. The book was a gift in that way; it allowed me, when I was back home in Brooklyn, to feel closer to L.A., to all I missed there.

Joanna Hershon: Rose and Lizzie are an unforgettable pair. Their connection isn't easy and it feels earned in a way that strikes me, as a reader, as particularly realistic. As a writer, it strikes me as particularly difficult to achieve! How do you think the ability to go back and forth in time affects their present-day interaction?

Ellen Umansky: First, thank you! As you know, I worried about the depiction of their relationship. I feared it might seem forced, given that they're decades apart and from completely different worlds. But at the same time, I felt strongly that they *would* be drawn to each other. They share similar traits: they can be walled off, from themselves and from others; they were both so irreparably hurt by their childhood losses. For Lizzie, Rose is a way to make amends for the disappearance of the painting. As for Rose, as much as she says she doesn't want to talk about the past, she's compelled by Lizzie's interest. And it's no accident that Lizzie is about the same age as a child of Rose's would have been, if Rose hadn't had those miscarriages. ▸

Ellen Umansky Talks with Joanna Hershon
(*continued*)

As for your question about the alternating structure: it didn't occur to me when I was writing the book, but I do think that the historical scenes deepen our understanding and sympathy for Rose. She can be curt and clipped, especially when she's talking about her past. But as readers, we were privy to those scenes in real time. When she tells Lizzie about not having kids, she's very controlled and unemotional—yet we know how torn up she was about that decision and how her miscarriages nearly destroyed her.

Joanna Hershon: Writing a novel can be an exercise in escaping one's life. Even if a novel isn't autobiographical, it seems that if one works on a book over the course of many years (as I know you did with this book), it can reflect the challenges and growth in one's own experience. Did you find that to be the case? Did the plot or emotional depth of the story ever reflect changes in your own life?

Ellen Umansky: Oh, absolutely. It's a completely different novel than the one I set out to write many years ago. I can pinpoint all kinds of shifts, large and small. My husband and I started thinking of having children and lo, my characters tried to have children. Rose and Thomas's marriage was much clearer to me toward the tail end of my work on the book, when I myself had been married for more than a decade, than at the start.

Sometimes plot decisions that I had already made became more personal and painful. Writing that terrible scene at the train station became all the more charged when I imagined putting my two young daughters on a train. Lizzie's father was always going to die at the opening—that was one of the few plotlines that did *not* change over the years—but when my own mother was diagnosed with a cancer that carried a grim prognosis, writing about Lizzie's loss of her father became harder. My mother passed away after I had finished writing the novel, but I look at the book now and it feels filled with her loss. I know that it was my anticipation and dread of losing her that animated much of that writing.

Joanna Hershon: Can you tell us how you decided to embark on researching the Kindertransport? Were there any stories you learned along the way that specifically inspired you?

Ellen Umansky: There are three moments I come back to. The first was during a seminar on Jane Austen I took with the great writer Lore Segal while I was in graduate school at Columbia. She told us that she became a fan of Austen's while living in England as a young ▸

émigré from Vienna. I later learned
that she had been on a Kindertransport.
She said that Austen's novels helped her
figure out how to be British. It was an
aside, but it stayed with me.

Another was from the documentary
Into the Arms of Strangers. A German-
born woman named Lory Cahn spoke
about what happened when her parents
took her to get on a Kindertransport.
She got on the train, and as they stood
on the platform, they were able to hold
hands with her through the train's open
window. When the train started to
pull out, her father was so upset, he
continued to grip her hands. He ended
up pulling her through the window,
out of the train, and onto the platform.
A few years later, they were sent to
Auschwitz. I don't think I truly
comprehended the agony of those
separations until I learned Lory Cahn's
story.

Then, when I was already deep in
my research, I came across the papers of
an older cousin of mine, Walter Porges,
in the archives at the Center for Jewish
History. Walter was married to my
mother's first cousin. He passed away
years ago. I had forgotten that he had
been born in Vienna and gotten out on
a Kindertransport.

He had a very successful career as a
TV news executive and spoke without a
trace of an accent. I remember hearing
stories about Walter producing the news
at ABC, Walter attending presidential

debates, but nothing about Walter fleeing Austria. I later learned that he and his sister had been put on a train when he was seven years old. Their parents made it out too, but their grandparents didn't. Among his papers were several Red Cross letters, responding to his request for information on his grandparents. They had been deported from Vienna during the war, and he never knew what happened. He wrote to the Red Cross through the years, asking for details. There was something so moving to me about those letters. They spoke of the private histories we all have.

Joanna Hershon: You've worked a great deal as a journalist and editor. Can you discuss some of the ways in which—positively or negatively—your other professions affect your life as a fiction writer?

Ellen Umansky: In some ways, I feel ill suited to fiction writing. I like talking to people and being out in the world. Doing research allows me to stay connected, and it is very much related to the features reporting I've done through the years. This is true for historical research, but also for the type of research one must do to write about unfamiliar worlds, like art theft or being a lawyer. (You were the one who encouraged me to simply call people and ask questions. ▸

Ellen Umansky Talks with Joanna Hershon *(continued)*

"But it's not for an article," I remember saying, skeptical. "No, it's for a book," you told me.)

But while I like and take pride in editing, I suspect it takes its toll on my fiction. The editor's voice in my head is more developed than I wish it were. It can impede me from simply pushing ahead. The way I write is through discovery, getting down that often-terrible first draft so that I can see, on paper, what I'm trying to say. From there I hack away, sharpen, and fine-tune. It's exhausting to hear that judgmental editor's voice—*that observation is trite; you're not getting to the point; who is this character again?* The voice might be right in the long run, but that doesn't make it useful in the moment.

Joanna Hershon: Chaim Soutine created the (fictional) painting that is so important to both Lizzie and Rose. How important is the shadow of Soutine's life story to each of their individual stories? Is the narrative of the painter—at least in this case— as significant as the painting itself?

Ellen Umansky: In a word: yes! Soutine's life is essential to the novel and to both Lizzie and Rose, though they might not realize it. Soutine himself was an outsider, a Lithuanian émigré in Paris, from all accounts a shy, awkward, volatile man. He didn't necessarily fit in with the other artists in Montparnasse, and his outsider status as a Jew during the Nazi occupation of France most likely shortened his life.

Lizzie doesn't know Soutine's history when she first arrives in L.A., but she's comforted by the painting. She sees the bellhop as someone who didn't quite belong, just as she too doesn't belong.

Soutine and Rose came from very different worlds—his family was dirt poor and religious, hers sophisticated and secular—and these distinctions were important to me. But they're both Jewish, of course, and because of that they're both swept up in dark forces well beyond their control.

Joanna Hershon: I'm always fascinated by what is left out of a novel as the story becomes more focused and refined. What is not there can often tell us so much about an author's creative process. Would you consider sharing anything that you wrote over the years that perhaps informed the book but didn't make it into the novel?

Ellen Umansky: Oh, there's so much. As you know, earlier drafts followed the painting every time it switched owners. I wrote a short chapter from Soutine's point of view: we see him, walking the streets of Paris and working in his studio, painting *The Bellhop*. Another chapter followed Rose's mother when she purchased the portrait. I even wrote about an American soldier, and his story explained how the painting made its way from Europe to the U.S. The book is so much better and more focused without those chapters, and yet writing that material was crucial. It helped me clarify the story I wanted to tell. Just as important, I had already brought those scenes to life. I knew the motivations for why they had occurred, what was at stake, the feelings they elicited. Cutting them and weaving in references in other parts of the novel was the easy part. The novel feels all the richer because of those excised scenes. They're the history of the characters, and you can never fully scrub away history. I wouldn't want to; I like the look of what remains. ᔗ

Reading Group Guide

1. Discuss how the meaning of the painting changes or deepens as the story progresses. How does Rose initially feel about the painting, and why does she look for it after the war?

2. What does Lizzie appear to have in common with Rose? Where do they differ? Think about their first meeting and how their relationship develops.

3. Though this story hovers around the Holocaust, the focus of the narrative draws our attention to the aftereffects rather than the atrocities themselves. How does the Jewish community recover after the years of devastation? Explain how Rose grapples with her sense of guilt and loss. Do other characters deal with it differently?

4. From what you can tell, how much of the information about the painting is based on historical fact? What do you think the author invented or adapted for this story?

5. The juxtaposition of Europe in the 1930s and '40s and Los Angeles in 2006 is a stark one. How do the two narrations play against each other? Do they seem to resonate? Try to connect the situations and conflicts across this time span.

6. Do you think the dual narrative is a good way for telling this kind of story? Why or why not? Can you think of other novels or films that use the same strategy?

7. Joseph's death and the search for the stolen painting bring Lizzie and Rose together. In what other ways are these characters drawn toward each other?

8. When Rose is a student in London, she feels a strong affinity for the work of Dostoyevsky, who writes that "one reptile will devour another." On page 158, Rose explains that this quote refers to the irrational side of the human soul, where all humans harbor dark, murderous impulses. She admits that she finds this "ugliness of the human condition" to be comforting, and that it makes her feel "understood." What do you make of Rose's ideas here? Why do you think Rose finds solace in thinking about the nature of evil?

9. On pages 104–105, Lizzie asks whether Rose ever sought reparations from the government for the loss and suffering her family experienced during the Holocaust. Rose refuses, saying, "I don't want that money, it's blood money. It makes what happened about property, and it most certainly is not. Besides, I'm not the victim ▶

here; my parents are." Think about Rose's refusal to seek compensation for her suffering, and then about her desire to recover the stolen painting. What is valuable to Rose? Can we see the painting as a "reparation"? Why or why not?

10. After Germany annexed Austria in 1938, life for Jews became even more restricted and difficult. Rose's father loses his business, the children aren't allowed to go to school or even to the movie theater, and most strikingly, the family has trouble securing visas to enter other countries. Can you name any other restrictions that the government imposed on Jews during the earlier stages of the Holocaust? Can you talk about other ways people tried to flee Nazi Germany and reach other countries?

11. How might Rose's experience fleeing from her home country resonate with current events? What are some parallels between her situation and the current refugee crisis in Europe?

12. The author never describes what actually happened to Rose's parents. What do you make of her decision to omit these details from the story? What do you think happened to them? What does Rose think?

13. Look up *The Bellhop* by Chaim Soutine. Does the painting appear like its descriptions in the story? Is it what you expected? How does looking at the original painting change the way you think about the characters' attachments to it?

14. Discuss the story's ending. Are you surprised by Rose's reaction to the discovery of the painting? Was this satisfying or frustrating for you?

15. People deal with grief and trauma in different ways. Discuss Rose's and Gerard's alternate responses to being separated from each other, relocated from their native country, and losing their parents. How does Gerard cope differently from his sister? How do their experiences compare with the way that Lizzie handles grief? ∾

Recommended Resources

I relied on many sources while writing *The Fortunate Ones*. Here's a partial list of those I suggest for further reading.
—Ellen Umansky

THE WORLD OF YESTERDAY BY STEFAN ZWEIG

Stefan Zweig wrote so much during his career—short stories, poetry, novels, plays, biographies—it's hard to suggest one title. *The World of Yesterday,* his autobiography, was indispensable to me as I tried to imagine the elegant city of Rose's birth. It's less about Zweig's life than the times he lived in. He paints an indelible portrait of Vienna before World War I—"the golden age of security," he calls it—when artistic and intellectual life reigned, and young men grew beards and wore glasses even if their eyesight was strong, as youth were "suspected of instability."

OTHER PEOPLE'S HOUSES BY LORE SEGAL

When I was a graduate student at Columbia University, I studied briefly with Lore Segal, who taught a seminar on Jane Austen. Segal had a crisp accent that I couldn't place. I later learned that she had been a refugee from Vienna, sent to England on a Kindertransport when she was ten. I thought of my former teacher and her work often when I was creating the character of Rose, not only for her life experience, but also for her ▶

sharp wit and intelligence. *Other People's Houses* is her first book, a semiautobiographical novel that follows her character from Vienna to England to the Dominican Republic and finally the United States, the same circuitous journey that Segal undertook. The novel is as clear-eyed, compelling, and insightful as Segal herself.

STILL ALIVE: A HOLOCAUST GIRLHOOD REMEMBERED BY RUTH KLUGER

Like Lore Segal, Ruth Kluger was born in Vienna. When she was eleven years old, she was ordered to Theresienstadt, and later to Auschwitz. She survived the war, becoming a professor of German language. Her memoir is short and bristling with intelligence and fury, particularly about the way the Holocaust gets talked about and memorialized.

INTO THE ARMS OF STRANGERS: STORIES OF THE KINDERTRANSPORT BY MARK JONATHAN HARRIS AND DEBORAH OPPENHEIMER

With first-person accounts of those who had been on the Kindertransports, this 2000 documentary (and the book by the same title) brings alive the campaign that rescued nearly ten thousand Jewish children on the eve of the war. More than a dozen men and women are interviewed, and they speak of all they left behind and what awaited them in England with frankness, humor, and grief. I couldn't get their stories out of my mind—particularly Lory Cahn's, who was pulled off the train as it was leaving the station.

LONDON 1945: LIFE IN THE DEBRIS OF WAR BY MAUREEN WALLER

Waller's engrossing account of the last year of the war focuses on daily life for Londoners—from the soot and the smells and the blackouts and the bombings to those who slept in the Underground during the bitterly cold winter of 1945. Her chapter on V.E. Day helped me picture what Rose and her friend Margaret would have done that night, and her discussion of fashion during the war was eye-opening; when I read about the stocking shortage and how women would cover their legs with makeup and drew lines to imitate the seams, I let out a little yelp, knowing that I would use the detail in my novel.

AUSTERITY BRITAIN: 1945–1951 BY DAVID KYNASTON

Britain's victory did little to lessen the deprivation and grim austerity its citizens grappled with in the years after the war. Shortages were rampant: meat, butter, cheese, and eggs were all rationed, as was bread, which hadn't been restricted during the war. Electrical outages were common. People stole lightbulbs off the trains on the Tube. This is a big book, both in length and in sweep, and Kynaston ably conjures up a bygone world where British were urged to "make do and mend" and the phrase "welfare state" wasn't yet an insult. ▶

Recommended Resources *(continued)*

THE RAPE OF EUROPA BY LYNN NICHOLAS

If you're interested in art theft, this is the book for you. It's a surprisingly suspenseful account of what happened to artwork during the Third Reich, from the Nazi effort to supposedly rid Germany of "degenerate" art (which they profited mightily from) and the systemic plundering of Jewish homes to the complex measures to safeguard treasures during the war. (I loved learning that the *Mona Lisa* was spirited out of the Louvre via ambulance.) Nicholas highlights matters of restitution and how refugees like Rose who had lost far more than possessions tried to track down the objects that were rightly theirs.

LIFE AFTER LIFE BY KATE ATKINSON

A great novel by the great Kate Atkinson. It's historical fiction—much of the action takes place in the 1930s and '40s Britain—with a twist. The main character, Ursula, keeps dying: as an infant, a woman during the Blitz, a mother in Nazi Germany. Each time Ursula dies, she is resurrected with little fanfare, and her life story is altered. I found this constant revision comforting and inspiring as I grappled with the writing of my own novel. Art is ever open to changes and possibilities. ❧

Discover great authors, exclusive offers, and more at hc.com.